T5-AGC-197

HER HEART'S DELIGHT

"You ever been sweet on a man?" The question slipped past Adam's lips before he was going to ask it.

Camille's grip tightened on her fork and she glowered at him. "What kind of question is that?"

"An honest one. I've been sitting here looking at you and I can't figure out how come a woman as pretty as you isn't hitched up to someone."

"You do have a bad habit of staring at me. Kindly cure yourself of it." She returned her attention to the potato on her plate.

So she had noticed. He felt better knowing she was neither bereft of vanity nor capable of wholly ignoring his presence. "Do I get an answer to my question?"

"No, I have never been sweet on a man," she said curtly. "And if you paid for my meal because you are harboring any romantic designs upon my person, you have wasted your money. I would rather be stomped to death by a herd of wild horses than fall in love and be tied down to some man."

"Don't lose any sleep worrying about my 'romantic designs,' Miss Kendall. I'm a confirmed bachelor. And even if I wasn't, the last woman on earth I'd set my sights on is a prissy little Evangeline," Adam said with a wink, "like yourself."

PUT SOME PASSION INTO YOUR LIFE . . . WITH THIS STEAMY SELECTION OF ZEBRA *LOVEGRAMS!*

SEA FIRES (3899, $4.50/$5.50)
by Christine Dorsey
Spirited, impetuous Miranda Chadwick arrives in the untamed New World prepared for any peril. But when the notorious pirate Gentleman Jack Blackstone kidnaps her in order to fulfill his secret plans, she can't help but surrender—to the shameless desires and raging hunger that his bronzed, lean body and demanding caresses ignite within her!

TEXAS MAGIC (3898, $4.50/$5.50)
by Wanda Owen
After being ambushed by bandits and saved by a ranchhand, headstrong Texas belle Bianca Moreno hires her gorgeous rescuer as a protective escort. But Rick Larkin does more than guard her body—he kisses away her maidenly inhibitions, and teaches her the secrets of wild, reckless love!

SEDUCTIVE CARESS (3767, $4.50/$5.50)
by Carla Simpson
Determined to find her missing sister, brave beauty Jessamyn Forsythe disguises herself as a simple working girl and follows her only clues to Whitechapel's darkest alleys . . . and the disturbingly handsome Inspector Devlin Burke. Burke, on the trail of a killer, becomes intrigued with the ebon-haired lass and discovers the secrets of her silken lips and the hidden promise of her sweet flesh.

SILVER SURRENDER (3769, $4.50/$5.50)
by Vivian Vaughan
When Mexican beauty Aurelia Mazón saves a handsome stranger from death, she finds herself on the run from the Federales with the most dangerous man she's ever met. And when Texas Ranger Carson Jarrett steals her heart with his intimate kisses and seductive caresses, she yields to an all-consuming passion from which she hopes to never escape!

ENDLESS SEDUCTION (3793, $4.50/$5.50)
by Rosalyn Alsobrook
Caught in the middle of a dangerous shoot-out, lovely Leona Stegall falls unconscious and awakens to the gentle touch of a handsome doctor. When her rescuer's caresses turn passionate, Leona surrenders to his fiery embrace and savors a night of soaring ecstasy!

Available wherever paperbacks are sold, or order direct from the Publisher. Send cover price plus 50¢ per copy for mailing and handling to Penguin USA, P.O. Box 999, c/o Dept. 17109, Bergenfield, NJ 07621. Residents of New York and Tennessee must include sales tax. DO NOT SEND CASH.

HER HEART'S DELIGHT

René J. Garrod

ZEBRA BOOKS
KENSINGTON PUBLISHING CORP.

To my son Benjamin.
You're one great kid.

ZEBRA BOOKS are published by

Kensington Publishing Corp.
850 Third Avenue
New York, NY 10022

Copyright © 1995 by René J. Garrod

All rights reserved. No part of this book may be reproduced in any form or by any means without the prior written consent of the Publisher, excepting brief quotes used in reviews.

If you purchased this book without a cover, you should be aware that this book is stolen property. It was reported as "unsold and destroyed" to the Publisher and neither the Author nor the Publisher has received any payment for this "stripped book."

Zebra, the Z logo Reg. U.S. Pat. & TM Off. The Lovegram logo is a trademark of Kensington Publishing Corp.

First Printing: April, 1995

Printed in the United States of America

Prologue

Helena, Montana
1885

Adam Carrigan burst through the door. Advancing on his quarry, he slammed his fist down on the barroom table. Half the whiskey filling Roy Higgins's glass sloshed over the side. "Higgins, you've got exactly three seconds to tell me the rumors I'm hearing are just that before I wring your scrawny, double-crossing, snake-in-the-grass neck!" Carrigan towered over the seated man, pinning him to his chair with his menacing glare.

Higgins cast a dismayed glance at the spill of whiskey soaking into the scarred, wooden tabletop. "Now, Adam, calm down," he whined. "It ain't like you reckon."

"Did you sell your land or didn't you?" Carrigan demanded.

"I sold it—but like I said, it ain't like you reckon."

"You promised if you ever decided to sell, that land was Josh's and mine." Grabbing Higgins by the collar, Carrigan pressed his face so close Roy was harrowed by the heat of his breath when he growled, "Seems me figuring you for a low-down, lying, two-faced son of a bitch is real accurate."

"That's because you don't know the details. Jack, bring

Adam here a whiskey," Higgins called over his shoulder to the bartender.

"I don't drink with liars."

"You and me been friends and neighbors for over nine years. Now sit down," Higgins grumbled. "All I done was take advantage of a fine opportunity to fill my pockets and extend the favor to you. The land is as good as yours."

"I'm listening."

"Well, I ain't explaining nothing until you let loose of my collar and stop looming over me like an irate grizzly."

Adam abruptly released him, slid into the opposite chair, and swallowed the whiskey in one gulp. "This better be one helluva explanation, Higgins."

"It is," Higgins assured him with a wide grin. "I sold the land to one Miss Camille Kendall—a woman with more money than sense." He shook his head pityingly. "I told her I was already obliged to sell the land to a friend, but she said she just had to have it. Followed me around like a hungry hound, dickering with me. I resisted, but she wouldn't take no for an answer, no matter how many times I said it. Before I know it, she's offering me double my original asking price—which from the start I'd set a helluva lot higher than the land is worth."

"And you accepted her money without even giving me a chance to match her price," Adam said angrily.

"Only a fool would pay what she was willing, and you ain't no fool."

"I wanted that land."

"And you'll get it," Higgins declared.

"How?"

"Miss Kendall's planning on turning the land into a horse breeding farm. Claims she's gonna work the place herself."

Adam raised a brow at the news, but curtly countered, "It's a rarity, but it's not unheard of for a woman to run a ranch."

"Miss Kendall ain't gonna run no ranch." Higgins chuckled. "She's a bored, high-society gal from Virginia. From the looks of her fancy clothes, she ain't never done an honest day's work. 'Sides that, she ain't no bigger than a half-growed child. She ain't gonna last a week out here, if she lasts that long. Once her starry-eyed dreams run smack dab into earthbound reality, she's gonna be so eager to sell, you'll be able to get the land for half of what I'd have been obliged to charge you for it."

"You sure she won't last?"

"I'd bet everything I own on it, that's how sure I am. Wouldn't have sold to her if I weren't." Higgins nursed his last sip of whiskey. "So you see, you wronged me accusing me of betraying our friendship. All along I've been looking out for your financial interests as well as my own. I'm selling the land to you, just like I promised. I'm just doing it roundabout. We're both gonna come out with fat pockets."

Though his blue eyes no longer flashed with fury, Adam remained skeptical. "What's to keep her from selling cheap to someone else?"

"She can't. I got it in writing. When she sells, she's gotta sell to you."

"I still don't like taking the risk. I've waited a long time to add that land to my ranch. You know my plans for it. Risking them on—"

"Ain't you been listening to a thing I've said? There ain't no risk." Higgins pursed his lips and massaged his chin. When Adam's features remained taut, he sighed loudly. "Tell you what, you ride on over to my place and introduce yourself to your new neighbor. After you meet her, if you still ain't convinced, I'll give you a clear shot at this old jaw of mine. Deal?"

Meeting Higgins's guileless gaze with a cold stare, Adam Carrigan tested his knuckles against his palm. "Deal."

One

Camille Kendall stood in the doorway, surveying the interior of her new home. Already she loved every chinked dust-covered log wall.

She stroked the fluffy white fur of the Persian cat cradled in her arms. "Well, what do you think of our new home, Lucretia?"

Lucretia twitched her tail and omitted a plaintive meow.

"I'll admit it's a bit rustic, but you'll get used to it. The important thing is that it's ours—every inch of this house, every acre of land, the barns, corrals, garden . . . *ours.*" She repeated the word with heartfelt satisfaction. "And there is no man on earth with the right to tell us what we can and cannot do."

When Lucretia didn't display the proper enthusiasm, Camille set her down on the plank floor. "Why don't you make yourself useful and catch a mouse or two? Considering Mr. Higgins's housekeeping habits, I'm sure we have more than our share."

Wrinkling her nose as she crossed the room, Camille located a broom and knocked a nest of cobwebs out of the corner. She had a thousand things to do before her horses arrived, and the last thing she wanted was to spend her time cleaning house, but neither was she fond of the notion of sharing her new home with vermin. The sooner she got started, the sooner she would be finished.

Camille decided the best way to tackle the task would be to drag all the furniture Mr. Higgins had left behind out into the yard. What she wanted to keep, she would scrub. The rest could be stored in one of the barns until she had time to sell it. Rolling up her silk sleeves and setting a lace kerchief over her flaxen hair, she immediately set to work.

The smaller pieces of furniture gave her little trouble, but many of the larger pieces proved too heavy and unwieldy for her to move alone. She allowed herself the indulgence of a few minutes of anger, first at the furniture, then at the men who previously had worked Mr. Higgins's ranch—almost all of whom he had informed her had expressed their preference to seek their wages elsewhere rather than take orders from a female boss. He had also informed her, without the slightest display of compunction, they were of the unanimous opinion she wouldn't last the summer, and they were loath to waste time with her before finding more secure employment.

Camille had been so vexed with the attitude of Higgins's men, she had foolishly dismissed the lot of then. Though it had always been her intention to do her own hiring, retaining one or two of the men who were willing to stay would have been pragmatic.

Camille had come out West hoping the men here would be less pigheaded than the men back East, but so far they weren't proving themselves much better. She hadn't been here long enough to completely give up on them, but they hadn't made a good first impression. The least they could have done was meet her before passing judgment on her.

Rather than discourage her, their lack of confidence made her all the more determined to succeed. Within a few years she was going to have the finest horse breeding ranch in

Montana. She had waited and hoped her whole life for this opportunity, and she would not fail. Her horses would be the best. Men who eschewed her authority today would tomorrow be begging to buy one of her fine mounts. And she would sell to them . . . for the right price. A smart businesswoman didn't let resentment interfere with making a profit.

But how could she be so sure she would succeed when she'd never tested her mettle? Perhaps she'd discover she wasn't as capable as she would like to believe. Camille fought to banish the self-defeating inner voice. She must not allow herself to have these thoughts. Let the world doubt her. She would remain stalwartly committed to herself and her dream.

Camille threw herself into the cleaning, exhausting her mind and body until the dark thoughts of defeat were forgotten.

The sun had set and the moon had risen high in the star-strewn sky before Camille allowed herself to surrender to fatigue and sink wearily onto a threadbare settee. The parlor, kitchen, bedroom, and ranch office had been scoured from floor to ceiling. That left only the storage attic for tomorrow. "A good day's work, don't you think?" she sighed to Lucretia, who sat in the corner meticulously cleaning all traces of the mouse she had eaten from her face and paws. Lucretia purred contentedly.

Though she felt almost too exhausted for dinner, Camille ate some bread and cheese washed down with two cups of strong, sweet tea, then crawled into bed and doused the lamp.

Weary as her body was, her mind would not be still. Even though all she needed to do was shift on the lumpy mattress or relight the lamp and look at the log walls surrounding her, she still was having trouble believing she was actually here in Montana in her own home.

She had spent over a year traveling around the country,

searching for just the right piece of land to buy. The moment she saw this ranch, her heart told her she had found it.

For years she had visited this ranch in both waking and sleeping dreams—the sloping hillsides, the wide river flowing into the mountains at the north end of the valley, the two barns . . . she had recognized it instantly. How she'd conjured so accurate a picture of a place she had never before seen she couldn't fathom—but she had. She considered it portentous. It was why she had been willing to pay too much to have it.

Not that she would miss the money. Her father had left her everything he had and he had been one of the wealthier men in Virginia. Her inheritance was managed by a man back in Virginia and was doled out to her in generous yearly installments. As her thoughts turned to her father, Camille drew her pale blond eyebrows together. A more old-fashioned, domineering man had yet to be born. If he were not already dead, her father would likely die of apoplexy if he knew what she was doing with her inheritance. Her father saw women as creatures to be cosseted, dressed in beautiful clothing, draped with jewelry. They were ornaments to be placed on a pedestal or worn on a man's arm. Cherished ornaments to be sure, but ornaments none the less.

His attitude had been an onerous burden on her soul since the day she had started to think for herself. That in itself had been an act of rebellion. Her father believed it unseemly for women to think. He also believed it unseemly for women to do anything else she found the least bit interesting. And most unseemly of all was her passion for horses.

One would have thought he would have been gratified his only child shared his affinity for fine horseflesh, but the opposite was true. If she had been born a son, he would not have forbidden her the pursuit of her passion. He had admitted as much on numerous occasions.

"A stable is no place for a young lady." Although her father had been dead nearly two years, his oft-spoken words still echoed in her head.

They constantly argued the point, or rather she railed against the strictures he imposed upon her and he thwarted her desires with calm, fatherly efficiency. He had the power of parental prerogative, the money to hire a legion of eager to tattle servants, and all of society on his side. She had only herself.

In hopes of appeasing her, he had eventually given her her own horse—a tiny ancient mare who even the threat of the glue factory could not persuade to a pace faster than a tedious walk. Even so, she was not allowed to ride without escort or personally provide any care for the animal. She was required to wait upon the front porch for her mount to be brought to her.

The only way she could visit the stables was to wait until the household was asleep, slip out her bedroom window, and climb down the oak tree growing beside her window.

She loved her midnight rides on horses worthy of her abilities, but despised the necessity to practice deceit . . . because despite everything, she loved her father and she knew he loved her. He truly believed he was doing what was best for his daughter.

When he caught her deliberately disobeying his will, he was never harsh. He merely shook his head sadly as he delivered a lecture on proper decorum for a young lady of her social rank and had her confined to her room. So she would know his disapproval for her behavior did nothing to lessen his affection for her, he invariably ordered Cook to have her favorite meals sent up on a tray. Often upon her release, he would gently remind her of her feminine role and gift her with a new pair of lace gloves or French bath soaps or some other frivolous folderol. Her life would have been easier if he had been an ogre.

Through the years she had grown more and more frustrated. Climbing out the window like a thief in the night might be seen as an adventure at fourteen. It was tolerable at eighteen. After she had passed her twentieth birthday, it was just plain degrading.

Though she often fantasized about packing her bags and making her own way in the world, leaving while her father was still alive wasn't an option her conscience would let her seriously entertain—especially after her mother's death. She was all the family her father had. It would hurt him too much if she turned her back on him. He was her father—and despite their differences—she dearly loved him.

"You look surly enough to bite the head off a rattler," Joshua Carrigan greeted his older brother between yawns. He padded down the stairs on bare feet. Pulling the blanket wrapped around his naked frame more snugly about his shoulders to ward off the chill air, he said, "Didn't expect you back till tomorrow. There some kinda trouble in town?"

Adam Carrigan slammed the front door shut behind him and sailed his hat to the hook on the wall. "Higgins decided to sell his property."

"That news oughta have you in a sunny—not sour—mood. We've had our eyes on that piece of land ever since we moved up here."

Striding into the parlor, Adam plunked himself down in his favorite chair, stretching out his long legs. His mouth settled into a deep frown. "He's not gonna sell it to us. He's already sold it to somebody else."

Josh took up the opposite chair. "Damn! I'd have bet money Higgins was a man of his word. I hope you beat the hell out of the bastard."

"I should have, but I haven't . . . yet."

"Why not?"

"He talked me out of it." Adam raked his fingers through his hair and blew out a breath. "Wants me to meet our new neighbor first."

"What's one got to do with the other?"

"She's a woman."

Josh jerked to attention, his anger at Higgins instantly evaporating. He licked his lips. "Single?"

Adam scowled at his brother's bright-eyed interest. He and Josh were the best of friends, but they had nothing in common when it came to the fairer sex. Making no effort to disguise his exasperation, he replied, "Of course, otherwise he would've sold the place to her husband, now wouldn't he?"

"How pretty is she?"

"How the hell should I know?"

"Well, you just spent half the night in the saddle coming home so you could meet her," Josh reasoned. "No man in his right mind would go to that kinda effort just to meet an ugly gal. Besides, why else would Roy reckon you meeting her will save his hide unless she's so pretty he figures you'll reckon he's done you a favor? Living this far from town, a woman is bound to need a man round the place to keep her company—"

"Then why don't you hightail on over there tomorrow and marry her, Josh?" Adam gibed. "We'll get the land we deserve, and it'll save me the trouble of checking her out."

Josh chuckled. "Me . . . marry? And disappoint all my lady loves?"

"I'm sure the painted cats in Helena will get over you," Adam said sarcastically.

"Nah. They'd miss me too much, and I sure as hell would miss them. Now, you . . . a wife might do you a world of good."

Easing his feet out of his boots, Adam crossed his thigh with his ankle and absently massaged his foot. "A wife would do me about as much good as a case of prickly heat on a trail drive. No matter how agreeable a woman is at the start, I've yet to meet one who doesn't prove herself more bother than she's worth and neither have you."

"You're too hard on women, big brother. Always have been. Every mama in the territory has her sights set on you for her daughter's husband, and every daughter is panting right beside her mama. And will you oblige them by falling in love? No."

Adam stroked the ends of his mustache. "Do I string them along?"

"You sure don't discourage them."

"There isn't a soul in the territory hasn't heard me say I intend to remain a happy bachelor until my dying day, and that includes every one of the ladies you mentioned. If they choose to think different . . ." He shrugged. "I don't see why I shouldn't have a little fun with them. If I see a gal is getting too serious, and I'm in hazard of breaking her heart, I just stop hanging around."

Josh pulled a long face, but there was a mischievous twinkle in his eye. "Poor noble Adam. You're cursed with the three virtues women find irresistible. You're handsome, have a goodly accounting at the bank, and you're content to be bachelor. Of course, they're compelled to marry you—it's in their natures. They can't help themselves."

"Well, I'm no more the marrying kind than you are." Adam chuckled.

"That mean you're planning on getting hitched someday, after all?" Josh waggled his eyebrows. "I sure am. Kinda like the notion of having a woman to take care of me. Yep, I intend to tie the knot all right, just as soon as I get finished sowing my wild oats."

"And when do you reckon that will be?"

"Years yet." Both brothers laughed.

"How long *you* gonna wait?" Josh prodded.

"Forever," Adam answered succinctly.

"Aw, come on, Adam. If you'd ever give a lady half a chance, you might find—"

"Drop it, Josh."

"I'm being serious, now. Sometimes you act as if women are all—"

"I said drop it."

Josh lifted his hands in a gesture of surrender. "Okay. It's your life."

"It is," Adam agreed. "Now if you're interested in getting back to talking about Higgins's land, I'll fill you in on what's going on. Otherwise I'm gonna wash up and bed down." He rose halfway out of his chair.

"I'm interested," Josh assured him.

"Good." Adam lowered himself back to the seat of his chair. "There's more important things in life than gambling, whiskey, and women."

Josh grinned. "Might be, but I figure a man oughta play to his strengths. I devote myself to sampling life's many pleasures because that's what I'm best at, and you devote yourself to this ranch because it suits you. That's why we make such fine partners."

It was an old argument, and one Adam had learned long ago he would never win. He wasn't even sure he wanted to. Josh had a flare for enjoying life. It didn't seem right to spoil his fun. Besides, when the chips were down, he could always depend on Josh to do what was necessary. There was no other man he'd rather have by his side. Still, he wasn't fool enough to admit it to him. Josh got himself in enough scrapes the way it was. Without preamble Adam offered up the facts. "Higgins claims our new neighbor is a bored little rich girl from Virginia who won't last out the week. If I agree with him, there's no harm done. He has it in writing she can't sell to anyone but us."

"Then why didn't he just sell to us in the first place?"

"Greed. He got twice what the land was worth."

"And he figures when she sells, she'll sell cheap." Josh supplied his guess of Higgins's reasoning.

"That's what he figures," Adam confirmed.

Joshua quietly ruminated on the information before offering his estimation of the situation. "Old Roy has proven he has a good head for business in the past. He's also been a loyal friend to us. Maybe he knows what he's doing."

"It's possible," Adam concurred. "That's why I agreed to give him the benefit of the doubt and postpone making him pay for his double-dealing with his hide."

"But you're still riled at him."

"I had a lot of time to think on the ride home. It's also possible he let himself be taken in by a wily woman."

"Can't be too wily if she overpaid for the land," Josh maintained.

"That's true." Adam thoughtfully accepted the logic of his brother's statement.

"My money says Roy wouldn't have sold out if he wasn't one hundred percent sure his land would end up in our hands. We've got nothing to worry about."

"Could be. But I'm not gonna take his word for it without checking her out myself. First thing in the morning, I'm paying a call on our new neighbor."

"If she's easy on the eyes, let me know. I won't mind helping you settle this matter by paying her a little visit myself."

Adam shook his head. "Let you around a good-looking woman and you're about as much use as a stallion near a mare in heat. If she said she wanted it, you'd likely sell her the house we're sitting in if you figured it'd get her into your arms. I'll be handling this myself."

"I'm crushed by your lack of faith." Josh hunkered deeper into his blanket.

"Am I wrong?"

"Naw. You've got my breed." He guffawed. "But I can't be selling our home out from under you without you signing the deed as well as me, so you quit fretting. A man's got a right to satisfy his curiosity."

"Leave Miss Kendall to me."

"You sure you can handle her all alone? What if you take one look at her and fall head over heels in love? Could be dangerous. Better take along a back-up man to protect you from her womanly wiles."

"The woman hasn't been born I can't handle, baby brother."

"Remember that bronc buster came round here last summer bragging how the horse hadn't been born he couldn't break? We both know what happened to him when we put him on ol' Tanglefoot. Your braying sounds suspiciously like his. Sure would tickle my ribs if some day you suffered a similar fate."

Rolling his eyes and shaking his head, Adam rose to his feet. "It's late. I'm going to bed."

"Night, Brother. Sweet dreams."

Adam adjusted his hat to better shade his eyes and stared across the Missouri River at the tendril of smoke rising out of the cookstove chimney of Higgins's house. He had neither the time nor the inclination to pay a call on his new neighbor, but procrastinating wouldn't improve the task—so there was nothing to be gained by putting it off.

Though the two ranches lay directly across the river from each other, the river was wide and deep between them, necessitating either the use of a skiff or a horseback ride upriver to a spot where the river was more shallow and narrow. The boat was faster, but since he was planning to ride out and check on his spring calves after he paid his visit, he opted for horseback.

Adam gave the cinch of his saddle a final tug, mounted, and spurred his horse.

By eastern standards it was too early in the day to be making a social call, but that didn't concern him in the least. Truth was, it pleased him. Around here, people rose before the sun and were ready to face whatever the day had in store by the first sign of light. If Miss Camille Kendall wanted to be a rancher, she best get used to doing things the Montana way, and in this valley the Montana way was his way.

His horse knew the path by heart, and Adam concentrated his attention on his ranch, making a mental list of the chores he wanted his hands to complete by week's end. As he did so, his face wore a contented expression.

It wasn't until he was riding into his new neighbor's yard

that he allowed his thoughts to return to Miss Kendall. His contented expression dissolved into one of irritation.

Roy had no right to sell his property to this Kendall woman without consulting him first. *He* ought to have been the one to make the decision whether to gamble she wouldn't stay or at least have the opportunity to match her price. He was as fond of money as the next man and not inclined to overpay for an investment, but adding Higgins's acreage to his was important. Its value could not be counted wholly in dollars.

The sound of approaching hoofbeats must have alerted Miss Kendall she had a visitor, because she stepped out onto the porch at the same moment he reined to a halt.

His eyes began to twinkle, and Adam grinned from ear to ear as he took in her elegant, dainty appearance with a sweeping gaze.

Miss Kendall was barely five feet tall, and he doubted she weighed as much as a hundred pounds. Wisps of silky flaxen hair framed her delicate finely boned features. Roy was right. A woman like her would never make a rancher. The land was as good as his.

With that worry off his mind, Adam relaxed and began to chew on the idea of taking advantage of the situation.

There was no denying the male in him had taken an immediate hot-blooded fancy to her feminine charms. Women as beautiful as Miss Kendall were a rarity in any part of the world, and in the territories they were nonexistent. A healthy surge of warm blood heated his veins, and he shifted on his saddle.

Josh claimed their new neighbor was going to be in need of company. There was no reason he shouldn't be the one to furnish it. She wasn't going to be around long enough to turn troublesome. Besides, who knew what kind of damage an inexperienced eastern filly might do to the place? He owed it to himself to keep an eye on the property. A few words of advice whispered in her pretty little ear could save his men and him the time and effort of undoing any disasters she begat.

Lord knew, greenhorns invariably proved themselves a fine source of entertainment, and lovely Miss Kendall was so green he imagined she'd top them all. Likely he'd be hooting over her blunders weeks after she packed her bags and headed on home.

He'd been working too hard of late and could use the diversion, especially when that diversion would be provided by a woman with a face so fair angels must envy her.

Yep. The more he thought about it, the more hanging around Miss Kendall was starting to appeal to him. His grin stretched even wider.

"Are you just going to sit there on your horse staring at me with that ridiculous grin on your face, or is there something I can do for you?" Camille inquired sharply when the stranger in her yard failed to introduce himself.

"Pardon me, ma'am. It's just that Roy's description of you didn't do you justice, and I was taken aback by your beauty." He delivered the line smoothly. Removing his Stetson, he revealed a head of thick russet hair.

His compliment had no effect on her. "I am assuming you are referring to Mr. Higgins."

"Yes, ma'am. He told me yesterday he sold you this place."

He was still staring and grinning at her, which didn't please Camille in the least. She stared right back, assessing him with the same bold regard he used on her.

The man knew how to sit his saddle, and his horse appeared healthy and well groomed—facts she'd noticed the moment she'd laid eyes on him. Any man who esteemed his horse couldn't be all bad.

His face was pleasant enough. Despite his fatuous grin, there was an intelligent gleam in his dark blue eyes. She suspected his nose had been broken once, but it had healed in a relatively straight line. His hair was long enough so that it brushed his collar. He sported a trim mustache. The tan color and texture of his skin was evidence of a life lived outdoors.

But his face was of little interest to her. What was of interest was the tall, well-muscled frame beneath his cotton shirt and denim trousers. She could put *that* to good use. "Are you looking for work?" she asked eagerly. "I'm planning to hire several men over the next couple of weeks. If you can follow orders, don't mind hard work, and can convince me you are of good character, I'm willing to offer you employment. You can start today if you like."

"Thanks for the offer, but I'm not here begging work. I'm your neighbor from across the river." He gestured toward the two-story, whitewashed house and assortment of outbuildings with a sweep of his arm. "I just rode over to be neighborly. The name is Adam Carrigan."

Camille immediately recognized the name and suffered a fleeting twinge of guilt. So this was the friend to whom Mr. Higgins had previously pledged his land. She hadn't been entirely certain he really existed. In fact, she'd been more than a little suspicious Mr. Higgins was making him up in order to justify his price. However, knowing for certain Mr. Carrigan did indeed exist wouldn't have prevented her from doing everything she could to secure the land. There was no use pretending otherwise, either to herself or him.

Camille wondered if Mr. Higgins had shared his opinion that her efforts at ranching would prove unsuccessful. She quickly concluded most likely he had. She also assumed the grin on Mr. Carrigan's face meant he was of the same mind.

Having spent a lifetime having her competence judged by

men before a shred of evidence for or against her was available to them, she was neither surprised nor hurt by her conclusion—but she *was* annoyed. A caustic comment sprang to her lips, but because she so recently had acquired land Mr. Carrigan wanted, and she preferred to be on good terms with her neighbors, she decided to be polite.

"I was just having my morning tea. Would you care to join me for a cup?"

"I'd rather have coffee if you have it," Adam replied. Dismounting, he looped his reins over the hitching post and joined her on the porch.

"I don't."

"I guess tea will have to do. I'll ride back over with a sack of coffee later on so you won't have to do without."

"No, thank you. I don't drink coffee."

"Most everybody else round here does—strong, hot, and by the gallon," he informed her in friendly tones. "If you don't want people to reckon you're unneighborly, you'd best have a ready supply when folks come to call."

"I appreciate the advice. Should I expect a lot of visitors?"

"Not likely this far from town. During the summer months if you get two or three visitors all season you'll be having an uncommon amount of company. Come winter, you won't see a soul till the spring thaw."

Camille rested a hand on her hip and tilted her head to one side. "Then why should I stock my larder with a supply of coffee?"

His eyes sparkled with roguish lights. "Because I like it, and being your closest neighbor, I figure I'll be paying frequent calls on you. Seems only right I help you get settled in."

Camille was no stranger to flirtation, and she gifted him

with a too-sweet smile. "Why would you think that? If anything, I should think you would resent my being here."

"Now why would I do that?"

He sounded genuinely perplexed. Perhaps Mr. Higgins had lied to her after all. "I was under the impression you wanted to purchase this property," she stated candidly.

"Sure do. With this land added to what we already own, my brother and I will own the whole valley. Higgins and I had an agreement, and I don't mind telling you I was mad as a hornet when I heard he broke his word."

"Then why help me?"

"Am I ever gonna get that tea you offered?" He avoided answering her question by asking one of his own.

"Of course. Please come into the house." Camille turned to hide the speculative look that stole over her face. There was a reason he hadn't answered her question, and it wasn't a desire for tea. "Do you take sugar?" she politely queried, opening the door.

"No, ma'am."

"Cream?"

"No, ma'am."

His eyes widened with admiration as he stepped over the threshold. "You've been busy in here."

"Yes," Camille replied, setting another cup and saucer on the table. She filled both cups with tea. After pouring another dollop of cream into her own cup, she emptied the cream pitcher into Lucretia's bowl. "I'm afraid I found Mr. Higgins's affinity for dust and cobwebs off-putting. I still have a lot to do to make the place feel like home, but at least it's livable." She motioned for him to take a chair at the table, then sat in the chair across from his.

"Now that you have your tea, I'll ask you once again: If

you are angry over the sale of this property to me, why offer to help me settle in?"

Camille had hoped to catch him off-guard, but his relaxed posture and even tone told her she had failed. "No sense in making you pay for Higgins's double-dealing now is there? Besides, what's done is done. What's to be gained by holding a grudge?"

"That's very generous of you," Camille replied. He was up to something. Camille was certain of it. The land meant more to him than he was letting on. Two theories immediately sprang to mind. The first was that he was a lovesick cowboy who had hopes of gaining the land by courting her and acquiring her hand in marriage. The second was that he was as certain as Mr. Higgins that her ranch was going to fail, and he was willing to wait for her to sell him the land. Camille decided to test her second theory first. Maintaining a cordial expression, she commented, "I'm sure your belief that I am not up to the task I have set for myself has nothing to do with your noble attitude."

Adam choked on his tea.

"I thought as much. More tea, Mr. Carrigan?" she asked sweetly.

When he caught his breath, he squared his shoulders and stated, "I didn't come over here to wish you ill-fortune."

"No—you came to evaluate me, to see if you agreed with Mr. Higgins's assessment of the likelihood of my success or failure. Of course, knowing I was a woman you had already made up your mind there was no possibility I would succeed, and upon seeing me, confirmed your opinion." Camille pinned him with her steadfast gaze. "Feel free to defend yourself if I'm wrong."

"You're right," he grudgingly admitted without looking away. "But you're only half right."

"Where have I gone astray?"

"I don't believe it impossible for a woman to make a success of ranching. I've met two such ladies over the years."

"But you don't believe *I* am capable of such a feat." It was a statement, not a query.

She could see he was struggling with the question of whether or not to tell her the truth before he stated, "No, ma'am."

"May I inquire why?"

"Look in the mirror." When she did not respond and persisted to stare at him expectantly, he elaborated. "Look at the way you're dressed: all silks and satins and furbelows. You obviously don't have the slightest idea what working a ranch involves. Eastern folks are always coming out here with their pockets full of money and their heads full of ignorance, figuring they've got what it takes to meet the hardships of making a living in the West. You're no different from the rest of them—worse if you want to hear the unvarnished facts. I'd be willing to bet that pearly white face of yours never has seen a full day in the sun. You're too skinny to be carrying any muscle to speak of. And if you had half a head for business, you wouldn't have paid Roy twice what his land is worth."

"My, aren't we forthright."

"You asked for the truth. I'm sorry if you don't like it." His countenance exhibited only meager sympathy. "And to prove to you I wish you no further injury, I'm willing to save you a lot of misery and buy the land off of you now . . . before you hurt more than your pocketbook."

Camille tightened her grip on her teacup and mentally counted to ten. When she spoke, her voice was deceptively serene. "Just how much are you offering to pay me?"

"Exactly half of what you paid Higgins. It's what the land is worth."

"I fear I must decline your offer."

He scowled at her. "If you expect me to pay the price of your stupidity, you have a higher opinion of me than you should."

"Oh, I doubt that is true."

His scowl deepened. "You've admitted yourself the land rightfully should belong to me. It's a wonder a high-bred lady like yourself can sleep at night, knowing you talked a principled man like Roy Higgins into imperiling his immortal soul by getting him to agree to break his word and betray a friend."

"My acquiring this property was purely a business transaction and perfectly legal. Mr. Higgins's soul is not my concern. No one forced him to sell me his land. My advice to you is to choose your friends more wisely in the future."

"That *la te da* voice might work on men back East, but out here we don't kowtow to sharp-tongued women." Leaning over the tabletop, Adam spoke in measured tones. Camille met him halfway, matching him glare for glare. "I'm right and you're wrong, and you know it. You can sell me the land now, or you can sell it to me later . . . makes little difference to me. I know I'll be getting it eventually."

"Don't count on it."

"I am, as surely as I count on the sun rising every morning."

"Then you will be sorely disappointed."

"Only person round here who's gonna be sore is you. Couple of days of honest labor and you'll be begging me to take this place off your hands."

Reaching across the table, Camille snatched up his teacup, then marched to the sink and poured out the contents. Returning to the center of the room, she placed the empty teacup on the table. "You've finished your tea, Mr. Carrigan. Kindly leave."

He rose to his feet. "You know where to find me when you change your mind about my offer."

"I said leave! Get out of my house—*now!*"

Settling his hat on his head, he smiled tightly. "Be my pleasure, ma'am."

Two

"Morning, Miss Kendall."

"What are you doing here?" Camille demanded. Standing on the porch, her feet planted firmly, she gave her uninvited guest a steely glare.

"I brought you that coffee I promised."

She watched him dismount. Wearing an irritatingly friendly grin on his handsome face, Adam Carrigan pressed a small sack into her hands.

"I thought I made it perfectly clear yesterday that I have no use for your company." She tried to give the coffee back, but he refused to accept it. She did, however, succeed in blocking his path when he attempted to join her on the porch.

Rather than retreat, he remained on the step. "That's true, and that brings me to the other reason I'm here."

"Which is?"

"I've come to apologize."

Camille eyed him suspiciously. "Why?"

"What kinda question is that?"

"Since I find it impossible to believe you underwent a miraculous transformation during the night, I am forced to concluded your apology is insincere, and you have another purpose for being here."

Though his amiable smile remained firmly in place, a shadow darkened his eyes. It was gone before she was sure it had been there. "That's not very charitable of you. Can't I just be here because I place a high value on being a good neighbor and want a second chance?"

"You could—but I don't think you are."

"Well, you're wrong, and I aim to prove it. I'm here to offer my services. You tell me what you want done, and I'll do it."

"What makes you think I need your help?"

"Before you learned who I was, you offered me a job. If you're as savvy about running a ranch as you claim, I figure you wouldn't be looking to hire me on if there wasn't work to do round here that requires a man's muscles."

Though she was loath to admit he might be right about anything, his argument was too logical to refute. And she could use the help. She felt confident when it came to raising horses, but milking a cow, tending chickens, and many of the other activities related to the day-to-day functions of running her ranch were entirely different matters. She had prepared herself by reading books, but book knowledge was not the same as experience. These past two days, she had found herself increasingly frustrated for not retaining at least one of Higgins's men to see to the everyday chores.

Camille didn't believe Adam Carrigan felt a whit of remorse for the things he had said yesterday, but as long as she knew that and stayed on her guard, why not take advantage of the opportunity he offered? Earlier this morning she had milked the cow and fought the hens for their eggs, but there was still plenty he could do. "All right, Mr. Carrigan, you may stay . . . as long as you understand *I* am the boss, and things will be done my way. The furniture in the yard needs to be carried to a barn. The one next to the chicken coop will do nicely. I've already cleaned out a stall at the far end on the left."

"Before I lift a stick of furniture, I've gotta hear that you accept my apology. I don't work for free, and my price is your agreement to let bygones be bygones."

"How can I accept something that was never given? You told me you came to apologize, but you never actually did."

"Geez! You're a hard woman."

"Thank you, Mr. Carrigan, but a compliment is not an apology, and if you want me to—"

"I'm sorry for the rude things I said yesterday. I oughta have kept my opinion to myself. There. Are you happy now?"

"Yes. And I thank you for being wise enough not to insult my intelligence by pretending remorse for your opinions. You are only sorry you spoke them aloud, and that I can believe. I accept your apology."

"Thank you." He muttered the words with clenched teeth.

"You're welcome." Camille smiled demurely, but her eyes sparkled with a self-congratulatory light. Turning on her heels, she left him to the furniture, pausing just before she closed the door to call out. "When you finish with the furniture in the yard, if you're still in the mood to do penitence, there's more in here that needs carrying to the barn."

"Damn ungracious, bull-necked woman," Adam grumbled under his breath after she closed the door. "She's lucky I'm such a gentleman, or I'd make that silky blond hair of hers stand up on end with a few choice words." He turned to face the furniture.

What the hell was he doing here anyway? He didn't even like Miss Kendall, and he sure as hell didn't want her here in his valley. So what demon had possessed him to offer to help her out? If he had any sense, he'd have stayed home.

However, having made the offer, Adam's pride demanded

he stay the rest of the morning and give his best to whatever tasks she set for him. In the long run it wouldn't make any difference. He was still absolutely certain she wouldn't be staying in Montana long. "Nothing but a bored little rich girl. More money than sense—won't last the week," he recited to soothe his rankled soul.

Hefting a scarred oak side table to his shoulder, he started for the barn, reminding himself that the only reason he was here was to make sure she didn't do anything to devalue the property. "She could burn down this barn," he muttered to himself, stepping from the sunlight into the shade of the building. "She could burn the whole place down, start a grass fire, and set the whole valley ablaze." That was it—he had to be here to make certain the overconfident Miss Kendall didn't leave a path of devastation in her wake.

Adam spun on his heels at the sound of footsteps coming up behind him. Speak of the she-devil . . . here she came with that fancy cat of hers prancing beside her. Her silk-clad arms held a tobacco-stained ottoman.

"I thought you were gonna leave the furniture hauling to me," he commented. She set the piece on the ground with a thud, swatted a mosquito off her arm, and wiped the sheen of perspiration from her brow.

"I was coming this way and thought to save you a trip."

"A woman your size shouldn't be lifting such heavy objects. You'll get yourself hurt," he warned.

"I appreciate your concern, and I am well aware I am not a large person—but I understand the best way to build up one's strength is to test its limits." Before he could reply, she pulled a pen and paper out of her pocket and strolled to the back corner of the barn.

Setting the table he carried down in the stall she had earlier indicated, Adam watched her. The corner of the barn contained a hodgepodge of bales of wire, fence poles and posts, tools, and tack—some stacked, some hanging on hooks on the wall, some dumped in jumbled heaps. She straightaway set to sorting everything into tidy piles, pausing now and then to write on her paper.

She was wearing a dress stitched of blue-gray grosgrain. Its skirt was pleated with a ruffled hemline, and a starched lace collar framed her face. The silk bodice snugly fit her trim figure, emphasizing the tiny waist and rounded breasts. Every time she bent over, his wayward mind conjured lusty images of the hips that lay beneath her petticoats and skirt. He sighed—she had the face of an angel, body of a temptress, and tongue of a serpent.

"Is something wrong?" Camille asked plaintively.

"No." Adam startled to attention. "Why?"

"You keep staring at me."

"Do I?"

"Yes."

He wasn't about to admit the truth—but having been caught in the act, he had to come up with a plausible excuse quickly. Adam's lips curved into a smile when his eyes lit upon her cat. "I hate to offend your vanity, having so recently earned my way back into your good graces, but it's not you I'm staring at. It's your cat. It's different from the kind we have round here."

"*She's* a Persian. My father gave her to me as a gift."

"She suits you."

Camille shook her head and laughed. Affectionately she scratched behind her pet's ears. "Lucretia suits no one but herself."

"Lucretia? What kinda name is that for a cat?"

"I named her after Lucretia Mott, a champion of women's rights," Camille explained. "I'm not certain if she would be honored by my choice, but I meant it as a compliment. Of course, if Father had ever guessed how I came by the name, he would have been furious."

"Why?"

"He was not a great admirer of those who advocate equality between the sexes."

Adam smoothed the ends of his mustache. "And you are."

"Yes. I believe a woman is capable of doing anything a man can do. Ofttimes she can do it better—*if* she is given a fair chance."

Adam changed the subject. "You speak of your father in the past tense. I assume that means he's deceased."

"His heart failed two years ago."

"And your mother?"

"She died when I was fifteen."

"Brothers? Sisters?"

"No. I have an aunt and an uncle and three cousins still living on my father's side. Two aunts on my mother's. There is also the usual assortment of second and third cousins." Camille arched a brow. "Is there anything else you would like to know about my family?"

"That'll do for now."

Exiting the barn, Adam returned a few minutes later with another piece of furniture. He glanced at Miss Kendall. She was totally absorbed in the task of organizing and cataloguing the contents of the barn. Lifting a halter, she examined it carefully before setting it into the appropriate pile.

She wasn't afraid to get dirty, he'd give her that. Every time he returned to the barn, he found her still hard at work. Grudgingly he acknowledged she had more gumption than he originally had assumed—no common sense to speak of . . . that was obvious from the way she was dressed—but her lack of sense was a separate matter.

She was still sorting and writing away when he had emptied the yard of furniture. He cleared his throat to gain her attention. "You'll have to stop and show me what you want moved out of the house."

"Finished with the other already?" she voiced her surprise, looking up from her task.

"Yes, ma'am."

Slipping her paper and pen into her pocket, she dusted her hands and led the way out of the barn. As they walked side by side, she perused him from head to toe. "Tell me, are all Montana men as efficient as you, or are you the exception to the standard?"

"Montana men are like men everywhere when it comes to work—some good, some bad, some indifferent."

She nodded. "I'll remember that when I do my hiring."

"How many men are you planning to hire?"

"A half a dozen to start with, mostly carpenters. The existing barns are large enough to house the mares and need only minor alterations, but I'll want a separate barn and corral for each of the stallions," she replied. "Once my livestock arrives, I'll require men who are skilled with horses. I haven't settled on an exact number just yet. I prefer to get by with as few men as possible in the beginning. The smaller my payroll, the faster this place will start to turn a profit."

"And if everything goes according to your plan, how long do you figure that will be?"

"A couple of years at least."

Adam succeeded in hiding the distress her answer caused him. She was being realistic, and that worried him. It didn't bode at all well for his hopes to rid himself of her presence before week's end. He didn't mind hanging around keeping his eye on her for a few days, but he sure as hell didn't want to waste his whole summer. Didn't matter how easy she was on the eyes.

They had reached the house. She led the way up the steps and through the door. "Everything in this room goes to the barn." She walked through the parlor and into the room that had previously served as Higgins's office. "And this one as well." Returning to the parlor, she crossed the floor with purposeful strides and entered the kitchen. "The table and chairs stay. That stays. That goes." She pointed to a sideboard, then a cabinet with a door hanging by one rusted hinge. Next she led the way into her bedroom. She frowned. Adam assumed she must be embarrassed to have him in the room, but her words quickly disabused him of the notion. "Unfortunately the bed stays until my own arrives. Leave the bedside table and my trunks. The rest can go." She swept back into the parlor.

"Is that it?"

Her gaze drifted toward the ceiling before settling back on his face. "I'm sure the storage attic is full of things I neither need nor want, but I haven't had time to sort through them yet. Since they're not in the way, they can stay where they are for the time being."

Adam wasn't sure he liked the way she looked directly at him with her big blue eyes. It made him feel peculiar inside. Every woman he knew kept her eyes downcast and her voice soft when she talked to a man. If she wanted to look at him, she stole covert glances. Seemed like someone forgot to read Miss Kendall the ladies' rule book. A part of him kind of admired her nerve, but the rest of him didn't know what to think. He shifted his weight from one foot to the other. "Well, I best get at it."

An expression of uncertainty clouded her eyes. "Do you need any help?"

"I can manage on my own."

"I know you can," she assured him. "But you've already done so much, and I don't wish to take advantage of your generosity and impose on you."

Now there was a pretty, feminine speech if ever he heard one, Adam cheerfully observed. He immediately felt back in full control of the situation, and he had no compunction about arranging circumstances to his advantage. Reaching for her hand, he patted it consolingly. "Tell you what. Make me a pot of that coffee I brought you, and we'll call it even."

Camille smiled wanly. "All right."

Adam paced himself so he would complete his task in the same amount of time it took to brew a pot of coffee. As he worked, he chided himself for allowing himself to get thrown off balance by Miss Kendall's forthright ways. He had absolutely nothing to worry about. Miss Camille Kendall might have a bit more backbone than most gals, but at heart she was just like the rest—except comelier. He was in for a fine time, after all.

When the last piece of furniture was in the barn, Adam stopped at the pump to wash up and slick his hair before presenting himself in the kitchen. "Smells good," he commented as he slid onto a chair.

Camille poured him a cup of the brew and set it before him. Adam looked at the pale amber liquid. He took a tentative sip. Despite his best efforts, he couldn't disguise his grimace.

"I didn't make it right, did I?" Camille pursed her lips. "I was afraid I wouldn't."

"Are you saying this is the first time you've ever made coffee?" Adam asked in disbelief.

"Yes—I told you before, I don't drink it. Did I make it too strong or too weak?"

"Weak," he informed her. "It tastes like muddy water."

"I used the same amount of coffee as I would tea."

"The rule is one tablespoon of coffee to each cup of water, then boil the lot until it's good and black." He studied her countenance for signs of chicanery. She looked innocent enough, but he felt compelled to ask, "Are you sure you didn't make it wrong on purpose to punish me for asking you to fix it for me? Seems to me even a high-toned eastern gal oughta know how to do something as basic as brewing a cup of coffee."

Anger sparked from her eyes, and she folded her arms across her chest. "Well, I don't. Cook did that sort of thing back home."

"Amazing. The next thing you'll be telling me is you don't know your way round a kitchen at all."

"If you're asking if I can cook, the answer is no, I can't. Not well at any rate."

Much to Adam's delight, she was getting hotter under her starched lace collar by the second. Suppressing the twinkle in his eyes and shaking his head pityingly, he confessed, "I expected you to be ignorant about ranching, but—"

Camille planted her hands on the table and leaned toward him until mere inches separated their faces. "I am not ignorant about anything. I merely lack experience in some areas. If I set my mind to it, I can learn how to do anything, and I'll match my skills against any man who cares to test me."

Adam grinned. "Sounds like a challenge to me. I'll expect you at my place tomorrow. Dinner's at noon on the dot, so don't be late. When do you want me to back here, so you can show off *your* skill with a skillet?"

Camille's eyes widened with dismay. "When I said I was willing to match my skills, I was referring to my skill with horses."

"You said you can learn how to do anything you set you mind to, or was that just bluster?" Adam countered.

"It's the truth—but you can't expect me to come by the required knowledge in a day."

"How long do you figure you'll need?"

After a moment's contemplation, she stated, "A week."

"Okay. I'm invited to dinner at your place a week from today." Rising to his feet, Adam settled his hat on his hat. "It's been a pleasure, but I best be on my way. Don't want to overstay my welcome. Be seeing you." Strolling out the door, he poked his head back inside. "Don't forget: my place, noon, tomorrow."

"No, wait," she called. "I can't come tomorrow. I have business to tend in Helena."

"The day after then," he invited.

Camille shook her head. "I'm not sure I'll be back by noon."

"Saturday?"

"Yes. I suppose I can come Saturday."

"Then Saturday it is."

Camille's hands gripped the sides of her skirt until the sound of retreating hoofbeats assured her she was alone. *"A week!"* she fumed throwing herself down on a chair. What on earth had possessed her to say she could become an accomplished cook in a week? That smug expression on his face, that's what! She scooped Lucretia into her lap. He had goaded her into it—the wretch! She didn't have time for this nonsense. She didn't even want to learn how to cook. And she certainly didn't want to have dinner with him at his ranch on Saturday.

What she wanted was for Adam Carrigan to stay on his

side of the river, and she would stay on hers. There was something decidedly unnerving about the man. Every time he came around, she felt queer inside. It wasn't normal.

"I don't have time for this!" she complained aloud to Lucretia. Camille continued to grumble while she poured out the rejected coffee and rinsed out the pot and cup.

There was no denying that she was infuriated with Mr. Carrigan, but she was far more infuriated with herself. From the first moment they had met, every instinct had warned her that Adam Carrigan did not have her best interests at heart.

He might say he was just being neighborly, but she didn't believe him. He watched her too closely, and she wanted to know exactly what sort of mischief he planned.

Exasperated, she pulled pen and paper from her pocket and surveyed her list. She had more important things to do than sit around pondering his motives. If she intended to be ready to leave for Helena at dawn, her time would be better spent completing her inventory.

"Not again," Camille grumbled when her ears picked up the sound of an approaching horse later that afternoon. Mr. Carrigan certainly knew how to make a pest of himself. He might be a man of leisure, but she had work to do.

Rounding the corner of the barn, Camille planted a grim smile on her lips, that was quickly replaced by an expression of surprise at the stranger riding up. So much for Mr. Carrigan's assertion she shouldn't expect many visitors.

"Howdy, ma'am." He tipped his hat. "I couldn't resist the temptation to ride over and see what kinda woman was capable of finagling a dinner invitation out of Adam Carrigan." Springing from his saddle, he tossed the reins over his horse's head, approached her with leisurely strides, and extended his hand. "I'm Joshua Carrigan, Adam's younger brother. Folks round here refer to me as the good-looking one of the pair."

Camille shook his hand. Now that he had introduced himself, she noticed there was a strong family resemblance. Joshua was a couple of inches shorter than Adam and his hair was darker, but his eyes and chin were the same. The shape of his nose and style of his mustache were also similar. She eyed him warily. "I did not finagle an invitation from your brother. It was a challenge—pure and simple."

"Meant no insult, Miss Kendall." Joshua grinned, revealing a row of straight white teeth. "And I sure didn't mean to imply I thought you did anything underhanded. It's just I've known my brother all my life, and not once has he asked a woman to our ranch for dinner. I judge him asking you nothing short of a full-fledged miracle. By the way, you're even prettier than Adam said."

Camille took a deep breath. "Mr. Carrigan—"

"I'd be much obliged if you'd call me Josh. Sounds friendlier."

"I didn't realize we were friends," she said warily.

"Of course we are. Or least we will be once we get to know each other."

The words were spoken with such disarming conviction, it was difficult not to believe him. She wasn't ready to let her guard down completely, but Joshua Carrigan seemed very different from his brother. She felt relaxed in his presence. "Then you're not upset I bought this property?" she asked.

"Not me. My brother is the businessman of the family. I say the territory can use all the beautiful women it can get."

"Why?"

He winked at her. "A man likes variety."

Camille groaned. "Mr. Carrigan, let me disabuse you of any false hopes. I am not of a romantic bent of mind."

"Really?" He appeared more amused than disappointed. "Well, that's all right by me."

"It is?"

"Sure. I'm only interested in looking at the scenery. Too tender an age to sacrifice myself on the altar of matrimony. Besides, Adam saw you first."

"Your brother should not be nurturing false hopes either," she stiffly counseled.

"Don't worry, he's not. Adam hasn't even figured out he likes you yet. So are we gonna be friends as well as neighbors?"

Camille wasn't certain what to make of his second statement, but she was positive she didn't want to ask him to explain it. She was also positive she wanted to be friends with this Carrigan. Unlike his brother, Joshua Carrigan was a *harmless* flatterer. His charm was almost boyish, and her instincts told her the friendship he offered was genuine. She could use a friend. Besides, it only made good sense to be on good terms with at least one of her neighbors. "I see no reason we shouldn't be friends." She met his twinkly eyed gaze with one of warm welcome.

"And you'll call me Josh?" he coaxed.

"If you will call me Camille."

"Cammie sounds less stuffy. If you've no objection, I'd rather call you that."

Cammie—she liked the ring of it. Camille did have a decidedly stuffy quality to it. A new life and a new nickname. The idea appealed to her. "Yes," she enthusiastically agreed. "Call me Cammie."

"I knew I was gonna like you," Josh proclaimed.

Cammie smiled at his declaration, but a moment later her expression turned serious. "Since we've decided to be friends, and honesty is the hallmark of fine friendships, I'm going to test ours by asking you to leave so I can finish my work."

He didn't act the least bit offended. "Hear you're headed into Helena tomorrow."

"Yes."

"I'll send someone over to take care of the place till you get back. Don't want a coyote getting your chickens or your milk cow drying up while you're away."

Camille was mortified that she'd overlooked such basic necessities. Lack of experience and having a million other things on her mind was a poor excuse for making stupid mistakes. "Thank you. I'll reimburse you for the wages paid for the lost work hours."

"No, ma'am. I know you'd do the same for us if we were in a similar fix, so I count us even."

She supposed what he said made sense. "All right. I appreciate your generosity. Thank you, again."

"My pleasure." Tipping his hat, Josh mounted his horse. "Guess I'll be saying goodbye for now since you asked me to go. Looking forward to seeing you on Saturday."

"Goodbye, Josh."

"Bye, Cammie."

Three

Cammie stepped out of the offices of the *Helena Herald,* crossed a line through the seventh entry in her notebook, and started down the street. She was making excellent progress.

She already had been to the Montana National Bank and the Montana Improvement Company's Mill and Yard. In addition, she had visited every store on her list: a grocers, a hardware store, the dressmaker's to pick up the blouses and sturdy split skirts she had ordered, and a general merchandise store where among other things she had purchased a cookery book which she hoped would help her show up one annoying Mr. Adam Carrigan. Arrangements were made at each establishment to have her purchases loaded on her wagon by seven a.m. the next morning.

The newspaper advertisement she had just placed, announcing her need for skilled horse trainers and grooms, was scheduled to begin running in the next issue and every issue thereafter until the date she had set for the interviews which would be conducted at her ranch.

When she was last in Helena, she had distributed handbills advertising for carpenters at every establishment in town serving male clientele, excepting saloons and brothels, and she was confident the generous salaries she was offering guaranteed a good response. Greed was a great motivator of men, and she intended to use human frailty to her advantage.

Since her handbills plainly stated the positions she offered were temporary in nature, she could afford to pay well. It wasn't fair her sex forced her to bribe men into her employ, but it was a reality she accepted. Once she established her reputation, she could pay the prevailing rate.

Cammie planned to interview and hire her carpenters later that afternoon at the International Hotel. As soon as she ascertained the mettle of man available, and if she was able to hire the number of men necessary to meet her timetable, she could telegraph her cousin in Virginia and confirm the date she had earlier wired him to transport the horses she had selected. They would be traveling to Helena by railroad car under the care of their best grooms.

Her next stop was Perkins's livery, where she had stabled her horse and wagon, to notify the proprietor to expect the deliveries and to hire mules and freight wagons to transport the building materials she had purchased. When he named his fee, her eyes narrowed.

"The price you are asking is outrageous! I could practically buy my own teams for that sum. If you insist on insulting my intelligence, I shall take my business elsewhere."

"But—"

"But nothing!" Cammie advanced on him, her finger pointing at his chest. "You have exactly five seconds to name a fair price, or it will be the last you will ever see of me and my money."

Mr. Perkins looked bewildered. "Ain't you the lady who just bought Higgins's place?"

"Yes, I am," she confirmed. "If that is why you think you can cheat me, you are sadly mistaken. Mr. Higgins had something I wanted that could not be had elsewhere—I was willing to pay more than his land was worth because the property was worth the price to me. You don't have his leverage. Wagons and mules can be hired at any number of establishments."

"Yes, ma'am."

"Your price, Mr. Perkins?"

"I guess half of what I quoted you will be enough."

"Make it a quarter of your original price, and we have a deal."

"Now you're the one trying to cheat me," he protested.

"Take it or leave it, Mr. Perkins. It is my only offer."

His bottom lip jutted out, and he ground the heel of his boot in the dirt while he considered his answer. "I'll take it."

Cammie arranged to have the wagons delivered to the Montana Improvement Company as soon as was convenient and left her encounter with Mr. Perkins thoroughly satisfied. The only way to deal with men of his ilk was to outbrazen them. Not only had she negotiated an excellent price, she had put him—and she hoped everyone he complained to—on notice that she was not a woman with whom to trifle. Some circumstances might call for her to spend more than she liked, but in all others she refused to spend a penny more than necessary.

Cammie glanced at the watch hanging on the silver chain about her neck. She would have to hurry if she wanted to make it back to the International Hotel on time for the interviews.

When Cammie reached the hotel, she was gratified to find twenty men waiting for her. On the way to town, she had rehearsed her speech—and although she knew she risked alienating a number of the men she hoped to hire, she didn't want any man coming into her employ with false illusions.

"Good afternoon, gentlemen," she greeted. "So I don't waste your time or mine, I am going to be blunt. My standards are very high, and if yours are not, you will find me a difficult woman for whom to work. I pay well and I expect to receive quality work for my money. If I have to speak to you twice about slipshod work, you will no longer be in my employ.

"You will find me firm, but fair. I brook no questioning of my authority. After the stallion barns are built and renovation of the existing barns is complete, I will be permanently retaining two men to see to routine repairs. If you want to be one of those men, I suggest you distinguish yourself with superior craftsmanship." Sitting down at the table, Cammie opened her notebook. "If anything I have said makes you feel abused, I suggest you seek employment elsewhere; otherwise, you may form a line and I will begin the interviews."

It was seven o'clock by the time Cammie had hired her six carpenters. She also hired two additional men. Though they both lacked an acceptable amount of building experience, each had impressed her with his eager-to-work attitude. One she hired to care for the farm animals and tend the garden. The other she hired on as a cook for the other men.

She would have to wait until morning to send her telegram to Virginia, but all in all, she was quite satisfied with all she had accomplished. Picking up her notebook, Cammie rose to her feet, intending to retire to her room.

"Oh, excuse me," Cammie apologized to the gentleman whose shoulder she clipped as she ascended the stairs. "I shouldn't walk around with my mind so preoccupied." Glancing up at his face, she stiffened, rolling her blue eyes heavenward.

"Apology accepted, Miss Kendall," Adam Carrigan graciously replied, tipping his hat and bestowing an elegant smile upon her.

She sighed aloud. "You again?"

Placing his hand on the small of her back, he guided her two steps up to the landing and out of the path of other hotel patrons wishing to use the stairs. "You sound less than delighted to see me."

"Perhaps the timbre you hear in my voice is merely the shock of surprise." She arched a brow. "I didn't expect you to follow me to town."

"I had business of my own to tend in town," he said breezily.

She was not so easily convinced. "It's curious that you invited me to dine with you in your home today when you had no plans to be there."

Adam met her penetrating gaze without flinching. "Not curious at all to my way of thinking. I would've been there if you'd accepted my invitation, but since you didn't, I decided to come to town. Have you eaten supper yet?"

"No."

"Neither have I. Care to join me at the Cosmopolitan? They serve the best steak in town."

"I take it they buy their beef from you?"

"Yes, ma'am."

"If I say yes, does it cancel Saturday's dinner invitation?"

Did he detect a note of wishful thinking in her voice? Adam contained his delight at her discomfort. He was looking forward to making her eat her words too much to be willing to let her out of the cooking contest. Of course, what he'd like even better was for her to be gone from his valley, which was why he was standing here on this landing cajoling her into having supper with him. A smart man never counted his chickens before they hatched, and he wasn't about to let her out of their bargain until he had the deed to Higgins's place in his hand.

"Absolutely not," he answered her question. "Neither of us will be cooking for the other tonight—which I believe is the point of our previous arrangement."

She sighed again. "I had planned to have a tray sent up to my room."

"Sounds like a lonely way to spend an evening."

"I enjoy my own company," she declared.

"Don't you get enough of it on your ranch? Seems to me, you oughta share a bit of company when you come to town." He was doing his best to make it impossible for her to say no. Indecision crinkled her smooth brow.

"Well, I have to eat . . . and I do like a good steak . . . so why not? As long as you let me pay for both our suppers as a thank you for lending me one of your men while I had to be away."

"That was entirely Josh's doing." His voice came out sharper than he'd intended. He wasn't any too happy with Josh for playing knight in shining armor. Fact was, he was furious with him, but he didn't want Miss Kendall to know that.

She looked at him intently. "You disapprove of his generosity?"

Recovering himself, Adam suavely stated, "Not at all. But knowing my brother as I do, I'm worried he'll claim I robbed him by accepting the reward for his good deed."

"I've only met your brother once, but he didn't strike me as a man who cares a fig for standing on ceremony. If he makes a fuss, next time we find ourselves in town at the same time, I'll pay for a supper for him, too," she assured him.

"Are you always so free with your money?"

"I am never free with my money. I just believe in paying my own way in the world." She rebuked him with her trenchant gaze. "Now do we eat together or alone? I'm tired and I'm famished. Give me your answer, or you will find yourself standing here alone."

Offering his arm, Adam replied, "Together."

The Cosmopolitan was not far, and the weather was fair, so they walked the distance. The restaurant was part of a handsome four-story hotel. The front of the building boasted brick verticals and three wrought-iron balconies. Inside it was equally elegant. The maître d'hôtel guided them to their table. His solicitous attention was promptly replaced by the waiter who took their order.

"Did you have a pleasant day?" Adam made conversation while they waited for their meals to arrive.

"I accomplished most of what I set out to do." She lay her hand upon her notebook. "The carpenters are hired, which was my prime task. The *Herald* will run an ad for the other men I need. I plan to interview them at the ranch after my horses arrive, so I can watch the two together."

"When will your livestock arrive?"

"In three weeks—assuming my cousin doesn't have any problems at his end. I doubt he will since I arranged everything but the last-minute details before I left."

Adam smoothed the ends of his mustache. Her expression was chary, but she didn't balk at his questions. It was a good sign. Maintaining his nonchalant mien, he continued to herd the conversation down the path he wished it to go. "Does your cousin approve of your starting a ranch here in Montana?"

"It is not his place to approve or disapprove," she curtly informed him. "I gave over the day-to-day management of my Virginia ranch to him, which pleased him well enough. He'd been after Father to do it for years. Cousin Shelby is under my thumb, not the other way around."

"Why aren't *you* managing the ranch in Virginia?"

"Because of narrow-minded men who prefer to conduct business with other men behind the closed doors of their all-male clubs." A flame sparked in her blue eyes. "On the rare occasions they were forced to deal with me, they were so patronizing I found it difficult to keep my temper."

"And you reckon it will be better here?" His words were half question, half statement.

"Yes. The competition will not be so keen. There are some good horses in the area, but none come close to matching my stable in quality. Too, here I am starting with a clean slate and will not be hampered with the burden of being Beaumont Kendall's pampered daughter."

"So you were pampered?"

"Smothered is a more accurate word."

"I figured you'd lived a sheltered life—which is why I've decided to up my offer for Higgins's property," he gallantly apprised her. "Having thought the matter over, I'm willing to pay what it's worth *and* split the difference on the amount you overpaid."

"How very charitable of you," she politely responded. "But as you know, the land is not for sale."

"I'm giving you a chance to change your mind." Leaning forward, he spoke in an exaggerated whisper. "I'm telling you as a kindness, whatever troubles you had in Virginia, you'd be better off living there. I've seen what life in the territories does to a woman. It wrinkles her skin, turns her hair gray, and ruins her figure years before her time. I'm sure you don't cotton to that happening to you. Be a crying shame to throw your beauty away for a few acres of dirt."

"I'm willing to take the risk. To be honest I find beauty more of a curse than an asset for a woman of ambition." Camille frowned. "If the only reason you asked me to join you for supper was to try to convince me to sell my property to you, you are wasting your time."

Adam could feel the muscles in his face knotting up. Damn mule-headed woman. If he didn't want the land so much, he wouldn't waste his time on her. Try as he might to be pleasant, every time he was around her, he found himself getting all steamed up. He knew the smart thing to do was to exercise a little patience, but he preferred this business over and done with and was willing to pay the price.

"I can see you aren't taking me seriously. I know I'm a softheaded fool, but I admire you too much to let you ruin yourself," Adam said, doing his best to sound compassionate. "If the only thing that will get you to behave sensibly is for me to pay you what you paid Higgins, I guess I'll have to do it."

"What you admire, Mr. Carrigan, is my land," she corrected. "Regrettably, I admire it as much as you. Obviously that causes you considerable distress." She picked up her notebook. "Perhaps I should leave now, so you can enjoy your meal."

"Ah, our food has arrived," Adam abruptly announced. Reaching across the table, he pried the notebook from her fingers. "Since you claim to be famished, it only makes sense you stay."

She clearly was displeased he had taken possession of her notebook, but after throwing him a withering glance, she picked up her fork.

Adam let the conversation lapse while both took the edge off their hunger. He was disappointed she hadn't accepted his more than generous offer, but only a little surprised. Though he tried to concentrate wholly on his meal, he couldn't help noticing several things about his dinner companion.

The first was the graceful way she moved her hands as she handled her knife and fork. When she tilted her head or brushed a wisp of hair from her cheek, it was the same. Though he would like to count the refinement of her movements against her, her grace was natural, not affected. Miss Kendall might not be a pleasure to do business with, but she surely was a pleasure to watch.

Another thing he noticed was that she didn't pick at her food like most women did when dining with a man. How she put all that food in that petite body was a mystery. She didn't wear an ounce of fat. She probably needed it to fuel her snippety tongue, he surmised, his lips twitching at his private joke.

His acute awareness of her enticing person brought him to another inconsistency. She appeared oblivious of the appreciative perusals of every man in the restaurant, and he counted a full dozen men who made no effort to be subtle about staring at her. It was as if she were unaware of her extraordinary beauty, or if aware, she chose to ignore it. She said she thought beauty a curse, but he'd never met a woman yet who wasn't at least a little vain. Her attitude confused him.

Lastly, he brooded over her conspicuous lack of need to fill every silence with idle prattle. She didn't scorn his questions, she answered them—sometimes with vinegar but always with a refreshing frankness. She even asked a few questions of her own. But she was certainly in no danger of being branded a chatterbox.

He wasn't sure what to make of her. She managed to be delectably feminine and thorny as a prickly pear cactus all at the same time.

"You ever been sweet on a man?" The question slipped past Adam's lips before he knew he was going to ask it.

Her grip tightened on her fork, and she glowered at him. "What kind of question is that?"

"An honest one. I've been sitting here looking at you, and

I can't figure out how come a woman as pretty as you isn't hitched up to someone."

"You do have a bad habit of staring at me. Kindly cure yourself of it." She returned her attention to the potato on her plate.

So she had noticed. He felt better knowing she was neither bereft of vanity nor capable of wholly ignoring his presence in favor of the food on her plate. "Do I get an answer to my question?"

"No, I have never been sweet on a man," she said curtly. Lifting a bite of steak to her mouth, she chewed it thoroughly, then deftly changed the subject. "This is good. I'll have to remember this place."

Adam leaned back in his chair. "Planning to come to town often?"

"I'll be making the trip more often than I'd like until I get my ranch up and running. You know, telegrams to send, trains to meet . . . that sort of thing." Now that they were discussing a topic she liked, her manner and voice mellowed.

"I'm sure you miss having all the modern conveniences within easy walking distance."

"Not really. Do you?"

"No, but a body can't miss something they've never had."

"Have you and your brother lived in Montana all your lives?"

"No. We grew up on a ranch in Wyoming."

"Do your parents still live there?"

He could feel his muscles tense. It was an innocent enough question, but he wasn't about to tell her the truth. Then again, he didn't know what he was going to say wasn't true. "They're both dead."

"I'm sorry."

"It was a long time ago." Adam dismissed the subject with

a shrug of his shoulders. The last thing he wanted was anyone's sympathy. This was a business meeting not a social event, and it was time to get the conversation back on track. "So when are you planning to head back to the ranch?" he casually asked.

"Tomorrow morning as soon as the telegraph office opens."

"Want company on the ride?"

She hesitated a moment before noncommittally replying, "I don't have anything against it."

Adam jumped on her answer. "I'll take that as a yes. Where is your wagon and horse stabled?"

"Perkins's livery."

"How about if we meet there at nine o'clock?" he suggested.

"I'm leaving at eight."

"Even better. Do you want dessert? The cherry pie is good here."

"No, I'm full, but you have dessert if you want some."

"Reckon I'll pass tonight, too."

Signaling for their waiter, he whipped out his wallet and pressed payment for the meal and a generous tip in his hand before his dinner companion had transferred her beaded reticule from her lap to the tabletop. "That should cover our bill," he informed the man.

Miss Kendall was staring daggers at him. He winked at her, quickly ushering her out of the restaurant before she made a scene.

On the street, she turned to face him. "Why did you do that?" she said angrily.

"I wanted to."

"That's not a good reason. We had an agreement."

He had been planning all along to pay for their meal. The

gentleman in him prevented him from even considering letting her pay. But he was not so much a gentleman that the opportunity to throw Miss Kendall off balance didn't hold great appeal. If she didn't behave in expected ways, why should he? "No, we didn't. You assumed we did, and I didn't tell you different."

She snatched her notebook from his hands. "If I ever have business dealings with you, I'll be sure to spell out every detail on paper and have several witnesses watch you sign." Turning her back on him, she started up the street at a brisk pace.

"Aren't you forgetting your manners, Miss Kendall?" Adam fell in beside her.

"What?"

"I don't know how they do things back East, but round here when a gentleman pays for a lady's supper she smiles at him and says thank you."

"A *gentleman* didn't pay for my supper. A liar did," she sputtered. "And if you paid for my meal because you are harboring any romantic designs concerning my person, you have wasted your money. I would rather be stomped to death by a herd of wild horses than fall in love and be tied down by some man."

Where did she come up with the idea he was getting sweet on her? "Don't lose any sleep worrying about my 'romantic designs,' Miss Kendall. I'm a confirmed bachelor and intend to stay that way till they bury me six feet under. And even if I wasn't, the last woman on earth I'd set my sights on is a prissy little Evangeline, like yourself."

"Can I have that in writing?"

"You bet! And I'll be glad to gather every soul in the territory to serve as witness."

Halting in midstride, she blocked his path, staring him

down like a bull about to charge. "Good night, Mr. Carrigan!"

"Good night, Miss Kendall!"

Cammie groaned aloud when she recognized the blood bay gelding tied to the hitching post in front of the livery. She had been confident after last night's heated confrontation that Adam Carrigan wouldn't be here this morning. She rubbed her temples. Now she would have to spend hours in his company. She didn't want to spend five minutes with him. What drove the man to plague her so?

He had been genuinely offended by her suggestion that he might be harboring romantic ambitions concerning her. Or at least she thought his outrage genuine, but with him she could never be sure. But what else was she supposed to think with all his talk about being a gentleman? And all through supper, every time she looked up at him, he had been staring at her with a covetous expression on his face. She had seen that look on the faces of other men, and it had always meant only one thing: trouble.

She wasn't up to another encounter with Adam Carrigan. She had been up half the night poring over recipes in the cookery book she had had delivered to her hotel room. Then she had risen early this morning so she could stop by the grocer's to pick up a few items she would need that her original list had lacked. But she hadn't suffered the lack of sleep because she was eagerly anticipating his company. She had done it because she had been so furious she couldn't sleep and because now—more than ever—she was determined to best him.

He sauntered through the door of the livery. "Telegram all

sent?" he greeted as if they had parted on the friendliest of terms last evening.

"Yes."

"Good. I took the liberty of having Perkins hitch your horse to your wagon, so we're ready to go."

Mr. Perkins led the horse and wagon out of the barn. Just in case he had any thought of handing the reins over to Adam Carrigan, Cammie snatched the leads out of his hands.

"Thank you, Mr. Perkins." She counted out what she owed him and took her seat on the wagon. Moments later she was guiding the wagon through the streets toward the edge of town. It took only a minute for Mr. Carrigan to catch up with her on horseback, but he remained silent until after they reached the outskirts of town.

"How long are you gonna stay mad at me?"

"I'm not angry. I'm annoyed." She kept her head facing forward.

"How long are you gonna stay annoyed at me?" he amended his question.

"Forever if you don't find something more productive to do with your time than hound my heels. I have things to do and more than enough on my mind to keep it occupied without having to constantly deal with you." She cast him a perplexed glance. "Why aren't you still angry with me?"

"Because last night when I got back to my room, I got to thinking about what you said and what I said, and I figured instead of being angry we oughta both be happy to know where the other stands. Makes it easier to be friends. Now we can enjoy each other's company without worrying the other is misinterpreting friendliness as romantic overtures."

She eyed him speculatively. "I have made it *more* than abundantly clear I am not interested in selling you my property for any price. And we can't seem to spend more than a few minutes together without getting on each other's nerves. Wouldn't it be more logical to abandon the idea of being any kind of friends at all?"

He dazzled her with a beguiling grin. "Nothing worse than not being on friendly terms with your neighbors. Besides, I have a notion sparring with you will keep my wits sharp."

"You enjoy arguing with me?"

"Enjoy is too strong a word. I don't enjoy taking a dose of cod liver oil, but every once in a while I need it."

It was the strangest compliment she'd ever received, but Cammie found herself pleased by it. It was certainly preferable to some lovesick idiot blathering on about the color of her eyes or the perfection of her complexion. "And what do I get out of this friendship?"

"Well, for starters I can provide you with useful information about the local customs."

Cammie thought it a great inconvenience God had seen fit to bless Adam Carrigan with more than ample brains and charm to compensate for his less appealing character traits. She really didn't need the distraction and would have been happier if she could develop an honest disliking for the man. Unfortunately she couldn't.

If truth be told, there *was* a certain satisfaction to be gained by sharpening her wits on him. Maybe they should be friends. Her eyes began to twinkle, and she smiled at him.

"Mr. Carrigan, I'm sure I will come to regret it—probably several times before we reach our respective ranches—but being friends does makes more sense than maintaining a lifelong feud."

"Thank you for seeing things my way, Miss Kendall."

"Don't look so pleased with yourself. I may be willing to extend the hand of friendship, but that doesn't mean I won't be counting my fingers."

"Appreciate the warning."

Except for the steady attacks of bloodthirsty Montana mosquitos which necessitated an embarrassing amount of swatting and slapping, the rest of the journey passed pleasantly enough, and Cammie found herself grateful for his company.

There was no question Adam Carrigan liked to twit her about her eastern origins, but he seemed to do so in the spirit of good fun, so she saw no reason to take offense. Besides, she contrived to poke his ribs as often as he poked hers, so she considered them evenly matched.

She'd never met a man who didn't feel compelled to treat her like a fragile flower, and she found it exhilarating to be dealt with as a peer. She'd rather face a thousand barbs than one more simpering, solicitous remark.

When the topic turned to ranching, Cammie listened far more than she talked and gained quite a bit of useful information in the course of the conversation.

Some miles neither of them felt obliged to say a word which was equally agreeable.

"Ouch!" Cammie exclaimed when her well-aimed whack came too late to prevent her target from taking a taste of her blood.

"Mosquitos always give you as much fits as they are today?" Adam inquired.

"They've been after me since the moment I stepped off the train," she complained, swatting another off the back of her neck.

"You should've told me sooner. I know just the thing to solve your problem."

"You do?" Her eyes lit with grateful expectation. "What?"

"Bear grease."

The bright lights immediately darkened, and she rolled her eyes. "Right."

"All the cowboys round here use it," he claimed. "You don't see any of the little blighters biting me, do you?"

Now that he mentioned it, she didn't. Maybe he was serious. "Are you wearing bear grease?"

"No, ma'am. After you use it for a while, its protective properties stick with you. I've been using it so long, all I have to do is smear it on once or twice a year and I'm set."

Not so much as a muscle twitched, and he sounded utterly sincere. She watched him closely for any telltale sign he was pulling her leg and saw none. She still wasn't entirely certain she believed him, but her desire for relief was great, and she pursued the topic. "If a person were so inclined, where would she get some bear grease?"

"From a bear."

She quirked a brow. "And where am I supposed to find myself a bear?"

"As a general rule they live in the forest. Of course, if you are too busy to go bear hunting right away, I could lend you a jar of grease. We have more than we need on a shelf at home."

"You do?"

"Every rancher in the territory keeps a good stock on hand."

His last two statements convinced her he was telling her the truth. He couldn't offer something he didn't have, and why would he have bear grease on his shelf if it didn't have a useful purpose. She was about to accept his offer, when he continued.

"Mind you, my offer is contingent on a promise from you that you won't get your hackles up just because I feel like being generous."

"You have my word," Cammie assured him.

"Then the jar is yours."

"Thank you, Mr. Carrigan."

"You're welcome, Miss Kendall."

Four

Cammie's nose wrinkled, and she shuddered as she spread a thin layer of pungent bear grease down her arm. "This stuff better work or I'm going to kill him," she vowed, setting the jar on her bedside table. "Kill him and feed his carcass to the crows." If she weren't covered with itchy red welts, she would never subject herself to this wretched remedy—but she was being eaten alive, so she had no choice. The sooner she started taking the cure, the sooner she could be done with it.

Presuming, of course, that it worked. Of course, it must work, she reasoned. If he had made the whole thing up, would he have had jars of the dressing ready and waiting on his shelf? And he had warned her to expect a less than pleasant odor. Even assuming he possessed a mind devious enough to plan the outrage out in advance, nobody went to that much trouble to play a practical joke.

"I may as well face it, I'm just looking for an excuse to get out of using this vile-smelling ointment," she scolded herself. "I ought to be grateful he told me about it."

Adam Carrigan had told her to cover herself from head to toe every morning and before she went to bed at night. What he had neglected to say was how long it would take before she would be able to confine her suffering to once or twice a year.

Lucretia had escaped to the opposite end of the cabin, but for Cammie there was no escape. She hadn't been particularly enthusiastic about going to the Carrigans for dinner. But now she was anxiously looking forward to the opportunity to find out how long it would be before she could stand to be in the same room with herself again.

The rasp of saws and the pounding of hammers greeted Cammie's ears when she awoke the next morning. She smiled and jumped out of bed. There was nothing quite so invigorating as the sound of industry.

The men she had hired and the wagonloads of lumber had arrived at the ranch several hours after she had yesterday. After allowing the men time to settle into the bunkhouse, she had given explicit instruction as to what she wanted done, how she wanted it accomplished, and her timetable for completion. She had appointed Quigley Culver foreman, and if today was any indication of his productivity, she had made an excellent choice.

Before dressing for the day, Cammie opened her jar of bear grease and diligently rubbed it onto her skin. Halfway through the smelly process, she decided it just wasn't in her to inflict her odoriferous person on her dinner companions. Whether it delayed the cure or not, she was going to make time to take a bath before dressing for dinner at the Carrigans.

She was about to set the jar aside, then changed her mind. It was hours before she had to leave, and she intended to spend most of them outdoors overseeing the construction of her stallion barns. Perhaps if she wore the nasty medicine until it was time to get ready to leave, she wouldn't set back the treatment at all. With stoic determination, she finished the task.

Tea and toast with jam sufficed for her breakfast. As soon as she cleaned up, Cammie stepped outside to see what progress her men had made.

"Mr. Culver." She waved from across the yard as she approached. "I'm glad to see you've wasted no time getting started."

"Morning, ma'am. If we hope to make your deadline, we've no time to squander."

Even before she reached his side, Mr. Culver's nose began to twitch and his lips pulled into a thin line. He said nothing about the bear grease while they leaned over the drawings she had given him yesterday, clarifying details to be certain they were in agreement as to what she wanted built and where. Cammie admired his gallantry.

All of her men remained politely silent in face of her assault upon their noses. She considered it a sign of good character, and it supported Mr. Carrigan's claim that wearing bear grease to ward off biting insects was common local knowledge.

Mr. Culver and she continued to remain side by side, walking the grounds and discussing the work to be done.

Most of her mind was focused on what the foreman was saying, but Cammie couldn't help but notice she had been outdoors nearly an hour and not one mosquito had taken a sip of her blood. She mentally apologized to Adam Carrigan for ever doubting his word.

They were in the midst of making a minor adjustment in the layout of the easternmost corral when Mr. Culver blurted, "Ma'am, I know it ain't my place to ask it, but why are you wearing that bear grease?"

Her brow knit. "Don't you know?"

"No, ma'am."

"Adam Carrigan told me it's what people out here use to keep the mosquitos away. It certainly seems to work."

"Yes, ma'am—it does—but by my reckoning the cure is worse than the affliction."

A distressed look puckered her face. "Will I have to wear it for a very long time then? Mr. Carrigan told me after a person wears it for a while, they only have to use it a couple of times a year to maintain its protective qualities—but I forgot to ask him how long 'a while' is."

Mr. Culver shuffled his feet in the dirt. "Ma'am, you ain't gonna be pleased with the answer."

"How long?"

"Forever."

"What!"

"I reckon ol' Adam is playing you for a greenhorn," he informed her. "It's an old joke, but it works because the stuff stinks so bad ain't man nor beast gonna come within a hundred miles of you if they can help it."

"Why didn't you tell me this sooner?" Cammie riveted him with a glare. "The moment you saw me you must have realized—"

"No, ma'am, I didn't." Mr. Culver rushed to his defense. "It's not the kinda trick I'd expect a man to play on a lady." He scratched his head. "Don't know what could have gotten into Adam. Anyhow, I figured you being a city gal, maybe you was wearing it for some reason a country-bred fellow like myself never heard of. You being my employer and all, at first I didn't want to risk giving offense, but after a while I just couldn't help myself."

"I suppose it was the same with the other men?" Cammie questioned.

"Like as not."

Both the manner and tone of voice of her foreman bespoke

utter sincerity, and Cammie decided she believed him. That decision made, her thoughts turned to Adam Carrigan. Her judgment of him was not nearly so charitable. She took a deep breath to control her rising temper. "Just to be certain I have not misunderstood you, let me restate the facts. Bear grease will keep away mosquitos, but only while you wear it. It possesses absolutely no lasting properties. Nobody in their right mind uses it. Mr. Carrigan has made a fool of me."

"Facts sound straight to me."

"Thank you, Mr. Culver. You can be certain I will put this information to good use."

Marching back to the house, Cammie picked up two buckets and headed for the well behind the cabin. She pumped the handle vigorously. When the buckets were filled, she stomped inside and set the water on the stove to heat. She was on her way to the bedroom to fetch soap and towels, when she stopped in midstride.

"Wait a minute! What am I doing?" Her eyes took on a malevolent gleam. *"I know exactly how I shall punish Mr. Carrigan for his crime."*

"Right on time. I'm impressed. Punctuality is a rare trait in a woman," Adam greeted when he opened the door to welcome his dinner guest. He jerked back as a foul odor assaulted his nostrils.

"Why thank you, Mr. Carrigan," Cammie cooed, extending a hand slick with bear grease. When he hesitated to receive it, she lifted it up to his face. Positioning it directly under his nose, she invited a gentlemanly kiss.

Adam declined. Giving her hand a quick squeeze, he lowered it to her side. Cammie swept into the room when he stepped aside to allow her to enter. Her eyes rapidly scanned the neatly appointed parlor.

Yesterday she had entered the house through the kitchen door and stayed just long enough to obtain the jar of bear grease. Today she could take a more accurate measure of the devious Mr. Carrigan's home.

Decorated in subtly patterned cream and tan wallpaper with cream-colored trim, the parlor was furnished with an assortment of tables and chairs. Some of the chairs were wooden, others upholstered in shades of burgundy and brown. A sofa matching the upholstered chairs sat against one wall. A bric-a-brac shelf stood in one corner. A large bookshelf filled with books graced the wall opposite the sofa. The floor was covered with floral carpeting woven from yarn of the same color tones found in the wallpaper. Damask curtains hung over the windows.

She was impressed by the tastefulness of the decor, although it seemed oddly out of character for a man as double-dealing as Adam Carrigan. Cammie glanced at the object of her ire and was delighted to see the thoroughly miserable expression on his face.

Joshua Carrigan entered the parlor, a welcoming grin on his lips. "Cammie, I've been looking forward to today more than—" Coming to an abrupt halt, he began to cough. A pained expression rumpled his features. "Phewee! What on earth have you put on that pretty skin of yours?" he choked.

"Lubin's perfume," she sweetly answered. "Did I use too much? I'm afraid I may be coming down with a cold, and my nose is a little stuffy. I thought I was careful, but—"

"It isn't any perfume I'm smelling. What I'm smelling is bear grease."

"Oh, I'd almost forgotten about that. I did put a bit on this morning." She feigned innocence, "I was having a dreadful time with the local insect population, and your brother kindly told me of this fine cure. I can't tell you how grateful I am."

"The smell doesn't bother you?" he queried.

She pretended not to see the reproving glance Joshua threw his brother or the warning glare Adam threw back his direction. "No, it's so subtle I barely notice it," she earnestly proclaimed. "I hope it doesn't bother you, because your brother said I must use it faithfully day and night, or it will not be effective."

"He did, did he?"

"Yes."

"Is he also the one who told you to slather the stuff on like butter on bread?"

She turned to the elder brother. "Oh, dear, did I use too much, Mr. Carrigan?"

"It really isn't necessary to use the whole jar at one time." Adam focused his eyes on everything but her. Cammie wished she knew exactly what was going on in his head, but was willing to settle for the knowledge that she was making him suffer.

"I'll remember that in the future," she vowed. "Do you think you could loan me another jar?"

Adam swallowed. "Be happy to oblige." It was well worth having her stink up his house for an hour or two. He wondered how many days she would keep using the stuff before she wised up. When she did figure it out, she was going to be one distraught little lady. Conceited as she was, her pride would force her to start packing her bag for home then and there.

He must be dealing with the dumbest woman alive, Adam snickered on the inside while he struggled to keep his outward expression one of gentlemanly consideration. After she left, he'd have to remember to thank Josh for playing along. Good old Josh—he was the kind of brother a man could always depend on in a pinch.

Adam hadn't had this much fun with a tenderfoot since 'seventy-one when that preacher rode onto their ranch in Wyoming and started passing out copies of a little blue book titled *Help the Heathen Cowboy of the West.* They'd obediently pitched the man a revival tent, but when he'd begun ranting that the brothels and saloons should be burned to the ground, he and Josh and the boys had strung the preacher up by the ankles and had themselves some fine sport. He'd run like a rabbit when they finally cut him down. Suppressing a chuckle, Adam wondered how fast Miss Kendall could run.

"I best check on things in the kitchen," Adam declared. "Josh, entertain our dinner guest till I come back."

Josh grinned. "My pleasure."

"Miss Kendall, if you'll excuse me . . ."

"Of course," she said graciously.

Once in the kitchen, Adam closed the door and allowed the laughter he was holding back to erupt into a kitchen towel. His entire person shook, and he was obliged to stick his head out the back door and gulp in some fresh air. When he had discharged enough merriment to trust himself not to give the game away, Adam turned his attention to the pots on the stove.

He'd prepared quite a feast for Miss Kendall. He didn't often have time to dally in the kitchen, but cooking had been a hobby of his since he was a young man. There was a science to combining just the right ingredients. He liked the challenge.

Today he was making cream of spinach soup, strips of veal marinated in a sauce of his own invention, garlic potatoes, peas from the garden, and yeast raised rolls. For dessert he'd baked a chocolate layer cake, spliced together with a thick filling of huckleberry preserves and frosted with sweetened whipped cream. And to make certain the meal left a lasting impression, he had a surprise dish in store for her. Not that he planned to tell her what she was eating until just the right moment.

He could hear Josh and Miss Kendall talking and laughing in the next room. They certainly sounded like they enjoyed each other's company. Come to think of it, when had they gotten to know each other well enough to be calling each other by their first names? Maybe he'd better get back in there. Josh was a sucker for a pretty face. Miss Kendall might stink, but she was as far from ugly as a woman could get. If the sight of her beauty stirred *his* lust, it was a sure bet Josh was in there drooling on her shoes. He didn't want his brother getting too friendly and unwittingly spoiling his fun.

Everything was just about ready anyway. After making a few last minute adjustments in the seasonings, he transferred the food to serving dishes and announced the meal.

Stepping through the kitchen door, Adam winced when the odor of bear grease assailed his nostrils anew. But the suffering was worth it he gleefully reminded himself. After placing the serving bowls on the table, he returned to the kitchen twice more for the rest.

"Miss Kendall . . ." He held out a chair for her at the end of the table farthest from the other two place settings.

"I'd rather sit next to you, if I may," she requested. "Josh, you don't mind trading places with me, do you?"

"Glad to oblige." Josh leapt at the invitation.

She smiled. "Thank you."

"Everything looks delicious," she complimented when they were all seated at the table. Adam thought he detected a note of disappointment in her voice, but he couldn't be sure.

"Adam likes to cook," Josh apprised her. "Makes him a handy man to have round the house."

They continued to converse as they passed the serving bowls and platters around the table, filled their plates, and began to eat.

"It's a wonder he has time for ranching, what with all the time he spends engaged in other activities—or are you the one who runs this ranch?" Cammie asked.

"Nope. I'm the devil-may-care younger brother. Adam is the responsible one."

"Really?" Her eyes widened and she lay her hand upon her bosom. "I would never have guessed."

"You'll never meet a man who works harder. Handsome, too. Every mama in the territory has her sights set on him for her daughter."

"Cut it out, Josh," Adam complained. "Miss Kendall isn't interested in listening to you recite a list of my virtues or hearing tales of my struggles to remain a single man."

"Yes, I am," she brightly interjected. "Not the first part—but I'd love to hear about your romantic escapades. Has your brother broken many hearts?" she asked Josh.

"Dozens. But he's not a cad. He never strings them on. They just fall in love with him in droves."

Adam set his fork down with a thunk. "Miss Kendall, one thing you oughta know about my brother is that he's an unconscionable liar."

"Family trait?" Cammie murmured sweetly.

Adam looked annoyed. "What's that supposed to mean?"

"Oh, nothing . . ." She gave a small silvery laugh. "It's just that a person can tell a lot about a man by the way he responds to a joke." She dabbed at her lips with her napkin. "This *is* delicious. I hope you don't expect something this good when you come to my house."

Adam was becoming more and more uneasy. Something

didn't smell right, and it wasn't just his dinner guest's person.

"Having trouble with your cooking lessons?" Adam asked.

"No. I haven't even had time to start them," she confessed.

"Overconfidence has been the downfall of many a greenhorn."

She ignored his comment. "Josh, I would invite you to join us for dinner at my house, but I'm rather fond of *you*. If I accidentally poison someone, I'd rather it be your dear brother."

"So you're planning to poison me," Adam stated, his eyes meeting hers. She met his gaze and stared back at him, assessing him with the same intensity as he assessed her.

When she replied, her voice was unnaturally honeyed. "No, even though we *both* know you deserve it. But I might poison you *accidentally*."

A look of understanding flashed through Adam's eyes and he groaned inwardly. "The bear grease?"

"The bear grease," she confirmed.

He threw his brother a damning glance. "Josh told you."

"No, though were he a real friend, he would have." She condemned his brother with her own glower. "Mr. Culver told me this morning."

"Then why are you still wearing it?" Adam demanded.

"Why—for you, Mr. Carrigan," she rejoined. "I'm going to sit here next to you all afternoon smelling like a pair of moldy riding boots, hoping you choke to death."

Josh hooted.

Adam scowled at her smug expression. She was supposed to get her feathers ruffled and hightail it back to Virginia in a pout. He hadn't counted on her calmly exacting a cunning measure of revenge. His face twitched as a fresh whiff of bear grease assailed his nostrils. "Here—have some more of these." He shoved a plate under her nose.

"Why?" She dubiously eyed the contents of the platter.

"They're a Montana delicacy. I'm interested in your opinion."

"Since I've already tasted them, I can tell you my opinion now. The flavor is a little unusual, but they're quite good. What are they?"

Adam smirked. "Mountain oysters. I made them especially for you."

"What's wrong with them?" She looked suspiciously from one brother to the other.

"Nothing."

"Josh, I know he's up to some kind of mischief. If you hope to ever find yourself back in my good graces, I suggest you tell me what kind of mischief it is."

"Mountain oysters are calf testicles, ma'am," Josh revealed.

Color bloomed on her cheeks, and the squeamish expression on her face as she recoiled from the plate was soul satisfying, but Adam's jubilation lasted only a moment. Taking the platter from his hand, she shoveled a large portion on her plate.

"Testicles, you say." She stabbed her fork into the meat with vicious force. Using her knife like a cleaver, she whacked a piece in two. The glee with which she chewed and swallowed the morsel made Adam squirm.

One bite followed another, each piece of meat eagerly assaulted with the same malicious stab, sever, chomp. The grin she wore upon her face was unholy.

Adam couldn't believe it. Every time he thought he had maneuvered her just where he wanted her, she turned the tables and gained the upper hand. At this rate he'd never be rid of her.

He tensely glanced her direction. There must be *something*

Miss Kendall found intolerable. All he needed to do was discover what it was. Even before he finished giving himself this good counsel, Adam realized he already knew. The one thing he *knew* Miss Kendall found off-putting was even the hint he might be interested in courting her. Though it was abhorrent to his bachelor pride, logic said the best tool to use to get rid of her was to pretend he had his heart set on having her stay.

"Eat up, Miss Kendall," he encouraged. "You know what they say about mountain oysters."

"No. What do they say?"

"They're an aphrodisiac. Make your blood run hotter than a Yellowstone geyser. Many a cowboy has used them to attain his heart's desire."

"You're lying," she maintained, but her fork wavered slightly on the way to her mouth.

"He's not," Josh vouched between chortles.

She dropped her fork on her plate. "Why didn't you tell me before?" Ignoring him, she rebuked Josh.

"Because I've been watching the two of you try to tie a knot in each other's tail ever since you walked through the door. I can't think of anything more entertaining than if you and my brother were to fall in love with each other. Heck, I could make a fortune selling tickets."

"That's not funny. Mr. Carrigan, kindly tell your brother what he said about us is not the least bit funny," Cammie snapped.

"Adam. I figure it's time you start calling me Adam," Adam mellifluously opined, puckering his lips and blowing her a bantam kiss.

"What's wrong with you?" she demanded, rising to her feet. "And why are you staring at me like that?"

"I enjoy feasting my eyes upon a beautiful woman." Adam

stood and traced her jaw with his forefinger. Batting his hand away, she took a step backward.

"Stop it! We're enemies, remember?"

"Naw. Playing a few silly jokes on each other doesn't make us enemies. I'd call what we've been doing love sparring. What do you reckon, Josh?"

"Looks that way to me, big brother."

For every step back she took, Adam took one forward.

"You're insane, the both of you! I'm going home!"

"So soon—before dessert?"

"The sooner the better!"

"Let me walk you to the door."

"I can see myself out, thank you." The words were barely out of her mouth when she slammed the front door behind her.

Adam raised a triumphant fist in the air and roared with laughter.

Five

Construction on the new outbuildings to house her stallions was proceeding at a satisfying pace. The quality of the work was excellent. Cammie was extremely pleased.

She had instructed Mr. Culver to assign two men the remodeling work she wanted done in the existing barns. When they finished with that, they would begin putting up the new fences she required.

Mr. Benjamin Fry, the man she had hired as ranch cook, prepared hearty nutritious meals for the men, supplying a plate for her as well whenever she requested. He was no master chef, and his cooking lacked imagination, but he provided enough variety no one complained.

Her new handyman, Steven Stewart, was proving similarly capable. Having grown up on a farm, he knew exactly what must be done, and how and when. Cammie was grateful to be freed of the routine tasks of milking the cow, tending chickens, and gardening so she could focus all her energies on preparing for the arrival of her horses.

During the day, that was exactly what she did. Over the years she had read every book her father owned on the subject of raising horses. The rest of what she needed to know she had learned by being a keen observer, and when circumstances had allowed, by firsthand experience. She was not so overconfident she thought she could avoid every mistake, but she was confident she could keep them to a minimum.

Speaking of mistakes, allowing Adam Carrigan to wrangle a dinner invitation was an imprudent decision. One minute he swore he was committed to remaining a bachelor until his dying day; the next he sounded like a lovesick swain. He was either the most fickle man on earth or he was playing her for a pigeon. As yet, she hadn't decided which it was.

The man definitely had an uncanny ability to drive her to distraction. Every time she was with him she became hypersensitive. She noticed things about him that she never noticed about other men—like the way he moved, how the color of his eyes darkened and lightened with emotion, the way the muscles in his broad shoulders relaxed or tensed.

Self-preservation: Cammie named the reason for her excessive attentiveness. It paid to be watchful around that man. The bear grease she could forgive because—as Mr. Culver had said—it wasn't the sort of joke a man played on a woman. Vexed as she was by the whole affair, it pleased her that Adam Carrigan had treated her on equal footing with a man. What didn't please her was when Adam Carrigan related to her as a woman.

His brother Josh wasn't much better. He could have told her the truth about the bear grease the moment she stepped through his door, but he hadn't. He had let his brother make her the brunt of his joke. Still, Josh had been genuinely pleased when he learned she had bested his kin at his own game. Whose side was he on anyway? *His own* was the answer that readily came to mind.

"It is just my luck to travel all the way to Montana to escape the stifling prejudices of men only to find myself neighbor to two of the most irritating members of that sex," Cammie complained to Lucretia.

After her abrupt departure the other day, she wasn't even sure Adam Carrigan would show up for dinner on Wednesday. She certainly hoped he didn't. She hadn't seen so much as a glimpse of him since Saturday. She considered it a good sign.

But just in case he did show up, pride demanded she had a passable dinner waiting. She didn't care about cooking—she cared about horses. Learning to cook was a bothersome waste of her valuable time. Even though she confined her culinary experiments to the evening hours, she still felt sorely abused.

More than once Cammie contemplated letting Mr. Fry cook the meal, pretending she had, but again her pride demanded she not cheat.

"Stupid, stupid man," she muttered under her breath as she pushed a wisp of hair from her forehead with a floury hand. "This is the one and only time I will ever cook for you."

The only worthwhile part of this whole culinary contest was the discovery that cooking was less an innate talent than it was a matter of reading and carefully following directions. She had settled on a menu of canapés à la crème, trout with mushrooms, baked potatoes, a green salad, and French apple pie—and she had successfully made each dish at least once.

The only item that gave her trouble was the pie crust. Every one she made came out of the oven resembling boot leather more closely than it did a flaky pastry. If worse came to worse, she could substitute a cobbler for the pie, but since the purpose of the dinner was to make a point, she preferred to master the more difficult dessert. For the same reason, she had prevailed upon Mr. Fry to teach her to brew a proper pot of coffee.

"All right. Pie crust number seven. You are going to come out of my oven so light you'll float off the pie tin," she ordered, slipping the pie into the oven. "I refuse to admit defeat."

Cammie greeted the arrival of Wednesday morning with both relief and dread. Whether it turned out well or awful, in a few hours the meal would be over, and her evenings would be her own again. In a few hours Adam Carrigan would have come and gone.

She already was annoyed with herself for spending so much time on this dinner. She wasn't the least bit interested in pleasing Mr. Carrigan, only in showing him she could do anything she set her mind to. Temper and pride were hard taskmasters. In the future she would have to learn to control both better.

Dressed in an everyday work skirt to display how little she cared about his visit and discourage any romantic overtures should his mind still be of that bent, Cammie set to work in the kitchen. She still clung to the hope he wouldn't bother to show up, but a tiny voice inside her head warned that Mr. Carrigan was possessed of as much pride as she. A knock at her door at twelve sharp confirmed her suspicion.

"I was hoping you wouldn't come." She stood in the doorway and greeted him with a barely civil nod.

"Glad to see you, too, Cammie." Adam Carrigan pressed a bouquet of wildflowers into her hand.

Cammie frowned. He was in *that* mood again. Scooping Lucretia up into her arms to occupy her hands and serve as a feline shield should he attempt to make any untoward advances, she gave him a stony look. "I don't believe I gave you permission to call me by my Christian name, and I know for certain I didn't give you liberty to use my nickname."

"You're right on both counts, but I'm gonna use it just the

same," he jauntily informed her, his lips twitching into a waggish grin.

Cammie kept both feet firmly planted in the doorway. She raised her chin a notch. "I would prefer you didn't."

"The other day, at our place, my brother called you Cammie, and I didn't hear you whine at him."

"That's different."

"How?"

She could hardly claim his brother and she were better acquainted, and she wasn't about to admit she found Adam Carrigan intimidating in a way his brother was not. She settled for a circumspect, "He's nicer than you are."

"I'm just as nice." He puffed out his chest and stretched his grin an inch wider. "Besides, you keep claiming you've a hankering to compete in a man's world. Ranchers round here are all on a first-name basis."

"All of them?"

"Every one."

"Fine, call me Camille."

"Sure thing, Cammie. So are you gonna invite me in, or are you planning on serving me my dinner standing in the doorway?"

This was going to be worse than she thought. Already he had her blood boiling, and as he had so "gallantly" pointed out, she hadn't even invited him inside yet. If she could think of any way she could get out of doing so without losing face, she would. Regrettably no brilliant inspiration sprang to mind. Cammie reluctantly stepped aside so he could enter. "Since you're here, you may as well come in," she grumbled.

"Enthusiasm like that is like to make a man wonder what he's letting himself in for." Doffing his Stetson, he threw her a wink and stepped past her. "Been having trouble learning to cook?"

"No—*you* showed me any idiot can learn to cook."

He lifted his nose and sniffed at the air. "It smells edible."

"If there is any doubt in your mind, you're welcome to leave. It won't hurt my feelings."

He shook his head. "A cowman never runs from danger."

"Then sit down. The sooner we eat, the sooner we will be done." Releasing Lucretia, Cammie marched to the stove. Discarding the flowers on the sideboard, she picked up the coffee pot.

She kept her back to him while she poured him a cup. "Stupid, stupid man," she repeated her earlier sentiment under her breath. "Don't let him get to you. It's what he wants." Pasting a stoic expression on her face, she served him the coffee.

She then dished up the rest of the meal and carried it to the table. After seeing her guest served, she filled her own plate. The food she served didn't have to taste better than what he had served her, it need only match it in quality. It looked right and smelled right, but the true test was in the tasting. Cammie deemed it irrational that she cared who won their silly contest, but care she did.

Refusing to let her inner trepidation manifest itself, she waited for him to taste the dinner. When he made no move to pick up his fork, she scowled. "Aren't you going to eat?"

"Yep."

"When?"

"After you take a bite of *everything*. Or have you forgotten that you threatened to poison me?"

She blinked at him. "You don't seriously think—"

"No." His tone remained polite. "But a man can never be too careful, especially where a spiteful female is concerned."

"That's the pot calling the kettle black if ever I heard it.

Or don't you think it spiteful to trick a person into smearing bear grease all over themselves?"

"Can't take a joke?"

"Certainly I can. I can also give as good as I get."

"Which brings us back to why I would be more comfortable if you tasted this food first."

"Fine." Lifting a forkful of trout to her mouth, Cammie chewed and swallowed it. She did the same with the each item on her plate. "Now are you happy?"

"Not quite. You served me coffee. You're drinking tea."

"For heaven's sake." She reached across the table, seized his cup, and took a sip. *"Now* are you satisfied?"

"Yep."

"Good—because if you aren't, you can leave."

"Wouldn't want to do that." He ate a bite of trout. "This is good," he said with surprise.

"I told you I was up to the challenge." Cammie sat a little taller. Meeting his discomfited gaze with her own victorious one, she said, "I am capable of doing anything I set my mind to."

"I'm assuming you're referring to running this ranch."

"Yes, I am."

The sheen in his eyes was no longer unsettled but penetrating. "Learning to cook and learning to ranch are not the same thing."

Cammie didn't turn away. "I didn't say they were. One big difference is that until a few days ago I knew next to nothing about cooking. I already know everything there is to know about raising horses."

"Is that so?"

"Yes, it is."

He looked at her speculatively, but he gave most of his attention to consuming the meal. After several minutes he casually asked, "What kinda horses are you bringing out here?"

"Quarter horses. Their build, speed, and ability to stop, start, and turn on a dime make them ideal for working cattle. Since I will be marketing my animals almost exclusively to cowboys, quarter horses are the most logical choice."

"How many times a year do you plan to breed your mares?"

He was testing her knowledge, and Cammie embraced the question with pleasure. She would rather talk horses than any other subject on earth. "Once. Any fool knows a mare can only produce one foal a year."

"When will your foals be saddle ready?"

"Since long-term health and quality are more important to me than short-term profits, I will be selling only four-year-olds. In order to establish my reputation as a trainer, I'm bringing out several animals that are old enough to be trained and sold immediately. I will be receiving a like number of yearlings, two-, and three-year-olds to be trained and sold in subsequent years. By then my mares and stallions will be steadily producing new foals every year."

"Who is gonna train your foals?"

"I will be hiring men to assist me, but I will be the head trainer. I want my horses to be the best, and the way to do that is to give them the best trainer." She pointed her forefinger at herself.

"Anyone ever tell you modesty is a virtue?"

"Yes, they have—more times than I care to count! I agree if modesty is justified. But what we are talking about is self-effacement, which is a curse imposed upon women by men to make them shrink from sharing their accomplishments with the world!"

"Whoa." He sat back. "You don't have to bite my head off. I was just tweaking your nose."

Cammie felt the heat of a blush stain her cheeks. She hadn't meant to lecture him. It was just whenever he was around she found herself on edge. She also found herself consumed with an overwhelming need to justify herself. "Sorry," she apologized. "You rubbed a raw nerve."

"Obviously," he agreed. "How about we change the topic of conversation?"

"To what?"

He shrugged. "Looks like your carpenters are making steady progress."

Carpentry was a comfortable topic. Cammie nodded. "Yes, they're already a day ahead of schedule."

"Lots of building going on. Must be expensive."

"I consider it a long-term investment."

He stroked his mustache. "Five new barns?"

"My stallions have to be housed separately."

"Are you planning on building a new house, too?"

"Eventually, but not for at least a year or two," she replied.

"I'd figure a city gal like you would hate living in a place like this."

"I'll admit it's not much to look at, but it's sturdy. That's all I require. My horses' comfort comes first."

The light in his eyes dimmed, and his forehead crinkled. Rubbing the back of his neck, he returned his attention to his food.

They finished the meal in silence. Cammie overtly watched her dinner companion. There was something going on in that handsome head of his, and she wanted to know what it was.

Most men were easy to read. Whether they were after her hand in marriage or wanted into her pocketbook or were laughing at her ambitions behind polite smiles didn't matter.

If she looked close enough, she could always tell what was on their minds.

There wasn't any question Adam Carrigan wanted her land. But that explained only some of his behavior, not all of it. He had made his offers to buy her out. She had refused them. That should have been the end of it. They could be civil neighbors without being friendly.

Then there were his sporadic attempts to court her—like the flowers he'd brought. Every instinct told her he wasn't sincere. How could he be if he believed she might try to poison him? If he thought to seduce her into selling her ranch to him, he was delusional. Marrying her to get the land was equally preposterous. She wasn't going to marry anyone. She wasn't sure why, but she believed him when he said he wasn't either.

Besides, if seduction or marriage were on his mind, the schoolboy prank of tricking her into wearing the bear grease made no sense. He had *wanted* to make her mad—she was certain of it.

It vexed her to have a man hanging about whom she couldn't neatly peg into an appropriate category and deal with accordingly. It was also intriguing—like a riddle that wouldn't leave her mind until it was solved.

She would have to keep a close eye on him. There was no doubt about that. Where doubt came to play was—

"Do you always stare at your dinner guests so boldly?"

The question startled her to attention, but she quickly recovered herself. However she did not avert her eyes. "When it suits my purpose."

Adam Carrigan met her direct gaze. "What is your purpose?"

"I'm trying to figure you out," she answered forthrightly.

"Oh."

" 'Oh.' Is that all you have to say?"

"At the moment."

Cammie cocked her head to one side. "In other words I am right to believe I should keep a careful eye on you."

His eyes darkened to the shade of a dark blue midnight sky. "A woman should always be careful when she's in the company of a gentleman."

"Do you believe yourself to be a gentleman?"

"Sometimes, yes. Sometimes, no."

Cammie moistened her lips. "That isn't a very comforting answer."

"I could lie if you'd like," he offered, moistening his own lips and shifting on his seat.

"No, thank you." Cammie vigorously shook her head to break the hold his eyes had on her. Pushing back her chair, she stood up and retreated to the other side of the room. "Would you like a piece of pie before you leave?"

"Am I leaving soon?" he asked.

"Yes."

"Then, yes, I would like a piece of pie."

Cammie served the pie, making an elaborate show of tasting it first herself. "Just in case you're still skittish about my cooking."

His eyes never left her face. "Much obliged."

Six

Cammie's days were filled to overflowing as the date her horses were to arrive from Virginia grew near. She was determined no detail would go overlooked, and the best way she knew to ensure that was to personally oversee every stage of the work.

She knew some of her men were whispering behind her back—calling her picky, interfering, overbearing—but she didn't care. As long as the work was done right and on time, they could think what they pleased about her.

Past experience had taught her well. If she revealed even a hint that she possessed a softer side, her authority would be undermined.

She got along well enough with Mr. Culver, and she had already decided to offer him a permanent position. Mr. Fry and Mr. Stewart would be asked to stay as well.

Her pesky neighbors, the Carrigan brothers, still plagued her on a regular basis with their uninvited presence, but she was becoming accustomed to having them underfoot.

Joshua Carrigan, with his ever present grin, was an easy man to handle. Though she didn't appreciate it when he teased her about his amorous ambitions for his brother and her, it was impossible to stay angry with him for long. He reminded her of a naughty dear little boy, with an ardent desire to have fun.

Adam Carrigan was a different matter. Whatever drove him

remained a mystery to her. He found some excuse to ride over at least every other day. Cammie had learned the best way to manage him was to pretend to ignore him and go about her business. Eventually he got bored with following her around and went home.

Being an honest woman, she had to admit that on the days he didn't show up, she found herself wondering where he was. Not that she wanted him hanging about her place, she assured herself. She got the feeling that for some reason of his own, he was attending the progress of the construction of the new outbuildings as closely as she.

Once or twice a week he insisted on renewing his offer to buy her property, which was vexing—but he accepted her refusals with a minimum of grumbling. She didn't believe he expected her to say yes. He just felt the need to keep offering. If not the land, they invariably got in an argument over something, heaven only knew what half the time.

In truth she preferred sparring with him to fending off his smooth-tongued blandishments. She wanted to drive him off her property with a bullwhip when he came to visit in one of *those* moods, but to do so would be undignified, so she resisted the temptation. Instead she parried his flattery with sarcasm.

It was always a challenge to guess which frame of mind he was in when he reined his horse to a halt in the yard. Everything about him was a challenge.

No, she definitely didn't *want* Adam Carrigan underfoot. He was more like a bad habit. Besides, it did give her a convenient opportunity to keep an eye on him—which she vowed she would.

* * *

The morning she was to return to Helena to supervise the unloading of her horses, Cammie was so excited she awoke before dawn. The horses wouldn't arrive until the next day, so she would stay the night in a hotel—but she wanted time to complete all her other town business before the train arrived.

Mr. Stewart was remaining behind to take care of the ranch, but every other man would be going with her. All had some experience handling horses. She might not like all of them, but she knew them, and she preferred to have them help in the transport of her precious cargo rather than take a risk with strangers. Along with the men from the Virginia farm who would be traveling with the horses, they should be able to manage the return trip to the ranch with relative ease.

Cammie was ready and waiting on the platform of the Northern Pacific Railroad Station a full hour before the train was scheduled to reach Helena. Mr. Culver stood by her side. The rest of her men huddled in a group a short distance away, smoking hand-rolled cigarettes and—from the occasional comment that drifted her direction—speculating on the quality of her horse stock. Their own horses were tied to a nearby hitching post.

The weather was warm and sunny, a perfect day for her horses to arrive.

"I'm looking forward to seeing them stallions I've been building barns for," Mr. Culver commented.

"So am I. I've missed my horses. Especially Bliss."

"She's something special, huh?"

"Yes, *he* is. I'll be riding him back to the ranch today."

"Have yourself a handsome gelding, do you?" he amended.

"Bliss is a stallion."

Mr. Culver's eyes bulged with surprise. "You strong enough to handle a stallion?"

"Controlling a horse is a matter of brains, not brawn," Cammie apprised him.

"I meant no offense," he promptly explained. "It's just taking a while for me to get used to the idea a small, fragile-looking woman like yourself is tough as nails."

Cammie smiled at the high praise. "No offense taken, Mr. Culver," she reassured him.

While she waited for the train, Cammie alternately tapped her foot and paced the length of the platform. It was a long trip from Virginia to Montana, and she hoped her animals would not be too distressed. She also hoped her cousin Shelby had followed her instructions for their transport to the letter. If not, he would be hearing from her, and he wouldn't like what he heard. He was living in her family mansion out of the generosity of her heart. She knew he didn't approve of what she was doing anymore than her father would have—but as she had happily informed Adam Carrigan—her cousin had no authority to stop her.

She was fairly certain Cousin Shelby would do nothing to try to thwart her plans, but one could never be absolutely positive where a man was concerned. He might send the wrong horses or—

Clenching her fists at the sides of her split skirt, Cammie scolded herself for succumbing to anxious speculation. Cousin Shelby wasn't a fool. He'd been coveting the family mansion since the day he was born and wasn't going to risk losing it by not following her orders. Besides, a telegram had been waiting for her when she arrived in town yesterday. Everything had been done exactly as ordered.

The sound of a train whistle elicited a sigh of relief from her lips. "Finally . . ."

A smile stretched across Cammie's face as the train rumbled toward her down the track. She counted cars as she waited, straining to catch sight of the livestock cars. When they came into view, her smile broadened.

For the first few minutes after the train's arrival, everything was chaos while passengers disembarked and others boarded. Cammie gathered her men around her.

A railroad agent approached. "You Miss Camille Kendall?"

"Yes, I am," she replied.

"I've got quite a shipment for you. Follow me, please."

A ramp was secured in place. Cammie ascended it. "How are they?" she greeted Mr. Hames, the groomsman charged with the welfare of the horses on the trip.

"As well as can be expected after being jostled halfway across the country."

"Any problems?"

"None," he grudgingly admitted.

"Good. Let's start getting them unloaded."

A man was riding in each car that held her horses. Cammie put each in charge of unloading his individual car while she supervised the whole. A cursory inspection revealed all the animals to be in excellent health. It was a relief, but even so she intended to give every horse a thorough examination once they were settled in at the ranch.

Cammie knew she wasn't the only one looking over her livestock. Every man present was making his own assessment and from their low-pitched whistles, covetous glances, and wistful sighs she knew their assessments were favorable. Besides her own men, a small crowd of admiring onlookers was beginning to gather. Cammie couldn't have been more pleased. Word of her fine horses would soon spread through town, then out to the neighboring ranches and farms. Word of mouth was the best form of advertisement, far better than anything for which she could pay.

A familiar neighing brought her attention spinning around. "Bliss," she joyfully cried. "You have no idea how much I've missed you." Taking his reins, she led him out of the way. He nuzzled her face as she stroked his chestnut neck and cooed words of welcome in his ear.

Though Cammie would have liked to throw on his saddle and immediately race him across the countryside, duty called—and after indulging in a few more minutes of loving welcome, she reluctantly handed Bliss over to one of the men.

Unloading the horses and preparing them for the journey to the ranch took the better part of the morning. In addition, wagons had to be loaded with tack and other equipment. More wagons were loaded with furniture and household items from her old home that she planned to use in her new one.

When all was ready, Cammie saddled Bliss, mounted, and signaled the procession to begin.

She assigned Mr. Culver to the front so he could guide the path of those who had no idea where the ranch was located. She took up the rear, where she could watch to make certain the horses were treated with proper patience and respect.

After being confined for so many days, Cammie didn't want to overtire the horses. She ordered a slow pace and frequent stops.

Even with the long summer days, it was almost dark by the time they arrived at the ranch.

The name of each stallion was already painted on a plaque over the door of each of the small barns, and they were bedded down in their new homes. The mares, colts, fillies, and geldings were divided between the two large barns.

The furniture was left on the wagons to be unloaded in the

morning, except for her bed. With a heartfelt good riddance, she watched as two men carried out Mr. Higgins's lumpy, moth-eaten mattress and bedstead and carried in her own mahogany four-poster with its clean, smooth, downy mattress.

Though it was well past midnight when Cammie climbed under the covers, it was a long while before she fell asleep.

This was it. Her horses had arrived. Now it was all up to her. She would fail or succeed on her own merit.

Cammie Kendall was determined to succeed.

Cammie had been hoping several of the grooms who had accompanied the horses on the train would fall in love with the Montana ranch, as she had, and want to stay on. Their experience would be an invaluable resource. Unfortunately not one of them would agree to stay when she asked. In the end she decided it might be for the best.

The last thing she needed was employees apt to question her proficiency and authority, and by the reasons they gave for their refusal to stay, she suspected that was exactly what she would have on her hands. She would be fighting an uphill battle to gain acceptance on her terms. The fewer ties she had with her old life, the better her chances to achieve that acceptance.

Cammie planned to give her horses a few days to recover from their journey and become accustomed to their new home. The advertisement she had placed in the *Helena Herald* set the date for the interviews for the positions of grooms and trainers three days hence. She was depending upon word of the quality of her horses—along with a salary that matched the sum being offered by the best-paying ranches in the area—to help ensure a large turnout.

Cammie wondered how long it would be before Adam Carrigan rode over to check out her horses. Not long, she'd wager. With their ranches positioned almost directly across the river from each other, it was impossible he didn't know they had arrived.

For once she unreservedly was looking forward to a visit from her neighbor. She wanted to see the look of admiration and envy on his face when he saw the quality of her horses. She wanted to watch him squirm.

Cammie didn't have to wait long for her opportunity.

"Morning, Cammie."

She greeted him warmly. "Good morning, Adam."

Reaching down, Adam absently rubbed behind Lucretia's ears before straightening to face her mistress. "Not that I'm complaining, but how come you sound so happy to see me? Usually you greet me like you figure I'm carrying the plague."

"Do I?" She pursed her lips. "And here I thought you were dense and hadn't noticed. My apologies."

"Feeling cantankerous again today, I see," he observed. "Never met a woman who could stay in a bad mood as many days running as you. Guess our Montana air doesn't agree with you."

"I'm not in a bad mood today—I'm in a wonderful mood. Would you like me to show you my horses?"

"Yep."

"You'll be disappointed," Cammie crowed.

"Why?"

"You'll see."

Leading him into the first barn, she strolled by his side, watching, while he traveled the length of the barn. He paused every few feet, peering into each stall they passed.

He didn't say a word until they had stepped back out in the sunlight.

"Good-looking horses," he casually stated.

"Yes, they are," Cammie proudly proclaimed.

"Are you gonna show me the rest?"

"Certainly. Follow me."

The trip through the second barn was a repeat of the first. They then paid a visit to each stallion. Adam took his time inspecting each one but refrained from commenting. The only clues she had to his reaction was the incandescent glow in his dark blue eyes and the taut set of his lips.

"So . . ." she prodded.

"So what?"

"What do you think?"

"Good-looking horses," he repeated.

"Is that all you have to say?"

"What do you want me to say?"

She scowled at him. "Something along the lines of 'Miss Kendall, I underestimated you. I can see by these animals that you are an expert judge of horseflesh. I apologize for ever questioning your abilities. Your ranch is sure to be a success' would be pleasant."

His expression remained closed and his voice murky. "Maybe."

"What's that supposed to mean?"

"It means I'm riding into town to pay a visit to a friend of mine." He abruptly turned on his heels. "See you later."

"Afternoon, Higgins," Adam said grimly when he located Roy sitting in a chair in the lobby of the Payne Hotel.

Higgins folded the newspaper he had been reading, put it on his lap, and sheepishly returned the greeting. "Afternoon, Adam. I figured I might be seeing you."

"And why is that?"

"Got a glimpse of them horses of Miss Kendall's what came in on the train yesterday. Not that I figure it to mean anything," he quickly amended. "I just reckoned when you saw them, you'd likely get a mite upset."

Adam sat down in the chair next to Higgins. "You said she wouldn't last the week," he tersely reminded. "By my count she's been here close to four . . ."

"I made a slight miscalculation," Higgins admitted.

"And the horses? If you've seen them, you know there's nothing in the territory that even comes close to the quality of those animals. If she's half as good a trainer as she is a judge of horseflesh and she charges fair prices, men are gonna be lined up for miles waiting to buy them," Adam continued to complain.

"She did surprise me with them horses, but that doesn't mean she'll stick around. Raising horses is hard work," Higgins argued. "You trying to tell me you reckon she's up to it?"

"I'm telling you she's been here four weeks. She's practically built a small town with all the new barns and corrals she's had put up on your old place—and her horses are the finest I've ever seen. You draw your own conclusions."

"I still say she won't last," Higgins contended with conviction.

Adam raked his fingers through his hair. "When I first met her, I agreed with you, but now—"

"Ain't nothing different today than there was the day she first stepped foot in town," Higgins insisted.

"She's bull-necked," Adam announced.

"I know that. I told you before how she badgered me into selling her that land."

Adam's eyes narrowed. "If I recall, you pocketed a tidy profit in the bargain."

"That's not the point."

"She's smart, too," he morosely added. "Bull-necked and smart—that's a dangerous combination."

"A little sage hen like Miss Kendall dangerous? You been kicked in the head by a mule lately?"

"No."

"Then you're talking nonsense."

"Am I?" Adam threw him a dark look. "I've had enough tastes of her wicked tongue to reckon otherwise. She's the type of woman who just might hold onto my land out of spite."

"Didn't strike me as the spiteful sort at all. Maybe you just rub her the wrong way."

"She sure as hell rubs me the wrong way!"

Higgins appeared startled by Adam's vehemence but his voice remained sympathetic. "Now ain't that an ungentlemanly thing to say. But I expect if it's true, it'll only help your cause. Women are sociable creatures. She ain't gonna want to live out in the middle of nowhere with nothing but a neighbor she don't like to keep her company. With her looks I imagine she was pretty popular where she came from, used to lots of attention. She's bound to get bored if she ain't already. Start missing all that gay city life. Tea parties, balls—you know how them kinda women are. Always needing to put on airs for someone."

"I don't know." Adam rubbed his jaw, running his hand down the column of his throat. "My head says it makes sense, but my gut says different."

"Your gut is probably just hankering after a thick, juicy steak."

Adam wanted to believe him. He'd been thinking about Camille Kendall far more than he liked ever since he'd laid eyes on her. All that unwilling thinking was getting on his nerves almost as much as the woman herself. It was against his principles to waste time pondering the whys and wherefores of the female of the species. "Maybe you're right," he optimistically considered.

"Sure I am. You'll see. Just give her another week or two, and she'll be eager to skedaddle on back to Virginia. All *you* gotta do is bide your time."

Seven

The day she had set for the interviews dawned sunny and pleasantly warm. Despite the fair weather and the knowledge she had done all that she could to assure a good turnout, Cammie couldn't help but be anxious.

She required good men to work her ranch, and she would settle for nothing less. If today went well, the fulfillment of her dream would remain on schedule. If not, she would be forced to advertise farther afield, which might mean a long delay before she could fully organize her operation.

In consideration of the distance it was necessary to travel to reach her ranch, the interviews were scheduled to begin at noon. They would last however long it took to hire the men she wanted.

At ten o'clock the first man arrived. By eleven o'clock the yard held close to two dozen men. Cammie smiled in satisfaction as she studied them through the window. For the most part they looked promising.

Cammie knew the men in her yard would judge her, just as she would judge them, and she had dressed to impress, choosing her dark green riding habit complete with top hat, matching kid gloves, and riding crop over her more practical split skirts. While she waited for the hands of the clock to reach twelve o'clock, she paced the floor and rehearsed her speech.

When the appointed hour arrived, Cammie smoothed her jacket, took a deep breath, picked up her riding crop, and stepped onto the porch. "Good afternoon, gentlemen." As the rehearsed words came smoothly to her mind, her nervousness vanished and she greeted the men with a polished smile. "I'm glad to see so many of you answered my advertisement. Those of you who have had time to look the place over have seen the caliber of my horses. I require men of equally fine caliber to care for them. If you have not had time to take a tour, please look around while you wait your turn.

"You may also feel free to ask any of the men who have been under my employ these past few weeks their opinion of me. I have instructed them to answer you frankly. Some may tell you I am an exacting taskmaster, but they also will tell you I am honest, deal with them fairly, and pay them in full and on time.

"There will be no drinking on the premises. What you do on your own time is your business, but do not make the mistake of showing up on this ranch drunk. Swearing I can tolerate if justified and done in moderation. You may smoke as long as you do not do so near me or my horses.

"If taking orders from a female offends you, now is the time to say so. My authority on this ranch is absolute." Cammie paused, casting her eyes over the men to measure the effect of her words thus far. No one appeared ready to bolt and she continued, "The salary I am offering was printed in my advertisement. Those who prove themselves worthy will be given raises as profits allow. I know horses and possess the skill and determination necessary to make this ranch a success. As I prosper, so will you.

"The order of business today will be as follows: I will conduct a brief interview with each of you in my office. We will then retire to the east corral so I may judge your skill in handling horses. After I have given every man a chance to prove himself, I will make my decision as to which ones I will hire. Are there any questions?"

"How long do you expect all this to take?" a cowboy standing in the center of the group asked.

"All day," Cammie replied. "Meals will be provided. Those of you who have traveled a long distance are welcome to bed down in the bunkhouse for the night."

"Who gets interviewed first?" another man inquired.

"I will conduct the interviews in the order of arrival. I trust you gentlemen to settle the matter fairly. It will be your first test. I do not tolerate bullies or cheats. Are there any more questions?"

After an encouraging nudge from his friend, a man in a tan hat stepped forward. "What if the place goes belly up?"

Cammie didn't flinch from the question. "You will lose your position, so I suggest if I hire you, you work hard to make this ranch profitable.

"Any other questions?" She scanned the crowd. When the men remained mute, she proceeded. "If you think of any other questions, please ask them during your interview. Mr. Culver, you may direct the first man to my office in two minutes." Turning on her heels, Cammie walked into the house.

"That went well, I think," she apprised Lucretia on her way to her office. It was now furnished with her father's wide, multidrawered walnut desk, two bookshelves filled with volumes concerning every aspect of horse husbandry, an Aubusson rug, an upholstered chair for herself, and a slat-backed chair for the interviewees.

Rather than dwarf her, Cammie felt the massive desk lent her an air of eminence and authority, which was precisely the image she wanted to project.

The first man was led into her office. Cammie assessed him from head to toe, nodded, then indicated he should take his seat.

One man followed on the heels of another. She asked each the same list of questions, noting their answers and her impressions on a separate sheet of paper. By design the interviews were brief. Their purpose was to allow her to form a first impression. The true test of each man would be how he interacted with her horses.

By midafternoon Cammie had taken up a position behind a small table at one end of the east corral. Tapping the butt of her riding crop against her palm at the end of each sentence, she instructed the men. "This afternoon's activities will consist of two parts. In the first you will ride your own horse. I'd like to see you circle the corral three times in each direction. You'll be judged on how you execute starts, stops, turns, and how comfortably you sit your saddle. Afterward you will be given three minutes to impress me with whatever skills you wish to show. For the second part, one of my horses will be let loose in the corral. You are to catch the animal and prepare it for riding with full tack. You will then mount and ride around the corral first at a walk, then a trot. Lastly, put the horse through the same sequence of starts, stops, and turns you performed on your own horse. Mr. Woodrow, you may go first."

By the time the first half of the men had ridden, Cammie was convinced she would be able to hire the caliber of men she desired. There was a wide range of skill, but by day's end she believed she would find more than enough possessed of the combination of expertise, experience, and horse sense she sought.

She continued to make notes on her sheets of paper as each man rode.

She announced the next name: "Mr. Larson, I believe it is your turn." During his interview, Mr. Larson had expressed an aspiration for the position of ranch foreman. Having worked as a wrangler on several ranches, he seemed to have the necessary skill and experience. Too, she admired a man with ambition. If he exhibited good horse sense, she would seriously consider him for the post.

Mr. Larson gave her a confident wave as he rode into the corral on his buckskin. She watched as he skillfully put his horse through the required paces. For his chosen demonstration, he treated his audience to an impressive display of trick riding—whipping his legs from side to side, jumping on and off while the animal circled the corral at a trot, and ending by balancing on his saddle with his feet and leaping to the ground with a bow. It was a fine performance, but something about the way his horse responded to his commands made her slightly uncomfortable. Notwithstanding, she applauded with the rest of the men.

"All right, Mr. Larson, let's see how you handle one of my horses," she said. His horse was led out of the corral, and Jewel, one of her favorite mares, was led in and released.

From the moment Mr. Larson began to approach the mare, Cammie sensed trouble. Rather than take the time to allow Jewel to familiarize herself with him, he swaggered toward the mare, talking loudly and waving his arms as he backed her into a corner.

When she became skittish, he threw a rope over her head and tightened the loop.

Cammie rose to her feet. "Mr. Larson!"

"I know what I'm doing," he called over his shoulder. "Gotta show these critters who's boss."

Before she could respond, he was shoving a bit into Jewel's mouth and cinching down the halter straps. This was more than clumsy handling, this was brutality. Jewel whinnied and reared. He yanked hard on the rope, bringing her front hooves back to the ground, and slapped her hard between the eyes.

"Enough!" Cammie shouted, knocking over the table in her haste to rescue her horse. "I want you out of this corral and off my property now!"

He refused to release the frightened mare. "A bad-tempered horse gotta be handled rough, or it won't learn no manners. I bet you knowed this mare would give me trouble and set me up."

Ignoring his huge size, Cammie squared off with him toe to toe. "I said off my property *now!*"

"Damn woman don't know nothing about handling horses." Larson sought support from his fellow cowboys.

Cammie brought her riding crop down on his hand, forcing him to release his hold on the rope. She smiled menacingly at his yelp of pain. "Mr. Larson, I am going to give you one more chance to leave this ranch with your miserable hide intact. I promise, I do not make idle threats and my aim with this crop is deadly accurate. You have to the count of three before I do the world a favor and save it the indignity of having you inflict your progeny upon it."

"I'd start running now," someone advised.

"You brought it on yourself," another opined.

"I'd take her at her word," somebody else counseled.

"One . . . two . . . three," Cammie counted out in measured tones, lifting the crop on three. Larson turned tail and ran for his buckskin.

His departure was accompanied by a goodly amount of catcalls and laughter. Cammie did not join them in their amusement.

"If any of the rest of you subscribe to Mr. Larson's methods of horse training, I suggest you get on your horse and follow him."

A couple of men quietly slipped away from the others, mounted their horses, and rode off on the same direction Mr. Larson had, though not at the same breakneck pace. "Anyone else?" Standing in the middle of the corral, Cammie slowly circled, scrutinizing the remaining men through narrowed eyes. When no one moved, she stated, "Fine. Gentlemen, I apologize for the interruption. If you will allow me a few minutes to see to the welfare of my mare, I will return and we can continue."

The rest of the afternoon proceeded without incident. When every man had had his turn to show his skill, Cammie stood and said, "Thank you all for your time. I will be retiring to my office to make my final decisions. Supper will be served by Mr. Fry from the kitchen attached to the bunkhouse. After you have enjoyed your meal, please gather in the yard in front of the house, and I will read the names of the men I have chosen."

Selecting a man for ranch foreman was easy. When she had first interviewed him, she had been impressed by the questions he asked but concerned that he lacked the range of experience of some of the other men. But the moment Carl Daley had ridden into the corral on his Appaloosa and Arabian mix, Cammie knew he had an instinct for horses. He exhibited exactly the kind of firm but gentle manner with horses for which she was looking. His love and respect for the animals were obvious in the glow of his eyes, the soothing tone of his voice, and in every movement he made.

The rest of her decisions were a little more difficult, but for the happy reason that she had too many, not too few, good men from which to choose. Because her horses were to be trained to be cow horses, experienced cowboys were given preference where all other qualifications were equal. In the end she was satisfied with her choices.

"The following men are now employees of the Kendall ranch." Cammie addressed them from the porch. "Mr. Carl Daley, Mr. Jordan Smith, Mr. William Woodrow, Mr. John Thorpe, Mr. Sidney Shanks, and Mr. Elias Rutley. I appreciate the time and trouble all of you have taken here today. As the ranch expands, I hope to be able to hire more of you in the future. Some of you undoubtedly will become customers, and I not only look forward to doing business with you, but can guarantee you will be purchasing the best horses in the territory. If I called your name, please stay and I'll give you further instruction. To the rest of you—good evening, gentlemen."

Every day Cammie rose before dawn and retired late. Though the men she had hired proved themselves to be more than competent, she liked to be personally involved with every aspect of the day-to-day operations of her ranch. She thrived on hard work.

Mornings she spent training her horses. The youngest ones required gentling to a foal-slip. The yearlings and two-year-olds needed lunging. Three-year-olds must be accustomed to wearing full tack and the four-year-olds saddle trained.

After the midday meal Cammie returned outdoors to participate in and supervise the exercising of the horses. At three o'clock she rewarded herself with a ride on Bliss. Evenings she spent whatever time was necessary in her office dealing with record keeping and planning out the activities for the next day.

Cammie had never been so happy.

Lucretia was having a grand time as well. If Cammie had

been worried about how her pampered pet would adjust to her new life, she needn't have been. Lucretia spent her days exploring, inveigling her favorite men into rubbing behind her ears, and dining on the mice she adored stalking.

The only thing that prevented Cammie from deeming her new life unequivocally perfect was her relationship with her nearest neighbors. Even though it had settled into one of cautious civility on the part of the older brother and authentic friendliness on the part of the younger, something about it unsettled her.

Joshua Carrigan rode over to see her at least once a week. He had his eye on a four-year-old mare. They had yet to settle on a price, but Cammie suspected that had more to do with the fact that haggling over the animal gave him an excuse to visit her than his claim she was trying to overcharge him. She liked Joshua Carrigan because she knew exactly where she stood with him. He was a mischievous boy in a man's body. And unlike his brother, he was perfectly content to have her for a neighbor.

In the weeks since her horses had arrived, she had seen Adam Carrigan only three times—twice in town and once at her ranch when he came looking for Josh. Both times he had acted decidedly odd.

One minute she could swear he was glad to see her; the next it was as if the mere sight of her had ruined his day. It was not so much what he said—he politely asked after the state of her health, the progress of her ranch, her immediate and future plans—it was the mercurial display of emotions in his eyes.

Why he suddenly had stopped making a constant nuisance of himself was an enigma as well. She couldn't think of anything in particular she had said that would put him off. Not that she had ever encouraged his attention. Just the opposite was true. But once he had said they ought to be friends if for no other reason than to keep their wits sharp. It was ridiculous, but she realized she missed bandying words with him.

It aggravated Cammie that she still couldn't neatly catalog Adam Carrigan as she was able to do with every other man she met. Sometimes she found herself watching him from across the river—which aggravated her even more than his erratic behavior toward her. With all the important matters she had to occupy her hands and mind, standing on the banks of a river pondering the conduct of some man was the last thing she wanted to be doing.

"So much for ignoring Miss Kendall in hopes her injured vanity will send her packing," Adam muttered under his breath while he cleaned his rifle. "At this rate I'll be an old man before she gets off my land."

"What's that you're saying?" Josh asked.

"I said our new neighbor is taking her sweet time about getting bored playing cowgirl and packing her bags for home."

Joining his brother under the shade of the cottonwood tree, Josh leaned against the trunk, chewing the end of the weed dangling from his mouth. "Maybe she figures this is home."

Adam continued to rub oil into the stock of his rifle. "Well, she shouldn't. She doesn't belong here."

"Why not?"

"She's an Evangeline."

"Nope. She's a helluva horsewoman. If I were you, I'd give up on getting my hands on that property of hers. It would've been nice to add the acres to our place, but we've gotten along just dandy without them for years. Besides, I'm kinda glad Higgins sold to her instead of us. I like having her for a neighbor."

"You would." Adam snorted. "Next you'll be telling me the two of you have fallen in love."

Josh laughed. "You reckon me to be weak in the head? She's too much woman for me to handle. When I take it in my mind to give up the bachelor life, I'm gonna settle down with a gentle, sweet-natured little filly who will treat me like the king of my castle. Cammie Kendall is a fine woman, but the man who falls in love with her better like a hard ride."

"Agreed. Underneath that pretty face and soft as silk skin of hers lives the most vexing woman God ever created. Her tongue is sharper than elk thistle with the temper to match. Figures she knows everything. She would have sold that property to me long ago if she weren't as stubborn as a mule." Adam sighted his gun. "Millions of acres in the territory to raise horses on, and she has to set up housekeeping in our valley."

"I see she's burrowed herself under your skin like a tick," Josh teased. "Hope you're not planning on shooting her to get rid of her?"

Adam hurled his brother a look that clearly said: don't think the idea doesn't tempt me. "No—I'm going hunting."

"Why don't you ask her to go with you?"

"Why on earth would I want to do that?"

Josh twirled his weed between his fingers. "Might be fun."

A light sparked in Adam's eyes. It might be fun at that . . . but not for the reason Josh had in mind. Ignoring Miss Cammie Kendall plainly wasn't working. As far as he could tell, she was delighted by the lack of his company. If she was getting bored or lonely, she sure wasn't letting on to anyone.

He never should have listened to Higgins. Couldn't even

say why he had except staying away was less troublesome than hanging around her.

He fingered his mustache. He should have stuck to his original plan and subjected her to the full greenhorn treatment. Then again, he was starting to wonder if that would work any better than ignoring her had. She hadn't exactly shrunk in horror when he'd played the bear grease trick on her. She'd fought back.

Pretending he had romantic designs concerning her had had its drawbacks, too. He knew it ruffled her feathers, but he didn't believe in stringing a woman along. It was a cheap trick, and he couldn't quite convince himself that the ends justified the means. Not that he thought she was in peril of losing her heart. She might not even have one.

What the woman did have in abundance was spunk. He'd been paying close attention to the gossip flowing between her men and his and watching her from across the river. She was a hard-working woman. She was also a tough boss. Her men already had nicknamed her "The Tiny Tyrant." But even as they complained about her bulldog ways, he could see respect and admiration in their eyes. He might not want her living across the river on *his* land, but it was difficult for him not to admire her, too.

As long as he was being honest with himself, he might as well admit he knew the real reason he had been willing to adopt Higgins's strategy when he knew his own was better—he had a healthy instinct for self-preservation. A smart man didn't tarry with a woman who didn't play by the rules, and Miss Cammie Kendall didn't act like any woman he'd ever met. Not that he was interested in her as a woman. Her body might inspire his lust and her nerve his admiration, but that was all there was to it.

However sensible as keeping his distance might be, Higgins's strategy hadn't worked yet, and he knew in his heart it wasn't going to work anytime in the foreseeable future. If he wanted Miss Kendall gone, it was time for decisive action.

Josh interrupted his thoughts. "You've been quiet too long, big brother, and I don't like that look in your eye."

Running his finger along the barrel of his rifle, Adam inspected his handiwork. "You'll be happy to know I've decided to take you up on your suggestion and invite Miss Kendall to go hunting with me."

"Something tells me I didn't do her any favor putting the notion in your head."

Adam grinned.

"Damn you, Adam." Josh scowled. "I made the suggestion because I wanted the two of you to spend some time alone together. Get to know each other—"

"I *know* why you made the suggestion. Subtlety is not your strong suit and neither is matchmaking."

"I just don't see why you're so hell-bent on being shabby to her. She bought the land fair and square."

"It was promised to us. She knew that when she bought it. The sale might be legal, but it wasn't fair," Adam argued.

"This isn't about the land, is it?"

"What's that supposed to mean?"

"I think you're afraid of her," Josh declared.

"I'm not afraid of any woman," Adam scoffed.

"Yep, I reckon you are. You're afraid Cammie is woman enough to melt your iceberg heart. That's why you're so determined to get rid of her."

Adam rolled his eyes. "You must have got hold of a batch of bad whiskey, brother. The only reason I want her gone is she's squatting on *our* land. She stole it out from under our noses. I want it back. It's the principle of the thing."

"You trying to convince me or you?"

"You. You're the one who's lost his mind over Miss Kendall."

"If I'm the one who's lost his mind, how come you're the one violating the code of a gentleman and resorting to dirty tricks?" Josh countered.

Adam feigned affront and stared at his brother with a guileless expression. "I don't recall saying anything about dirty tricks. I just said I was gonna invite her to go hunting."

"Where?"

"Thought we'd take the boat downriver into the canyon."

"That's rough country."

"Yep."

"If you let a mountain lion or bear chew on her, I'll be obliged to borrow that rifle and shoot you," Josh warned.

"I'm not gonna let her get hurt. I just figure if she's determined to stay, she oughta get a true taste of the country so she knows what she's up against. If we have a hard winter, there's no telling what kinda wild animals might come down from the mountains to prey on the livestock. She oughta know what she and her horses are up against. If she gets scared and decides to run back home . . . well, I can't help that."

"Maybe she won't get scared," Josh said.

"Then that worried frown you're wearing on your face will be wasted, and the laugh will be on me."

Eight

"I've never been hunting," Cammie said when Adam appeared on her doorstep shortly after dawn the next morning. "I don't have the slightest idea how to go about it."

"Really?" Adam replied. "I was under the impression there was nothing a man does that you don't know how to do—*usually better.*"

"Is that what they are saying about me?" Eyes twinkling, Cammie cocked her head to one side. "How delightful."

Adam expelled an exaggerated sigh. "I hate to disappoint you, but I believe it was you who told me of your prowess."

"I've never claimed anything of the sort." She serenely set him straight. "What I claim is there is nothing a man does I can't learn to do if I am so inclined."

"Are you inclined to learn to hunt?"

Cammie ran her gaze up and down his frame before settling it on his face. His posture was stiff, his expression insouciant. She was fairly certain he was up to something, but her mood was such that curiosity overwhelmed caution, and she tendered him a noncommittal, "I don't know. I've never really thought about it."

"You oughta," he earnestly counseled. "It's important to lay in a good supply of meat for the winter. I always make it my top priority."

"I can see how your advice might apply to me, but you have a huge herd of cattle," Cammie reminded.

"Can't profit off a steer I eat."

"That's true."

"If you're afraid, just say so," he prodded.

"I'm not afraid."

"Squeamish?"

"Certainly not. Though I have never killed my own supper, I know the meat on my plate didn't appear there by magic."

"Then why is it taking so long for you to say yes?"

Not wanting to admit the chief cause of her hesitation was discomfort with the genuine excitement she felt at the prospect of agreeing to go with him, she continued to pretend disinterest. "I'm just surprised at the invitation, that's all. I haven't seen much of you around here lately."

"I have a ranch to run," he glibly stated.

"As do I, which is another reason I am hesitant. I had planned to go over the drawings I made for the exercise barn with—"

His jaw started to drop. "Building *another* barn?"

"Yes." Cammie clasped her hands together. "I considered doing without, but decided it would be an ill-advised economy. Working my younger horses outdoors in the dead of winter is an unnecessary risk of their health. I can afford to build the barn now, so it seems foolish not to do so."

"Getting started can't wait till tomorrow?"

"I suppose it could. I'm not in any hurry. All that really matters is that the building be completed before bitter cold weather sets in. I believe that won't happen until late November or early December."

"So are you coming?" he asked again.

Though common sense recommended a negative answer, Cammie preferred to follow her natural inclination. "Yes, I believe I will. I could use a break from my usual routine, and learning something new will do me good."

His eyes brightened. "Beginning to feel bored living out here with nothing but horses and roughneck cowboys to talk to?"

"Not at all. I've been too busy to be bored."

"Oh . . ."

"Don't sound so disappointed. I've told you more than once I'm here to stay. Look around you—" Her arms swept over the orderly yard and wealth of new outbuildings. "Why can't you just accept the fact you were wrong about me and my ambitions?"

"I'd have an easier time accepting it if you didn't insist on being right in my valley."

"Our valley," she corrected. "Didn't your mother ever teach you how to share?"

His eyes narrowed and his nostrils flared. "No."

It was painfully obvious she had hit a raw nerve, and Cammie had the feeling it had nothing to do with their dispute over the land. Though she was honestly looking forward to the excursion, she graciously offered him an out. "Maybe you'd rather not take me hunting, after all."

"I wouldn't have invited you if I didn't want to take you, now would I?" he said tersely.

"I'm not sure."

"Well, I am. You agreed to go and you're going. The skirt you're wearing is fine, but you oughta change into sturdy walking shoes if you have them."

"Should I bring my rifle?"

He appeared slightly startled. "You own a rifle?"

"Yes. I've never actually shot it, but since I am living alone and a considerable distance from town, it seemed prudent to own one. I purchased it shortly after moving here."

"Do you have bullets?"

"Of course."

"Bring them both."

"All right. Allow me twenty minutes to tell Mr. Culver and Mr. Daley of my change of plans, give them instructions for the day, and saddle Bliss."

"You won't be needing your horse. We'll be taking my boat downriver."

Despite her growing pique at his brusque manner, Cammie's eyes lit up. "Into the canyon? I've been wanting to go there for ages!"

The corners of his lips sagged. "You have?"

"Yes. Every day I see the river flow between those two mountains." She gestured toward the point. "A person would have to be totally lacking imagination not to wonder what lay beyond."

After dragging his gaze over her person as if trying to determine what species of creature she was, he squared his shoulders, turned, and walked down the steps of the porch. "I'll wait for you at the dock."

Cammie arrived at the dock, rifle in hand, in half the time she requested.

"That's not loaded, is it?" His eyes riveted on the rifle.

"No, why?"

"Wouldn't want you to accidentally blow a hole in my skiff, especially when I don't even know if you can swim."

"I can keep myself afloat should it become necessary," Cammie stretched the truth to what she hoped would prove true while silently praying she wouldn't be put to the test.

After handing Adam the gun, she stepped into the boat and settled herself on the seat opposite his. Adam picked up the oars and began rowing toward the tree-studded bluffs marking the Missouri River's entrance into the mountains.

Cammie studied her companion. His eyes were shaded by the brim of his hat, and his mouth was set in a rigid line. Muscles rippled beneath his cotton shirt as he pulled at the oars, but he appeared oblivious to the effort he expended.

She would be far happier if she could believe his invitation was nothing more than a simple, straightforward act of neighborliness, but with Adam Carrigan nothing was ever simple or straightforward. She supposed that was why she found him intriguing.

One minute he was smooth talking, the next rude. When he wasn't making himself a neighborly nuisance, he made himself so scarce their ranches might as well have been a thousand miles away. And he kept looking at her funny. She was used to the stares of men and was expert at disregarding them, but she couldn't disregard Adam Carrigan's stares. Whether exhibiting male admiration of her person or disapproval of something she said or did, his eyes seemed to bore right through her.

He was doing it right now. He was watching her as closely as she was watching him, as if he expected her to suddenly do something stupid. She met his penetrating gaze without flinching.

He didn't blush, break the awkward silence, or turn away. He kept on staring. So did Cammie.

Adam Carrigan was like a column of figures that wouldn't add up right. She knew if she looked long enough, she would find where she had gone astray in her calculations, and until she did it was impossible to get the problem off her mind.

Another woman might be nervous about spending the day alone in the wilderness with a man as confusing as Adam Carrigan, but she wasn't the least bit nervous. There wasn't a man or woman in the territory who had anything bad to say about him. She had made a point of casually working his name into the conversation whenever the opportunity allowed. What she heard from everyone from her banker to her handyman was that her neighbor was honest, well-respected, and headed the smoothest-running cattle operation in the area. Even if their opinions hadn't been so universally favorable, her own head and heart told her he wasn't capable of evil. Mischief was a different story, but she didn't find that particularly threatening. It merely kept her on her guard.

Rather than sit there staring at him, wondering whether or not he had mischief in mind that day, Cammie asked, "Why did you ask *me* to go hunting with you? Your brother seems a more logical choice."

"I told you before, I wanted to ask you," he informed her.

"Yes, you did," Cammie agreed. "But why . . . ? If you are planning some mischief, I would like to know now."

He was all provocative smiles. "If I'm planning mischief, telling you would spoil the fun."

"So—I'm right to be suspicious."

"Are you?"

"That's what I'm trying to get you to tell me."

He leaned forward as he pulled on the oars. "I suppose I could tell you, but I'd rather let you sit there and fret about it."

Cammie refused to be intimidated. "I'm not the sort to fret."

"What sort are you?"

She matched her grin to his. "The sort who wants to know what you're up to, but knows she can handle anything you have up your sleeve."

"Always full of confidence, aren't you?"

"Yes." Her eyes reflected the fire of the sun on the water. "Without confidence I would be sitting in a parlor in Virginia twiddling my thumbs while life passed me by."

"Why is it you figure your life there was so bad?" Adam asked, the teasing tone of his voice overlaid with open curiosity.

"My sex condemned me to a cosseted life," Cammie replied.

"I thought women liked to be cosseted."

"Many do, but I'm not one of them."

"Why not?"

"I have no idea," she answered him truthfully. "I only know I despised living a life devoid of usefulness or challenge."

"So you moved out here."

"Exactly."

"I would've figured a resourceful woman like yourself could've found something useful and challenging to do a little closer to home."

She shrugged. "Possibly."

"Did you even try?" he pressed.

"I don't see how that is any of your business."

"You sitting on my land makes it my business."

"We're back to that again?"

"Yes—my offer to buy the place still stands. I'll even reimburse you for the improvements you made."

"How kind of you, but as I have told you more times than I care to remember, I am not interested in selling my land."

"A woman is allowed to change her mind," he cajoled.

"Don't you ever get tired of having the same conversation?"

He stopped rowing. "As a matter of fact, I do. Wouldn't have to keep having it if you'd stop being so mule-headed."

"You're calling *me* mule-headed?" Cammie guffawed. "You're the one who bears a striking resemblance to a mule. I assumed you were up to something when you asked me to accompany you, but I had counted on you doing me the courtesy of being a little original when it came to vexing me. If negotiating a sale is your sole reason for inviting me on this excursion, you are wasting your time and mine."

He glared at her. "You want to go back?"

"If you're going to harangue me about buying my property all day, yes. But I'd much prefer you give me your word you'll not mention the subject of my land for the rest of the day and we keep going. I'm eager to see the canyon, and learning to hunt strikes me as a desirable skill to acquire."

Adam growled, pulling on the oars with unnecessary vigor for a full dozen strokes before he answered her. "Okay. You have my word."

"Thank you."

They were passing through the steep hills that marked the river's entrance into the mountains. The view of the rolling grass-covered hills of the valley was left behind and replaced by sharp limestone cliffs.

In some places a narrow band of conifers grew along the river's edge, but many of the cliffs rose straight up from the water. More trees dotted the top of the cliffs. Others had taken root in patches of soil collected on minute buttresses.

From a distance the huge rock walls appeared to block further passage, but as they drew near, a bend in the river exposed the illusion. Overhead eagles, ospreys, and falcons soared on the updrafts. Squirrels scampered across the rocks. Mountain goats grazed high above their heads, balancing on ledges so narrow they were invisible to Cammie's eyes.

"This is magnificent," she rhapsodized.

"Yep."

"Do you come here often?"

"Whenever I can spare the time. Usually I come alone."

"I can see why you would. It's like being in a cathedral carved by God's own hand."

"You don't find it overpowering?" he queried.

"Absolutely. That's what makes it so sublime. It takes away my breath and makes my heart beat so fast my limbs are tingling."

He started to say something, then abruptly clamped his lips together.

She smiled. "Thank you."

"For what?"

"Biting your tongue before you pricked me with some jibe."

"You're welcome."

He swung his head away from her, and for a long while they floated along in silence, each absorbed in the resplendent scenery.

When he was of a mind to, Adam Carrigan made an excellent companion. Cammie realized that of all the people she had met since moving to Montana, Adam Carrigan was her favorite. Although he exasperated her more often than he pleased her—and she didn't come close to comprehending him—she felt deliciously alive in his presence. He was the only man she had ever met who would rather goad her to prove her mettle than coddle her. That alone tipped the scales heavily in his favor. And who could help but like someone willing to share with her a place as glorious as this river canyon?

Cammie stiffened. Admitting "like" was too close to admitting she was attracted to the man who sat opposite her. She slammed the door on her thoughts, retreating behind a shield of conversation. "So what are we hunting?"

Her question plainly jarred him out of musings of his own, but if the reflective smile on his face was an accurate indication, he didn't seem to mind. "Whitetail deer. Not too much farther downriver there's a spot where we can beach the boat and hike into the hills."

"It seems a pity to disturb such serenity." Cammie spoke her thoughts aloud.

His voice lowered to an ominous timbre and his eyes darkened. "Nature's serenity can be deceptive. We won't be the only predators in the forest. Every day is a life and death struggle."

"What other predators stalk this forest?"

"Mostly bears and mountain lions. The forests are crawling with them. But that's not the worst of it. When the weather turns, they come out of the forest and stalk anything with meat on its bones." He grimaced. "You'll have to guard your horses every minute and watch your own back as well."

"This occurs when?" Cammie inquired evenly.

"Soon as the snow starts to fall . . . sometimes sooner," he somberly stated.

"At least I'll have plenty of time to prepare," she commented. Her eyes scanned the forest. "Do you think we'll see any bears or mountain lions today?"

"Might."

"I hope we do."

Adam scowled at her.

Cammie's brow knit. "Did I say something wrong? I only meant I think it would be thrilling to observe wild creatures in their habitat."

"Aren't you afraid of anything?" Adam complained.

"Yes."

"What?"

"I'm afraid of dying before I have the chance to live."

He squinted at her. "Am I supposed to understand what you mean by that?"

"Being a man, I suppose you wouldn't." Cammie smiled wanly and proceeded to explain. "I am twenty-six years old, but I feel as if I've been alive only a few months because up until my father's death, I had no life except for what he allowed me and the snatches I stole when no one was looking. You have no idea how frustrating it is to sit on a settee, draped in jewels, serving tea to a roomful of gossips when you would rather be out in the stables working with the horses."

"Can't say as I've ever been subjected to that particular trial," he admitted.

"Of course you haven't because you were born a man. Men are allowed to have ambitions. Women are expected to devote their lives to the comfort of men. If a young girl tries to pursue her own ambitions, she is confined to her room."

"Spent a lot of time locked in your room, did you?"

"More time than I care to contemplate."

He chuckled. "Figured as much. Can't imagine a bull-windy like you letting anyone, including your own daddy, tell you what to do."

"If you had been subject to like treatment, you wouldn't think it funny."

He immediately sobered. "So now you're an independent woman with your own ranch and a bunkhouse full of men who gotta take orders from you."

Cammie's eyes glowed with pride, and her lips curved into a puckish grin. "Yes, and I love every minute of it."

"Vengeance is mine sayeth Miss Kendall."

"Vengeance has nothing to so with the pleasure I take in my present circumstances," she said without rancor. "I merely enjoy having power over my own life."

"I hear you wield that power with an iron hand."

"I'll not deny I do," Cammie confirmed. "I have no choice if I hope to prove myself in a man's world."

He changed the subject and rowed in to shore. "This is the spot I was telling you about. I figure we'll hike in a ways till we find a good place for a little target practice. After you've got the feel of your rifle, we can do some earnest hunting."

"All right."

When the bottom of the boat scraped the gravelly shore, Adam stepped out and pulled the boat high enough on the beach so that Cammie could climb out without getting her shoes wet. Before disembarking, she handed him his rifle and the knapsack her nose told her held their lunch. Together they dragged the boat out of the water.

He settled the knapsack on his back. "If you've no objection, I'll lead the way."

"Since you know where we're going, it only makes sense for you to lead."

Nodding, Adam started up a trail.

"You must come here often, or the area is used by others as well to have worn a path," she remarked.

"Deer made the path down to the water."

"And if we follow it, we'll find the deer?"

"Exactly. Or at least that's how it's supposed to work. They've got trails all through these hills. There's no guarantee we'll find anything worth shooting at the end of the one we're on, but it gives us a place to start."

"To be honest, I don't really care. I find just being surrounded by raw nature exhilarating."

"It's the altitude," he declared. "If you start getting too winded just holler, and we can sit a spell till you're up to going on."

Cammie winced at his comment, but she was well aware that proving herself an equal in a man's world involved more than standing her ground and profitably running her ranch. It involved proving her mettle in every arena in which the male of the species traditionally excelled. She resented the feeling, but she acknowledged proving herself to Adam Carrigan was important to her in a way proving herself to other men was not. There was something about the man . . .

She shook her head to banish the thought because she had no notion how to end it.

They squeezed their way through dense thickets and crawled over large rocks, always moving uphill and rarely slowing their pace. At one point Cammie found herself with her back to a stone wall, edging along an eight-inch ledge. At times she was forced to cling to branches, the base of small bushes, rocks embedded in the earth, anything she could wrap her hands around to pull herself up a steep hillside. She was glad she had had the foresight to buy a strap for her rifle. More often than not, she found herself needing both hands free. Unfortunately the butt and barrel took turns whacking her shoulder and backside as she climbed.

Other than to ask the name of a bird or plant or some small animal that scampered across their path, Cammie didn't even try to carry on a conversation. She needed all her breath to keep up with her guide. She knew she had only to ask and he would stop, but her pride wouldn't allow her to admit she couldn't keep up with him. It didn't matter that his longer legs, well-hewn muscles, and years of experience gave him unfair advantage. She just couldn't do it. Every time he looked back over his broad shoulders, she forced a blithesome smile to her lips.

"Do you need to rest?" he sporadically questioned.

"Do you?" Cammie asked.

"No."

"Then neither do I," she said.

They had been hiking up the hill for well over an hour when he finally stopped and turned to face her, an incensed expression on his face. "When I said you were mule-headed, I was understating the facts. What are you trying to do—kill yourself?"

"I don't know what you mean," Cammie panted.

"Like hell you don't. If your face gets any redder, somebody is gonna mistake you for a tomato and cut you up for their salad."

"You don't look all that comely yourself. I know for a fact it's not raining, so that must mean that moisture is sweat I see trickling down your brow."

"You're evading the issue."

Laboring to keep her gasping breaths as quiet as possible, Cammie gazed at him with wide-eyed innocence. "What issue is that?"

"You know damn well what it is, and I'm not any too fond of the notion of having to lug your corpse out of these woods because you're too damn mule-headed to admit you can't keep up with me."

"But I did keep up."

A strangled groan rose up from his throat while he glared at her. "Let's have some lunch and do some target shooting."

"Let's." The delight she took in holding her own was magnified by the certain knowledge he purposefully had been testing her endurance from the beginning. Her delight however did not preclude the gratitude and relief she felt that they had finally stopped. Her heart was pounding so hard she felt as if her ribs were bruised and her head was so light, if not for the tree she leaned against, she doubted she would still be standing. Slipping her rifle from her back, Cammie cautiously sank to the ground. "This looks to be a lovely place for a picnic to me," she professed.

Adam moistened his kerchief with water and slapped it on

her forehead before handing her his canteen. "Take small sips or you'll puke all over yourself."

Her eyes thanked him for the warning, but she couldn't push the words past her lips.

The lunch consisted of fried chicken, potato salad flavored with onion and bacon, and a loaf of sourdough bread. Cammie was tempted to ask Adam if he had made the meal himself, but his dark looks kept her quiet.

Rising to his feet as soon as they had finished the meal, he gruffly asked, "Are you ready for your lesson?"

"Yes."

"Good."

"I'm gonna scratch a circle into the trunk of that tree over there with my knife—then I'll show you how to sight a target."

Brushing the crumbs from her lap, Cammie picked up her rifle and stood, eager to face this new challenge. "Do you want me to load the rifle now or later?" she called as he walked toward the tree.

"I'd be much obliged if you'd wait till I'm standing behind you."

"Fine," Cammie muttered under her breath. She had no quarrel with his instruction, but the tone in which he gave it rankled her. It inferred she hadn't enough sense not to fire the gun while he was in harm's way.

He returned to her side. "Now you can load up."

"Thank you."

He mutely watched while she slipped the bullets into their chambers. Lifting his own rifle, he demonstrated while he spoke. "Spread your feet apart so you have a steady base and brace the butt of the rifle against your shoulder. Close one eye and line up the front and rear sights with your target." He pointed to the sights on her rifle with his forefinger.

"When you're ready, gently squeeze the trigger. It's gonna kick, so be prepared."

Having explained each step, he physically went through each one again, but this time he pulled the trigger. His bullet hit the center of the circle. "Now you try."

Cammie carefully duplicated his movements. She sighted the target several times before she was satisfied with her aim. Just as he had instructed, she gently squeezed the trigger. The rifle went off with a deafening roar, and she found herself sitting in the dirt.

"You forgot to brace yourself for the kick." His lips twitched as he offered her his hand.

"I did exactly what you did," Cammie protested. Refusing his help, she picked herself up off the ground.

"I've got more weight. Try setting your feet farther apart, and hold the butt up tight against your shoulder."

"First I want to see where my bullet hit the tree."

The grin he was struggling to suppress fixed itself upon his face. "You didn't come within a mile of the tree. Came mighty close to hitting that cloud overhead though." He gestured skyward.

"Don't look so smug. That was only my first attempt. I don't imagine you were an expert marksman the first time you fired a rifle."

"Sure wasn't, but at least I didn't end up on my backside with my jaw hanging open. But don't let that fluster you. You look kinda cute that way."

"Very funny," she snapped.

Her second shot was an improvement over the first only in that when she landed on her posterior, she did so with less force. Her instructor didn't laugh aloud, but his whole frame shook with repressed merriment. Cammie reloaded her rifle, planted her feet firmly on the ground, and gritted her teeth.

This time when she squeezed the trigger, she kept her footing, but she still missed the tree by a wide margin.

"Try again," he chortled.

Cammie did, with equally dismal results.

She fired off ten more shots with no discernible improvement.

"You're terrible with a rifle," Adam observed, the pleasure in his voice as plain as the grin on his face.

"I am well aware my performance thus far has much to be desired," she stated with as much dignity as she could muster. "But perhaps my lack of success reflects more on the skill of my teacher than on me. If you spent less time laughing at me and more time helping me hone my skills, I might do better."

Adam stepped behind her. Reaching around her, he elevated her right elbow with his hand. He was standing so close his front side pressed against her backside, but she didn't dare complain for fear he would refuse to help—and despite her biting criticism of his teaching methods, she knew her poor showing was more her fault than his.

"Try now."

She did. There was a little improvement but not much.

"Are you remembering to close one eye?"

"Yes."

"Okay. Let's try this. You sight the target, and I'll hold both your arms level and steady."

Cammie nodded. This time—though she didn't actually hit the tree trunk—she did wing a branch.

"Better." He reloaded the rifle for her.

Cammie found that as long as Adam steadied her arms, she could come reasonably close to hitting the tree, but whenever he let go and stepped away, she couldn't keep the bullet in the same county.

Though she had to give him credit for trying, the wretch couldn't stop laughing at her. He did everything he could think of to help her improve her aim, but that only made things worse, because it left her with no one but herself to blame for her miserable performance. She wanted to scream in frustration. In deference to what little dignity she had left, she resisted the urge—but she couldn't prevent herself from muttering a heartfelt "damn" each time she bungled a shot.

To add injury to insult, every time Adam stepped behind her and put his steadying arms around her, she became increasingly aware of him as a man. The strength of his muscles, the evocative masculine scent of his skin, the whisper of his warm breath against her neck . . . all of them assaulted her senses, stirring them to intemperate awareness.

Even if she hadn't already humiliated herself enough in front of him for one day, she wouldn't welcome these perverse sensations. Having never let a man this close to her, for any reason, Cammie had no idea if a man could tell if a woman's body was reacting to his. She hoped not. She had no idea what was going on in his insides and that gave her hope the same was true of her for him. However, assuming such was the case provided small comfort. The feelings themselves chafed her. She certainly didn't plan to act on them, so why have them?

He interrupted her thoughts. "We're just about out of ammunition. We better stop and head home."

She stepped away and turned to face him. "What about hunting?"

"With all the shooting we've been doing, I doubt there's a wild creature within ten miles of us. Besides, it's getting late."

Cammie glanced at the sky. "You're right. I didn't mean to make you waste your entire day teaching me to fire a rifle. I'm sorry."

"Don't be," Adam counseled. "They say laughter is good for the soul."

"I don't think it qualifies when it's at someone else's expense."

"Can't say how the original speaker meant his words to be taken, but I know today has done my soul a world of good."

"You would."

"And so would you if you were the one teaching me and I was the one shooting everything but the tree."

"What a beastly thing to say." Cammie pursed her lips. "I would be highly insulted . . . if it weren't true."

They both laughed at their mutual lack of penitence concerning their fondness for getting the better of the other.

Gathering up their gear, Adam started down the hill. "Best be nice, or I'll make you row us home."

"I think not." Cammie fell in beside him. "Home is upriver."

"I can't believe my ears. Miss Cammie Kendall admitting she's not up to a task? I may not have been able to teach you to hold a rifle steady, but I did manage to teach you something." He paused for dramatic effect. *"Humility.* The world is gonna be clamoring to have me nominated to sainthood."

Cammie cast her gaze heavenward, then anchored it on him. "I am perfectly capable of rowing us upriver. I simply choose not to be goaded into doing something I don't want to do. In the future if you want to share rowing duties, you will have to play fair and not take the easiest way for yourself. We will flip a coin for the honors *before* we start off."

Adam grinned. "Were you born ornery or did you spend years developing it into an art?"

"A little of both I believe."

"A lot of both is more like it."

Nine

She never had enjoyed a day so much and disliked it with such equal intensity. Cammie rubbed her bruised shoulder and backside. While she dressed herself for the day and prepared her usual breakfast of tea and toast, Cammie contemplated the previous day.

The sights and sounds she had seen and heard on the trip downriver had been fascinating: the cliffs, the burbling water, the mingled scents of pine, cedar, and humus. Trudging up the mountainside had pushed her strength to its limits and past. Stretching those limits was invigorating. She had eaten the best fried chicken and potato salad she had ever tasted.

As a friend Adam Carrigan had much to recommend him. Their conversations might be liberally salted with barbs directed at each other, but for the most part it was a game of wits. They were like two children playing at king of the mountain. He introduced her to new experiences, kept her on her toes—and not only allowed her opportunities to prove herself but engineered them.

Cammie hadn't ever had a really good friend, even when she was a child. The girls she knew were all interested in staging mock tea parties or balls or playing house, activities that bored her senseless, and she wasn't permitted to play with the boys.

She would like to have Adam Carrigan for a friend, but

friendship was all she wanted from him. Platonic friendship. She didn't want to feel tingly when he touched her. Not that she blamed him for her incommodious reaction. He had done absolutely nothing to elicit it. She had only herself to blame.

The trouble with blaming herself was that she had no idea why her body had reacted the way it had—therefore she had no way of knowing if it might happen again or how to prevent the possibility. She didn't approve of lust without love, and she didn't intend to fall in love with anybody. She had her life planned out in minute detail, and nowhere did those plans include a man.

Love and marriage were death for a woman. She had seen too many young women exchange the oppressive rule of their fathers for that of a husband. The thought of her making a similar mistake made her shiver. A woman of ambition must be ever vigilant, or she would find herself losing her hard won freedom.

Perhaps it hadn't been her at all but the altitude. She borrowed the explanation Adam had given her the day before when she had expressed her wealth of feeling for the forest. It made far more sense than believing a woman of her ilk—who had never before felt the slightest attraction for any man—would suddenly find her body turned traitor. Altitude sickness, she mulled the theory over in her mind. With a sigh of relief, Cammie decided she had hit upon the proper interpretation of her behavior.

With that settled, her thoughts turned to the other reason her memories of the day vexed her. She was a dreadful markswoman.

Cammie knew it was unrealistic to expect to succeed at everything she tried, but knowing and accepting were two different things. Being able to accurately fire a rifle was a skill she might someday need, especially if what Adam said about the threat of predators from the forest stalking livestock was true. She'd never forgive herself if something happened to one of her horses because of her incompetence.

The only sure way to become competent at anything was to devote yourself body and soul to learning the skill, and keep on working at it no matter how slow or discouraging the progress. Patience, perseverance, and a healthy measure of raw nerve had seen her through before—and she was confident they would do so again. As she recalled yesterday's abysmal performance, she amended her bold assertion with the word *eventually.*

Cammie considered herself a woman of many virtues, but a willingness to advertise her failures to the world was not one of them. Her practice would be conducted in private, far enough away from the ranch that no one would hear the report of her rifle.

Her afternoon rides on Bliss changed so they began at noon. Often they lasted until the sun slipped behind the western mountains. No one asked why she always strapped a rifle to her saddle, and she didn't say a word.

Taking Cammie Kendall hunting had been an unmitigated disaster, Adam glumly concluded before the skiff had reached the dock on his side of the river. Not that he hadn't enjoyed her company. He had—but the purpose of the outing had been to scare Miss Kendall out of her wits. How was he to know she had a passion for wild animals? On the trip home they had seen a number of black bears. The fool woman had practically jumped out of the boat in her eagerness to get a closer look at them.

His attempt to prove she lacked the stamina necessary for life in the territory proved equally frustrating. She had been considerably worse for wear when exhaustion had finally forced *him* to stop, but she had matched his killing pace without complaint.

Even the rifle lesson—entertaining as it was to watch her try so hard and fail so consistently—rankled him because the fact was that he had called a halt to the lesson, not her. Her arms had to be aching, her shoulder battered black and blue, and her ears ringing—not to mention the wounds to her pride. What kind of woman was he dealing with here? The kind of woman that drove a man loco, that's what kind.

Even if his plan had been a good one, he hadn't stuck to it as well as he ought to have, which wasn't like him. He prided himself on being both decisive and tenacious. But she kept distracting him by refusing to react the way she was supposed to. He had set out determined to prove to Josh that he wasn't afraid of any woman—never had been, never would be. But Miss Kendall made him nervous. Real nervous.

Adam continued to brood about the trip over the next few days. No matter how hard he worked, he couldn't keep his mind off her.

He was even starting to dream about Cammie. Nice dreams, until he woke up and realized how much he had been savoring her company. Then all he felt was a hollow pit where his stomach used to be. It was bad enough she had invaded his valley. Now she was invading his head.

Of all his grievances against his new neighbor, the one that disconcerted Adam most—and the one he spent the greatest energy trying to avoid acknowledging—was that spending the day with her in the forest had the unforeseen effect of causing him to start admiring her too much. And it wasn't just her pluck, though he couldn't help but give her credit for that, too. The woman had a body made for a man to love—sweet smelling, soft in all the right places, eyes so big it was hard not to drown in them. When he'd nestled up to her backside to help her steady her rifle, he'd liked the way they had fit together.

He'd recognized his physical attraction to her before the day he had taken her into the canyon, but either he'd forgotten how strong it was or what he'd felt earlier lacked the intensity of what he was feeling now.

The woman was a hazard—there was no doubt about it. He knew the rules. A man was free to take his pleasure with women who sold it, but he best keep his hands off proper ladies unless he had marriage on his mind . . . and marrying Miss Kendall was the last thing he had on his mind.

He'd made up his mind long ago not to step into the same trap his father had. He'd watched him die by inches, and he would take a swift bullet through the heart any day over the agony he'd seen him suffer. Cammie Kendall was just like *her*—eastern born and bred, delicate boned, beautiful. Not that he thought himself in jeopardy of falling in love, which had been his father's true downfall. What he felt for Cammie Kendall was good old-fashioned lust. But too much liking and lust had a way of turning ugly on a man, and he wasn't inclined to trust his future happiness to luck. Women were too fickle to be trusted. He hadn't remained a bachelor all these years by being careless.

No, he wasn't afraid he might fall in love with her. That was so preposterous, Josh was lucky he hadn't laughed in his face when he'd made the statement. He just didn't want his life complicated.

One night Adam dreamed he saw himself standing at the altar in a flower-filled church—and who should sashay down the aisle but a smirking Cammie Kendall. Adam awoke in a cold sweat.

The next night he had the same dream, and he awoke feeling even more unnerved.

Josh might not be right about his heart, but if he was starting to have nightmares about marrying Miss Kendall, he considered it a bad omen. He wanted her out of his valley *now.*

He didn't like himself for feeling how he felt, but his desire to rid himself of her took on new urgency. Setting his mind the task of coming up with a solution to his problem, Adam endured days of unproductive cogitating and as many sleepless nights. Finally his weary brain offered up an idea.

Cammie Kendall might not be afraid of bears or mountain lions, but he didn't recall snakes coming up in the conversation. There wasn't a woman alive who wasn't terrified of snakes.

It wasn't the best plan in the world, but it was all he had. Its chief appeal was that he could carry it out without having to exchange a word with his nemesis.

"What the hell are you doing?" Josh demanded, staring at his brother as he sat at the dining room table wrangling with a garter snake. On the table sat a bottle of whiskey, a saucer, a leaf heaped with pitch, some string, and the box of rattles they'd collected from snakes they'd shot as boys.

"I'm making a rattlesnake," Adam replied without looking up. "Sit down. I could use some help here."

Josh sat. "It won't work."

"Sure it will. All I gotta do is spread this fella's tail with pitch, tie on the rattle with the string, then get him good and drunk so he'll sleep till morning."

"I didn't mean you won't get the snake to cooperate, though my bet is you won't." Josh gave his brother a pitying look. "I meant whatever you're planning on doing with that snake, it won't scare Cammie into selling you her land."

"What makes you figure she has anything to do with what I'm doing?"

"She's the only person I know who inspires you to make an ass of yourself, so there's no doubt in my mind she's involved in this."

Adam dropped his pretense and concentrated on the snake. "Name me one woman you know isn't petrified of snakes."

"Don't know any," Josh granted. "But that's beside the point. You could scare her right out of her bloomers, and she's not gonna give up that ranch of hers. All you're gonna do is ruffle your own feathers just like you did on that hunting trip. Then I'll have to put up with your lousy mood—and to tell you the truth, brother, you've been getting on my nerves more than I can tolerate lately."

"I wasn't aware I was behaving any differently than I always do."

"You aren't aware of *anything* but Cammie Kendall. Why don't you just stop fighting it and admit you've taken a fancy to her."

"Because I don't fancy her—at least not in the way you keep pushing me to. What I fancy is getting her out of our valley."

Scratching his head, Josh rose to his feet. "I can see my time would be better spent trying to talk sense to a rock. I thought you were supposed to be the responsible brother, and I was the one who couldn't keep myself out of trouble."

"Avoiding trouble is exactly what I'm doing," Adam insisted, continuing to grapple with the snake.

"Right, and I bet you have a three-legged horse you'd like to sell me, too."

* * *

"What is that?" Cammie asked, stretching her hands high over her head and yawning as she sat up in her bed. She blinked at the early morning sun streaming through the window. The sound resembled a cricket, only it was different enough she couldn't quite convince herself that's what it was.

Slipping on her wrapper, she padded on bare feet toward the direction of the sound. Lucretia skulked at her heels.

"It's coming from inside my boot." Cammie whispered her discovery. In the same instant Lucretia pounced. Wrestling the boot onto its side, she stuck her paw inside and pulled out a writhing snake.

Panic seized Cammie's breast. The only snake she knew that made a rattling sound was "No, Lucretia! Get back!" she shouted. "You'll get hurt! It's poisonous!" Before the last word of her frantic cries left Cammie's lips, Lucretia bit off the snake's head. She lay the body at her mistress's feet.

Lucretia appeared unharmed.

Cammie quaked with relief. "Don't you ever frighten me like that again," she began to scold her cat, but as she bent to lift Lucretia into her arms, Cammie noticed something odd about the snake.

She'd never seen a rattlesnake before, but she felt certain their rattles were not tied on with string. Her eyes flashed. Someone had crept into her room while she slept and placed the mock rattler in her boot. The question was why and who?

The why was easy. The snake was supposed to scare her. If someone had meant her real harm, they would have used a real rattlesnake.

As for the who . . . it might be one of the men she had hired . . . but she didn't think so. There was only one man she knew who had the audacity to do such a thing and his name was Adam Carrigan.

He'd been making himself absent lately, and she'd been wondering what he was up to. Still trying to test her it seemed.

Picking up the remains of the snake between her forefingers, she examined it more closely. "You certainly went to a lot of bother, didn't you?" Cammie began to laugh. Tears of mirth streamed down her cheeks long before she could sober herself.

The next time Adam came to visit Cammie, she was wearing a snakeskin band with a rattle for decoration around her riding hat. He tried not to stare. He'd been waiting on his side of the river for over a week to hear an account of her harrowing encounter with the snake. When none of her men when visiting his said a word, he concluded the snake had awakened early from its whiskey-induced nap and slithered off before she found it. Now he knew different.

"Is something wrong?" she asked her voice sounding suspiciously merry.

There was no way he could tell the truth without divulging his guilt, which he wasn't going to do. "No."

She cocked her head to one side. "You keep looking at me funny."

"Must be your imagination."

"I'm sure you're right." She continued to smile at him agreeably. "Now why was it you said you wanted to see me?"

"I want to take a closer look at that four-year-old Josh is thinking of buying from you." He repeated the excuse he had used earlier to justify his presence.

"She's out in the north pasture. I was just about to go for a ride, so my horse is already saddled. I'll take you out there myself. On the way we can talk about the cattle I want to buy from you. I need a few head to help keep my pastures clean of parasites and to use to train my horses to cattle. Perhaps we can negotiate some kind of trade."

"How many head do you want?"

"A dozen. They needn't be your best cattle. As long as they're healthy, they'll suit me well enough."

"Cattle are worth thirty dollars a head. A saddle horse goes for thirty-five," Adam stated when they were both mounted and well on their way to the north pasture. Hoping a heated negotiation would distract him from the fine way her seat fit her saddle, he proposed, "We can trade the mare and one head straight across. Then you can pay for the rest of the cattle less five dollars."

Cammie shook her head. "Market-ready cattle are worth thirty dollars a head. I have already indicated my willingness to take animals in less than prime condition. Also an ordinary saddle horse is worth thirty-five dollars. My mare is far from ordinary."

"What do you want for her?"

"Six head."

"That's a ridiculous price."

"Wait until you see my mare." She nudged her horse to a canter.

Adam didn't want to wait to see the mare. He wanted to hightail himself back to the safety of the other side of the river. He'd only come over to satisfy his curiosity about the snake. He didn't know if she knew he was responsible, but the confrontation obviously hadn't fazed her. Josh could negotiate the price for his own damn horse.

Miss Cammie Kendall was in too fine a mood to his way of reckoning. Her whole face was lit up like a chandelier as she sat proud as a peacock on her high-stepping stallion.

She was riding astride, like a man, and he kept finding himself wishing she weren't so damn attractive. He tried not to pay her any mind, but a man would have to be dead to do that.

By the time they reached the north pasture, his jeans were so tight the buttons of his fly were straining against their threads. It was a helluva condition to be in on a horse.

"There she is." Cammie pointed out the mare in question. "Your brother has excellent taste in horses."

Adam couldn't argue with the truth.

The mare had bold, intelligent eyes and perfect conformation. Her coat was glossy. Dismounting, he slowly approached her and checked her teeth, ankles, and knees. All the while the mare cooperated with his attentions as though she could read his thoughts.

Though the mare's manners were as impeccable as her structure, there were some thoughts in his head Adam didn't want to share, even with a horse. Those thoughts concerned Cammie Kendall, and the kind of inspecting of her conformation he'd like to be doing. Adam flicked his tongue across his lips. He smoothed his mustache. Noticing he was starting to breathe too heavily, he throttled his imagination and did his damndest to concentrate on the mare.

"So are you willing to pay my price?" Cammie prodded.

It was the chance for escape he'd been waiting for, and Adam sent a thank you heavenward. Patting the mare's neck, he strode back to his own horse and mounted. "I'll have to talk it over with Josh and get back to you."

"All right."

"I know you're busy, so don't bother riding back with me." He tipped his hat. "Be seeing you around."

* * *

If a snake didn't work, maybe a skunk would. They were a common problem in the area. Many was the unsuspecting greenhorn who left his door open to catch the summer breeze and found his home invaded by one of the malodorous creatures. Miss Kendall had yet to experience the delights of one of these unwelcome visitors. In the interest of speeding her departure, Adam decided to make the introduction.

All that was required was a warm day, a few strategically placed pieces of raw fish, and good timing. His biggest worry was that her cat would eat the fish before a passing skunk got wind of it, but since the feline spent most of her day at her mistress's heel in the barns and pasture, he was reasonably confident of success.

Miss Cammie Kendall might be able to handle a snake, but nobody won a contest with a skunk.

The sun set red, promising warm weather the next day. An early morning fishing trip provided the rest. After cutting the fish into bite-sized pieces, Adam rowed upriver from her house and tied his boat to a bush.

Since no man was ever allowed to be idle during daylight hours on the Kendall ranch and Cammie worked herself as hard as her men, he doubted his presence would be noticed—but as a precaution Adam brought along his fishing pole. If he got caught with the bucket of chopped fish, he could always say he was using it for bait, which was true. Adam grinned at his own cunning. The only place he wouldn't be able to cover himself was while he was actually inside her house.

He began laying his trail.

Cammie entered her cabin, tossed her riding gloves on the small table near the door, and stopped cold. A skunk was standing in her parlor. Scooping Lucretia up into her arms, she gulped a breath and held it. Ever so slowly she backed out the door.

Out in the yard she stood staring at her house in consternation. She had put in a long day and she was tired. This was the last thing she needed. No, she amended, the last thing she needed was for the skunk to spray her or her furniture. She was grateful she had discovered the skunk's presence by sight, not smell.

There was little question how the skunk had gotten into the house. Even on rainy days she was in the habit of leaving the doors to her house open to keep the air from becoming stale.

Having no experience in dealing with this type of situation, and fearing a mistake on her part would lead to putrid consequences, Cammie went in search of some advice.

"Gentlemen, I have a skunk in my parlor," she announced to the group of men gathered in the kitchen of the bunkhouse.

"Happens now and then," Jordan Smith remarked.

"Can anyone tell me how to get him out?"

"Has he stunk up the place?" John Thorpe asked.

"No."

"Then the best thing to do is open all the doors and wait for the critter to wander out on his own," Mr. Daley recommended.

"Your other choice is send in a man to shoot it, but likely you'll end up with a bullet hole in your floor, and if he misses, neither man nor beast is gonna want to step foot in that house for a good long while," Elias Rutley added his opinion.

"I believe I will follow Mr. Daley's counsel. Thank you, gentlemen. I apologize for interrupting your supper."

"Ma'am?"

"Yes." She turned back to face the room.

"If I were you, I'd think about locking that kitty of yours up somewhere. She's a mighty curious cat and . . ."

"Yes, you're absolutely right. Thank you, I will."

After stopping to put Lucretia in a tack shed, Cammie retraced her steps to the house. The front door was already open. She assumed the back door still was as well, but she walked around to the back of the house to check to be sure the afternoon breeze hadn't blown the door shut. It hadn't.

Hoping the skunk might have already left, Cammie returned to the front of the house and warily peeked inside. The skunk was still there.

A couple of old chairs that had previously belonged to Mr. Higgins sat in the yard. She plopped down in the pine rocker to wait out the skunk.

Benjamin Fry brought her a plate of food.

Cammie had planned to spend the evening working on her accounts in her office after supper, but after a few minutes of pique at having her plans thwarted, she allowed being forced to sit and relax was not all that bad.

The weather was as close to perfect as a person could wish. Gradually the sky darkened, and one by one stars began to twinkle overhead until the sky glowed with tiny white lights.

It had been a long time since she had taken the time to appreciate the beauty of the night sky. Montana's sky made the sky back in Virginia seem pale by comparison.

It was approaching ten o'clock when the skunk finally poked his black and white striped head out the door and waddled away. Cammie reluctantly rose to her feet.

After walking from room to room, sniffing the air to assure herself that the skunk hadn't seen fit to leave her a memento of its visit, she fetched an extremely indignant Lucretia from the tack shed and retired.

* * *

For something that happened now and then, finding a skunk in her parlor soon became an almost daily occurrence. Cammie was beginning to think the first skunk must have informed all his friends and relatives he had found a lovely spot to pass the time. It was getting so bad, she was beginning to recognize some of the more frequent visitors.

She was following every piece of advice she was getting, but nothing seemed to have any effect. She closed her doors, and the skunks climbed in the windows. She closed the windows, and invariably she forgot to shut a door properly and the wind would blow it ajar. She kept her kitchen spotless, so the scent of a free meal wouldn't attract the creatures. She didn't allow so much as a bread crumb to litter the yard within a hundred feet of the house, but still they came.

Mr. Culver thought it must be a sign that a hard winter was coming. Some of her men agreed. Others had their own theories, ranging from the skunks being attracted to Lucretia to some sort of social upheaval in the skunk population. But other than posting a man to stand sentinel on every side of the house and shoot the creatures on sight, everyone had run out of suggestions to make them go away.

Cammie hated to resort to such drastic measures. Thus far none of the skunks had done any real damage. Lucretia had come perilously close to being sprayed on several occasions, and she had had more than one close call, but shooting the creatures seemed too harsh.

Cammie knew she couldn't let the skunks take over her house, and she would do whatever she must—but before losing the labor of four able-bodied men to the task of skunk patrol, she decided to watch the house herself. Maybe if she could discover how and why they got in, she could devise a way to keep them out.

There was a cluster of wild rose bushes growing near the southeast corner at the back of the house. Cammie chose the spot to hide herself. She wasn't all that optimistic anything would come of her efforts, and unwilling to waste an entire day, she took a new book on cattle driving she had been meaning to read.

The first day not a skunk came in sight, but on the second, her vigilance was rewarded. Her eyes flashed, and her hands clenched the cover of her book.

She should have known a human skunk was behind the sudden invasion of her home, she silently fumed as she watched Adam Carrigan carefully lay a trail of raw fish to her back door! He swiveled his head from side to side, obviously checking to see if anyone was watching him, then disappeared inside. A few moments later he emerged from the house, a satisfied grin on his face. Leaving the door ajar, he started back the way he had come.

When Cammie thought of how many times she had been tempted to ride over to his ranch and solicit his advice on how to deal with her skunk problem, she felt her blood boil. Thank God, she hadn't given him the pleasure of playing her for more of a fool than he already had. Her first impulse was to leap from her hiding place and confront him immediately, but a small voice in her head stopped her.

Raining curses upon his head might vent her frustration, but that's all it would do. She had something far more effective in mind . . .

"Mr. Woodrow, how are your skills as a fisherman?" Cammie approached the first hired hand she came across as soon as it was safe to leave her hiding place.

"Good as the next man's."

"Excellent, I would like you to take the rest of the morning off and go fishing."

He stared at her, clearly startled by her suggestion he quit work and spend the day being indolent. "You sure?"

"Yes. I find I have an acute craving for fish."

"Okay. How many fish do you want?"

"I think two or three will be sufficient . . . and Mr. Woodrow, please don't gut them. I'd like to do that myself."

"Yes, ma'am."

It was certainly nice of Adam Carrigan to show me exactly how this is done, Cammie mused as she tied Bliss to a tree hidden from view from the Carrigan ranch. All I have to do is follow his example and hope there are as many skunks on his side of the river as there are on mine.

The Carrigan ranch was as busy as her own, and a minimum of stealth was all that was necessary to lay the trail of fish parts from a promising-looking grove of trees to the back door of the house. Cammie pressed her ear to the door, listening carefully to determine if anyone was inside before opening the door and continuing the trail inside. Leaving the door wide open, she found a hiding place close to the house and sat down to wait.

She supposed it was undignified of her to be engaging in adolescent pranks, but she didn't care. Adam Carrigan had started this. She could not let this latest mischief go unavenged. There was no telling what he might do next if she did.

She didn't have solid proof, but she knew as surely as she knew her own name that he was behind the "rattlesnake" in her boot. She had thought to unnerve him by letting him wonder just what had happened between her and the snake, but she could see now she should have taken stronger measures from the start.

What on earth possessed a grown man to stoop to these boyish shenanigans? She didn't know why she put up with him. The sensible thing to do would be to call in the sheriff and have him arrested for trespassing. But calling in the law would be admitting she needed a man's help handling him. She would drown herself in the river before she would admit to that.

Adam Carrigan was obviously unbalanced. That was the only rational explanation for his ability to be charming one minute and exasperating the next. Someone had to stop him from harassing his neighbors and that someone was her.

As she sat in the shade of the dogwood thicket, Cammie tried to work herself up into a lather of righteous fury, but she fell far short of her mark because—much as she hated to confess it—there was a certain diabolical exhilaration to be found in baiting a trap and lying in wait, especially when her intended victim was Adam Carrigan. And if all went according to plan, she would do him one better.

Cammie fingered the pebbles in her pocket. She wished she could be here to see the look on his face, but she planned to be back on her ranch long before he discovered what she had done to him.

It was a long wait, but late in the afternoon, Cammie's patience was rewarded. She chortled with glee as not one but two large black and white skunks marched into the Carrigans' kitchen, their fluffy tails high in the air.

It was time to make her move. Scampering across the distance between herself and the house, she cautiously followed the skunks through the door. The kitchen was empty. Her heart was beating so rapidly it was difficult to breathe, but she made herself tiptoe through the room into the next.

The trail she had laid ended in the parlor in a small pile of fish. It was there she found the skunks—which was exactly where she wanted them. They nibbled contentedly, unaware of her presence.

What she intended to do next required perfect timing, or she would become the victim of her own revenge. Cammie paused to steady her nerves. One . . . two . . . three—she mentally counted off the seconds.

Reaching into her pocket, Cammie lobbed a volley of pebbles at the skunks and ran. As soon as she was out the kitchen door, she slammed it behind her. She was less than a half-dozen steps away from the door when Adam Carrigan rounded the corner of the nearest barn.

"Cammie? What brings you to this side of the river?" he called out and waved, crossing the yard with long, steady strides.

Cammie's heart dropped to her toes. She clasped her hands tightly together and pasted on a smile. "Good afternoon."

He fixed his gaze upon her. "You feeling okay? You look . . . twitchy."

"I'm fine."

"Everything okay at your ranch?"

"Couldn't be better," she chirped.

His brow knit. "You sure look like something is bothering you. Why don't you come into the house, and we can talk about it."

"Ah, no thank you, I can't spare the time."

"You must have come over for some reason."

"No. I was just out riding, and I thought I'd stop by to say hello. When I knocked on the door, no one answered. I waited, hoping someone would come home, but now I find I've used up all the time I had allotted for the visit."

Adam glanced toward the hitching post, then around the yard. "Where's your horse?"

"Over there." Cammie tilted her head in the general direction of the spot she had left Bliss. "I found a nice patch of grass in the shade. I know I spoil him, but . . ." She shrugged. "I really do have to go. Perhaps another time. Goodbye."

Beating a hasty retreat across the yard, she left him staring at the empty spot where she had been standing.

Bliss was a considerable distance from the house, but Cammie covered it before Adam Carrigan opened the door to the kitchen. She knew the exact moment he did, because a string of the bluest cuss words she had ever heard rent the air like a knife.

Ten

"She's ruining my life," Adam Carrigan complained to the peacefully grazing herd of cattle he was surveying. Unwilling to concede any woman could ever have that much power over him, he brusquely corrected his statement. "Okay, ruin is too strong a word, but she sure as hell knows how to stink it up."

He'd been spending a lot of time out on the range with his cattle lately. Everyone was staying as far away from the house as practicality allowed. He didn't blame Cammie Kendall for what she'd done to him. He knew he deserved it, and he was willing to take his punishment like a man. What chafed him was she had the cheek to carry out the deed. How was he ever going to get rid of her if she was forever reacting in the opposite way he expected her to?

Adam lifted his hat and raked his fingers through his hair. He was tired of being routed. If he had to listen to one more chiding remark from Josh's grinning mouth, he was going to kill his own brother. But he couldn't give up. There was too much at stake: his land, his peace of mind, and after suffering another defeat at his irksome neighbor's hands—his vanity.

The woman definitely had the whole damn animal kingdom on her side. He may as well accept it and give up on that avenue. This time he wanted what he did to work.

Adam searched his mind, pondering and discarding a succession of ideas. His conscience tied his hands, preventing him from embracing many of the most effective means of driving her from the valley. He was frustrated enough to bend his own standard of conduct and morality, but he wanted to be able to live with himself after she was gone.

He continued to chew over his dilemma while he tended his herd. After a good long while, he hit upon an idea he could stomach.

If wild animals didn't daunt her, maybe he should try to spook her with wild men. What Indians were left in the area were peaceful, and he wasn't of a mind to bring them any grief, but as long as he took a few precautions, nobody would get hurt. Desperate times called for desperate means.

He knew she gave her men Sundays off. Most of them would be spending their pay in town and wouldn't be back until Monday morning. He'd plan a Sunday night "attack."

Getting word to whoever stayed at the ranch not to pull their guns wouldn't be all that difficult. There were plenty of men from both ranches who were good friends. And there were few things cowboys liked better than a good joke. That's how he figured he'd present his scheme. Anyone who balked, he could bribe with a bottle of whiskey, or if that failed to secure their cooperation, his own men could sneak over and hogtie and gag any rebels. That would leave Cammie alone to defend herself, and he had firsthand knowledge she couldn't hit the broad side of a barn standing three feet away.

He and his men could ride around her house a few times, whooping and hollering, wearing a bunch of feathers and war paint until they had her good and scared. The next day he could stop by, reinforce her dread of an Indian uprising, and help her start packing for home.

If she tried to stir up the locals against the Indian population before she left, he'd quietly confess his little prank to the right people and stop any trouble before it got started.

Adam spent considerable time contemplating his plan and every possible resulting complication, working out satisfactory solutions to deal with every contingency. He would have been a lot happier not to be sitting on his horse thinking the thoughts he was, but her stubborn refusal to succumb to his other schemes forced him to it.

When Sunday night arrived, everything was arranged according to plan. Anticipating Josh's disapproval, Adam had kept him ignorant of his intentions. To make certain Josh stayed out of the way, he had persuaded him to take a trip to Deer Lodge to check on some bulls they were considering buying. The two men remaining on the Kendall ranch were in cahoots with him. The cowboys who would be riding with him were his most trusted men.

As he and his men shed their shirts, blackened their hair with charcoal, and spread on the war paint he had concocted by boiling down berries and barks and mixing the extracts with lard, in the back of his mind a persistent voice kept telling him what he was about to do was beneath his dignity—but Adam ignored it. This was his valley. The land rightfully belonged to him. Again and again he had offered her a more than fair price to move on. He was only doing what he had to do to set Higgins's mistake to rights.

Sunday evenings were the one time during the week that Cammie allowed herself the luxury of indulging herself. Filling her brass tub with the hottest water she could bear, she scented the water with perfume and settled in for a good long soak.

The heat of the water soothed her aching muscles, and these days her muscles always ached at the end of the day. She was getting stronger, but her lack of physical endurance was a chronic irritant, and she constantly tested her limits in hopes of stretching them.

Closing her eyes and leaning her head against the back of the tub, she thought of all the burly girls who longed for dainty beauty. If such a thing were possible, she would trade her fair features and delicate frame for one of their plain faces and robust bodies without hesitation.

She wondered if God had purposefully set out to mismatch souls and bodies to build strength of character or if it was an accident of nature.

Cammie's philosophical musings were abruptly interrupted by a sudden burst of noise outside her door. It sounded as if a hundred men with an equal number of horses had converged on the house. They were riding in circles, surrounding the house, and screeching gibberish.

Bounding from the tub—and without bothering to dry herself or waste time dealing with undergarments—Cammie pulled on the skirt and blouse she'd relegated to the laundry pile only minutes before. She grabbed the rifle from its rack in her office, loaded it, then inched the front door open a crack.

Indians! She peered into the darkness at the half naked, painted bodies sitting astride the thundering horses. She had been told Indians had ceased to be a problem in the area years ago. *Renegades* . . . the dread word resounded in her head. Easing the door shut, Cammie pressed her back against it. Her heart climbed into her throat.

"Don't panic," she sternly whispered to herself as every grisly tale of Indian savagery she had ever read flooded her mind. "There aren't as many of them as you originally thought out there. No more than a dozen, if that many. Take a deep breath! *Think!*"

Cammie hadn't heard a single gunshot, and that could only

mean one thing: Jordan Smith and Sidney Shanks already had been murdered, and she was next. A shudder racked her frame, but she forced herself to stiffen her spine. If she was going to die, she wasn't going to do it without a fight.

After wedging a chair under the latch of the front door, Cammie dashed to her bedroom and dragged her bed in front of the back door. Supplying herself with an extra box of bullets on her way back to the parlor, she positioned herself at the edge of the window.

The din was deafening. The pounding of her pulse in her ears added to the ominous rumble. Lucretia rubbed against her skirts and nervously meowed.

The only reason Cammie could think of to explain why renegades would attack her ranch was her horses. Somewhere she had heard Indians valued good horseflesh. She knew word of the quality of her horses had rapidly traveled throughout the territory. She'd made a point of making certain that it did. It had never occurred to her that the news would spread to anyone but potential customers. Rather than simply steal what they wanted, it was clear these thieves didn't want to leave her alive to come after them. Cammie stifled a scream of mingled rage and terror.

Her beautiful horses in the hands of miscreants and her brief taste of independence snatched from her grasp so soon. It was too terrible to contemplate.

She couldn't just stand here with her knees quaking, waiting for them to attack. She had to do something!

Taking a deep breath, Cammie used the butt of the rifle to break out a windowpane and fired off two shots in rapid succession. Reloading the rifle, she fired again. She missed all four times, but her last shot blew a feather off one Indian's headdress.

"Hey! You said she didn't know how to use a gun," the man squealed in unbroken English.

Cammie stood dumbfounded. It couldn't be . . .

Staying carefully hidden behind the window frame, she squinted into the darkness. There was a half-moon, and now that she took the time, she saw her enemy in more detail. With all the war paint they had smeared on themselves, it was impossible to recognize the men, but when she scrutinized them, she immediately recognized several of the horses. One in particular was unmistakably familiar.

Cammie was so furious she sputtered. Reloading her rifle, she fired off two more shots. She kept reloading and firing as fast as she could take aim. As irate as she was, she possessed enough presence of mind not to actually hit anyone, but she came as close as she dared. The effect was immediate chaos.

"I ain't gonna get myself killed playing no joke on a woman!"

"Me neither!"

"Let's get outta here!"

"I'm right behind you!"

Cammie kept firing as the band of Indians retreated. Adam wheeled on his horse to join them in the same instant Cammie aimed a shot to his left. A yelp of pain pierced the air as he grabbed his arm and tumbled off his horse.

He lay motionless on the ground.

"Oh, my God—I've killed him!" Cammie cried. She threw down her rifle, kicked the chair aside, and flew out the door. Halfway across the yard, her toes caught the hem of her skirts and sent her sprawling in the dirt. She was up and running again before the first mote of dust settled. When she reached Adam's side, she dropped to her knees. "Don't be dead," she pleaded, cradling his face in her hands.

"I'm not." He stared up at her. Peeling her hands off his face, he pushed himself to a sitting position. "You just winged me."

"Then why were you lying on the ground?" Cammie persisted to search his person for mortal injury, worry creasing her brow.

"You caught me off balance. When I grabbed my arm, I fell and got the wind knocked out of me."

Combing her fingers through his hair, she felt for lumps. "Are you sure?"

"Yes! Stop fussing over me," he ordered. Retrieving his hat, he slammed it on his head and hunkered beneath it. "I think I've suffered enough for one night."

Cammie sat back on her heels. Now that she knew he wasn't in imminent danger of dying, her wrath surged afresh. "And that's *my* fault?"

"Yes," he insisted with irresolute conviction, keeping his gaze averted from hers. "When the hell did you learn to shoot that rifle?"

"I've been going off by myself and practicing every afternoon since the day we went downriver," she curtly informed him.

"Figures."

"Is there something wrong with that?"

"No, it just would've been nice if you'd have let someone know you'd become a crack shot."

He didn't deserve the truth, but she offered it in her own defense. "I'm not. I didn't mean to hit you."

Whipping his head around, he gaped at her with horrified disbelief. "Are you telling me you were just firing every which way and hoping for the best?"

"No," Cammie retorted. "I'm much better at hitting my target than I was at the river. If you hadn't turned at precisely the wrong moment, the bullet would never have hit you. I'm just saying that as yet, I'm not as skilled as I would like to be." She gingerly examined the bright red gash bloodying his upper arm. "Come into the house. I want to look at your arm in the light."

"I don't want you looking at my arm."

"Ask me if I care what you want." Wiping her hands on her skirt, Cammie stood up and none too gently prodded him to do the same with her big toe. "Now that I know I didn't kill you, I'm thinking of remedying the situation."

"Thanks for the warning." Mutinously he fell in beside her.

"Don't give me that look," Cammie chastised. "We both know you're more responsible for your injury than I am. Of all the stupid things you've done, this is the stupidest. What if I hadn't overheard one of your men speaking English? I might have killed the lot of you before I figured out who you were."

"I didn't know you had learned to use a gun," Adam lamely proffered.

"And you think that makes scaring me out of my wits okay?"

His eyes and voice brightened. "You were scared?"

"For about two minutes before I realized it was *you* again. Sit down." She pushed him down in a chair.

The light in his eyes extinguished. "You're enjoying this, aren't you?"

"You think I enjoy patching up idiots? Not hardly."

"You enjoy bossing me about like I was a fractious chore boy," he gruffly clarified his complaint.

"If you don't like being treated like a fractious child, my advice is stop acting like one."

"What do you want me to say?"

" 'I'm sorry' would do nicely for starters," she suggested over her shoulder as she lifted a tin of bandages and salves from the shelf. "You can follow that with a promise to stop these lame attempts to get me to sell you my land. For the life of me, I don't know how you ever got the reputation of being an upstanding member of Helena society." Setting the tin on the table, she fetched a bowl, two washcloths, a towel, and a bucket of water. "The only way you are going to get me off this land is if I'm carried off it in a pine box, and as poor as my opinion is of you, I don't think you're willing to imperil your immortal soul to gain a few hundred acres of land." Cammie poured some of the water in the bowl, handed him one of the washcloths, and indicated he was to use the water in the bucket to wash the war paint off his skin.

"The land isn't worth it, but getting rid of you might be," he muttered, applying the washcloth to his face.

Dipping her cloth into the bowl, Cammie sponged the blood and war paint off his injured arm. As she did so, she couldn't help but notice the strength of the muscles beneath her fingers or the appealing way the russet hair covering his bare chest tapered toward his waistband. A lack of notice might be beyond her ability, but scorning the sensations assailing her body was not. She diligently focused her thoughts on the issue at hand. "What is it about me that compels you to behave like such a boorish oaf? Just because I'm a woman—"

"It's got nothing to do with your being a woman."

"Then what is it?"

His furtive glances were none too subtle, and every time his eyes lit upon her, they darkened. He also seemed to be having trouble sitting still. "It's you."

"Other men in the territory seem capable of tolerating me—" Cammie stopped in midsentence as a thought occurred to her. "Speaking of other men—what have you done with mine?"

Adam took a keen interest in scrubbing his forehead, refusing to meet her accusing gaze.

Rinsing out the washcloth, Cammie continued to cleanse his wounded arm. "You may as well tell me. I'm going to find out eventually anyway."

With considerable reluctance he admitted, "I bribed them with whiskey."

"Really?" she kept her voice devoid of emotion. "How many bottles?"

"One each."

"They sold their loyalty cheap. I hope you are prepared to provide them employment, because you just cost them their jobs on this ranch."

Catching hold of her wrist, he locked his eyes on hers. "Don't go taking your anger at me out on them. I convinced them that I was only playing a prank."

Cammie didn't turn from his potent gaze, but neither was she swayed by his sincere tone or his conscience-stricken mien. "I will not pay good money to men I cannot trust. Nothing you say is going to change my mind."

"Nothing anybody says ever changes your mind about anything," he disparaged, his eyes continuing to hold hers captive.

Cammie shook his hand from her wrist. "Some people think constancy is a virtue. *I* happen to be one of them."

"Then why'd you let Higgins sell you his land? I thought women of virtue were supposed to help men keep on the straight and narrow, not lure them into abandoning integrity."

"I see no reason why I or any other woman should be held responsible for the behavior of any man—and I'm surprised to hear you claim otherwise." She raised a brow. "Or are you claiming the female of the species is inherently superior to the male?"

"No."

"I thought not."

He slowly ran his gaze up and down her person. "You, of course, hold to that opinion."

"No. I hold the opinion that individuals should be judged on their own merit or lack thereof."

"Is that so?"

"Yes, it is."

"I bet you judge yourself as first-rate."

"Of course."

"And how do you judge me?"

Cammie's shoulders lost some of their starch. She had no idea how to answer his question without completely losing her dignity. Telling him she found his naked arms and chest rather breathtaking would never do. Neither was she willing to divulge that she found stroking the washcloth over his well-muscled arm stimulating in ways she wished it wasn't. She could refuse to answer his question, but that seemed cowardly. Clearing her throat, she guardedly replied, "I'm not certain. Sometimes I hold you in high esteem. You are obviously intelligent enough to run a profitable cattle ranch, and you have a fine reputation among the other ranchers. And I do find you amusing. Then other times, like tonight, I am absolutely convinced you are dangerously deranged." Without warning she poured tincture of iodine directly on his open wound.

"Ow!" Adam flinched from the unexpected sting.

"Sorry."

He perused her through narrowed eyes. "You don't look very sorry."

"I lied," Cammie confessed. "I still haven't heard you promise you will stop trying to get me to sell you my ranch."

"I don't make promises I have no intention of keeping," he apprised her.

"So you're going to keep coming up with progressively asinine schemes until someone gets seriously hurt?"

His bottom lip protruded slightly. "I didn't say that either."

Corking the bottle of iodine, she tied a bandage around his arm. "I dislike riddles. Just tell me if I need to post armed guards on the perimeter of my ranch or not."

"That's not necessary. Any further negotiating I do for the land will involve you and me, face to face. No more sneaking around."

"How do I know you're telling me the truth?"

Adam raised his right hand. "I swear." When she persisted in looking dubious, he added, "I'm getting mighty tired of getting caught in my own loop. You've made it plain you're meaner than you look. Even this dumb ol' cowboy knows when it's time for a change of tactics."

Determined not to be fooled again, Cammie leaned toward him, and when they were nose to nose, she plumbed the depths of his eyes, searching for the truth. After a long moment she murmured, "I probably shouldn't, but I believe you."

"Good." His voice was low, almost a growl, only not physically menacing. What it did menace was her senses. The sound rippled through her like the caress of a breeze. The scent of his skin filled her nostrils. She could feel his warm breath on her face. Her head told her to retreat, to look away from his deep blue eyes, but Cammie couldn't seem to muster the will.

"Is it good?" her voice came out barely above a whisper.

"Yes."

"Why?"

"I'm telling you the truth, Cammie," he said as he stroked the sides of her arms.

"I hope so," she sighed. "Both our lives will be much less complicated if we learned to get along."

"I don't reckon so." A ragged edge seeped into his softly seductive tone.

Cammie's tongue dampened her bottom lip. "Why do you say that?"

"We'd still get under each other's skin."

She wasn't sure what to make of his statement, but she knew it was past time to put a healthy distance between them. His gaze was too intense, and her reaction to his closeness too disconcerting. "I'm finished with your arm. I'd appreciate it if you would leave." She started to stand upright, but before she could, he caught her shoulders in his hands and held her in place.

"Before I do, I'm gonna give you a little friendly free advice."

"What's that?"

Pulling her onto his lap, he covered her lips with his, kissing what little breath she had away. His mustache tickled her upper lip. The heat of his mouth seared her. As suddenly as he had seized her, he set her on her feet, at the same time rising to his own. "Next time you invite a man into your cabin, wear something more than skin beneath your blouse."

Before Cammie recovered from her shock enough to reply, he was gone.

Eleven

"Hear you've got yourself a little war going on in your valley," Roy Higgins said with a grin when Adam joined him at his table in his favorite saloon.

"Shut up."

Higgins made a valiant attempt to hide his mirth and failed.

Adam waved his hand, signaling the bartender to bring him a beer. "You must be forgetting you said I get to beat the hell out of you if you were wrong about Cammie Kendall, Higgins, or you wouldn't be grinning like the business end of a jackass. Or was that just another convenient lie?"

Higgins ignored Adam's threat. "Cammie Kendall? Sounds like you two are on friendly terms."

"Humph. Saying we're at war is closer to the truth."

Higgins raised a brow. "Josh says—"

His beer arrived, and Adam tossed a swig down his throat. "Josh says a lot of things that have nothing to do with the truth. Put a woman in the same room with him, and he loses what little good sense he has."

"To hear him tell it, you're the one who's lost his good sense. I'm inclined to agree. Never thought I'd see the day *you* caught calico fever, but the way you've been acting . . ." Letting his words trail off, Higgins took a sip of his whiskey.

Adam might be willing to admit to himself Cammie Kendall was the driving force behind his recent misadventures, but he'd be damned if he'd admit it to anyone else. And he wasn't suffering from calico fever. There wasn't an iota of affection in the equation between Cammie and him. What he felt for her wasn't any different than what a bull felt for a cow in season. But that wasn't any of Higgins's business either. "I may be behaving a little peculiar lately, but it isn't because of a woman. It's because of a piece of land—land that you promised to sell to me."

"Are you sure *she* don't got something to do with it?"

Adam glared at him.

"Just asking." Higgins retreated behind his whiskey glass, but Adam was certain he still detected the shadow of a grin.

"The only interest I have in Miss Kendall is that she owns land that by rights oughta be mine. I want her off my land. You said she'd be gone long before now." Adam pinned Roy with stormy eyes. "You're the one who created this mess. I want to know what you're gonna do about it."

Higgins shrugged. "Nothing I can do except admit I made a mistake selling the land to her in the first place and say I'm sorry."

"That's it?" Adam set his mug down with a thud. "A shrug and an apology?"

"What is it you'd have me do?"

"Hell if I know. I just don't cotton to the notion I'm the one paying the price for your mistake."

"Ain't none of us perfect," Higgins defended. "The way Josh tells it, hear you've made a few mistakes of your own concerning Miss Kendall."

Adam's lips thinned. "Just exactly what has my brother been saying about me?"

"Oh, he's full of tales about hunting trips, snakes, skunks . . . heard some of them from his own lips. Some

Maggie at Lillie McGraw's parlor house repeated to me. Some Jack—"

"I get the picture," Adam indignantly interrupted. "If a body is breathing and has ears, my brother is blathering into them."

Higgins nodded. "Josh always has been fond of good gossip, and you've been providing him with a steady supply. Don't reckon there's a soul in town don't know you've taken to dressing up like a wild Injun. Wish I could've been there to see that."

"Josh is gonna find himself minus a tongue if he doesn't learn to keep his locked behind his teeth."

"Aw, he's just having a little fun at your expense 'cause you haven't been acting like your usual self lately. 'Sides you getting yourself shot by Miss Kendall was all over town long before he said a word."

Adam grimaced and pulled a long draft on his beer.

"Why don't you just accept the fact Miss Kendall is here to stay," Higgins advised. "She's not your conventional woman—but the way I see it, and a lot of folks agree with me, she makes a fine addition to the community. Men who work for her, even the two you got fired, got nothing but respect for her. They say she's got a magic touch when it comes to horses."

"I hear they call her The Tiny Tyrant behind her back," Adam rebutted.

"Yep. Nobody's pretending she's all sugar and spice, but they respect her just the same. She's got her rules and expects them to be followed—but she treats every man fair. Same as you and me when I owned my own place. Plenty of folks would hate to see her and her horses leave the county."

"I don't care what other folks think of her. She isn't strutting about with her nose in the air in their valley. Woman has got calluses from patting her own back. I want her gone!"

"Josh is right." Higgins rubbed his chin. "You ain't a rational man where Miss Kendall is concerned."

There was enough truth in what Higgins said to make Adam's gut clench. "What's that supposed to mean?"

"Nothing. Nothing at all—except it's not like you to waste time fighting what you can't change. I'm man enough to admit I was wrong about Miss Kendall, and I know you are, too. If I was you, instead of kicking like a bay steer, I'd try to make friends with the lady."

"Make friends with the lady? Hah!" Adam Carrigan muttered on the ride home from Helena. Did Higgins take him for a beaten dog? He wasn't about to go slinking about his valley with his tail between his legs.

Thus far he'd exercised gentlemanly restraint when dealing with Miss Kendall. Well, he was through being a gentleman. She kept claiming she wanted to be treated on a par with a man. It was past time he granted her the wish.

He didn't like the idea of violating the law his father had set for both his sons when dealing with a lady, though he always had thought his father far too generous in his opinion of the fairer sex. Even after what his wife had done to him, his father never spoke a word against her. But his father was long dead, and he was his own man. Besides, Miss Kendall hardly qualified as a lady. She sure didn't fight like a lady. The woman was down right unnatural.

Adam believed every word of his own argument, but he was leaving out one important detail. He'd kissed her. He hadn't meant to do it, and in the days since, he hadn't been able to figure out why he had. Oh, he knew watching her traipse around her house with her blouse clinging to her bare breasts and her pretty little toes peeking out from beneath her skirts would sorely tempt any man. And there was something incredibly sensuous about having her wash him, even if she was only cleansing blood from a wound she'd inflicted. No, it wasn't kissing her that bothered him so much as the fact he'd done it without thinking.

All his life he'd been a man who believed in thinking first and acting second. He wholeheartedly approved of this sensible approach to life. It kept a man out of trouble and on track.

He adjusted the brim of his hat against the setting sun. Cammie Kendall was as good at kissing as she was at everything else she did. She'd been too startled to kiss him back proper, but the movement of her soft sweet lips against his was like being licked by a flame. Having her round little bottom snuggled in his lap and her breasts crushed up against his bare chest was an experience worth remembering on cold winter nights, too. But what had given him the most pleasure was the disappointed look on her face when he'd let her go. That was one memory he intended to savor for the rest of his life.

That brought him to his other objection to the kiss. Besides startling him as much as it had her, he'd liked it too damn much.

His immediate plans didn't include playing with fire, but if he ever decided to kiss her again, he was determined to be in full control of the situation. Eyes wide open, no underestimating his enemy, no more kissing her unless there was a solid, well thought out purpose behind doing the deed.

What his immediate plans did include was a bottle of whiskey and a deck of cards. If he'd learned one thing about Cammie Kendall, it was she couldn't turn down a dare.

This time when they met on the field of battle, he was going to take full advantage of her boundless bravado. This time he would be victorious.

"What are you doing here?" Cammie demanded when she opened her door. She had been enjoying a relaxing evening of her own company, and the sight of Adam Carrigan brought only one question to mind: *What now?*

"Is that any way to greet your neighbor?" He grinned guilelessly.

"When the neighbor in question is you, yes."

Lucretia wandered out onto the porch to investigate the commotion, sniffed Adam's boot, then twitched her tail and pranced back into the house.

Adam held up a bottle of MacBriar whiskey. "I brought you a peace offering."

Cammie gave his gift a dubious look.

"You do drink whiskey, don't you? You seem to do everything else a man does, so I just assumed you'd drink like a man as well. If you'd rather, I can return with something more ladylike. Perhaps a cordial would better suit your delicate constitution."

"Are you insinuating that I don't possess the intestinal fortitude for whiskey?"

"Am I?"

"Yes, I think you are."

"Care to prove me wrong?"

She continued to bar the doorway. "I have better things to do with my time than play games with you. I would have thought that being shot the other night would have taught you a lesson, but I can see you're even more thick-skulled than I conceived."

"Diversionary tactic," Adam declared.

"What?"

"You know you're not 'man' enough to drink whiskey, so rather than admit you can't do it, you babble about everything but the challenge at hand."

What Cammie knew was that she didn't want him in her house. The memory of his kiss was too fresh in her mind. "There is a world of difference between can't drink whiskey and won't. There are many things I *can* do that I choose not to do."

"You can tell yourself anything you want, and you're free to believe it as well. Just don't expect me to be fooled by your little speech. Truth is it's kinda nice to know there's something we men are better at than you. Plenty of fellas in town will be glad to hear it, too." He paused, drawing in a sighing breath and subtly shaking his head. "Though there are some gals in town will be disappointed. You've become something of a heroine to them, but you never asked for the honor, so there's no reason for you to feel obligated to take their feelings into account. I'll send over that bottle of cordial. Be seeing you around." Turning, he strode toward his horse. He mounted and reached the edge of the yard before Cammie's vanity overcame her common sense.

"Wait."

Adam reined to a halt. "Why?"

"Don't think I don't know exactly what you are about, but I refuse to let you have the satisfaction of thinking I'm refusing because I don't have the stomach for your game. Bring the bottle inside."

"Yes, ma'am."

Abandoning him in the yard, Cammie marched into the house, leaving the door open behind her. She didn't say a word when she heard him close the door and his footsteps follow her across the floor.

Instead she retrieved a glass from the cupboard, grabbed the bottle from his hands, and poured a half inch of liquid into the glass. She took a small sip. Her nose wrinkled and her lips drew back in disgust. "I've never tasted anything so horrible in all my life. Why on earth would anyone willingly subject themselves to anything so vile?"

"You're not supposed to sip it. You swallow the lot in one gulp."

Once while hiding in the loft of one of her father's stables, she had witnessed a groom consume whiskey in this fashion, so Cammie knew he wasn't lying. Even if she had thought he was, the chance to be done with the contents of her glass in a single swallow was too tempting to resist.

Taking a deep breath, she raised the glass to her lips and drained it. The whiskey burned a river of fire down her throat, causing her to turn bright red and gasp repeatedly. Between gasps she coughed so hard she feared she would hack up her lungs. Tears filled her eyes and spilled down her cheeks.

Adam was immediately at her side. He took the glass from her hand and set it on the table, slipping his arm around her shoulders to lend his support. "Take a couple of deep breaths."

"I'm trying to, you oaf," Cammie choked out. When she recovered herself enough to formulate lucid thought, she shoved away the support of his arm and collapsed onto the nearest chair.

"There! I drank your whiskey. It certainly wasn't a pleasant experience, but as you can see, I did it. I trust I have proven my mettle to your satisfaction."

"No." He looked amazed she would say such a thing. "I thought you invited me in for a contest."

"I don't recall you saying one word about any contest," Cammie protested.

"When men get together with a bottle of whiskey and something to prove, the idea is to see who can drink the most without getting drunk. One little swallow of whiskey doesn't prove a thing."

Her eyes widened. "You expect me to drink a whole bottle of whiskey to prove myself?"

"Only half." He fetched another glass from the cupboard. "I'll be drinking the other half. Of course, anytime you want to call it quits is fine with me."

"We'll end up sick," Cammie argued.

"Likely we'll both feel like our heads are split open by a hatchet come morning, too."

"And the point of practicing this self-abuse is?"

"To prove who's the toughest rancher in this valley. But I want to be a gentleman about it." He patted her hand and smiled sympathetically. "As I said before, I'll understand if you want to call it quits before we get started."

Cammie didn't pretend that what she was about to do was wise. It was the height of stupidity. If she had any sense at all, she would damn her pride and show the man the door. And she would, too, if it was any other man but Adam Carrigan. He drove her crazy when he was with her, and tormented her thoughts when he was absent. Besides—every time they had a confrontation, she had come out the winner. She was gambler enough to believe her luck would again hold. The satisfaction of besting him once again was too enticing to resist.

"If you can bear it, then so can I," she said coolly. "I never quit something I start."

Motioning for him to take the chair on the opposite side of the table from her, she skewered him with a steely gaze.

"Before we begin this contest, I want you to tell me the rules. All the rules. Any trickery on your part and the contest ends, and I am declared the winner. In addition, if I catch you cheating, you will dung out each and every one of my barns. Agreed?"

"Agreed. And if I catch you cheating, you will polish my boots every time I ask for as long as you live here."

"The penalties are mismatched in your favor, but as I know myself to be completely trustworthy, I will agree to your terms. However, I will require you to put your pledge in writing." Rising to her feet, she strode to her office, fetched paper and pen, and set them in front of him. When he finished writing down the terms, he signed them. Cammie added her own signature, folded the paper, and tucked it into her pocket. "Now tell me the rules."

"We drink glass for glass until one of us gives up or passes out."

"What if we run out of whiskey first?"

"Then it's a draw."

"Okay." Cammie's eyes narrowed. "If your intention is to cloud my judgment with alcohol and get me to agree to sell you my property, you're wasting your time. There isn't enough whiskey in all of Montana to get me to agree to sell out."

"Then you've got nothing to worry about, do you?" he said smoothly. Reaching into his pocket, Adam placed a deck of cards on the table.

"What are those for?"

"May as well play a friendly game of poker while we sip our liquor."

"You said a person is not suppose to sip whiskey."

"So I did." He poured them both a glass. "Drink up."

"I already have. Until you catch up with me, I'm not touching another drop."

Picking up his glass, he downed the contents without so much as a twinge of discomfort.

Cammie wasn't pleased, but she tried not to show it. She carefully measured out another glass equal in contents to hers.

Each watched the other over the rim of their glasses as they simultaneously emptied them. The whiskey burned on the way down Cammie's throat, but the fire was not so breath-stealing as the first time.

Adam refilled their glasses, and they raised them again.

"Five-card stud?" he asked, picking up his deck of cards.

Cammie looked from his face to the cards and back to his face. Counting from one to ten forward and backward to test how much the whiskey had thus far impaired her mental acumen, she found her mind intact. Other than a numb throat and tingling lips, the whiskey seemed not to have affected her at all. "How is it played?"

Pouring them each another glass of whiskey, Adam shuffled the cards while he spoke. "Dealer lays a hole card face-down, the next face up. Then we make our wagers. High hand goes first. Three more cards are dealt face up, one at a time, with a round of betting between each one. You can fold anytime. Hands are ranked straight flush, four of a kind, full house, flush, straight, three of a kind, two pairs, one pair, high card."

"What will we be playing for?"

"Favors . . ."

Cammie had harbored more than her share of suspicions concerning his motives for being here ever since he had knocked on her door, and his suggestion did nothing to decrease her wariness. "What kind of favors?"

"Housecleaning, ditch digging, that sort of thing. We can bet minutes of chore time. Winner gets to choose the task."

"Legitimate tasks only?"

"I wouldn't think of suggesting anything else. If either of us figures the other is taking unfair advantage, we'll call in an impartial third party to settle the matter."

The terms seemed safe enough, but Cammie took an extra measure of time to be certain she wasn't overlooking some loophole. "All right."

He handed her the deck to cut, then dealt them each two cards. Cammie received the ace of diamonds facedown and the three of spades face up. Adam showed the ten of clubs.

"Five minutes," he opened.

"I'll match your five minutes and up it by two."

"You call my five and raise it two," he instructed. "I call your two." He dealt them each another card. Cammie's was the ace of spades. Adam's was the king of hearts. "You have the highest card showing, so it's your bet."

"Ten minutes."

"I'll call."

Cammie's next card was the three of diamonds. His was the king of spades. "You have a pair of kings showing, and I have a pair of threes, so this time you bet first, right?"

"You're a fast learner."

She smiled. "Yes, I know."

"I'll up the pot seven," Adam stated.

Cammie studied the cards on the table and the one in her hand. "I'll call."

Adam dealt the last cards. Cammie's face was a blank mask as he lay the ace of clubs on the table. His card was the eight of diamonds.

If she bet too high, he would know her hand beat his and fold. By her calculations she already was guaranteed to win twenty-four minutes of free labor, but she preferred to take him for all she could. "Ten more minutes."

"I'll call and raise you ten more."

Pursing her lips, Cammie replied, "I'll call . . . and raise . . . another ten . . ."

"You asking or telling?" Adam queried.

Feigning apprehension, Cammie hesitated, then said, "Telling."

She could feel his eyes intensely perusing her expression, but she refused to meet his gaze. He rubbed the card in his hand. "Okay. I'll call your ten and raise fifteen."

"Fifteen?" Cammie emitted a flustered gasp. "That seems awfully high."

"You can fold if you want."

"No. Having played this far, I believe I'll call."

Adam turned over a king and grinned. "Three of a kind. That beats the two pair you've got showing. Show your other card."

Cammie turned over her ace. "A full house tops three of a kind. I win," she announced. "Let's see, that means you owe me—" she calculated the figure in her head "—one hour and nine minutes." Flushed with success, she gaily opined, "I think I better get some paper to keep track of our bets. Before the night is over, I fear you will owe me so much time, adding in my head will be too big a burden."

"Beginner's luck," Adam credited her triumph. "But the paper does sound like a good idea. Don't want to lose track of my winnings."

"You don't have any," Cammie waggishly reminded.

"Yet . . ." Adam countered.

When she stood up to fetch the paper, Cammie noticed that it took a second for her to feel completely stable on her feet, but the sensation was fleeting. She silently congratulated herself on her ability to handle hard liquor.

Returning to the table with several sheets of paper, another pen, and a pair of scissors, she cut the paper into small squares, handing Adam half the stack and pushing the pen in his direction.

Cammie dealt the second hand. Adam won it and the next. They continued to play, taking turns winning and losing. At the end of an hour, Adam was ahead by twenty minutes.

The whiskey was starting to make Cammie light-headed, and much to her chagrin she couldn't stop herself from giggling every time she won a hand, but otherwise she felt totally in control of her thoughts and actions. She watched Adam carefully for signs of drunkenness, but he exhibited no untoward behavior.

They played another hour, prodding the other into drinking another dose of whiskey whenever they remembered—which out of concern for her throat and stomach Cammie made a point of doing as infrequently as possible. At the end of the second hour, the minutes won and lost were dead even.

"In the mood to make the stakes more lively?" Adam asked.

Cammie coolly met his bright-eyed gaze. "What do you propose?"

"You bake me one of your French apple pies once a week for a month, and I'll take you back into the canyon and teach you tracking skills."

"Agreed."

Cammie easily won the hand with a flush to Adam's pair of fours.

"Your turn to name the stakes," he declared without any sign of disappointment at his loss. Cammie admired his sportsmanship.

"Your skiff for my settee. I understand the skunks ruined your sofa."

"Deal."

Again she won. "It seems your luck has deserted you."

He leaned toward her, a glint in his eye. "How about your betting that mare Josh wants to buy from you against the cattle you want from me."

"Are we talking six head or twelve?"

"Six. Straight bet. High hand wins."

"Deal."

Cammie won the hand again, this time with three queens. "I'll take delivery tomorrow. Care to call it a night?"

"No. It's your turn again."

She thought hard. The whiskey was making it difficult for her to focus her thoughts, but she persevered. "Loser buys the winner a ticket to the next production at the Ming Opera House."

"Not a very daring wager."

"I'm starting to feel guilty about winning so often." Cammie preferred to lie rather than confess the tickets were the only idea her fuzzy brain would conjure.

"I'm man enough to take it."

"I never said you weren't. Do you accept or not?"

"I accept."

Cammie won yet again. Thinking any thought for more than a few seconds seemed beyond her—but she was delighted that her luck was holding.

"Your land for an equal number of acres of mine," Adam casually named his next wager.

"De—" Cammie clamped her teeth on her tongue when what he said fully registered. She glared at him. *"No!"*

"Why not? With the streak of luck you've been having, you could double your acreage."

"I could also lose my ranch. No deal."

"Too scared to make a man-sized wager?"

"Too smart. Everything I've risked so far I was willing to lose. My ranch doesn't fall into that category. For that matter, neither does your land. You must be very drunk or you would never consider risking it."

"Do I look drunk?"

"No, but why else would you—"

"High stakes make the thrill of victory that much sweeter."

"It also leaves the loser desolate."

"But you're on a winning streak," Adam cajoled.

"No deal." She firmly repeated her refusal.

"Then I'll take a kiss."

When her whiskey-soaked brain failed to come up with some intelligent response, instinct took over, and Cammie demanded, "Why?"

He shrugged. "You can't yak at me while you're kissing me. Besides, I'm kinda curious to know if you *can* be sweet to a man. My guess is the reason you're so all-fired determined to prove yourself equal to any man is you're afraid someone will find out you don't know how to act like a woman."

Cammie stiffened at the insult. How dare he! He didn't know what she thought or felt about anything. She was capable of doing anything she set out to do—including being sweet to anyone to whom it suited her fancy to be sweet. Just because she didn't fawn all over every man who crossed her path didn't mean she was lacking normal female feelings. When he had kissed her the other night, she had responded as befitted her sex. The last thing on earth Cammie wanted to do at the moment was kiss him, but she couldn't let his statement go unchallenged. Besides, she had to kiss him only if she lost, and there was no reason to think she would. "If

I agree to wager a kiss, in exchange, when I win the hand, I want to be declared winner of our drinking contest as well. I also want you to go home immediately thereafter."

"Agreed. One card, high card wins?" he queried.

In the interest of getting the hand over as quickly as possible, Cammie nodded.

Adam watched her as he shuffled the deck, fanning and tapping the cards for an exorbitantly long time.

"Are you going to deal?" Cammie impatiently inquired.

He started to lay a card in front of her.

"I want to cut the deck."

He handed her the cards. After cutting them, she handed them back. Adam lay one card in front of each of them, then set the rest of the deck aside. "Ready?"

They turned over their cards in unison. Cammie's eyes lit on his card first. It was the jack of spades. Twelve cards in the deck could beat it. Not the best odds—but as Adam had said, she was having a lucky streak. However, when her gaze raised to his face, she knew it had just ended. The ire that had goaded her into making the wager abruptly deserted her, leaving nothing but trepidation in its wake.

"Aren't you gonna look at your card?"

Cammie glanced downward. "It's the two of hearts."

"Kinda fitting, don't you think?"

She chewed her bottom lip. "I lost."

"Yep."

Glancing at the smug smile on his face, she slid a little lower in her chair. "I think you cheated."

"How?"

"I don't know—but you must have."

"We both know I didn't cheat. If a body loses, it's always best to lose with grace."

"I don't want to kiss you," she said.

"I don't want to give you tracking lessons, my skiff, my cattle, or a ticket to the opera, but you don't hear me bellyaching."

He hadn't complained, and she really didn't have a right to either. She could have refused this wager just as she had refused to risk her land. Fair was fair. "When do I have to do it?"

"I'll take delivery right now." He pursed his lips and polished them with his fingers.

Cammie smiled wanly. "I suppose I may as well get it over with."

"That's the spirit."

Rising to her feet, Cammie was dismayed to find the floor no longer stayed in one place, and no amount of blinking persuaded it to remain stable. Charily walking around the table, she stood in front of Adam, trying to decide how best to approach the required kiss. A quick peck and retreat to her side of the table held enormous appeal, but Cammie knew he would name her a coward, and he would be right. Too, his accusation that she didn't know how to act like a woman still stung. She didn't really want to kiss him at all. She couldn't fathom why she had agreed to the wager in the first place.

"Are you just gonna stand there growing roots, or are you gonna kiss me before we both grow gray?"

"I'm going to kiss you."

Adam made an ostentatious show of moistening his lips and smoothing his mustache.

Cammie starched her shoulders and took a deep breath. Wrapping her arms around his neck, she moved her lips against his, gently tasting his top lip before settling both her lips squarely on his. Then caught up in the heat and enjoyment of the moment, she kissed him with far more hunger than she ever intended.

She combed her fingers through his hair, pulling his lips tighter against her. Her skin flushed. The room began to swirl around her. An odd numbness assailed her limbs. Cammie steadfastly attributed it all to the excess of alcohol she had consumed, but she knew in her heart that the fire in her veins had more to do with the man whose lips she devoured than any amount of amber liquid.

She kissed him again and again, though in truth one kiss melted into the next so seamlessly each had no true beginning or end. Adam moaned beneath her kneading fingers, drawing her closer.

The voice of reason called out for her to end the kiss, but passion drowned out the counsel of reason. She didn't want to stop. It felt too wonderful. She kissed him again.

From the beginning he had cooperated with the kiss, giving caress for caress, but Cammie suddenly found the role of aggressor snatched from her grasp. Even if had she possessed breath enough to protest, she had no desire to do so. The only desire she felt was desire for the man wrapped in her arms.

Her heated blood surged through her. Every cell felt charged with electricity.

Adam slipped his tongue into her mouth, stroking her senses to even greater heights. The taste of him was divine. The scent of his skin like heady incense. The sound of his heavy breathing was music.

Cammie's hands splayed across his chest, not to push him away, but to stroke his firm muscles. She could feel the beating of his heart beneath her fingers. Its pounding matched the cadence of her own, which resembled the thunder of a horse's hooves at a full run.

His hands were everywhere, and everywhere they touched she wanted more. She clung to him, whimpering encouragement when his lips trailed down her chin to the base of her throat. Adam unfastened one button of her blouse, then another, forging his trail of hot kisses ever lower with each new inch of skin revealed. Impatient for more, Cammie grasped both sides of her blouse in her fists and dispensed with the rest of the buttons in a single motion. The sound that arose from Adam's throat made her tremble with exultation.

His hand dipped inside her corset and chemise, cupping her breast, his callused thumb strumming the tip to a rigid peak. Cammie went limp in his arms, dropping her head back to give him fuller access, while she was engulfed in carnal sensation. He treated her other breast to similar delights, stoking the flames burning within her so white-hot that passively receiving pleasure beneath his exploring hands became impossible.

Cammie made quick work of the buttons of his shirt, nuzzling her face into the soft hairs of his chest. She circled his nipples with her tongue, then kissed them. She could feel his fingers struggling with the lacings of her corset, but she was too busy burrowing against him to help. However, when she felt her bosom spring free of the constricting garment, she sighed with relief. The next sensation she felt caused a sharp intake of breath. Lifting her up, he suckled her nipple through the fabric of her chemise. Cammie briefly wondered if it was possible to die of ecstasy, deciding in the same instance she was willing to find out.

Adam continued to lavish her breasts with attention, and Cammie continued to cling to him, kneading the muscles of his neck, arms, torso. Her fingers brushed across the line her bullet had made on his upper arm. She traced it, then moved on to caress the smooth flesh of his shoulders.

When he scooped her up into his arms and carried her toward the bedroom, the only sound of protest that escaped her lips was protest that his lips had abandoned her breasts.

Laying her on the bed, Adam discarded his clothes in a pile on the floor. His eyes never left hers, and the fire in them reflected the heat consuming her. Her gaze traveled downward to his aroused manhood, but no alarm bells rang in her head. She wanted this. She wanted *him.* She wanted him more than she had ever wanted anything in her life.

He tugged off her skirt, then loosened the string of her chemise and lifted it over her head. Her drawers were next to join the pile of clothes on the floor. Lastly, he removed her garters and stockings, dancing his fingers down the inside of her leg as he rolled her stockings over her knees and off her toes. He then retraced the path of his fingers with his lips, nibbling her toes, the arch of her foot, her ankle—and the higher he traveled, the tighter the coil of passion between her thighs wound. Her hips rose slightly off the bed, and her thighs opened in invitation. She began to writhe, but his hands steadied her as he kissed across her belly, up through the valley of her breasts, over her throat and chin to her lips.

This time when his tongue entered her mouth, it plunged in. His tongue withdrew and she followed it with her tongue, invading his mouth with the same urgency. Their tongues pursued each other from mouth to mouth, laving each other with long, languid strokes.

Cammie was convinced she would die if the tension in her body wound any tighter. She would explode into a thousand fragments of herself. The thrusting motion of her hips became more insistent. Cradling her face in his hands, Adam matched the rhythm of the mating of their tongues with the thrusting of her hips. Cammie clutched the quilt covering the bed.

When he finally entered her, her gratitude was so overwhelming that her conscious mind didn't even register the stab of pain accompanying the tearing of her maidenhead.

Their hips strained together, Adam bracing the weight of

his upper body on his elbows. Cammie kissed him everywhere her lips could reach. Perspiration beaded on both their brows. Their breaths became gasps. The heat building within their coupled loins escalated . . . until it erupted with volcanic force, contorting their faces with the pain of pleasure.

Cammie cried out. Adam roared with his final thrust. Their passion spent, they collapsed into each other's arms and fell into a deep and dreamless sleep.

Twelve

Adam yawned. Slowly lifting one eyelid, he quickly closed it again. His head felt ready to explode. His mouth tasted like someone had stuffed it with quilt batting. A heaviness weighed down his chest. Damn whiskey, he muttered in his head, but even the sound of a thought was too loud. He started to roll to his side and pull his blankets over his head when the realization struck him. *He wasn't alone, and this wasn't his bed.*

The weight on his chest was the body of a naked woman. Please make her be some whore from Helena, he prayed—but even as he prayed, memory of the previous evening flooded back into his aching skull. He didn't need to open his eyes to know who lay sleeping in his arms.

Cammie Kendall—his lips formed her name as they would a curse. She lay directly on top of him, her face nestled into the crook of his neck and her lower limbs tangled with his.

Good Lord! What had he done? Though every thought felt like a knife stabbing through his head, Adam forced himself to think. He knew exactly what he had done. He had bedded the enemy!

He had never intended to do anything of the sort. He had come to her house to get her drunk in hopes of cajoling her into gambling away her land. He'd even cheated to make sure she won when it suited his purpose. As small as she was, he'd been sure she would be numb from the neck up long before the whiskey he consumed had any effect on his judgment.

From the start he'd known getting her drunk was a rotten thing to do, but he'd eased his conscience by promising himself he would insist on paying her what the land was worth before she left. Besides, she'd entered the contest knowing full well what he was up to. And he wouldn't have stacked the deck in his own favor to win her land. He would have won it fair and square or not at all. Just because the acreage he would have given her if he had lost was up near the Canadian border didn't mean he'd completely lost his sense of honor.

Why—when she refused to be coaxed into betting the deed to her ranch, he had insisted she wager a kiss was beyond his comprehension. As he thought back over the events leading up to the ill-fated kiss, he remained bewildered. Even drunk he ought to have known it was a fool thing to do. He recalled wanting to take back the words the moment they had slipped past his lips—then she had kissed him like no woman had ever kissed him before—and the next thing he knew, they were tearing off their clothes and making love.

Lying here skin to skin, heart to heart, snuggled up together, Adam wanted to make love to her again. But every fiber of his being was committed to his going to his grave a bachelor. Marriage was the one arena of life he had solemnly vowed to himself that he would never venture near. Now . . .

Moving with the care of a man extracting himself from a bedroll full of scorpions, he inched toward the edge of the mattress, disentangling Cammie's limbs from his and replacing his body with a pillow. She mumbled in her sleep, frowning as her arms encircled the pillow, but she didn't open her eyes.

Adam vigilantly watched the rhythmic rise and fall of her

chest to reassure himself that she continued to sleep soundly. In slumber, with her thick blond lashes against her cheeks, and soft rounded body only partly concealed by the snowy sheets, she appeared too vulnerable. Adam felt like a cad sneaking out on her—but he needed to put some distance between them until he figured out what to do.

As soon as he was dressed, he picked up his boots and tiptoed out of the bedroom into the parlor. The whiskey bottle and cards still lay on the table, unwelcome reminders of last night's folly.

He caught a movement out of the corner of his eye. Lucretia leapt from the seat to the back of the overstuffed chair where she had been dozing, flexed her spine, and began to meow loudly.

"Shh." Adam lay his finger to his lips. "We don't want to wake her." He scratched behind the cat's ears and down her back. She immediately quieted and began to wash her paws.

Crossing the floor to the front door, he eased his feet into his boots, opened the door, and slipped outside onto the porch.

He looked back over his shoulder. Maybe it was wrong to leave without waking her—but not nearly so wrong as bedding her in the first place.

If God felt he needed punishing, he would have preferred a swift lightning bolt to waking up in Miss Kendall's arms.

Not that Adam had any complaints about the physical aspects of their impassioned union. His mind might be reeling, but he couldn't remember ever engaging in so satisfying a bout of lovemaking. Having seen her in nothing but her skin, now even more than before he believed Cammie to be the most beautiful woman ever to set foot in Montana. It was the repercussions of what they had done that left him feeling wretched.

Untying his horse from the hitching post, Adam led it a few yards from the house, mounted, and swiftly rode away.

The sound of a giant trying to knock down her door jerked Cammie from a deep sleep. She groaned, burrowing lower in the bed and pulling the covers over her head.

"Miss Kendall, you okay? Miss Kendall?" She recognized Carl Daley's voice calling her name.

"Go away," Cammie mumbled into the mattress. "And stop that infernal pounding."

She felt the mattress give when Lucretia jumped onto the bed. Her meows as she pawed at the covers and paced back and forth near the head of the bed sounded more like shrieks to Cammie's ears.

When Mr. Daley persisted in knocking, Cammie reluctantly poked her nose out from under the covers. The light pierced her bleary eyes like shards of glass. She scrunched her eyes closed, cautiously reopening them a mere slit. Crawling on all fours to the edge of the bed, she dropped her feet over the edge.

The pounding and hollering at the front door continued. She had to do something to stop it or her head would burst.

"I'm coming," Cammie started to shout, but the volume of her voice was too much to bear, and it diminished to a barely audible whisper halfway through the sentence. The next instant she was on the floor on her knees, frantically reaching under the bed for the chamber pot.

After casting up the contents of her stomach into the pot, she started to wipe her mouth on the back of her sleeve and realized she didn't have one. Cammie stared numbing at her own nudity.

"Oh, no!" She buried her head in her hands, her eyes filling with tears as the reason for her naked state hit her like a slap in the face. "I didn't. I couldn't. I wouldn't . . ."

But she had.

It suddenly occurred to Cammie she might not be alone in the bedroom. She would die of humiliation if Adam saw her crouched naked on the floor babbling and heaving like a common drunk. She furtively scanned the room.

Thank God, it was empty. Cammie didn't know when or why he had left, she was only grateful he had.

She rubbed her head. She needed to think, but first she needed to get rid of Mr. Daley.

Pushing herself to her feet, Cammie retrieved her wrapper, tied it around her waist, and unsteadily made her way to the front door. When she reached it, she opened it a crack and peeked around the edge. "Yes, Mr. Daley. How can I help you?" She forced the words past her thick tongue.

"I started to get worried when you didn't show up at the—"

"What time is it?" she interrupted.

"After ten o'clock."

Cammie opened the door a little wider, sticking her head out the door to peer first at the sun then him. "I won't be working with the horses today. I'm sick."

He nodded, his expression full of concern. "You look awful. Do you want me to send someone to town to fetch a doctor?"

She hadn't looked in the mirror, but if she looked half as bad as she felt, his concern was not unfounded. Telling him the truth was out of the question, but an outright lie wasn't necessary. Cammie took a deep breath and tried to sound convincing. "No. My stomach is upset, that's all. I ate something that disagreed with me. I'll be all right by tomorrow."

"Are you sure?"

Cammie wasn't at all sure, but she stoically replied, "Yes."

"Well, you go back to bed then. Me and Mr. Culver will see to it everything that needs doing gets done."

"Thank you." Cammie shut the door.

When she returned to her bedroom, the first thing Cammie did was get dressed. She was grateful it took all her concentration to perform the routine task without retching again, because as yet she wasn't ready to think too much about last night. After a painstaking trip to the necessary to empty the chamber pot and make use of the facility, she shuffled into the kitchen to make herself a piece of dry toast in hopes of settling her stomach.

On the way to the stove, she passed the table. Her gaze fell upon the whiskey bottle and cards.

She had heard strong spirits referred to as demon rum, and now she was convinced it was true. A demon must have possessed her last night or she would never have— Cammie couldn't finish the thought. She had been so busy vigilantly guarding her ranch from Adam Carrigan that she had neglected to guard herself. Except it wasn't him who— Staring at the chair where he had sat, she shook her head to banish the vision of her kissing him. She immediately regretted the ill-advised action, and sank into the nearest chair, clutching her throbbing forehead with both hands.

When the agony in her skull abated, she gingerly rose to her feet. Grabbing the whiskey bottle by the neck, she carried it to the back door and poured the remaining liquid in the bottle on the ground. Shuffling back to the kitchen, she discarded the bottle, burying it deep in the trash tin. She retraced her steps to the table, intent on discarding the deck of cards as well so no evidence of the previous evening remained.

Cammie swept up the cards. All but the two of hearts. She couldn't bear to touch it. She threw away the other cards, then returned to the table. Pulling out a chair, she sat down, eyeing the card as she would a vile enemy. She had no idea how long she engaged in this morose pastime, but at length, she forced herself to assess her situation logically.

The only person on earth who knew what she had done besides herself, and the only person who ever would know if she had any say in the matter, was Adam Carrigan. Cammie wanted to lay the blame for this disaster entirely at his feet, but she knew she was at least partly responsible. She shouldn't have kissed him the way she had, and when he had pushed the kiss beyond a kiss, she should have resisted his advances. She didn't care how drunk she was or how seductive she found being held in his arms, she most definitely should have resisted.

But she hadn't resisted. She had encouraged him. If memory served, and she hoped it didn't and instead she was suffering from some alcohol induced delusion, she had practically ripped both their clothes off so eager was she to have him touch her.

Lucretia jumped into her lap. Cammie snuggled her, hiding her face in her fur. "Oh, Lucretia, I was a very reckless woman. What on earth am I going to do now?"

The answer to her question was obvious to Cammie. First, she was going to secure Adam's promise that he would never breathe a word about what happened here last night; then, she was going to go about her business and pretend last night never occurred. Releasing Lucretia from her grasp, she picked up the lone card remaining on the table.

Pretending the evening never occurred was a fine plan as

long as she didn't cozen herself into believing it could never happen again. It might not be a very prudent sentiment to admit, but she relished the act of lovemaking. If not for the strictures of society and conscience, and the fear she might produce an illegitimate child, she would be delighted to take her neighbor for a lover.

The admission startled her and she resisted it. Dangerous thoughts led to dangerous deeds. Perhaps she needed protection from herself as much as from Adam Carrigan.

Cammie decided the card in her hand should not be relegate to the trash pile, after all. She'd frame it and hang it over her bed as a constant warning of her own stupidity. The two of hearts would be her talisman against future acts of madness.

Adam pulled on the oars of the skiff, guiding the boat upriver. He'd spent the day alone in the canyon avoiding Josh, walking off the aftereffects of the whiskey, but mostly just thinking.

He knew what he had to do. He'd known it from the moment he had awakened in Cammie Kendall's bed. He'd just needed time to work up the courage to face it.

It wasn't that he disliked his neighbor—truth was, he would be a lot happier if he were contemplating marrying a woman he loathed. He would do his duty by her and go about his business unscathed. But it would be different with Cammie Kendall. She wasn't the kind of woman a man could ignore. She was the kind of woman that made a sensible man turn rash. He was afraid he'd get too close, too used to having her around. He knew what would happen. About the time he got to figuring everything was all love and undying devotion between them, he'd ride in from the range one day and find her gone. Adam's grip on the oars turned white-knuckled—he wasn't going to sacrifice his heart to any woman. He didn't care how beautiful or how smart or plucky or lively in bed she was. He was going to keep fighting the attraction. She could live her life, and he would live his. Maybe, they wouldn't even have to live them under the same roof . . .

When Adam reached the shore on Cammie's side of the river, he didn't waste time sitting in the skiff, dreading the task at hand. He was already feeling guilty for leaving her alone all day to sit and fret whether he was man enough to make an honest woman of her. What he was about to do wasn't going to get any easier no matter how long he put it off.

Securing the boat, Adam adjusted his hat, and focused his eyes on the front door. Halfway across the yard her foreman stopped him.

"Miss Kendall is feeling poorly today. I don't know if she's up to receiving visitors."

"If she's not happy to see me, I won't stay," Adam assured him.

Reaching the door, he knocked softly. Cammie answered it almost immediately. Her face was pale and her eyes listless.

Adam removed his hat. "How are you feeling?"

"Like a horse kicked me in the head."

"Me, too. Can I come in?"

"Yes. I need to talk to you." Turning her back on him, she led the way to the parlor. She brushed Lucretia to the floor and stiffly took a seat on the overstuffed chair. Gesturing for him to sit, she folded her hands tightly in her lap, focusing her eyes on a spot on the floor.

"I'm sorry I ran out on you this morning without saying a word, but I needed time to think." Adam fingered the hat on his lap.

"I was glad you were gone."

"You were?"

"Yes."

"Why?"

A blush stained her pale cheeks. "It's not important."

Now that he was here staring her in the face, Adam suddenly felt tongue-tied. Poor little thing looked like a rag doll with all its stuffing knocked out. If he had been feeling like a lout before, it was nothing compared to this. Adam cleared his throat. "Well, I didn't come here to beat around the bush. I'm gonna come right to the point. Considering last night the only gentlemanly thing for me to do is marry you. So I'm asking, Cammie Kendall, will you marry me?"

"No."

"What?" he exclaimed, certain he couldn't have heard her correctly.

"I told you before how I feel about marriage."

"But that was before we—"

"I know what we did. I'm sure most women would insist on marriage, but as we both know, I am not most women. As long as you keep our little indiscretion secret, I see no reason to ruin either of our lives."

He couldn't believe what he was hearing. She sounded as serious as he had ever heard her, but what she said didn't make sense. She must be so distraught, she didn't know what she was saying. "You're letting me off the hook?"

"No—I'm looking out for my own interests."

"Then you have to marry me," he argued.

Cammie shook her head. "I don't have to do any such thing."

"But you were a virgin," he protested.

She looked at him directly. "I know. Did you think I made a habit of getting drunk and taking men to my bed?"

"To tell the truth, I wasn't thinking at all last night or we wouldn't have ended up in your bed."

"Exactly. We were both drunk and incapable of rational thought. Now that we have come to our senses, I see no reason to worsen our folly by getting married."

Adam knew he should rejoice at her words, but his pride and sense of propriety were highly offended by her pithy speech. He had come here offering to sacrifice his very soul for her honor. The least she could do was act a little grateful. "I own up to my obligations. Having bedded you, I'm obliged to marry you."

"I disagree. You were obliged to make the marriage offer. My refusal absolves you of any further obligation."

"How come you're being so 'understanding' about this?" he demanded.

"Why are you being so insistent? You told me once you intended to stay a bachelor until they buried you six feet under."

"That's my preference—but scruples sometimes have to take precedence over desire."

"I wish you would have practiced that bit of wisdom last night."

"So do I, but wishing something true and making it true aren't the same thing."

"No, it isn't. We can't rewrite the past, but we certainly can do a better job with our futures."

Why was she lecturing him like a Sunday school teacher when he was the one trying to do the right thing and she was the one turning her back on propriety? The only answer that made any sense at all was despite his proposal of marriage she was still just too upset about last night to reckon straight. She sure made it tough to be a gentleman, but he was determined not to take the coward's way out. "Maybe I oughta give you time to mull things over before I take no for your final answer."

Cammie exhaled a sharp breath. "Either your self-opinion is without bounds or you're deaf. I don't want to marry you. Not today, not tomorrow—not ten or a hundred years from now. I'm beginning to believe this proposal of yours is nothing but another thinly disguised plot to get your hands on my land."

His blood began to boil. Throwing his proposal back in his face was one thing, but claiming it was motivated by greed was insulting. Adam fought to control his anger. "My proposal is a matter of honor."

Cammie came out of her chair like a screeching barn owl. "Really? If you're so damn honorable, why were you willing to get me drunk and try to steal my property from me?"

"Hell if I know," Adam shouted. "I don't know why I've been doing half the things I've been doing lately. For some reason you bring out the worst in me."

"Which is all the more reason we shouldn't marry. I don't plan to spend the rest of my life being blamed for your shortcomings!"

"Since you're dead set against marrying me, you won't have to, will you?"

Cammie's face contorted. "No, I won't!"

"And there's no sense in me sitting here cluttering up your parlor with my presence!"

"Precisely!"

Adam rose to his feet and slammed his hat on his head. "Good day, *Miss* Kendall."

"Good day, *Mr.* Carrigan!"

Thirteen

When Cammie's temper cooled she wasn't very pleased with herself.

How could she have behaved so badly? Snarling like some cornered animal was beneath her dignity. All he had done was propose marriage to her, and she had known he would feel required to make the offer long before he knocked on her door. She thought she was prepared for it.

True, her hideous headache fueled her reactions, and she was demoralized to find the mere sight of him rekindled the lust of the night before—which had thrown her even more off balance—but that still didn't excuse her behavior.

He may have goaded her into drinking the whiskey that caused her throbbing head, but he hadn't pinned her down and poured it down her throat. It wasn't fair to take out her ire on him. . . . He had come to her door prepared to pay the price for his trespass upon her person. She could have been more gracious.

Unfortunately, it was difficult to be gracious to a man whom one liked and hated at the same time. Her feelings toward her neighbor had always been confused, and now they were in absolute bedlam. Cammie didn't know whether to laugh at the irony of her situation or weep with despair.

She had come to Montana knowing exactly what she wanted out of life: independence, her horse ranch, relief from the strangling strictures of Virginia's male-dominated society. She'd also known what she didn't want: *a husband.*

She still didn't want a husband. But she hadn't counted on a man like Adam Carrigan riding into her life.

She had absolutely no good reason to like him, and plenty of reasons to dislike him, but she liked him all the same . . . far too much . . . enough to have risked her entire future for a few minutes of lusty pleasure in his arms. She may have been beguiled by the demon rum, but Cammie knew she wouldn't have given her body to a man she cared nothing about.

Again and again she had tried to work herself into a fury over his attempts to wrest her land from her grasp, but she never quite succeeded. While his attempts might be aggravating, they weren't truly vicious, and they certainly made life entertaining. She tried to work herself into a lather of righteous indignation that he had bedded her—but she hadn't been able to do that either. . . . Maybe a person could possess an instinct for telling a good man from a bad one, just as her instinct distinguished good horses from bad—or maybe she'd just plain lost her mind.

Her hatred for Adam was easier to explain. She didn't wish him ill-fortune—she hated him for making her aware of her own lust. Lust had no place in the life of a single woman, and heretofore denying herself the carnal benefits of marriage hadn't felt like a sacrifice. Now . . . to never again experience the physical delights of lovemaking made the price of freedom seem dear indeed.

But she would pay that price because she had no choice. Never again would she live under the thumb of a man . . . but that didn't mean she would suffer no regrets.

* * *

The next day the six head of cattle she'd won—along with the six additional head she wished to purchase and a bill of sale—arrived on her side of the river. Later that day she noticed the skiff tied to her dock.

Cammie worked from dawn until dusk, driving herself at a mind-numbing pace in an attempt to keep all thoughts and emotions at bay. When darkness forced her indoors, she closeted herself in her office and devoted herself to her account books until her eyes refused to focus.

She kept up this grueling schedule for over a week, each day accomplishing the work of two days in the space of one. It benefitted her ranch but was of little personal benefit to her. Even though she told herself she was glad Adam Carrigan hadn't stepped foot on her property since the day she'd turned down his marriage proposal, she kept finding herself glancing across the river, hoping to catch a glimpse of him.

A week's absence stretched into two. Cammie was beginning to wonder if she had seen the last of Adam. Her head told her it would be for the best, but she couldn't stop thinking about him.

Life had settled back into a predictable, if less than exciting, pattern when early one morning she opened her door to find Adam on her doorstep. He was dressed in a flannel shirt, blue jeans, and his black Stetson. Her heartbeat quickened, and before she could stop it, a welcoming smile spread across her face.

He pressed a ticket to Ming's Opera House in her hand. "I've come to pay off the rest of my debt."

"Thank you, but it's really not necessary."

"It is to me."

"Then I'll not argue with you."

"Now there's a first."

Cammie was so glad to see him, she ignored the remark. "How have you been?"

"Fine."

"You?"

"Fine."

She hated the awkwardness between them. He looked stiff enough to use for a fence post. "I've been meaning to ride over to your place to thank you for the prompt delivery of the cattle and skiff . . . and to apologize for the way I behaved the other day. I know I didn't act like it, but I really do appreciate your willingness to be a gentleman."

"You change your mind about marrying me?"

"No."

His relief might have insulted Cammie if her own ambition to avoid the matrimonial state had not been so great. She twisted a wisp of the hair at the nape of her neck, trying to think what she should say next. "Do you want me to make you a cup of coffee?"

"No," Adam brusquely replied. "I told you before, I'm here to pay off my debt. My new skiff is tied up at the dock. If you can fit it into your day, I figured I'd give you that lesson in tracking you won."

Cammie's initial inclination was to refuse, but she could tell by the set of his lips that he would never be able to put that evening behind them until he paid his debt in full. Having no desire to drag things out and make either of them any more uncomfortable than they already were, she said, "I'll meet you at the dock in five minutes."

As soon as the words had left her mouth, Cammie started to regret agreeing to go, but she didn't call him back. She would have to accept his payment sooner or later, so it may as well be sooner.

She still found him as handsome and provocative as ever,

but she was going to have to learn to live with her lascivious feelings for him. After all, they were neighbors and were bound to find themselves attending the same civic and social functions.

If she spied a bottle of anything stronger than water in the skiff, she would run back to the house and bar the door, but as long as both of them remained sober, she had complete confidence in their ability to behave.

After a brief conversation with Mr. Culver and Mr. Daley to let them know she would be gone, Cammie returned to the house for her rifle.

"Are we going to the same spot you took me to before?" she asked, trying to make cheerful conversation when she arrived at the dock.

He glared at her. "I haven't decided."

Abandoning her attempt at congeniality, Cammie queried, "Are you planning to scowl at me all day?"

"I haven't decided that either."

"Let me know if you do. In the meantime, I will avoid looking at your sour expression." She settled herself in the boat.

After untying the skiff, he started to lay hold of the oars, but Cammie stopped him with a firm "No."

Reaching into her pocket, Cammie produced a coin. "Heads or tails?"

"Heads."

She flipped the coin in the air, caught it, and popped it on her wrist. "It's heads," she announced. "You win the right to row with the current."

Adam lifted the oars and began to row.

The sun felt good against Cammie's skin, and she closed her eyes and tilted her face skyward. She listened to the steady slap of the oars against the surface of the water. Cammie didn't know how she expected Adam to act toward her, but she saw no reason they couldn't behave civilly toward each other. She was even optimistic enough to believe they could learn to be friends. As long as they never allowed a drop of liquor past their lips when in each other's presence, there was no reason to believe they couldn't control their carnal urges.

They were two intelligent adults. They were both capable of understanding the risks involved in indulging in acts of unrestrained passion. Neither of them wanted to get married, and Cammie was sure they'd both learned from their mistake.

Peeking at Adam from beneath hooded eyes, Cammie was tempted to repeat her self-assurances to him, but she decided against it. He didn't look like he was in the mood for a lecture, especially a lecture that would tell him nothing that he didn't already know.

The river canyon was as sublime on second sight as it was on the first. Cammie found it impossible not to be affected, and the serenity of her surroundings seeped into her. Before long she was pointing out a curiously twisted tree trunk, an unusual rock formation, a badger scampering along the shore, and asking questions to enhance her knowledge of the area.

Adam answered her questions without complaint. He seemed as distant as ever, but the flow of river water had the effect of wearing down the sharp edge of his tension.

Spying a section of river where they could pull the boat out of the water and hike into the forest, Adam rowed ashore.

Tracking, it turned out, was merely a matter of being extraordinarily observant of one's environment. The greener the wood of a broken branch, the more recently whatever had snapped it had passed that way. A tuft of hair caught in the bramble could be used to identify the species of the traveler. Upon close examination, the earth beneath their feet revealed a multitude of footprints, ranging from tiny to the size of her hand. Droppings divulged the identity of an animal and how long ago it had used the path.

Adam was a thorough teacher and Cammie an adept student. She didn't plan to take up hunting as a pastime, but she found the information and mental challenge fascinating nonetheless. So immersed was she in the study at hand, she almost was able to completely disregard the fact the man walking beside her was more than the platonic friend she wished him to be.

It really was a pity Adam was so handsome, and that his muscles undulated beneath his clothes with every movement. She wished she didn't remember with such vivid clarity what those muscles looked like without the cloak of clothing. If the whiskey was potent enough to lead her down the road to perdition, one would have thought it should be potent enough to provide a convenient case of amnesia as well.

Equally distracting, the man possessed a mind as fine as his body. As far as she could discern, there was nothing he didn't know about the plants and animals living in the area—every time she was with him, she was impressed with his knowledge.

It was a shame the world was a place a woman was forced to choose between freedom and love. Not that she thought Adam would ever fall in love with her—even if she were so foolish as to allow herself to become enamored of him. Men didn't fall in love with strong women. They fell in love with women they could readily bend to their will. Cammie exhaled a sighing breath. Would that she could order the universe to her liking, but as yet God hadn't seen fit to assign her the task.

The excursion was proceeding well—far better than she had any right to expect. She was experiencing certain intense wanton physical reactions to her instructor, but Cammie was feeling proud of the way she was handling them, which was to say she disguised them from him and dismissed their significance to herself. . . .

They were climbing up a steep hillside when her foot slipped, and she started to slide. Cammie was in the lead, and she knocked Adam's feet out from under him, sending them both tumbling down the hill. They landed on a soft patch of wild grass at the bottom. Adam sprawled atop her, their faces inches apart. He closed the span between them with a feverish kiss.

Even as Cammie told her arms to push him away, she found herself pulling him closer. His lips tasted like the sweetest honey she had ever savored. Cammie was consumed with desire and bereft of reason. It was as if the fall not only had knocked the breath out of her, but her mind—and with it all will to resist temptation.

A voice in Adam's head reminded him that he had promised he would never do this again, but rather than heed it, his kisses became more ardent and urgent. In his skiff he had watched the delightful play of emotion on Cammie's winsome face, the flutter of her hand, the tilt of her head, the rise and fall of her chest with each breath. Squatting on the ground, shoulder to shoulder to examine a hoof or paw print with her had been pure torture. Watching the sway of her hips while she tramped up the hill, their round firmness within arms' reach, had filled him with lust. Every puff of breeze teased his nostrils with the seductive scent of her femininity. Relief awaited him in her silken limbs. His driving need was too great to resist. When she met his kiss not with protest but with a desire as immoderate as his own, he gave up trying. He became kin with the beasts of the forest with no more thoughts of right or wrong.

His lips devoured hers while his hands worked the buttons

of her blouse and lacings of her corset. He ripped the fabric of her chemise, exposing her breast to the sun and his lips. Her want of him was gloriously evident in the hardness of her nipples, and knowing she craved him intensified his own lust.

Burying his face in the valley of her bosom, Adam dragged his lips up one pillowy mound to the pink-tipped summit. He circled the nipple with his tongue, relishing the way she squirmed beneath him, then pulled the taut nub into his mouth and suckled her passion to greater heights.

So intent was he on giving her pleasure, he was barely aware of her unbuttoning his shirt and sweeping it off his shoulders. He was aware only of how magnificent it felt to be skin to skin.

Neither needed any further urging to discard the rest of their garments. Rolling atop them to shield their naked flesh from tickling blades of grass, they kissed and caressed each other with abandon. The air was cool, but the heat of their bodies made the whisper of a breeze welcome. The musky scent of intimacy joined that of the earth beneath them, drowning them in erotic balm. The rush of the nearby river echoed the surge of blood through their veins.

Adam kissed down one exquisite ivory arm, across her palm, to Cammie's fingertips, suckling each finger as he had her breasts. She kissed his neck and chest, her hands stroking his belly, reaching ever lower with each caress until they cradled his sex. He trembled, murmuring encouragement of her exploring touch.

She was exciting his already wild appetite to savage rapacity. Rolling to his back, Adam pulled her with him. Straddling his hips, Cammie leaned forward, teasing his lips with the tips of her breasts while her hands kneaded the muscles of his chest. She rocked against him.

Adam caught her hips in his hands. Lifting them, he guided them to his throbbing erection. She cried out with pleasure as she sheathed him. Half her hair had escaped the strictures of her chignon. Leaves adorned the golden strands.

She was no longer a lady proper but a creature of the forest. Wild . . . beautiful . . . unrestrained . . .

Arching her back, she took him deeper within her with every thrust until each thrust enveloped him full length. Cries rose from their throats in a duet of carnal celebration unsullied by the dictates of civilization.

The vigor of their movements increased with their passion as they rushed to fulfillment. Nothing existed except each other. A thin sheen of perspiration covered their skin, giving a salty taste to their kisses.

The climax to their union came in an explosion of mutual gratification. Limp, Cammie collapsed upon him. Adam sheltered her in his arms as they both gasped for breath.

The first time they had made love, whiskey had lulled them into a deep sleep. This time, they were afforded no such respite. The haze of bliss retreated with each restorative breath. When enough lucidity returned to make them aware of what they had just done, they sprang from each other's arms as if they had been lying on a bed of hot coals.

Clutching her skirt in front of her, Cammie stared at Adam, a horrified expression on her face. Adam waited tensely for her to accuse him of bringing her to the canyon for the purpose of seducing her, but she said nothing. She just kept staring at him in wide-eyed dismay.

Not knowing what to say, he began to dress. When he finished, she was still standing there like a statue. After an eternity of staring at each other, he mumbled, "I shouldn't have taken advantage of the situation. I'm sorry."

The only effect his words had was to cause her to cover her face with a hand.

"Are you gonna get dressed?"

She nodded affirmatively but didn't budge.

"Would it make you feel better to yell at me?"

Cammie shook her head.

"Well, it would make me feel a helluva lot better. I can't stand all this silence," Adam confessed, raking his hands through his hair. He hadn't meant this to happen; he was older and supposed to be wiser. "I take full responsibility for—"

"What just happened between us was both our faults." Her voice was clipped and pitched unnaturally high. "Please don't make matters worse by being a martyr. And if you are feeling compelled to renew your marriage offer, don't. If you do, I'll grab my rifle and shoot you—and this time it won't be an accident."

Her speech left him totally nonplussed, but the glint in her eye told him she was serious about shooting him. "Okay," he guardedly replied.

"Turn your back."

Adam did as ordered.

He could hear the rustling of fabric and was relieved she was putting on her clothes. Trying to carry on a conversation with her was unwieldy enough without her being naked. He was sure there must be something a man in this particular predicament should say to the lady involved, only he hadn't an inkling what it was. He'd never stood in these boots before. Adam was grateful she didn't want to exact her revenge for his trespass by marrying him, but if she didn't want him to renew his offer to make the honorable sacrifice, it left him without anything to say.

Cammie tapped his shoulder. He turned and she threw her torn chemise against his chest. "Bury that!"

"Okay," Adam acceded, catching the undergarment in one hand.

"Bury it good and deep, so no one will ever find it," she instructed.

Adam used a sturdy stick as a shovel and dug the hole between the roots of a tree. After laying the chemise in the bottom, he covered it with dirt, then hefted several rocks and tossed them on top. Sweeping the dirt with a branch and sprinkling pine needles over the area to erase his footprints, he turned to face her. The strain in her blue eyes had not lessened. Her arms crisscrossed her chest and hugged her waist.

"Thank you," she mumbled.

"You're welcome."

"I want to go home."

"I understand."

She raised her chin a notch. "I also want your solemn oath that you won't say a word to a single soul about what happened here between us today—and that constraint includes me."

"You don't need an oath to secure my silence on the subject when I'm around others. I'm not the kinda man to bandy about a lady's reputation." Adam centered his weight and tensed his shoulders. "But if it'll make you more comfortable, I'll give you one just the same. You and I are a different matter. I figure we need to talk."

"I don't want to talk." Cammie snapped, averting her gaze from his. "Besides, there's nothing to say."

Mind reading would be a handy talent when dealing with a woman like Cammie Kendall, Adam mused. Her stance, her expressions, the words she threw at him, were even more incomprehensible to him, than his own behavior. He truly wanted to make amends but because, as rattled as he was, he saw no hope of that, he was willing to settle for not making things worse. "Are you sure?"

"Yes," Cammie stiffly responded. "It's obvious we are both physically attracted to each other. It's also obvious we both just exhibited a shocking lack of self-control that cannot be blamed on a bottle of whiskey. I don't want to marry you. You don't want to marry me. Sexual intercourse, though undeniably pleasurable, has been known to result in the conception of a baby—which for some couples might be a consequence as pleasurable as the act itself . . . but for us would be a disaster. We are not to engage in it again."

Adam's eyes dilated. "For a woman with nothing to say, you just said an awful lot."

Cammie clamped her lips firmly together.

He cleared his throat. "I'm in complete agreement with everything you said, but—"

"What's to keep us from succumbing to temptation again?" Cammie finished the sentence for him and answered it in the same breath. "We will avoid each other's company."

"That's gonna be kinda hard to do living directly across the river from each other."

"I know we can't avoid all contact. Thanks to your little escapades and your brother's wagging tongue, there are already enough rumors circulating about us without giving people further reason to speculate on our relationship. I just think it would be wise if we avoid situations like this—" she gestured to the trees "—where we might find ourselves alone and for too long."

He knew it shouldn't, but it bothered him she was capable of applying logic to their plight. There was also a question that had been nagging at him since the first time he had let his passions overrule his head. "What if that child we both don't cotton to is already in the making?"

She flinched, then a stony expression descended upon her face. "I'm trying not to think about the possibility, but if that is true we will have to reassess our situation."

"If you don't want the baby, I'll take it," Adam tautly informed her.

"We don't know if there is a baby," Cammie shot back.

Adam could tell by the set of her lips that she'd rather be torn to shreds by a mountain lion than be burdened with caring for his child.

Fury boiled up in him, tingeing his words with venom. "Didn't say there was. I just figure as long as we're being so cold and businesslike that I oughta let you know I'm willing to raise the baby alone—so you can get on with the grand life you've got planned for yourself without being burdened."

"That's very generous of you, but—"

"*I* take my responsibilities seriously," he interrupted, looking down his nose.

"Are you implying I don't?" Cammie indignantly demanded.

"You sure don't sound any too thrilled about the idea of having a baby."

"Of course, I don't," she fumed. "I'm not married. A man may be free to sow his wild oats, but women who do so are ostracized, and more often than not, so are their children."

"At least you have the good grace not to pretend you want children, then decide you don't!"

"I never said I don't want children! What I don't want is marriage. Since I can't in good conscience have the first without the second, the decision whether or not to bear children has never been mine to make." Cammie advanced on him a step. "I don't even know why we're having this conversation."

"Because if you are with child, I don't want you to playact like you love him, then run out on him," he shouted at her.

"I would never do that! I can't imagine any woman doing such a thing!"

Adam's eyes narrowed. "It's happened before."

"When?"

"Twenty-eight years ago my mother walked out on Josh and me without so much as a 'nice knowing you'!"

Cammie gaped at him. "Oh . . ."

"I rest my case." He spat the words, pronouncing judgment.

Cammie's resentment rebounded. "I'm sorry your family was not a happy one, and I have no idea what compelled your mother to abandon you—but I am not her!" Cammie sighed and brushed an angry tear from her cheek. "All I want to do is go back to my house. If you don't want to accompany me—*fine!* I'll take the boat, and you can swim home."

Fourteen

Cammie scowled at her reflection in the mirror. The eyes staring back at her didn't appear to be those of a starry-eyed fool. They glimmered with the light of intelligence. She glanced at the framed two of hearts hanging on the wall over her bed, then returned her gaze to her own eyes. So why had she been so stupid that day on the hillside?

When Adam had landed atop her, she should have shoved him off and started back up the hill. She should *not* have responded to his kisses and rolled around on the ground like a lust-crazed wanton. This time she hadn't been drunk—she'd been fully aware of what was happening. Cammie slapped her hairbrush against her palm. *Why . . . ?* She had asked herself the question a hundred times and could not come up with a suitable answer.

Oh, she knew she liked lovemaking. The second time had been even more delicious than the first, but that didn't excuse throwing reason to the wind. She liked strawberries, but she resisted eating them because she knew they gave her a rash. Making love to Adam Carrigan would result in consequences far more grievous than itchy skin.

Cammie replayed the scene and their conversation following their latest act of passion in her head. At first the shock of what she had done had left her tongue-tied. Then she had used logic as a shield because she didn't know any other way to handle the situation without making a total fool of herself. Adam had accused her of being cold, but the opposite was true. So many emotions assailed her that she feared she would burst into tears.

She was distraught about what had occurred between them. She'd spent much of her life hiding her true feelings from others for fear they would use any show of weakness against her. Perhaps Adam had been disguising his feelings, too—her instincts said it was a distinct possibility.

Then there was his revelation about his mother. Cammie was sad as she envisioned the pain of the two young boys deprived of their mother's care. But that had nothing to do with the present predicament—and she hadn't appreciated Adam comparing her to his mother.

Frustrated, Cammie vigorously brushed her hair, pulling the silky flaxen tendrils flat against her head and twisting them into a severe bun at her neck. Whatever Adam Carrigan's manner and motives, her own were where she should place her concern. She couldn't do anything about him, but she could and would learn to control herself—assuming it wasn't already too late.

She might be foursquare against marriage, but she wasn't so selfish she wouldn't grit her teeth and sacrifice herself on the altar of matrimony to provide a name for any offspring produced by Adam and her illicit union. Cammie harbored no illusions she would make a good wife, but despite what Adam might believe, she *would* be a good mother.

Of course, her overriding hope was that she wasn't pregnant, and she saw no reason to pretend she felt differently. Any woman in her position would feel the same.

At one time she had lulled herself into complacency by believing the whiskey had been the cause of her undoing. Now she knew better. Forewarned was forearmed—and she intended to keep an arm's length between her and Adam at all times.

"Lucretia, you see standing before you a woman who is committed body and soul to the principle of chastity. I don't care how seductive and satisfying lying with the man is, I shall resist!"

Jabbing the last pin into her hair, Cammie marched out of the house to meet the day.

She recognized the sound of his horse's approaching hoof-beats immediately. Cammie's pulse quickened. Drying her hands, she left the rest of her supper dishes to soak in the pan in the sink.

It had been several weeks since she had seen Adam. Though she had missed him far more than she cared to admit, she wasn't all that happy with the prospect of being face to face with him again.

Many was the night that she'd lain awake, struggling unsuccessfully to subdue her lustful longings. Not that she intended to do anything about them—but, still, they left her feeling ill-prepared to face her *ex*-lover.

Adjusting her skirt and smoothing her hair, Cammie waited for the sound of his knock. When it came, she counted to ten both to steady her nerves and prevent him from knowing her hand was already on the knob of the door.

"Good evening," she coolly greeted.

"Good evening," Adam returned. His face wore an uneasy expression.

Cammie stood blocking the doorway.

"Can I come in?"

"I don't think that's a good idea."

He doffed his hat, holding it against his chest, crushing

the brim in his hands. "I'll stay only a minute. I need to talk to you about something . . . *privately.*"

After a lengthy internal debate, Cammie reluctantly relented. "All right, but just for a minute." She stepped aside to permit him entrance.

Closing the door behind him, he followed her into the kitchen. Cammie stood with her back pressed to the sink; Adam stood soldier-stiff a few feet away. He came right to the point. "I figured it's been long enough for you to know if you're with child."

"I'm not."

"That's good news."

Cammie nodded, her eyes never leaving his. Having him in her house was too unnerving to allow anything other than wary stoicism.

"I've been worrying about it . . . and you," Adam said.

"I appreciate your concern, but it was unnecessary. We were lucky."

"Yes—damn lucky."

He fell silent but kept watching her apprehensively, as though he expected her to rip off her clothes and throw herself into his arms at any moment. She supposed he had good reason to fear such an occurrence—the urge to do so had assailed her the instant she'd seen him standing at her door. However, she was determined to be strong for both their sakes.

The silence between them lengthened. Cammie tried to think of something to say, but her brain refused to cooperate. The longer they stood there, the more agitated she became. She began to fear the reason he said nothing was that—like herself—the only thoughts filling his head were ones of erotic surrender.

She should never have let him come in. She wanted him

out of her house, but her mouth wouldn't form the words. She licked her lips, hoping the moisture would lubricate them as oil did a rusty wagon wheel. It didn't help.

She glanced at the door. Why had he shut it? In a clearer frame of mind, she might have reasonably concluded the answer was to keep out the brisk evening breeze, but her head was far from clear. The only reason that came to mind was that he had prurient purposes for doing so. His eyes were so dark she could see herself in them, and the rise and fall of his chest seemed too labored.

What if she were wrong to assume him an innocent victim of their mutual lust? That his marriage offers were sincere? Maybe he knew all along she would refuse him, and that was the only reason he had asked. She *had* told him in no uncertain terms she never wanted to marry. What if he was the worst kind of womanizer? The type of man who would use a woman's ambitions and emotions to his own advantage? Both times they had lain together, *he* had initiated the circumstances.

Panic seized Cammie's mind. It was caused in part by her suspicions, but even more by the realization that her qualms did nothing to mitigate her sexual appetite for him. She had to do something! Save herself before it was too late!

Grabbing a bucket of cold water sitting on the floor near the stove, she threw the contents over him.

Adam sputtered, shaking the water from his hair. "Why the hell did you do that?" he demanded.

"I thought you needed some cooling off," Cammie shrilly informed him. "I want you to get out of my house. I didn't want to invite you in in the first place. How dare you come here to seduce me! Go back to your side of the river and stay there!"

"I didn't come here to—"

Cammie yanked open the door and jabbed her forefinger in the direction she desired him to take. "I said *go!*"

"Fine!"

"And don't come back!"

"I won't! You're a crazy woman!" Adam stomped past her. "Man tries to own up to his responsibilities and look what he gets for his troubles—ice water and insults. It's no wonder why I'm partial to staying a bachelor."

"Morning, Cammie. Nice looking animal you've got there," Josh hailed. Dismounting, he tied his horse to a rung of the corral where Cammie was lunging a two-year-old.

"Yes, he is," Cammie agreed. Giving the lunging reins over to Elias Rutley, she strolled across the corral and stepped out the gate. Josh met her there, and they walked side by side toward the house. "What brings you here? I haven't seen much of you recently."

"Been busy with the fall cattle sale," he explained. "But mostly it's Adam. He doesn't like me fraternizing with the enemy."

Cammie grimaced. "Is that how he refers to me?"

Josh shook his head. "Won't talk about you at all. Sure wish the two of you would settle whatever is eating at you both so the rest of us can get back to living peaceable lives."

"He's not planning another idiotic stunt to try to get his hands on my property, is he?"

"Naw. At least not that I know of, and I've been keeping my eye on him. I reckon your shooting him cured him of that monkey business." His lips twitched into a crooked half smile before settling into a more sober expression. "What I'm bellyaching about is the fact a body can hardly say three words to him without him trying to bite your head off. Already had one cowboy up and quit and a couple more are threatening to. You sure know how to put Adam in a stew."

Cammie's muscles visibly tensed, but she hid her reaction by pretending to stumble over a small stone. "I'm not responsible for his bad temper."

"Sure you are," Josh amiably insisted. "He hasn't been the same since you moved here." He chuckled. "But I didn't come here to talk about my brother—I came to invite you to the dance."

With more caution than enthusiasm, Cammie queried, "What dance?"

"Big shindig they have in town every year this time. Next to the Christmas Ball, which is a bit highfalutin for my tastes, it's the biggest social of the year. Everyone will expect you to be there."

"Everyone" had an ominous sound to it. She couldn't risk going if Adam was attending. Her cheeks reddened with embarrassment as she recalled her last meeting with him. She'd acted so unfairly, so impulsively—and the only reason he had come to her door was out of honest concern. How could she have imputed her own wanton desires onto him? Cammie had no wish to face him anytime soon.

When she asked her next question, she carefully schooled her voice to convey indifference. "Is your brother going?"

"No. Adam doesn't put much stock in prancing around on a dance floor in fancy clothes," Josh confided. "I used to try to talk him into going to these affairs, but I gave up years ago. Wild horses couldn't drag him to town on a dance night."

Attending the dance immediately increased in appeal. Cammie had been so busy getting her ranch up and running, she had sorely neglected her social obligations, which wasn't wise. It was bad for business. Too, fostering a few new friendships might help keep her mind off Adam Carrigan. He and Josh were the only people of her social standing she had taken the time to get to know, and it struck her her reclusiveness might be partly to blame for her obsessive preoccupation with the eldest Carrigan brother. "When's the dance?"

"Next Saturday."

After giving the matter a bit more thought, she said, "I believe I will go."

Josh beamed. "Good. I'll pick you up in the skiff bright and early Saturday morning, then drive you to town in the buggy."

Cammie frowned. Though she liked Josh and generally felt at ease in his company, appearing too friendly seemed inadvisable, in light of her turbulent relationship with Adam. "I'll drive myself to town."

"As long as we're going the same direction, we may as well have someone to talk to on the ride," he coaxed.

It was a sensible suggestion. If not for Adam, she wouldn't hesitate to accept. Cammie remained undecided until she was jolted by the realization that if she refused, she would be allowing Adam to dictate her behavior. The concept was so offensive, she blurted, "I would love to keep you company on the ride to town."

If he was surprised by her sudden eagerness, Josh didn't show it. "Be sure to pack a bag. Dance sometimes lasts till dawn. Most folks who live a fair distance from town plan on staying through till Monday morning."

Cammie nodded. "What time should I be ready?"

"If we arrive a little ahead of time, it'll give us a chance to get settled in at the hotel and clean up before the fun begins . . . six o'clock too early?

"Six o'clock is just fine."

* * *

Adam Carrigan scanned the festive crowd, stopping every time his gaze lit upon a head of pale blond hair or an uncommonly petite figure. His sighs of relief were audible when he discovered they didn't belong to *her.* Josh had assured him Cammie Kendall wasn't coming to the dance, but it wasn't unheard of for a woman to change her mind at the last minute.

He'd debated whether or not to come—but in the end had decided to attend just like he had every year since they moved here. If he didn't attend, people were bound to ask why, and he wasn't about to tell them he'd stayed home because of a woman.

Speaking of Josh, he hadn't seen him yet. He was usually one of the first to arrive so he could get his name on the dance card of all the comeliest ladies. Adam hoped he didn't have any trouble on the way to town. He'd already been in town tending to some business for two days, but Josh hadn't wanted to come early, claiming he needed a break from his company. Adam didn't blame him. He hadn't exactly been in the best of moods lately. Who could be with Cammie Kendall living across the river?

He kept telling himself he ought to be grateful she didn't want to marry him. He didn't want to marry her. But he sure would like to bed her again. He didn't know what she'd done to him, but he couldn't keep his mind off of her—and all that unrelieved passion was making him testy.

He'd tried slacking his lust at Chicago Joe's, but that had proved about as helpful as scratching his arm when his leg itched. Worse, he'd felt guilty for going there at all, like he was betraying a sweetheart—only he didn't have a sweetheart. What he had was Miss Camille Kendall. Except he didn't have her, he reminded himself. She didn't want him.

It wasn't that his ego was so puffed up he believed himself irresistible to the fairer sex, but he wasn't exactly the town derelict. There were any number of ladies who would marry him in a minute if he asked them. Not that he wanted Cammie to demand he marry her. He didn't. But she could have been polite and at least thought about it a while before rejecting his offer.

And he wanted her to stop being so damn desirable. She'd poisoned his blood, turning it into fire. A fire only she could put out. Not that he was ever going to put himself in a situation where he'd have the opportunity to make love to her again. He was smarter than that. But he was in desperate need of relief. It just wasn't fair for a man to suffer this way.

If she had any decency, she would move out of his valley. He was sure once she was gone, he would return to his former coolheaded self. But she wasn't going anywhere—and he knew it. She was going to keep waving her delectable little self under his nose until he went stark raving mad.

His thoughts kept churning in tight little circles, leading nowhere except to a bad mood. Determined to have a pleasant evening, Adam straightened his tie and waistcoat, squared his shoulders, and took a step toward Mr. Kohrs and his wife. His second step froze in midair.

Sweeping into the room in a dress of periwinkle blue striped silk fashioned with enough ruffles, lace, and bows to decorate three dresses, was Cammie Kendall *on the arm of his own brother.* She nodded her head and graciously extended her hand as Josh introduced her to first one couple, then another. Her skirts flowed gracefully about her with each step she took. Josh was grinning like he'd just won a silver-mounted saddle at a rodeo. She was smiling, too . . . until her eyes met Adam's across the room.

It took every bit of Cammie's self-control to keep a gracious smile pasted on her face, while inside she was screaming with fury and frustration. Her grip on Josh's arm tightened, and she dug her fingernails into the fabric of his coat-sleeve. "You told me he wouldn't be here," she hissed in his ear.

"Did I?"

"You know perfectly well you did."

"I'm not one to argue with a lady. If you said I did, I guess I must have—but I just can't remember the conversation."

"Liar."

Josh just grinned.

As satisfying as it would be to smack the grin off Josh's face, there wasn't a lot Cammie could do without causing a scene. The last thing she needed was more gossip involving her and the Carrigan family, which a hasty retreat was sure to generate. She would just have to ride the evening out.

Adam didn't look any happier to see her than she was to see him. That meant he would be as eager to avoid her as she was him. For appearance sake she would be obliged to exchange a cordial hello, but the rest of the evening she would contrive to stay on the opposite side of the room from him.

The ballroom was gaily decorated with swags of gold, rust, and pumpkin colored fabric tied with contrasting ribbons. Garlands of fall flowers draped the front of the platform, where the musicians played popular dance tunes. Some men wore tailored suits and ties; others wore dress shirts, trousers, and black silk kerchiefs tied around their necks. The ladies created swirls of color as they spun around the dance floor bedecked in their finery. Everyone appeared to be having a grand time.

Since her primary purpose for attending the dance was to make new acquaintances, Cammie suffered Josh to guide her around the room, introducing her to his friends and their mutual neighbors. He seemed to be friends with everyone, and politeness dictated they stay and exchange at least a few words. They moved forward at a snail's pace. Cammie didn't mind. The longer it took before she was required to engage in social amenities with Adam, the more pleased she would be.

Though she had met a few of those present in the course of conducting business, most of the faces were new to her. Cammie enjoyed meeting the local ladies, especially those who openly expressed admiration for her daring to run her own ranch. The gentlemen she met and some of the older women were not so enthusiastic about her bid for equality and independence in the male world, but they nonetheless treated her respectfully and generously wished her well.

Whenever Josh introduced Cammie to one of his single friends, the gentleman invariably asked for a spot on her dance card. Cammie readily agreed, hoping to fill her card well before they reached Adam, just in case he felt socially compelled to sign up for a dance. She wasn't certain who she distrusted the most, him or herself, but she preferred not to put either of them to the test.

As she and Josh proceeded around the room, Cammie kept casting surreptitious glances in Adam's direction. He was moving through the crowd in the same direction they were, at a casual though slightly faster pace. She was grateful for his cunning. With any luck they would never catch up with him.

Though she was ever aware of Adam's presence in the room, Cammie did her best to concentrate on memorizing the names and faces of those she met and the conversations at hand.

They had worked their way halfway around the hall, when Josh snorted in disgust. "Stay right here," he ordered, making a beeline for his brother.

Faced with an imminent meeting between Adam and herself, Cammie turned coward. What if they got in another argument in front of all these people? She would like to believe herself able to bite her tongue no matter how sorely provoked, but with Adam Carrigan her behavior was far from predictable. He made her feel sensations and emotions that threw her totally off balance. Even from across the room she was all too aware of his virility.

Seizing the opportunity to lose herself in the crowd while Josh's back was turned, Cammie slipped away from the spot where she had been told to stand. She paused to speak with several people on her way to the corner she had selected, and when she turned back to face the room, Josh was completely hidden from her view—which she hoped meant she was completely hidden from his. She was about to congratulate herself for a job well done, when to her dismay she realized she was standing next to Jay Larson.

"Evening, Miss Kendall," he tipped his head.

Cammie had neither forgiven nor forgotten his treatment of Jewel, and she barely managed a civil, "Good evening, Mr. Larson."

"Care to dance?"

"No, tha—" Spotting Josh headed directly toward her, a stone-faced Adam in tow, she quickly amended her answer. "Yes!"

Mr. Larson appeared slightly bemused by her eagerness, but he rapidly recovered himself. The musicians were playing a waltz, and they settled into the steps.

Mr. Larson was an excellent dancer—a fact, judging by the smug expression on his face, of which he was all too aware. He further annoyed her by trying to hold her too close. Cammie was forced to stiffen her arms and exert considerable pressure against his shoulder and hand in order to maintain a respectable distance.

"I hear you hired Carl Daley on as ranch foreman," he commented during a series of turns.

"Yes."

He fixed his gaze directly upon her face. "We both know my riding was more impressive than his."

"Yes, it was." She met his gaze without flinching. "But I shudder to think what you did to coerce your horse into cooperation."

"Just showed him who's boss."

Cammie refused to be drawn into a public altercation with a man of Larson's ilk. She knew his kind well, and as long as he stayed away from her horses, keeping her temper was simply a matter of reminding herself he was too uncouth to expend her energy upon. "Personally I find gentle persuasion far more effective than violence."

"Everyone's entitled to their own opinion, but yours is dead wrong. That ranch of yours is gonna go bankrupt faster than you can say 'I sure wish I'd listened to ol' Jay Larson'—unless you get yourself an expert like me in there to teach them horses some manners. Don't matter how pretty they are, no cowboy is gonna buy a spoiled horse."

"As you said, everyone is entitled to their opinion," Cammie coolly replied.

"After the way you treated me, I know I'm softheaded for saying this—but I'm Christian enough to let bygones be bygones. A green little gal like you needs a man who knows what he's doing around the place to run things for her. If you want me for foreman—and I know in your heart you do—I'm yours."

Cammie couldn't believe her ears. Was the man drunk or merely excessively dense? She discreetly sniffed the air. Not smelling alcohol on his breath, she concluded it must be the latter. "Mr. Larson, not only do I not want you as my foreman, I wouldn't hire you to dung out my stables—even though I am sure your odious nature makes you well suited for such a task."

Her words finally seemed to penetrate his thick skull. "You calling me shit?" he stammered.

"Yes, Mr. Larson, I believe I am."

"I don't gotta take that from no woman."

"Then how very convenient for you that the dance has ended." She peeled his hands from her person. "Good evening."

Cammie was so intent on escaping Mr. Larson that she paid little attention to the path she chose to exit the dance floor. When it was too late to change direction without the reason being evident, she realized she was heading straight for Adam. Josh was nowhere in sight, and for that she could be grateful. There was no telling what further mischief he had planned for the evening.

Maintaining an air of dignified detachment with Adam was a far more difficult proposition than doing so with Mr. Larson. Cammie drew in a deep breath.

"Good evening, Mr. Carrigan," she crisply greeted.

"Good evening, Miss Kendall." He accepted her hand when Cammie extended her hand, but quickly released it. Rather than remain face to face, she took up the piece of floor beside him. "I didn't expect to see you here tonight," he tautly informed her, keeping his gaze focused on the dancers. Cammie did the same.

"Nor I you. In fact, I was specifically told you were not planning to attend."

"I assume your source of information was the same as mine."

"If you are referring to your dear brother, yes."

"I intend to make him pay for this."

"As do I. He finagled me into letting him sign up for several spots on my dance card. Rest assured, I shall be dancing on his feet more often than the floor."

"Good."

"Well, now that we've said the required hello, I'm going to spend the rest of the evening in other company. You stay on your side of the room, and I'll stay on mine. Agreed?"

"Agreed," Adam said, and a look of understanding passed between them.

Relieved the encounter was over, Cammie started to leave, but he caught hold of her arm. Startled and dismayed, she turned to face him.

Adam cleared his throat. "Before you go, can I give you a little free advice?"

Cammie wasn't at all certain she wanted to hear whatever he had to say, but she forced an impassive shrug of her shoulders. "Why not?"

"I wouldn't get too friendly with Larson if I were you."

"Trust me—I have no intention of doing any such thing. The man disgusts me."

Adam's brow wrinkled. "Then why did you dance with him?"

"To avoid meeting up with you," Cammie said flatly, wishing Adam didn't look so handsome in his suit of black wool, waistcoat, and starched white shirt. Not waiting for a reply to her comment, she beat a hasty retreat to the other side of the room. Glancing at her dance card, she saw there was a name filled in for the next dance. Its owner arrived at her side just as the musicians struck up the first measures of a schottische.

One dance followed another, each with a new partner.

While they danced, Cammie gave her partners her full attention, but in between dances she discreetly scanned the crowd to make certain Adam was nowhere in her vicinity.

For a man whose brother claimed he disliked dancing, she noticed Adam had as many dance partners as she. On those occasions when her next partner was slow to find her in the crowd, she was afforded brief opportunities to observe Adam dance. His skill and ease made it glaringly obvious he was no stranger to the dance floor. She wasn't particularly surprised. She already knew Josh to be an unconscionable liar.

Speaking of the devil, his name was the next on her dance card. An evil smile spread across Cammie's lips.

"I believe the next dance is mine." Josh presented himself before her.

"Yes, it is." Cammie eagerly gave him her hand.

"I'm glad you've gotten over being mad at me," he remarked, leading her out onto the floor.

Cammie broadened her smile.

Much to her delight the dance was another waltz, which meant his feet would be within striking distance throughout the dance. Her eyes glimmered as they took up the required position. The first step forward she took, she landed on his right toe.

"Pardon me," Cammie apologized.

"No need to beg my pardon," Josh assured her. "I've stepped on a few toes myself."

She let a measure pass, then stepped on his toes again. "Oh, dear."

"Don't worry about it." Squeezing her hand, he gave her an encouraging smile.

As they executed a turn, she brought her heel down hard on his instep.

"Ouch!" Josh muttered.

"Sorry."

"It's okay." He subtly attempted to put a safer distance between his toes and hers, but she refused to cooperate and follow his lead.

She let three measures go by and stepped on him again. This time, and the next three, she let a contrite expression suffice for an apology.

The fifth time in the space of six measures that she stomped on him, he narrowed his eyes. "I spoke too soon about you not still being mad at me, didn't I?"

"Whatever makes you say that?" Cammie cooed.

"The fact that you're trying to lame me might have something to do with it."

Cammie gave up all pretense of innocence. "You deserve to be punished."

"For what?" Josh guided her through another turn, deftly sidestepping another attempted assault on his toes. "For trying to get you and Adam to spend some time together? The two of you are made for each other."

"We are not."

"Sure you are."

Cammie wanted to strangle Josh on the spot and be done with his romantic delusions about his brother and herself—but getting hung for murder was a bit drastic. Adam and she knew exactly where they stood with each other, and where they both preferred to stand was miles apart. She skewered Josh with a reproachful glare. "Your opinion is insupportable. You don't have one good reason—"

"I have a couple of good reasons," Josh interrupted. "First off, you make a fine-looking couple, and secondly, you're both so bull-necked and bossy I wouldn't want you inflicting yourselves on any other member of the opposite sex."

"Very amusing."

"You want to hear another reason?"

"No."

"My brother is in love with you."

"He told you this?"

"Of course not. He's spent so many years telling himself and everybody else he's a happy bachelor, it'd kill him to admit otherwise unless he was sure the woman returned his affection." Twirling her through a series of rapid turns, Josh suspended her response.

"I'm no more in love with your brother than he is with me," Cammie succinctly stated the moment they settled back into a less dizzying mode of the dance.

"Exactly," Josh triumphantly declared. "I've seen the way the two of you look at each other—like the other is a canteen of water in a bone-dry desert six weeks into a cattle drive. Your 'no more in love' is more in love than most folks ever have the nerve to get."

That Josh believed every word he said was indisputable—that he had noticed Adam's and her propensity for each other's person was mortifying. Hiding her distress behind a scornful tone, Cammie demanded, "And what makes you such an expert on love?"

"I was born with the gift."

"What you were born with is a giant hole in your head."

"Okay—then prove me wrong," Josh challenged. "I'll give all my dances on your card to Adam. If the two of you don't end up all moon-eyed and breathless by the end of the evening, I'll shut up."

"I don't have to prove anything to you or anybody."

Josh chuckled. "What you mean is you won't do it because you know I'm right."

"That's not true." Cammie focused her defiant gaze on his collar.

"I say it is—and there's only one way to settle the argument."

"You are not going to goad me into doing something I don't want to do."

"Fractious as you look, I reckon I'm not. So I'll just have to resort to plan two." He guided her through a quick succession of traveling steps. "Howdy, brother . . . Miss Mullin." Josh plucked Miss Mullin from Adam's arms and pushed Cammie into them. "I've come to steal your partner." Before either could protest, he danced away with Miss Mullin.

"I'm gonna kill my brother," Adam stated, his tone seething with menace.

"Not if I get my hands on him first." Cammie stood rooted to the spot, her lips compressed into a grim line. "There is no reason we have to finish the dance."

"Except everyone is watching us."

She glanced around the room. He was right—they did appear to be the center of attention. Cammie swore under her breath. "Don't they have anything better to do?"

"Obviously not."

"So you think we should dance?"

"I think we oughta stop standing here like a couple of statues. Finishing the dance will cause less speculation, but we can retreat to the punch bowl if you'd rather."

"We'll dance. It will give us an opportunity to plan Josh's demise."

Despite Cammie's suggestion, they didn't exchange more than three words during the remainder of the waltz, and they were the same word, twice from his lips, once from hers, "Smile."

Dancing within the circle of Adam's arms was exquisite torture. She could feel the strength in the hand gripping hers.

The spot on the small of her back where his other hand lay radiated fingers of fire up her spine and down her buttocks. His breath titillated the hairs on the top of her head. His scent roused her. Riveting her gaze on his broad chest forestalled a discomfiting meeting of their eyes, but it begat risqué fantasies in her head, and she was forced to swallow the lump of desire rising in her throat.

As soon as the waltz was over, Adam delivered her into the hands of her next partner. Cammie's pulse slowed to a sensible rate until the time came for Josh to claim her for another dance. Instantly the three of them became the center of attention once again.

"You're spreading gossip to make it impossible for Adam and I to evade your machinations, aren't you?" she accused as she followed Josh onto the dance floor.

"Yep."

This time instead of handing her over to Adam, Josh joined the square where his brother stood, effectively achieving similar results since the dance called for near constant interchanges between the couples. Cammie did her best to concentrate on the dance steps and ignore her body's betrayal whenever she found herself in Adam's arms. Luckily the dance was vigorous enough so that the heightened color of her cheeks could easily be attributed to exertion.

When the dance was over, Cammie counted the number of times Josh's name was entered on her dance card. Three more dances were all she had to survive. It was three too many, but having been caught in Josh's trap, Cammie was determined to put the best face on the situation.

Pretending a gaiety she was far from feeling, she swept around the dance floor on the arms of her partners and engaged in animated conversations with the ladies on subjects she cared little about. If the name Adam Carrigan ever came up in these conversations, she casually excused herself and moved on to another group. Josh claimed her for another waltz and glibly engineered her into his brother's arms.

Cammie and Adam exchanged collaborative glances and planted vacant smiles on their faces. Adam made a comment about the musicians. Cammie complimented the punch. They discussed horses, cattle, the weather whenever a bit of conversation seemed called for. They behaved neither as enemies nor friends and certainly not like lovers.

Cammie had no idea what Adam was feeling as they performed their little act. She tried not to think about it—besides, it took all her resources to manage her own feelings and appear composed when dancing within his embrace.

To circumvent Josh, the next time it was his turn to collect her for a dance, rather than permit him to claim her hand then make a show of handing her over to Adam, Cammie told her present partner Adam's name was next on her card. It was a small victory, but satisfying. While they danced the two-step, Adam voiced his approval, recommending she do the same next time.

With only one more dance with Adam to go, relief was in sight. If she had not promised two more dances after Josh's, Cammie would have left before it came. Keeping up the charade was exhausting, and it was late enough that her departure would not seem odd.

Unfortunately she had promised the dances, and she had no wish to slight the gentleman in question.

Cammie didn't have to seek Adam out. He came to claim her for the designated dance. She noticed Josh grinning at them from a few feet away. Adam glanced in the direction of her exasperated gaze and glowered.

"I used to think I liked having a brother," he muttered, guiding her onto the dance floor.

The musicians were playing another waltz. Cammie was convinced Josh had consulted with them beforehand to make certain he signed his name in exactly the right spots.

"He really is getting out of hand," she commiserated. "Can't you do something about him?"

Adam's eyes darkened and he whispered, "What do you suggest? Short of telling him the unvarnished truth—which I'm not about to do—I don't know of a damn thing that would work."

"No. We don't want to tell him the truth," Cammie emphatically agreed in hushed tones.

They continued to converse in voices audible only to each other's ears.

"Knowing Josh, it might not work anyway. He'd probably get it in his head to load up his shotgun and make us do the decent thing."

Cammie winced.

"Try to look a bit less like you're at the dentist's having a tooth pulled out and more like you're enjoying dancing with me, would you?"

"Sorry." She curved the corners of her lips upward.

"That's better." Adam exhaled a breath. "No sense in giving people any more to chew on than they already have. If we're both gonna live in this county, which I don't recommend, we've gotta learn to act natural around each other. Enough people see us behave with each other like we do everybody else, it'll make Josh look like the saphead he is, and folks will stop listening to him."

"He told me you're in love with me," Cammie disclosed.

Adam's cheeks bloomed cherry red, and he stumbled on the step.

"Oh, don't worry. I didn't believe him for a moment," she reassured him. "I just thought you ought to know the sort of things he's saying about you—so you can better defend yourself against them."

Adam nodded.

"Do you know what he's saying about me?"

"No."

A twinge in her gut told Cammie he wasn't telling her the truth, but she didn't press the issue. It was easy to guess what Josh was blathering in the ears of others, and hearing her worst suspicions confirmed would serve no useful purpose.

She was already so furious with Josh that she didn't know how she was going to be able to sit in the same buggy with him on the ride home. He had no business meddling in their lives. Their relationship was complicated enough the way it was.

Adam was right. The best way to thwart Josh was to let enough people see them behaving unremarkably, often enough, everyone would realize Josh was insane to believe she and his brother had the slightest romantic interest in each other—and they would stop listening to him. In any case the strategy was well worth thinking about.

When the waltz ended, Adam left her at the side of her next partner. Cammie provided him with good company and did the same for the man who came after him.

Having fulfilled her social obligations, she discreetly made her way to the door. Once outside she breathed a sigh of relief and immediately hailed a carriage.

Fifteen

Starting with the night of the dance, Cammie's indulgent opinion of Joshua Carrigan began to rapidly deteriorate. Tales of the very worst matchmaking mamas paled in comparison to his efforts to persuade anyone who would listen that she and Adam would make a perfect couple.

Josh seemed to have committed his life to the task of ruining hers. She despised being the object of gossip, and it certainly didn't help her establish the reputation she aspired to in the community.

Cammie tried to distract herself with work, but it was impossible to ignore the incessant whisperings. She had lost count of the times she had sat Josh down and told him in no uncertain terms to stop, but she may as well have been talking to a fence post. She knew Adam was doing the same with like results because Josh delighted in telling her the details of his brother's attempts to "blind himself to the plain as the nose on his face truth." He treated them both as if they were willful toddlers, even though his brother was four years older than him and she was only a few years younger.

Adam and she were more than capable of determining the course of their own lives, and they had both rightfully decided that their potent physical attraction to each other was a poor reason to give up their independence.

Whenever Cammie pondered her unconventional relationship with Adam, her brow knit and her lips quirked into an expression halfway between a frown and a grin. Since the night of the dance, they were getting along better than they ever had. She supposed it had a lot to do with having a common goal and a common enemy. They still made a point of avoiding each other's company whenever possible—which was most of the time. And they never put themselves in situations where they might find themselves alone. But on those occasions they were in the same place at the same time, they discussed strategy instead of arguing.

If she were the marrying kind, Cammie knew Adam was the type of man she would choose for a mate. He was intelligent, responsible, possessed a droll sense of humor, and was an enthralling bedmate. But as she was always quick to remind herself, even a man with Adam's sterling qualities was still a man—and by nature, men were compelled to dominate the women in their lives. She had only to conjure visions of her father to quail at the thought of love and marriage.

The strategy Adam and she used to deal with Josh's interference in their lives was the one they had discussed at the dance. Both attended the functions they would normally attend, and whenever they found themselves at the same affair, they treated each other nonchalantly. There were some people who would always prefer rumors over truth, but the more intelligent members of the community slowly seemed to be getting the message that there was no great romance brewing between Adam Carrigan and herself.

October waned and the chill of each day in November increased as the calendar marched toward the end of the year. Cammie's ranch was fully prepared for the winter. The exercise barn was complete, a good supply of feed was laid in to supplement her horses' diets when snow made grazing on the hay provided by the native grasses too difficult. She had sold every one of the four-year-olds she had hoped to sell, all for a good price. The men who bought them were extremely pleased with the horses and provided excellent word-of-mouth advertising for the sales she would be ready to make in the spring.

The first snow arrived on the eighteenth of November. By Saturday there was a thick blanket of white on the ground, and midmorning of that day two dozen people bundled head to toe in fur and wool, driving horse-drawn sleighs, filled her front yard.

The unexpected noise of jingling bells and clamor of excited voices sent Cammie hurrying onto the porch.

"Morning Cammie," Josh greeted, hopping down from the sleigh he shared with Adam. "We've come to fetch you for a snow picnic."

"A picnic in the snow?"

"Yep, and the ladies have already elected you captain of their team for the snowball fight, so you've gotta come."

Despite her vexation with Josh, the outing sounded delightful. The size of the group was fortifying, and it only took a few moments contemplation to decide what her answer would be. "Give me two minutes to put on my wraps, and I'll join you."

Adam held the reins. Cammie hoped to seat herself to Josh's right, but Josh nudged her into the sleigh so that she was sandwiched between the two brothers. Adam and she exchanged fatalistic glances and polite hellos.

Though sitting between Josh and Adam was not her place of preference, it was the warmest spot in the sleigh, and Cammie felt quite cozy as they glided across the glistening fields of snow. Adam kept as far to his side of the bench seat as practical, and their thighs brushed against each other only occasionally. Every time they did, the friction sparked a flame within her, but Cammie stoically pretended to feel nothing. She had come to regard the bodily sensations Adam ignited within her with the same forbearance she accepted the discomfort she felt the first two days of her monthly. There was nothing that could be done about it, so she lived with it and went about her business as usual, trying not to think about it.

Everyone was in a gay mood with conversations constantly flowing between the sleighs and impromptu races to the top of a hill or bottom of a hollow engaged in every few minutes. The majority of those who formed the party were young married couples, but three sleighs contained courting couples, and one held the two eldest Taylor sisters, Janice and Beth.

The sky overhead was a patchwork of gray and pale blue. The sun played peekaboo with the clouds. The day was cold but not bitterly so. Cammie's eyes sparkled as they trotted past snow-encrusted pines and bare-branched bushes where snow had melted and refrozen, making them appear to be sculpted of ice.

She and Adam took turns introducing innocuous topics of conversation to waylay any hopes Josh had of steering the dialogue to the subject he loved most: them. Since both judged any topic other than themselves suitable, the exercise didn't produce undue strain.

They traveled a considerable distance before Josh—who seemed to be the leader of the band of merrymakers—announced they had arrived at the perfect spot for the snowball fight. There were plenty of trees and bushes to hide behind and more than abundant snow.

"Shall we eat first, or bury the ladies in snowballs?" Josh asked the gentlemen.

"Eat," the men proclaimed in unison.

"You're a bit overconfident, don't you think?" Cammie

chided Josh as she climbed out of the sleigh. "We'll be burying you."

The ladies enthusiastically seconded her opinion.

While the men got a fire started and put coffee on to boil, the ladies retrieved the picnic baskets. Cammie contributed the one she found waiting in the Carrigans' sleigh.

The meal was consumed standing around the fire. As soon as it was over, the men gathered in one group and the ladies in another. Without warning snowballs began to fly from the direction of the men.

"Ladies!" Cammie herded her troops behind the nearest cluster of trees. From their sheltered positions, they lobbed snowballs back at the men, who took up strategic positions of their own.

Cammie threw her snowballs at any available target, but she took special glee whenever a snowball landed on Josh. It was a pleasure to have a socially acceptable opportunity to vent her spleen upon him. She had planned to avoid making Adam an intended mark, but the heat of the battle proved too much, and she pelted him with the same enthusiasm as she did the others.

Shouts and laughter peppered the air. Cammie threw snowball after snowball in rapid succession, totally absorbed in the fun of the moment. The ladies' team was holding its own, but ten minutes into the contest, Cammie was certain they could do better. Sprinting from tree to tree, she whispered instructions in the ears of her confederates. They readily agreed with her plan.

On signal from her, three ladies stepped out from behind their trees, hurling snowballs as fast and furiously as they could, creating a diversion that allowed two others to slip away unseen. They continued to do this until half their troops were stationed behind the men and half remained in their original positions.

The ladies that remained with Cammie had been piling up a steady supply of snowballs, saving two for every one they threw. She had asked Beth Taylor to general the ambush troops. When Beth's ladies had ample ammunition, she let go a war cry.

Caught by surprise, the gentlemen had no place to hide. Snowball after snowball pelted them, giving them little chance to return fire. The ladies cheered each other on, remorselessly escalating the attack.

"Ready to surrender, Frank?" Ida Peterson called to her husband after catching him square in the forehead.

Wiping the snow from his face with his coat sleeve, he hollered, "Never!"

There was so much noise as everyone yelled taunts and calls for submission back and forth, Cammie could not imagine the pandemonium of a true battle. The ladies were closing in on a decisive victory when several of the husbands stormed their wive's positions, carrying them off like prizes of war. The foray deprived both sides of an equal number.

The men were on the move, forcing the ladies to do likewise, running from tree to tree to take up advantageous positions. Soon it became impossible to tell who was behind what tree, and often a snowball was set flying before the thrower realized it was aimed at a member of the same sex.

Adam scored a satisfying strike on Cammie when, while hiding on the opposite side of the same tree trunk, he reached around and shook a branch above her head, precipitating a miniature avalanche. Cammie counterattacked by pretending to retreat, then abruptly stopping and sticking her leg out so he tripped and landed face first in the snow.

Joe Cassidy caught his wife and slipped a handful of snow down the back of her dress.

Beth and Janice Taylor joined forces. Disregarding the snowballs he pitched their direction, they relentlessly advanced on Josh, causing him to roll head over heels down a small knoll.

Eventually everyone was laughing so hard, it was a rare snowball that reached its target, and a truce was called.

"Well, you did pretty well today, ladies," Frank Peterson complimented.

"Only because we were outnumbered," Josh grumbled good-naturedly.

"Isn't it just like a man to look for excuses when things don't go his way," Beth Taylor teased.

"Just for that, I'm gonna punish you and Janice by riding in your sleigh on the way home," Josh proclaimed. "You're gonna have to listen to me yak at you on all my favorite subjects."

They fell into each other's arms and moaned, but obvious to all present, the two sisters were overjoyed by the prospect.

Cammie and Adam were not—but as every other sleigh held an established couple and the Taylors' sleigh wasn't large enough to accommodate four people, they were stuck with each other.

The fire was doused and the sleighs loaded with the remains of the lunch. Cammie settled into the sleigh next to Adam. She knew she should probably be distressed to find herself in these circumstances, but she was in such a fine mood, she experienced only a twinge of trepidation.

Two of the men challenged each other to a mile race. Another man asked to join them, and the three sleighs sped off. The rest followed behind at a more relaxed pace.

The destination now being home, one by one farewells

were bid and sleighs turned off to take the shortest route. Before long there were only three sleighs left in the group: Ben Bridger and Elizabeth Brown, Josh and the Taylor sisters, and Adam and Cammie.

The clouds had been thickening all afternoon, and a light snow began to fall. Cammie entertained herself by trying to catch snowflakes with her tongue.

"Anyone up for a race to the river?" Josh asked.

"Sure," Ben replied.

"How about you, Adam?"

To say no was to be left behind alone, and Adam promptly agreed to join in. They lined up the sleighs and were off!

Cammie and Adam shot ahead but were almost immediately overtaken by Ben and Elizabeth. Josh and the Taylor sisters kept up a few yards behind, but the added weight in their sleigh made it impossible for them to compete on an even standing. The racers kept up these positions for a quarter mile.

"Ben will wear down his horse at the start of the race, and we'll make up the lost time and pass him long before we reach the river," Adam assured Cammie of their victory.

It was difficult not to be caught up in the excitement of the race, and Cammie shouted encouragement to their horse. They were starting to slowly gain on the lead sleigh when a troubled expression pinched Adam's face. The sleigh began to wobble. Josh and the Taylor sisters whizzed past them.

The rocking became progressively more pronounced, forcing Adam to pull back on the reins. As they slid to a halt, the right back corner of the sleigh sagged to the ground.

They shouted for Josh to stop, but he didn't seem to hear them. Adam climbed out to inspect the damage while Cammie held the reins.

"We've lost most of the bolts holding the runner," Adam informed her after a brief examination.

"Do we have any extra bolts with us?"

"No. But I can loosen some of the others and space them out to hold the sleigh up well enough to make it home as long as we take it easy. It shouldn't take that long to make the repairs." He opened a small compartment built into the seat box. "We keep a . . . Damn that Josh!"

Cammie startled. "What?"

"The tools are missing—and there's no reason anyone would remove them, so that rules out someone taking them and forgetting to put them back," Adam fumed. "I don't reckon the runner coming loose was an accident."

"He purposefully stranded us out here?" Cammie cried. "The wretch!"

Adam grimly nodded. "Probably leave us out here an hour or two. Then show up with a guileless grin on his devious face and the bolts and tools at the ready, claiming he figured we must have had some kinda trouble with the sleigh, and he figured it best to let the Taylor sisters drop him off at the house before riding to the rescue."

Cammie had no doubt Adam's assessment of the situation was close to the truth, and her heart sank to her toes—all the pleasure of the day fading before the prospect of facing an hour or two alone with temptation. She could kick herself for allowing Josh to do this to them. "We should have anticipated something like this."

"Well, we didn't," Adam stated, stomping the snow beneath his feet. "I figured arranging it so we drove home together was all the mischief he'd planned for today."

"What are we going to do?"

Shaking the snow from the brim of his hat, he met her apprehensive countenance with one of matching unease.

"Nothing to do but sit here and wait for him to come back for us."

"Why not unhitch the horse and ride back?"

"He's trained to the harness, not a saddle. There's no chance both of us could ride him. One of us could try, but my guess is we'd end up with a broken sleigh *and* no horse."

Cammie knew without asking that it was too far to walk without the aid of snowshoes. Having no other suggestions to offer, she agreed they had no choice but to sit and await rescue.

After lifting the back corner of the sleigh up onto the runner and bracing both sides by heaping snow against them, Adam climbed back into the sleigh. He and Cammie sat stiffly side by side, neither saying a word.

Considerable time passed. It had begun to snow in earnest, and the wind was picking up.

"Are you warm enough?" Adam inquired.

The pink of Cammie's cheeks brightened. She knew his question was innocent, but she couldn't prevent her lascivious mind from jumping to the wrong conclusion. The answer she gave was accurate for both interpretations. "Yes."

He kept his gaze focused straight ahead.

Cammie was glad Adam didn't feel obliged to engage her in conversation. It was awkward enough just sitting here, knowing what kind of thoughts were filling the other's mind.

More time passed. Adam tucked the lap robe more snugly about them.

It was now snowing so hard it was difficult to see more than a few feet in front of the sleigh. The wind blew through their layers of clothing like a knife. Cammie gritted her teeth to keep them from chattering.

"We're gonna freeze to death if we keep sitting here,"

Adam apprised her, wiping the snow from his mustache. "We're gonna have to take shelter."

"Where?"

"There's an old line cabin not too far from here."

"Will Josh know to look for us there?" Cammie asked.

"Unless I'm guessing wrong, in about five or ten minutes we're gonna be looking at a full-fledged blizzard. He won't be able to come looking until it's over."

She tried to sound calm. "How long do you think it will last?"

"There's no saying. Could be less than an hour—could be days."

"Days!" Cammie abandoned all efforts to maintain outward composure. Adam's eyes met hers.

"I don't like it any better than you do. All we can do is hope for the best."

Following Adam's instructions, Cammie stayed under the blanket until he unhitched the horse, then joined him on the ground. They started to walk into the storm using the animal's bulk to block the piercing wind.

Being caught in a blizzard was dangerous, but all Cammie could think about was the danger that lay ahead when they reached the line cabin. She could lecture herself from here until doomsday on how she and Adam should behave, but . . . It was difficult to have confidence in one's good sense when the memory of failure was so enticing—and too much privacy was soon to be theirs.

The new snow was dry, causing them to sink with every step, and their progress was slow. They trudged for what seemed forever.

"Are you sure you know where you're going?" she called against the wind.

"I'm sure."

"How much farther?"

"Not more than a few hundred yards."

When they reached the line cabin, Adam pointed to a lean-to built next to it to indicate his intention of stabling the horse, then opened the door and pushed her inside.

Cammie closed her eyes to speed their adjustment to the darkness. After a minute she could make out the shadow of a small table and a narrow bed, but nothing else. The door opened and closed behind her.

"I'll have a fire started in a few minutes." Adam carried an armload of wood past her. Laying it on the floor and dropping to his haunches, he busied himself across the room. A match glowed in the darkness. Soon the tiny flame grew into a crackling fire, lighting the room. "Keep stoking the fire while I carry in a few more loads of wood."

"I will."

The fire felt wonderful, and Cammie warmed her hands while she fed it more fuel. The firelight allowed her to see the room more clearly. The cabin was about nine feet square with a dirt floor and clay-chinked log walls. There was one shuttered window. The fireplace was built of local stones. A couple of hooks hung on the wall near the door, but the cabin contained no other furniture besides the table and bed.

Adam came in with another armload of split wood.

"Where are you getting that?" Cammie queried.

"The lean-to. I send a man up here every summer to split a cord if the one from the previous year was used up. Sort of a courtesy for stranded travelers."

"Thank heaven for your generosity to strangers."

"People in these parts look after each other." Adam dismissed her heartfelt praise and headed back out the door.

Several trips later he removed his hat and gloves, holding his hands out to the fire. "As soon as it gets a little warmer in here, we can take off our coats and spread them out to dry. We may need them for blankets if the storm doesn't let up before nightfall."

He spoke the words casually, but Cammie could hear the underlying tension beneath them. If she knew what to say to reassure him, she would say it—but at the moment her brain wasn't conjuring reassuring phrases.

"What do you think Josh will do when he realizes he stranded us in a blizzard?" Cammie asked, feeling compelled to say something.

"I reckon he's already realized it," Adam said. "I'd like to picture him pacing the parlor mad with worry, but he knows I know how to take care of myself and you."

"Great," Cammie groused. "He puts us in this untenable position, and I don't even get the pleasure of imagining him wracked with guilt, believing that he's murdered us."

"He's probably suffering a few pangs of remorse, but I'm sure he's not suffering as much as we'd like him to."

"If it's enough to make him stop meddling in our lives, I'll be satisfied."

Adam turned his hands over to warm their backs. "I wouldn't get my hopes up."

Cammie didn't. There was room for only one all-consuming hope in her breast, and that was that she maintain her dignity and remember her vow to resist giving in to any and all carnal urges. She had failed to live up to her own high standards before, and even now a part of her was singing the siren song of surrender. She wanted to discard reason and make love to Adam. But she couldn't. She wouldn't. Her gaze stroked his broad shoulders. At least she prayed she wouldn't. "You don't think we'll—"

Adam read the rest of her question in the pitch of her voice and the hunted look in her eyes. "No. I'm not gonna try to seduce you."

"I didn't mean to imply I thought you might," she defended. "Despite what I may have said to you in the heat of anger, I've never really believed my own words. I just panicked. I think you know that."

Adam's voice softened, and he smiled wanly. "I guess I do."

"I'm glad—I really am a fair person, and I'm willing to take the blame for my own weaknesses."

A thin sheen of perspiration was beginning to form on Adam's brow, and he pressed his lips together. He rocked his weight from one foot to the other, then back again. A pained expression darkened his eyes. "Can we change the subject?"

"Yes, of course. I'm sorry," Cammie apologized. "You choose a subject."

"I don't know what the hell to talk about," he protested.

"Maybe we shouldn't talk."

"Good idea."

They both clamped their lips together and stared at the fire. When necessary, Adam added another log. Cammie walked to the window several times, opening it a crack to check on the progress of the storm. It was getting worse outside, not better.

When the room was sufficiently warm, Adam carried the table nearer the fireplace. They spread their coats on it, adjusting them occasionally to be certain they thoroughly dried. Cammie held her gloves, hat, and scarf up to the fire in turn to dry them as well. Adam did the same with his outer garments and the lap robe.

When their clothes were dry, they were deprived of all useful occupation for their hands. Cammie found the compulsory idleness disconcerting. How was she supposed to ignore the stirrings of lust if there was nothing to do but stare at its source? The air between them vibrated with sexual tension. Her skin might feel cool, but there were parts of her person that were exceedingly and demoralizingly warm. Each minute felt like an hour. Hoping it might in truth be much later than she believed, she asked, "Are you carrying a watch?"

Adam reached into his pocket. "It's quarter past six."

"Oh." Cammie walked to the window again to check on the storm. It was as bad as ever. She returned to the fire, a grimace on her face. More time passed. She asked the time again.

"Six twenty-eight," Adam announced.

The third time she asked, he pressed the watch into her hand. She glanced at the face, then started to hand it back to him. "Keep it," he ordered.

"I have to find something to do," Cammie pleaded. Slipping the watch into her own pocket, she stood before him, lacing and unlacing her fingers. "You don't happen to be carrying a deck of cards?"

He raised a brow.

"Solitaire. I want them to play solitaire."

"I don't have a deck."

"Why didn't you just say so?"

He shrugged. After a while he asked, "Do you want to play tic-tac-toe? We could scratch a board in the floor."

"Anything is better than nothing."

They knelt on the floor before the fire. The game proved less than satisfying as both knew how to place their first mark to assure the best the other could achieve was a draw. They added two more lines and required four in a row to win. This too grew boring, and eventually they scratched out a checkerboard, snapping a piece of kindling into short pieces to provide one player's checkers and peeling bark from a log and breaking it into small chunks to supply the other's.

With nightfall the temperature began to drop dramatically. By ten o'clock, even with the fire, it was cold enough inside the cabin to require wearing their coats, and that was sufficient to ward off only the worst of the chill, not keep them warm.

At length, Adam cleared his throat. "I was planning on us sleeping in shifts, but . . . I know you're not gonna like to hear this—but if we hope to keep from freezing to death before morning, we're gonna have to share our body heat."

He was right. She didn't like hearing it, but having already come to the same conclusion, she stoically mumbled, "I didn't expect it to get this cold."

"Neither did I." Rising to his feet Adam dusted his hands and dropped his gaze to her boots. "I'll pull the bed as close to the fire as I dare, then turn my back till you've stripped down to your chemise and drawers."

"What!"

He didn't look up. "With all the clothes we're wearing, we're not gonna be able to do each other any good unless we strip down and pile all our clothes on top of us."

"Do you think that's wise?" Cammie demurred, her voice pregnant with misgiving.

Adam raked his fingers through his hair. "Hell, no. I don't think it's wise, but it's either stare temptation in the face or wake up icicles—except, of course, we won't be waking up at all."

"What will you be wearing?"

"My red woolens."

Considering past experience, crawling into bed with Adam with nothing but their undergarments between them was crazy, but so was willfully freezing to death. Cammie didn't like it—and she clung to no illusions that their good intentions were guaranteed to last the night—but she was too pragmatic to ignore reality. Taking a deep breath, she said, "If it must be done, it must be done. My ranch is turning out too well for me to be willing to freeze."

Adam dragged the bed across the room, flipped the mattress to the less dusty side, and presented his back.

Cammie quickly disrobed, piling her garments on top of her and covering the whole with her coat. "You can turn around now."

Adam stoked the fire and banked it. "Whenever you're ready, you can close your eyes."

Cammie shut them tight. She didn't open them again until Adam's clothes, coat, and the lap robe joined her clothes and coat, and he slipped under them, pulling her against his chest. The warmth of his body was welcome, but the fiery blush that stained her checks was not.

"I will do my utmost not to take unfair advantage of you," he gruffly promised.

"And I you," Cammie pledged in return. She covertly glanced at his face at the same moment he surreptitiously glanced at hers. Their eyes met. Both hastily looked away.

"I figure the best thing for us to do is try to go to sleep right away," Adam opined.

"Yes."

"Good night, then."

"Yes, good night."

He closed his eyes, and Cammie did the same. Unfortunately, depriving herself of the sight of his too enticing person only sharpened her other senses' awareness. Her ears pricked at the sough of his breathing. Her nostrils quivered as each inhalation drew in the heady scent of his skin. She could feel his heart beating against hers; was aware of each twitch of his muscles.

Cammie concentrated on breathing deep rhythmic breaths, hoping to induce sleep by mimicking it.

Next to her Adam was devising and mentally enacting a series of heinous crimes upon his brother . . . when he could tear his thoughts away from the woman lying so temptingly in his arms.

Up until this afternoon when the sleigh broke down, he had enjoyed the day—and what he had enjoyed most was watching Cammie rally the ladies to give their all to the game. Usually the snowball fights between the gentlemen and ladies were insipid, the men holding back and often as not stepping in front of the snowballs tossed their direction to be sporting. One of Adam's chief grievances with the fairer sex was their lack of spunk. Cammie Kendall had spunk enough for herself and plenty to share. He respected that—just as he respected the way she ran her ranch, her willingness to embrace new experiences, and the sensible way she insisted on dealing with their indiscretions. Trouble was, he didn't want to respect her—or rather he didn't want to feel the admiring, smitten kind of respect he was feeling. It made resisting her abundant physical charms that much more arduous.

The curves of her body fit his too well. The heat of her blushing skin beckoned him. How was he supposed to lie here next to her and do nothing? He was a flesh and blood man, not a rock.

Human or not, he wasn't going to breach faith with her or himself. It was important—neither of them wanted marriage. He'd sweated out the days wondering if their previous sexual congress had gotten her with child. He imagined she'd done the same. Once was more than enough.

In the silence Adam could hear his watch ticking off the

minutes. He counted them . . . then tried counting sheep. He opened his eyes and stared into the fire, hoping the flickering flames would mesmerize him to sleep.

The hour was past midnight before either drifted off into a fitful sleep.

Cammie snuggled closer to the source of heat next to her and burrowed her face against his chest. Despite the twinges of embarrassment she knew she would suffer when she awoke in the morning, she welcomed these dreams. They hurt no one, and since the price for taking Adam as a real-life lover was too steep, having him as a dream lover was better than no satisfaction at all.

He was kissing the top of her head. She liked it when he did that, but not as much as she liked it when he captured her lips for a soul-searing kiss. As if reading her thoughts, he rolled her to her back and covered her lips with hers. She thrust her tongue into his mouth. He deepened the kiss. It went on and on—a blissful eternity that caused her to tingle from head to toe in anticipation of what was yet to come.

Cammie stroked the sides of his face, splaying her fingers and dragging them through his thick hair. Their tongues danced a languid waltz, punctuated by long shuddering sighs of pleasure.

Adam's hands kneaded her back from her shoulders to her buttocks. Releasing her lips, he trailed his mouth over her chin down the column of her throat to the tip of one breast. He kissed it, then proceeded to kiss her entire breast, radiating out from the tip in a spiraling circle and up again. Reaching the peak, he pulled her nipple into his mouth, nibbling and sucking until she writhed beneath him. He swallowed up more of her, laving her skin with his tongue.

Cammie clung to him, drowning in his worshiping caress, loving the weight of his body on hers. He kissed her again full on the mouth before turning his attention to her other breast.

Adam suckled on the breast, filling his mouth, contented as a babe—except his sensations were far from those of an innocent child. He was a man on fire with lust and he stoked that fire by tantalizing his mate, preparing her to receive him.

Her uninhibited want of him drove him wild. She touched him everywhere: his head, his neck, wrapping her arms around his torso to coax him upward, urging him to take her. Her thighs were open in invitation. Her hips raised from the mattress, seeking his sex. He kissed her eyelids, her nose, her passion swollen lips.

Her hand captured him, guiding him where she wanted him to be, but he brushed it away, kissing her again and again, prolonging the moment until he could restrain himself no longer.

He plunged into her. She cried out her delight. They arched together in a frenzied race to the pinnacle of intimacy. The bed frame creaked beneath them. The air was heavy with the musk of lovemaking. Her muscles contracted around him, drawing him deeper into her with each thrust.

He rode her over the crest of rapture, trumpeting his climax as she sang out hers, reveling in the erotic spasms that spilled his seed into her.

Sagging against her, he rolled them to their side, still keeping her cradled against his body. He opened his eyes just in time to see hers blink open.

They both turned to stone.

Sixteen

"I'm not dreaming," Cammie stated numbly as reality stared her full in the face. She remembered drifting off into an exhausted sleep, but she had absolutely no memory of removing her underclothes. The rest of what had occurred between them, she vividly recalled. Her cheeks flamed.

Adam stared at her mutely before murmuring, "No."

It was too cold to crawl out from beneath their makeshift covers, and she was too naked to make doing so more than a fleeting notion. The mattress was too narrow to allow putting any distance between them. Cammie told herself it didn't matter—the damage was already done. It wasn't a very comforting thought. Another filled her head. Though the possibility mortified her to depths of soul, she had to know. "Did I . . . seduce you?"

Unlike her, Adam chose to brave the biting cold and his nakedness. Escaping the bed, he lay several logs on the fire, keeping his back turned toward her while he stirred up the coals. "I don't think so."

Cammie's gaze fixed upon his bare buttocks. "Did you seduce me?"

Adam abruptly stood, and she averted her gaze. Approaching the bed, he sifted through the jumble of clothing, yanking on his woolens when he found them. The rest of his clothing followed. "I don't remember."

Ducking her head under their coats and the lap robe, Cammie located her chemise, then her drawers, and pulled them on without leaving the bed. Next she rolled on her stockings. Adam presented his back while she finished dressing. "If you don't remember, you probably didn't," she consoled.

"You're generous to say so." His shoulders sagged. "I'm sorry . . . whoever's fault it was."

"This is Josh's fault. We were doing very well until—"

"Yes, we were."

Cammie joined him in front of the fire. They stood shoulder to shoulder, staring into the flames. "I didn't know a person could . . . you know . . . while they slept."

"I'm not all that sure we were asleep. Maybe through the first kiss or two, but after it was probably more a case of not wanting to stop."

Unfortunately, Cammie agreed. She rubbed the bridge of her nose. "Why are we capable of being logical after, but never before or during?" she plaintively queried.

"Hell if I know. If you figure it out, tell me."

"I suppose we ought to rethink our strategy."

Adam glanced at her, then returned his gaze to the fire. "You still dead set against marrying me?"

"Yes—but it's not you personally."

"It's okay by me," he gruffly rejoined.

"We both have our reasons for preferring the single state. I don't fully understand yours, but I respect them," Cammie elaborated. "And there is no need to try to stifle your sigh of relief. It won't hurt my feelings."

"What does hurt your feelings?" Adam asked.

"Not being taken seriously," Cammie replied, grateful he didn't try to deny he was relieved she wouldn't be requiring him to marry her.

Adam looked at her more seriously than anyone had ever looked at her in her life. "So what do you want to do?"

To stand beneath his penetrating gaze without turning away took every bit of nerve Cammie possessed, but she made herself stand fast. This was no time to be fainthearted. Both their futures depended on them facing their situation head on and dealing with it with logic, not emotion. If she felt the need to quail and wallow in an excess of feeling, she could do so when she was alone. Schooling her voice to reflect her resolve, she responded, "As I said: rethink our strategy. I detest being the object of gossip, but I would rather have people whispering behind my back than risk the possibility of being maneuvered into a situation where one or both of us loses sight of our goals. I think from now on we should avoid each other's company altogether, even if we have to be obvious or rude."

"If that's what you want, that's what we'll do—but what about last night?" His eyes darkened and he smoothed his mustache several times before he continued. "If word gets out we spent the night stranded together, even if we lie and claim we behaved like saints, you'll pay the price with your reputation. Men start figuring you're free with your favors—they'll give you nothing but heartache, and I'm none too fond of the notion of having to fight them off for you."

A picture of Adam valiantly defending her honor formed in Cammie's head, causing a whimsical smile to flit across her face. Refusing to be beguiled, she briskly shook her head. The image and the smile evaporated. Cammie swallowed the lump in her throat. "I'm perfectly capable of defending myself, but I'm not convinced I'll have to. Josh will know we spent the night together, and my men will know I spent the night away from home, but they won't know it was with you. Surely we can think up something politic to tell them to explain my absence—unless Josh has already broadcast the truth all over the county."

Adam brushed a wisp of hair from her cheek and tucked it behind her ear. Cammie's lips quivered. Jerking his hand back, he dropped to his haunches and poked at the fire with a stick. "I doubt he has. Josh has been doing a lot of things I don't cotton to lately, but ruining a lady's reputation would be going too far, even for him."

"I hope you're right." Cammie squared her shoulders. "I'm afraid he might see this as a perfect opportunity to further his ambitions to bring us together."

"It's possible, but I still don't figure he'd do it."

"You know him better than I do," Cammie replied. If Adam was right, it was one less worry. Ignoring her conscience, she proposed, "So we'll think up a good story, stick to it, and no one will be the wiser."

Adam's grip tightened on his stick. "Unless I got you in the family way."

"We were lucky before. Hopefully our luck will hold."

"I'll be on my knees praying every night it does."

"So will I."

"What if it doesn't?"

He certainly didn't believe in dropping a subject before thoroughly discussing the details. They needed to have this conversation, but they didn't have to commit to any firm plan for every possible contingency. She turned her back to the fire and him. "We'll cross that bridge when we come to it."

She couldn't see his expression, but his voice sounded as strained as her own. "Assuming I'm right about Josh, we come up with a convincing story, and there's no baby on the way—"

"I like those assumptions," Cammie ardently interjected.

He continued, "I know you figure avoiding each other altogether and putting up with the gossip is the best way to handle our predicament—but it seems to me, it'd make both our lives a lot simpler if one of us left the valley."

"And I'm the logical choice," Cammie dully finished the thought for him.

"I've been here for years, and I was here first. I'd pay a fair price for your land and all the improvements you've made. But if you won't go, I'm gonna have to seriously contemplate selling my place."

"I don't want you to have to do that," Cammie protested, turning to face him.

Adam tossed a log on the fire and rose to his full height. "Then sell your place."

"I can't. Oh, I know there's plenty of other land, and I could make a profit elsewhere."

"Then why won't you sell?" he asked when she paused to collect her thoughts.

"If I tell you, you'll scoff at me."

"Try me."

Under any circumstances admitting the truth to him, or anyone else for that matter, would be difficult. She had worked day and night to build her reputation as a no-nonsense person. But having recently offered "a dream" as her excuse for lovemaking, revealing the truth was now ten times harder. However, Cammie felt she owed it to him. "I dreamed the land. I've been dreaming about it since I was a little girl. When I saw Mr. Higgins's ranch, I recognized it instantly. I *know* this is where I'm supposed to be. It has absolutely nothing to do with logic; it's a gut instinct."

He didn't laugh, but he looked at her strangely.

"You think I'm crazy, don't you?"

"No."

"Why not?"

Adam hesitated a long moment before answering her question. "Years ago I had a similar dream, only in it I owned the whole valley. I'd never dreamed a piece of land before. Even Josh doesn't know about it. I gave him a list of practical reasons, and he figures they're the only reasons I wanted to settle here."

"Oh."

"I'd appreciate it if you didn't tell anyone differently. I've always felt kinda stupid about it."

"I won't tell a soul, but it does complicate things."

"How?"

"I would never ask you to do something I wouldn't—and if a dream brought you to this valley, there must be a reason."

"What?"

Her brow knit. "I don't know."

"Maybe there isn't one. People have dreams about lots of things. Ours were probably just coincidences."

"Is that what you believe?"

"If I knew what to believe, I'd be a happy man. All I know is you and me in the same valley spell trouble. The first time we lay together, we were both inebriated, the second time we fell into the trap because we deluded ourselves. A man makes a mistake three times, he oughta learn something from it."

"We have," Cammie argued. "What we've learned is we need to stay away from each other—far away. You'll stay on your side of the river, and I'll stay on mine. If you wish to attend a social function, send one of your men across with a note, and I will make my excuses and avoid the affair. I will send a note to you whenever I accept an invitation, and you can absent yourself."

They stood toe to toe and gazes locked, taking stock of their own resolve and each other's measure.

"You figure that will work?" Adam queried.

"We can hardly fall prey to temptation if we are never in the same room," she reasoned.

"Makes sense."

"Yes, it does."

"I guess I'm willing to give it a try if you are."

"I think we should. Our ranches are important to both of us. Giving either of them up is too drastic."

Crossing the room, Adam opened the shutters. "The storm has stopped."

Cammie sighed with relief at the sight of the clear blue sky. "Thank goodness."

"I'll bring in enough wood to keep you warm, then hike back to the sleigh. Josh may already be there. If not, I'll give riding Jonas a try. If he throws me, I'll hike back to the ranch, get what I need to fix the sleigh and come back for you. While I'm gone, try to think up that story to tell your men to explain why you didn't come home last night. I'll be doing the same."

Cammie started to suggest she go with him, then decided having time alone to compose herself before facing the world was preferable. Despite sounding reasonably rational, her thoughts and emotions were still a jumble. She nodded her agreement.

As soon as Adam finished carrying in an ample supply of wood, he set off.

Josh was leaning over the runner, tightening down the bolts when Adam spotted the sleigh. The two horses Josh had with him whinnied as Adam approached. When Josh looked up, he wore a contrite expression.

"Howdy, brother," Adam balefully greeted, advancing on

him with a murderous glint in his eyes. The two brothers squared off in the snow.

Josh held up his hands and took a step back. "Before you say anything, I want to let you know I never meant—" He glanced around, peering behind Adam. "Where's Cammie?"

"Staying warm in the old line cabin."

"She okay?" Josh hesitantly queried.

"As well as can be expected," Adam snapped. The cold fury that gripped him upon seeing his meddlesome brother made it impossible for him to be charitable. Shamefaced or not, he didn't know if he'd ever be able to forgive him. Right now he wasn't even going to try.

Josh squirmed beneath his brother's pitiless regard. "The blizzard blew in without warning."

"That's no excuse for what you did!"

"I know," Josh admitted. "I tried to ride back to fetch you, but I couldn't see a thing and had to turn back."

Adam growled.

"I always hoped you two would get together, but I never planned for you to *have* to marry her. I'm sorry, Adam."

"We're not getting married," Adam icily informed him.

Josh gawked at him, then his penitent expression turned reproving. "I don't know what happened between you two in that cabin, and I'm not gonna ask. I wouldn't have been able to keep my hands off of a woman like her, but it was you in there, not me. Only you and she know what you did and didn't do. My point is, we both know she deserves to be treated like a lady."

Adam closed the distance between them with a single stride. "You oughta have thought of that before you stranded us for the night."

"It's not fair to make her pay for my mischief," Josh asserted.

"We're not getting married," Adam repeated.

Josh narrowed his eyes and jutted his chin. "I know I'm already in danger of getting my face smashed in by your fist, and if beating me to a pulp will make you feel better, go ahead and do it—but it's my duty as a gentleman to remind you of *your* duty. You've compromised her. Your bachelor days are over. You've gotta ask her to marry you whether you want to or not."

Adam didn't flinch. "I know my duty."

"Then do it!"

"You stranded us. You marry her."

"If it comes to that, I will before I let her be branded a fallen woman," Josh proclaimed.

Watching Josh's face redden with anger was small compensation for the misery he'd caused them, but Adam was determined to milk the moment for every ounce of agony he could inflict upon his brother. Stone-faced, he continued to taunt him. "She won't have you."

"How do you know?" Josh demanded.

"Because she doesn't want to marry anyone."

"How do you know?" Josh repeated.

"She told me."

"I'm sure that was before you compromised her! You can't hold the woman to some opinion she once expressed just because it suits you. I bet if you asked her to marry you now, she'd jump at the chance!"

"I bet she wouldn't." Adam maintained his aloof tone and bearing.

"Adam, I've always respected you more than any other man on earth besides Pa when he was alive. But you're fast losing that respect." Josh was so disillusioned and outraged by his brother's indifference that his eyes glistened with tears. Adam relented a little.

"I have asked her to marry me."

"Thank God!" Josh sighed with relief. "What did she say?"

"No."

Josh pursed his lips, scowling as he pondered this information. "She's probably just too upset to think straight."

"She knows exactly what she wants," Adam curtly replied.

"How can you be sure?"

"I asked her more than once. Unless she's with—" Adam clamped his lips shut, appalled at the slip of his tongue. A fiery blush spread up his neck.

Josh's eyes widened. "Something *did* happen between you two."

"Shut up, Josh!"

"Why didn't you tell me?"

"I said shut up!" Adam hunched his shoulders, wishing he could retract his head into a shell like a lake turtle. "It's none of your damn business! It's nobody else's damn business either!"

Josh chortled. "I knew you liked her all along."

Adam slammed his fist into his brother's belly, depriving him of wind for further comment. It felt so good, he did it again before readjusting his hat and fixing Josh with a steely gaze. "Now that I have your attention, I want you to listen to me. First, you're gonna swear off matchmaking for life. Second, you're never gonna mention Cammie and me again in the same sentence to anyone. Third, you're gonna tell me what you've already said and to whom about last night."

Josh gasped in a breath and wheezed. "Nobody but me noticed you didn't come home, so I kept it to myself and let them figure you were in the house. When the blizzard turned me back, I stopped by Cammie's place and told Culver she was spending the night with a friend."

"Did you mention a name?"

"No."

"Good. I'll tell Cammie if anyone asks to keep it vague. It'll lessen the chance of getting caught in a lie."

"What about—"

"Cammie and I will deal with things *our* way," Adam interrupted. "The only thing you're gonna do is keep quiet. Understood?"

Josh slowly straightened and nodded his head.

"No more meddling. No more advice."

"Okay, but I still figure you oughta—"

Adam cut his words short. "I said no more advice. I'm warning you Josh, we've been partners all our lives. If you want to keep it that way, butt out!"

Josh didn't look happy, but he promised. "No more meddling. No more advice."

"Good." Adam turned his back on him. "I've got enough on my mind without putting up with more trouble from you."

Seventeen

Cammie glanced up from the book she was reading and frowned at the white flakes falling outside her window. Lucretia was curled up in her lap, and she absently stroked her back. Lucretia began to purr.

"I'm starting to think winter is going to last forever," Cammie complained aloud. It wasn't really snowing that hard, and she knew most of the snow that fell during the night would melt away by midday, but Cammie was feeling lonely and gloomy and inclined to look on the darker side.

It wasn't that she didn't have any friends. She had made quite a few since moving to Montana, and they often visited back and forth. She had the daily companionship of her men as she worked side by side with them. She had Lucretia and her horses. She was lonely because she missed Adam.

Cammie groaned. She wasn't supposed to miss him. She should be happy that they were staying away from each other. She knew the consequences of their spending time together, and the price was too high.

After the night they'd spent in the line cabin, she had waited anxiously for her monthly to arrive. It was nearly a week late, and it was the longest, most agonizing week of her life. She never wanted to put herself through that again.

If they kept making love, it was only a matter of time before she ended up pregnant, and they would be forced to marry.

Adam didn't want to marry her, and she didn't want to marry him—all they would ever do was fight. She was too ambitious. He was too bossy. She listed just a few of the reasons they shouldn't marry.

Over and over she told herself being lonely was preferable to being oppressed. She believed herself, too—but she wished life would offer her another choice.

When Cammie was feeling particularly low, she tried conjuring pictures of Adam and herself in love and living happily as man and wife. Her mental musings always started pleasantly enough, but after the passage of an imaginary year or two the pictures turned ugly. She would see herself standing at the door in an apron while Adam rode off to have adventures. Or she would be sitting in the parlor while he loomed over her, lecturing her on the duties of a proper wife. Or she went to the stables to train her horses and there were padlocks on all the doors. No matter how hard she tried, she couldn't make the story turn out right in her head.

If she couldn't even conjure a picture of a fulfilling marriage in her mind, she knew there was no hope that she could accomplish it in real life. There was no point in deluding herself. Marriage was not for her, and without marriage spending time with Adam was hazardous. She would get over her infatuation for him eventually and be her old self again. It would just take a little more time.

Adam stood on the banks on the river, watching Cammie walk from her house to the barn. At least once a day he found himself standing here, hoping for a glimpse of her.

He knew she didn't need him or want him, but he couldn't help worrying about her. It was ridiculous. She was the most competent woman he knew. Hell, most men couldn't hold a candle to her—but he worried just the same.

He had waited to receive word from her about the "results" of their latest night of passion, but it had never come. Knowing her to be a sensible woman, he confidently assumed that meant there were no results. He was glad their luck had held, or at least the rational part of him was glad. The irrational part of his mind kept whispering that if she had gotten pregnant, they would be forced to get married—and he wouldn't find himself staring across the river, missing her and wishing her a thousand miles away all at the same time.

He'd thought about asking her to marry him again. Not like the other times, but on his knees accompanied by romantic declarations. More than once he'd even gone so far as to saddle his horse to ride over, but he just couldn't make himself do it. He never got past throwing on the saddle blanket before his palms got sweaty and his gut clenched with panic.

He had to face facts—and the fact was he didn't really want to marry her. He was already too enamored with her the way it was. If they shared the same roof, made love every night, sipped cups of coffee sitting across the breakfast table every morning, he would just keep getting more enamored until he was inseparably in love.

He didn't try to kid himself he wasn't half in love with her already, but half in love meant half of him was still safe from the kind of pain he was willing to do anything to avoid.

Sometimes he wished he could talk to someone about the fearful feelings that welled up in him every time he thought about getting close to a woman, but he didn't know who he could talk to. All his life he'd hidden his feelings from his family because he didn't want to make things worse than they were. Josh was a man now—but he still didn't figure he was the right person to give him the kind of wisdom he needed. Josh was . . . Josh. He'd be sympathetic, but he wouldn't understand. Josh had been a lot younger when—

Adam massaged the back of his neck. Josh was a good brother, and he'd kept his word about staying out of Cammie's and his lives, but Josh's method of dealing with problems was to act on his first impulse and ride out the consequences. It worked for him, but Adam was different. He needed to think out his actions and weigh their results before he jumped in with both feet.

He had plenty of friends, but it just wasn't the sort of thing a man shared with a friend. He'd be too embarrassed to even try.

Since he couldn't talk it out, and he couldn't solve the problem on his own, Adam figured the only thing he could do was make the best of a bad situation, which meant doing exactly what he was doing—staying away from her.

It'd been months since he'd seen her up close, and he intended it be months more before he ever did. He'd keep busy and stay away. Adam nodded his head and turned his back on her ranch. It was the only sensible thing for a man to do.

April arrived and with it the first of the foals. Cammie kept a sharp eye out for the signs of impending birth: restlessness, waxing up of the mares teat's, small excretions of milk, a slacking of the body on either side of the tail. When a mare exhibited one or more of these signs, she was moved to a foaling box filled with sweet straw.

Cammie made a bed for herself next to the foaling box. As a precaution she spent many nights sleeping in the barn, but all her mares did fine on their own, and the foals they produced were healthy and beautifully conformed.

With the warming weather and the arrival of the foals, activity on the ranch picked up, allowing little time for pondering life's problems. Cammie was grateful for the respite.

Her method of training being based on gentleness and mutual respect—after allowing a few days for mare and foal to bond—she began to spend a little time every day with each new arrival. Rubbing her hands in the stable bedding, she offered them for sniffing, gradually working up to stroking the foal's neck—and when she was sure she had gained the animal's trust, introducing a foal slip.

Quite a few of the local cowboys and ranchers stopped by to see her foals. Though it would be years before they were ready to sell, the comments made were gratifying and boded well for the future.

During the long winter days, Cammie had charted which mares she wished to breed to which stallion to attain the best characteristics for next spring's foals. After the foaling, as soon as the mare came into season, she let her loose with the stallion she had chosen to serve her.

The breeding went as well as the foaling. Only one young mare, who was being bred for the first time, refused to allow her stallion to cover her.

By the first of June, a near constant stream of visitors were stopping by the ranch to check out the rumors concerning the quality of her new foals. Some were so pleased with a specific foal that they contracted to purchase it the year it would be old enough to sell. Others bought one of the four-year-olds that was ready this year.

It was an exciting time for Cammie. She was living her dream, and reality matched her long-nurtured hopes. The only thing to mar the perfection of her days was the conspicuous absence of one particular man.

She didn't expect him to come see her foals. In truth, she

would have been angry with him if he had come. They had an agreement, and they were both sticking to it. She just wished she could share her success with him.

She knew he was busy with his own ranch. Josh didn't visit as often as he once had. Their friendship had been sorely strained since the day he had stranded Adam and her in the blizzard. But he had stopped by a few times. She always discreetly inquired after Adam's health. Josh sometimes grumbled about his brother's lack of cheer, but he assured her he wasn't sick and that their ranch was prospering.

As long as Cammie kept busy—something that was easy to do these days—she could harness her desire for Adam's company. It wasn't going away as she hoped it would, but neither did it interfere with her efficiently running her ranch. The only times she really suffered was at night, just before she drifted off to sleep and her iron grip on her thoughts relaxed . . . and those times when she woke up from a deliciously erotic dream.

Cammie judged she had three options. She could throw away her independence and tell Adam she had changed her mind about marrying him. She could abandon her belief that this was where her ranch was meant to be—sell her land and move away; hoping the old adage 'out of sight, out of mind' was true. Or she could go on as she was. Every time she seriously contemplated doing either of the first two, a black mood descended upon her, so she chose to do the third.

Another morning dawned sunny and comfortably warm. Before going out to work her horses, Cammie decided inasmuch as she was down to her last pair of drawers, it was time to stop putting off doing the laundry piled up in the basket in her bedroom.

Before fixing her breakfast, she set water on the stove to boil. As she scrubbed then rinsed her clothes, Cammie promised herself one of the first things she would do when she had a larger home built was hire a maid to take care of the laundry and all the other domestic chores she loathed doing but felt uncomfortable asking one of her hired hands to do.

The only good thing about spending the morning doing laundry was that Cammie knew she wouldn't have to do it again for a while. It was with considerable satisfaction that she hung the last garment on the line behind the house to dry.

Cammie spent the rest of the day with her horses, and her mood was buoyant when she strode into the house to clean up for supper. Mr. Fry knocked on the door, delivering the plate of food he now habitually prepared for her. She thanked him, then set the plate on the table.

She had used all the water in the house for the laundry. Needing some for tea and doing the dishes, Cammie picked up a bucket and headed for the pump. What she saw when she stepped out the back door stopped her in her tracks.

Her once clean laundry was now smeared with streaks of brown. For a moment she could do nothing but stare. When she recovered herself enough to approach the clothesline, one sniff of the air revealed manure, not dirt, had been used to soil her clothing.

"He wouldn't do something like this," she protested when Adam's name immediately came to mind. She probed her thoughts for someone else to blame, but try as she might, no name came to mind.

All the evidence pointed to Adam. Cammie knew he still wanted her out of his valley, and this was exactly the kind of smelly trick he had used before to try to persuade her to sell. She knew he had promised not to do this sort of thing again after she had inadvertently shot him—and she didn't want to believe he was up to his old tricks—but he was the only suspect she had. No one else had motive, and she already knew him capable of sneaking over unseen.

However, before Cammie believed it of Adam, she intended to question every one of her men. Hopefully one of them had seen someone else lurking about the ranch, but she was afraid it was him.

Cammie was angry, but more than that she was sad. After all they had been through, what he had done was cruel.

Returning to the house, Cammie composed herself before she faced her men. When she was calm, she called them to the back of the house. The sight of her manure-stained laundry instantly evoked their outrage.

"Did anyone see anybody who shouldn't have been here on the ranch today?" Cammie asked.

Every man searched his memory and came up with the same answer. "No.

Cammie knew they hadn't had a single visitor, and she trusted her men, but she felt compelled to ask, "Are you certain?"

"Yes, ma'am," each man responded in turn.

The next question she asked nearly choked her, but she pushed it passed her lips. "Did anyone see Adam Carrigan or his horse or boat on this side of the river today?"

Again their answers were no, but the expressions on some of the men's faces revealed they harbored the same suspicion she did.

Cammie expelled a weary breath. "Thank you. If anyone remembers something later, please inform me immediately. In the meantime I'd like everyone to keep a sharp eye out."

Eighteen

By the time Cammie finished rewashing her laundry, she was still undecided whether or not to confront Adam about it. No one saw him commit the deed, but no one had seen him luring the skunks into her house day after day. She tried to find reasons to convince herself it could be someone else, but with no success. Logic said it had to be him.

Though she remained opposed to a direct confrontation, what Cammie did—after several days of contemplating the matter—was send Elias Rutley across the river with a note for Adam. It simply said: *Please remember your promise to stay on your side of the river. Cammie.*

Cammie did her best to put the incident out of her mind and concentrate on her work. She nearly had succeeded in doing so, when a few days later, she was awakened before dawn by a frantic pounding on her front door.

"Miss Kendall, wake up! The horses are gone!" Carl Daley yelled.

Cammie jumped out of bed so fast, she sent Lucretia flying off the covers. "*What!* The horses are gone?" she cried.

Mr. Daley's cheeks bloomed bright red at the sight of her with her hair down and in her nightclothes, but he wasted no time explaining. "Something woke me up. I don't know what. I was trying to go back to sleep, and a funny feeling came over me, so I got up and went to check on the horses. All the stalls were empty, the corral gates were open, and there's not a horse in sight. I didn't check the pasture fences, but I got a feeling when I do, I'll find someone has been messing with them during the night, too. I ran back to wake the other men, then came here to get you."

"I'll meet you at the east corral in five minutes." Slamming the front door, Cammie raced to her bedroom and yanked on her clothes.

"If anything has happened to one of my horses, I'll strangle the villain with my bare hands," she vowed as she shoved her feet into her boots. Sprinting across the yard, Cammie met Mr. Daley and the rest of her men a minute ahead of schedule.

"I know it's still dark, and we don't have any horses to ride, but we'll start the search immediately. Light lanterns, take a rope, and work in pairs. As soon as you find a horse trained for riding, bring it back, saddle up, and resume the search on horseback. If you find any injured animals, don't move them unless you're sure it won't cause further injury. Come get me as soon as possible, and I'll assess what should be done. I'll be searching south along the river if you need me."

It took all day and half of the next to round up her horses, but eventually they found every one. Cammie was relieved to discover that none of them had suffered any harm except for a few scratches. When she had reassured herself of their health and assigned men to repair the damage done to the pasture fences, Cammie turned her thoughts to the perpetrator of the crime.

The fact that none of her horses had been stolen or injured convinced her she knew who was responsible. She might be able to overlook an assault upon her clothing, but this time

Adam had gone too far. She didn't care how badly he wanted her out of his valley, he was going to be stopped. If that meant calling in the sheriff and pressing charges, so be it.

Saddling Bliss, Cammie headed for the Carrigan ranch.

"What are you doing here?" Adam's eyes widened with dismay when he opened his door and found her standing on his porch.

Ignoring his startled look, Cammie tersely informed him, "This isn't a joke anymore."

"What isn't a joke?"

"You know very well why I'm here," she insisted.

"No, I don't."

"Don't play innocent with me!"

He raked his fingers through his hair. "I'm not playing anything."

"Where were you two nights ago?" she grilled.

"Camping up in the canyon. I just got back not more than an hour ago."

"Can you produce witnesses?"

"No—I went alone."

Her eyes narrowed. "Isn't that convenient."

"I wish you'd tell me what the hell you're talking about because I don't have the slightest idea."

Cammie remained unconvinced. "I thought we agreed you would stay on your side of the river and I would stay on mine."

"We did, which is why I'm gonna ask you again: What are you doing here?"

She glared at him. "I'm here to stop you."

"From doing what?" he demanded.

"Two nights ago you sneaked over to my ranch and ran

off my horses! A week before that you smeared manure into my laundry while it hung on the line!"

His jaw dropped and his expression changed from vexed to concerned. "So that's what your note was about."

"Yes!"

"It wasn't me."

Cammie's gaze met his. In it she read nothing but utter sincerity. The anger filling her breast slowly began to drain, leaving a void in its place. "Then who was it?" she mumbled.

"I don't know, but I reckon you oughta get the sheriff out here right away to find out."

"You're serious, aren't you?"

His lips forming a grim line, Adam nodded. "I know I'm guilty of doing a lot of things to you, but that was a long time ago. I swear it wasn't me—which means someone else is trying to drive you off your ranch. I want to know who."

"Why?"

"There's a big difference between mischief and malice. By my reckoning what's happening now falls into the second category. I don't like it. We don't know how far this fella will go." His brow furled. "I won't lie and pretend I wouldn't be more comfortable if you were gone from my valley, but whether you go or stay oughta be your decision."

Adam was right—these two recent raids on her ranch had a different feel to them than the pranks he had played. There was also the fact *he* was the one who had brought up contacting the sheriff. It made no sense for him to make the suggestion if he was guilty.

The more she came to believe him, the more nervous Cammie felt. Tangled as her feelings were for Adam, she had never judged him evil. Once she had considered him her friend. She had given herself to him three times and loved every minute of it. She had even entertained notions of marrying the man. Cammie was afraid she believed him because she wanted to believe him.

Adam was watching her, his eyes fathomless pools of dark blue. When Cammie had arrived at the Carrigan ranch, her fury had shielded her from the too potent attraction she felt for the man standing before her. Now she was all too aware of his thick russet hair, mesmerizing blue eyes, inviting lips, wide shoulders . . . Cammie jerked her gaze away when it drifted below his belt.

Rather than wane during their long separation, her passion for him had bottled itself up. The sight, sound, and scent of him uncorked the bottle. Her mouth went dry. Her heart thudded against her ribs. Every inch of her skin pleaded for his caress.

Cammie had no idea what Adam was feeling for her—or if he felt anything at all—but she knew *she* had to get away.

"Well, if you're not at fault, I guess I have no business here." She took a quick step back. "I apologize for violating the terms of our agreement. I won't do it again without just cause."

"You'll contact the sheriff?" he queried. There was a husky tinge to his voice, and he looked as though he was about to add something more, but he didn't.

"Yes. I'm going to town on Friday. I'll do it then."

"Have you thought about posting a night watchman?"

"My men are taking turns sleeping in the main barns."

"That's smart." He tucked his hands behind his back. "I'll keep my eyes open for anybody acting peculiar and order my men to do the same."

Cammie took another retreating step. "Thank you."

"If anybody sees anything, I'll send a note."

"Yes." Backing down the porch steps, she untied Bliss's

reins from the hitching post and mounted. "If I need to communicate with you, rather than ride over, I'll do the same."

"I reckon that's wise."

Cammie drew a deep shuddery breath, shoving down the surge of desire rising in her bosom. "Goodbye."

"Goodbye," Adam gruffly replied.

Adam stood on the porch watching Cammie ride away, fighting the urge to call her back. It wasn't like he hadn't thought of her at all since the last time they were together. He thought about her at least ten times every day. But seeing her—having her so close he could reach out and grab her—had just about undone him. She was even more beautiful than he remembered. The fiery gleam in her eyes more keen. Her body more enticing.

And as if all those things weren't plenty to upset him, now someone was causing trouble at her ranch. Considering the things he had done when Cammie first moved here, he knew it was hypocritical of him to want to hunt down the son of a bitch and hang him from the nearest tree, but that was exactly what he felt like doing.

She'd worked damn hard to make her ranch a success. He'd never known anyone who worked harder. And she knew horses. He hadn't seen her new crop of foals, but just about everybody else in the territory had. The men who had bought horses from her last year swore they were the best cow ponies they'd ever owned. A couple claimed she taught her horses to read their riders' minds. He'd never seen anybody move to an area and build a first-class reputation as quick. Cammie was doing exactly what she wanted. Nobody had a right to take that away from her.

Adam wondered who wanted to. As far as he knew, he was

the only one who had anything to gain if she sold out. It was prime land she owned, but when she did sell, she couldn't sell it to anybody but him. Everybody knew that. Higgins had never kept the terms of his contract with her a secret.

Adam scowled. No matter which way he added up the facts, he kept coming up with the same answer. He'd played tricks on her before. He'd told anyone who would listen that he wanted her out of his valley. He was the only one who would gain if she left. It was little wonder she thought him to blame. If he was in her boots, he would have jumped to exactly the same conclusion. That was why her accusations hadn't made him angry. They'd hurt his feelings. But she'd believed him when he'd said it wasn't him, and that had meant a lot to him.

He tried to remember what his life had been like before Cammie had moved to his valley. When he slept all night. When he woke up every morning, knowing exactly what he thought and how he felt and why. When the only person he ever worried about was Josh. When life was simple. Those days were shrouded in a haze.

Adam knew it wasn't any of his business, and the less he was involved in Cammie's life the better it would be for him—but he just couldn't stay out of it. The laundry and the horses might just be a couple of isolated incidents, but if someone was out to cause serious harm, he wanted him stopped. He had to do something to help her.

Trouble was, there wasn't much he could do from his side of the river. But he could contact the sheriff for her. He hadn't been planning to go to town until next week, but he decided to go today. It wasn't much, but it was better than doing nothing.

* * *

"Good afternoon," Cammie greeted the law officer she found standing on her porch when she returned from her ride on Bliss.

"Afternoon, Miss Kendall. Adam Carrigan said you've been having some trouble out here."

Cammie stiffened. Why had Adam contacted the sheriff when he knew she was going to do so on Friday? Was he just trying to be helpful or did he have another, less noble reason? Cammie hated herself for being so suspicious, but she possessed too prudent a nature to completely ignore the whisperings in her head. "Yes, there has been some trouble," she replied staidly.

"Why don't you tell me all about it?"

It was a reasonable request, and the man was the sheriff. Even if he was good friends with Adam, Cammie could see no harm in telling him everything she knew. She didn't believe Adam guilty of anything, but she wasn't ready to unconditionally commit to the belief he wasn't. Proceeding with caution was the sensible approach. "I see Mr. Fry has already brought you a cup of coffee. Would you like to come into the house to drink it?" she asked.

"Sure."

Cammie led the way into the house, inviting the sheriff to sit in the overstuffed chair and she positioned herself on the settee. "What did Mr. Carrigan tell you?"

"He said someone wrecked your laundry with manure and let your horses out. He didn't know many of the particulars."

Filling in the exact times, dates, and details, Cammie calmly answered the sheriff's questions about the incidents. He dutifully recorded the information she gave him in his notebook.

The sheriff was a pleasant man. His questioning was thorough and his manner businesslike. Cammie read both intelligence and concern in his eyes.

"Well, I guess I have only one more question before I take a look around and ask your men a few questions." He took a sip of coffee. "You have any idea who might be out to get you?"

Cammie hesitated a moment before replying. "No."

The sheriff eyed her over the brim of his cup. "You don't look too positive about that answer."

Focusing her gaze on the toes of her boots, Cammie contemplated how much, if anything, she should say. She decided to tell the truth. "That's because my only suspect is the man who sent you here, and I don't really think he's responsible."

"Adam Carrigan isn't our man," the sheriff confidently assured her.

Cammie nodded in agreement but found herself asking, "Why do you say that?"

"Two reasons. I've known him too long to believe any differently, and he's too worried about you for it to be him." He drained the last of his coffee. "Oh, I know all about the little war you two were waging when you first moved here. Whole county knows. But Adam says that's all behind you. No reason for me not to believe him, is there?"

"No."

"Didn't reckon so." Rising to his feet, he handed her his empty cup. "I best be getting the rest of my evidence gathered and head off. I'll let myself out."

Despite his offer, Cammie walked him to the door. "Thank you for your prompt attention to this matter."

"Just doing my job. To be honest with you, I don't know how much good my coming here will do. Unless I find some clue to the culprit's identity when I take a look around the place, there's not much to go on. Might just have to be satisfied knowing no hurt was done you couldn't set back to rights."

The sheriff uncovered nothing.

Two days later Mr. Fry found rocks jammed into the well pump. It had to be completely dismantled. Cammie paid a visit to the sheriff's office when she went to town to buy new parts to replace those that were damaged beyond repair. The sheriff rode back to the ranch with her, but there were still no clues leading to the identity of the villain.

A few more days passed and Mr. Woodrow discovered several slashed bridles in the tack shed. The vandalism was subtle, done so the cuts wouldn't break completely through the leather strips until a rider pulled hard on the reins. A less observant man might not have noticed until it was too late.

The next Monday, Steven Stewart found the coup filled with dead chickens. When the sheriff came to investigate, he confirmed Cammie's suspicions that their feed had been poisoned.

Cammie seethed with frustration. After Benjamin Fry had discovered the damage to the pump, she had set up two-man patrols to guard the grounds day and night. In addition to the men already sleeping in the main barns, she assigned a man to every stallion barn as well.

All her precautions didn't seem to make any difference. Nothing ever happened where she had a man stationed, and they couldn't keep every inch of the ranch under surveillance at all times.

The niggling suspicions she had harbored concerning Adam dwindled with each new onslaught. She now knew with absolute certainty he couldn't be behind the attacks. She refused to believe she could misjudge any man she knew as intimately as Adam that badly.

Cammie knew Josh was keeping Adam apprised of the situation. He carried offers of help from his older brother every time he came to see how she was faring. Judging she was already doing all that could be done, Cammie politely refused them, but knowing Adam was concerned lightened her spirits a little. So did knowing he was just across the river should she really need him.

No one was getting much sleep and even less work was getting done. Cammie considered hiring more men, but logic told her she would have to hire a small army to have a man every place at all times. Besides, she was afraid to trust anyone she didn't know well.

She was beginning to be afraid to trust her own men. She knew her manner could sometimes be abrasive. Had she inadvertently offended one of them without knowing it? So much so he was bent on revenge? One of her own men undeniably had more opportunity than anyone else would. And it would explain why no one had seen anything out of the ordinary. But no matter how many nights she lay awake, Cammie couldn't recall any encounter worthy of the ire she was receiving. She would swear her men respected her. She would also swear they were as upset as she was about what was happening.

As abruptly as the attacks had started, they suddenly ceased. One week passed, then two. When no new assaults occurred in the ensuing days, Cammie began to relax a little.

A full month passed without incident. It bothered Cammie that they hadn't caught the man responsible, but she was grateful the siege appeared to be over.

With a man sleeping in the barns, her horses were safe, and that was what was most important to her. Everyone continued to remain alert, but Cammie no longer felt it necessary to keep up the constant patrols. She gradually reduced them, and when no havoc befell the ranch as a result, eventually stopped them altogether.

Nineteen

Adam paced the shore on his side of the river, his hands balled into fists. He was going mad with worry, and there wasn't a damn thing he could do about it. She wouldn't let him help, and he felt compelled to respect her wishes.

More than once he'd been tempted to ride over to her ranch with a band of his men and insist she accept his assistance. Independence was an admirable trait, but there were times even the most self-sufficient person could use a helping hand. He wouldn't think less of her, and neither would anyone else. Neighbors were supposed to look out for each other. It was the unspoken law of the West. The land could never have been settled without it.

However, much as he would like to believe otherwise, Adam knew Cammie wasn't just being mule-headed. It wasn't help in general—she regularly consulted the sheriff—but his help in particular she rejected. She regarded him as a greater danger to her well-being than the person behind the raids against her ranch.

He couldn't honestly argue he wasn't. Even armed with the best intentions in the world, he couldn't seem to keep his hands off of her. He was worse than a drunk with a bottle of whiskey in his hands—only it was Cammie Kendall who enticed him to abandon common sense and besotted his mind. She was smart to keep him at arm's length.

It didn't soothe Adam's conscience one whit knowing every time they had lain together, her desire for him had been as great as his for her. Or that after months of separation, he saw his persistent passion reflected in her eyes the day she rode over to accuse him of the first two attacks. What it did do was make it that much harder to resist her more than abundant charms.

She had reduced him to a smitten, lust-crazed, sad excuse for a rational man—and the worst of it was, he was absolutely sure she was as unhappy about it as he was. Adam wished he didn't care what happened to her, but he did.

As he continued to gaze across the river, Adam's fists clenched even tighter. There was another reason besides her justifiable fear they might succumb to temptation, Cammie wouldn't accept his help. Every time he thought about it, it felt like someone had stabbed a knife in his gut and was twisting the hilt.

He'd been certain he'd convinced her he didn't have anything to do with these new assaults upon her ranch but he'd been wrong. In the course of conducting his own inquiries, he'd discovered a private detective was quietly asking questions all over town about him and Josh. When Adam had confronted the man, he'd refused to tell him who had hired him, but it didn't take a genius to figure out who or why.

Regardless of what Cammie might be pretending to Josh and the sheriff, it was painfully obvious that she didn't believe him.

Adam tried not to let her lack of faith get to him, but it did. He could accept her refusal to take him for a husband, because he knew she was rejecting the notion of marriage more than him—and he was as eager to avoid the depressing consequences of that state as she. But this was different. It was a personal spurning of his integrity. He may have behaved badly last summer, but the mischief he had made had been a temporary lapse of good judgment. No one had been hurt except him.

Besides, that was before they'd made love. That had changed everything between them. Except for a couple of glaring incidents when carnality had overwhelmed self-restraint, he'd been a perfect gentleman since, . . . and he'd never made love to her purposefully, it'd just happened. Too, he'd swear on a stack of Bibles she was as willing a participant as he. It didn't make sense to him for a woman to want to make love to a man she didn't trust. Then, women never did make sense to him. There was no predicting what they would do. Wasn't that the reason he'd avoided falling in love with them all these years?

Adam commanded his thoughts away from his confusion concerning her feelings for him and back to his overriding worry: keeping Cammie and her ranch safe. No matter what she thought of him or why, his regard for her made it impossible for him to accept her troubles as none of his concern.

Since she didn't want him or his men on her side of the river, he had to settle for only doing things he could accomplish from his side. He organized patrols of the riverbank. Through the sheriff and Josh, he was keeping a sharp eye on the progress of the investigation. At night he lay awake trying to figure out a pattern and who might have a motive. These were small things and not proving effective, but it was better than doing nothing.

Adam also knew by way of Josh and the sheriff the precautions Cammie was taking, and though they were exactly what he would be doing in her place, her efforts weren't stopping the trouble either. The problem was with the size and isolated location of the ranch and ample cover of trees. A lone man, or even two or three, watching the movements of her men could come and go without anyone being the wiser. He'd done it himself more times than he cared to remember.

With the stream of visitors who came to check out her horses, there were too many tracks to distinguish one set from another without asking to inspect the hooves of every horse in the territory. More than a few people would take offense at the notion that they were under suspicion just because they'd called at the ranch. He was a savvy enough businessman to know better than to even suggest she alienate her present and future customers in hopes of catching the culprit, especially when he didn't even know if it would work. For all he knew, one of her own men was responsible.

News of each new attack increased Adam's frustration and weakened his determination to stay on his side of the river. Each day he recited a long list of excellent reasons why he should continue to keep his distance, but one thought outweighed them all. He might not be able to stop the attacks, but he could make certain nothing happened to Cammie. Nothing was more important to him.

Adam's resolve to behave sensibly was near its breaking point when a day passed and then another with no bad news from across the river. Two days became three, then four, then a week.

He remained on edge, but after several uneventful weeks, he was able to worry less and focus most of his energy on running his own ranch.

Life was back to normal—or as close to normal as Adam deemed it ever would be with Cammie Kendall living across the river from him—when he answered a knock on his front door one afternoon late in July to find an expensive buggy in his yard and a younger version of Josh and himself standing on his porch. The resemblance was so startling, that for a few minutes both men just stared at each other.

The stranger was the first to speak. "Are you Adam or Joshua Carrigan?"

"Adam. I know I don't know you, but I get the feeling I should."

"My name is Samuel Carrigan." The man held out his hand and Adam shook it.

Adam supposed there might be branches of the family tree he knew nothing about, but it seemed odd his father had never mentioned them. His brow knit. "I assume we're relatives?"

"Yes—but what I have to tell you may come as a shock. May I come in?"

"Sure." Adam stepped out of the doorway and led the way to the parlor. "I apologize for my manners. It's just you look just like—"

"You." Sam supplied the last word. "I was prepared for a family resemblance, but this is uncanny."

"Who are you?"

"You might want to sit down before I tell you. When I learned of your existence, I certainly needed a chair."

Adam sat. "Okay."

Sam did the same before announcing, "I'm your younger brother."

Adam's jaw dropped. "What?"

"I'm the youngest son of Barnett and Margaret Carrigan. I wish there was a better way to tell a person this sort of news, but if there is, I don't know it."

A thousand questions filled Adam's head. He believed him—how could he not when looking at Samuel's face was almost like looking into a mirror? Adam had always wondered what had become of his mother. Now he knew. She had been living back East with a brother neither his father,

Josh, nor he knew existed. Did she love this son better than her first two? Why had she kept Sam a secret from them, and apparently them a secret from him? How could she? Adam sat rigidly in his chair, his hands gripping its upholstered arms. "Is she still alive?" he dully asked.

"No. I learned of you and Joshua during the reading of her will. She divided her estate equally between her three sons, which is one of the reasons I'm here. I have the legal papers in my bag in the buggy. The other reason is because I would like to get to know my brothers. But I'll understand if you would rather not."

His mother was dead. The news neither shocked nor saddened Adam. She had been dead to him for twenty-eight years. The rest of what Sam said barely registered. "When?"

"When what?"

"When did she die?"

"A year ago last spring. I set out to find you immediately, but I ran into some trouble when I tried to find you in Wyoming, which was where I initially believed you to be."

"What kinda trouble?"

"It's a long, complicated story. I mentioned it only to explain the delay." A wry grin curved Sam's lips. "In the end I had to resort to hiring a private detective."

Adam sat up taller. "*You* hired the detective who has been asking about me, not Cammie?"

"Who is Cammie?" Sam queried.

"That's another long story, and right now I'm more interested in what you've gotta say," Adam prompted.

"I hired a man named Richard Dover," Sam supplied a name.

"That's the one."

"You look relieved."

Adam nodded.

"I hope my hiring him didn't cause any problems for you or this Cammie," Sam remarked.

Adam knew it was ridiculous to feel so elated that it hadn't been Cammie who hired the detective after all. It didn't change a thing between them. But he had never been so glad to be mistaken in all his life. However, his feelings for Cammie were a private matter, and he wasn't ready to discuss them with anybody. Besides, facing a full-grown brother who was a stranger and all the long-avoided emotions his arrival stirred up was more than enough for a man to deal with. He cleared his throat. "I jumped to the wrong conclusion, but that's my fault, not yours. As far as I know, Cammie doesn't know anything about Dover," Adam assured him.

"It's kind of you to shoulder the blame, but please accept my apology and extend it to the lady as well should you discover I have discomfited her in any way."

Adam changed the subject. "Why don't you tell me about yourself?"

Sam signaled his willingness with a bob of his head, but politely inquired, "Is Joshua around?"

"Last I saw him, he was out in the barn grooming his horse."

"I don't mean to be impatient, but I'd like to meet him if I may. That way I can tell you both everything you want to know at the same time. I'd also like to ask a few questions myself, with your permission, of course."

Rising to his feet, Adam said, "You stay here and make yourself comfortable. I'll go get him."

Leaving his new brother, Adam strode out of the parlor, through the kitchen, and out the back door. Once outside he slackened his pace. He didn't know how he felt about finding Samuel on his doorstep, but it wasn't happy. And how the hell was he suppose to break the news to Josh?

Adam didn't have anything against his newfound brother. He seemed a nice enough sort. It sounded as though he'd gone to a lot of effort to make sure they got their inheritance, and that said something about his character. Adam just didn't know if he was ready to face the answer to the question that had haunted him since he was seven years old: *Why had his mother run out on them?* After all these years he'd never been able to come close to forgiving her. He suddenly felt seven years old again. His eyes filled with tears and he furiously blinked them back.

When he reached the barn, it was empty. Adam sighed with relief. He needed to have a few extra minutes to compose himself. The truth was waiting for him in the parlor, and he couldn't run away from it, but he didn't mind delaying the moment of reckoning.

"Hey, Adam, I thought you said you were going up to the house to work on the ranch books this afternoon," Josh hailed when he rounded the corner of the barn.

"We have company." Adam gravely informed him.

"Who?"

Adam opened his mouth to reply, then clamped it closed again. "I'll let him introduce himself."

"Why? Something wrong?" Josh questioned as the two brothers walked side by side toward the house. He eyed Adam's face. "You look a little pale. It's not bad news, is it?"

"No, but I reckon you oughta prepare yourself for a helluva shock."

"What kinda shock?"

Adam rubbed the back of his neck. "If I knew how to get the words out, I'd come right out and tell you, wouldn't I? You'll know what I mean as soon as you step foot in the parlor."

When Josh entered the parlor, Sam was already on his feet.

Josh stood dumbstruck in the doorway. Adam glanced between the two brothers. Sam favored Josh even more than he did Adam—so much so with the two of them standing in the same room, they could pass themselves off as twins. He had a good idea what Josh was feeling right now, and he thought it best to let him have a minute or two to get over it.

"Did you tell him who I am?" Sam queried.

"No," Adam admitted.

"I didn't think so. I can see now that I probably should have written a letter announcing my arrival in advance."

Josh kept staring at the stranger. "If I didn't know better, I'd swear—"

"He's our brother." Adam finished the sentence for him. "That's exactly who he is. Samuel Carrigan meet Joshua Carrigan."

The two men shook hands.

"I'm pleased to finally meet you, Joshua." Sam smiled earnestly.

Josh returned the smile. "I go by Josh."

"And I, Sam."

Josh continued to grin. "Pleased to meet you, Sam. Have a seat, and tell me where you come from."

All three brothers sat. Josh leaned forward, his eyes dancing with curiosity. Sam's posture was formal but congenial. Adam sat stiffly, his fingers splayed on his thighs.

"Originally I'm from New York City," Sam said. "That's where I was born, raised, and built my business. More recently I've been residing in Wyoming with my wife's grandmother."

"A married man, huh? Adam and I are both bachelors."

"Yes, I know."

"How? Adam and I didn't even know we had another

brother. This whole thing is mighty strange. If you weren't such a handsome devil, I'd never believe it."

Sam chuckled. "As I've already told Adam, I had to hire a private detective to find you. He's the one who supplied me with my current information. Our mother—or rather her will and diaries—supplied what I know about you when you were children."

"She's dead, is she?" Josh received the news with little show of emotion.

"Yes."

"I don't remember anything about her except that she was pretty, and even that I'm not sure if I'm remembering or it's because of the portrait of her Pa kept on his bureau till the day he died. I sure would like to know what she was like."

Josh was accepting the arrival of a new brother into their lives with his usual happy-go-lucky resilience. Adam could tell that he and Sam were already hitting it off and was glad for them. Adam wished he could do the same, but he couldn't. He could understand Josh's curiosity about their mother, but he couldn't handle hearing about her—leastways, not yet.

"I'd rather hear about Sam," Adam interrupted. "How long have you been married?"

"About a year. My wife Ella and daughter Josephine are staying at the International Hotel in Helena."

"You oughta have brought them out to the ranch with you," Josh said.

"I wasn't sure what kind of reception I'd get, so I thought it best I come alone," Sam explained.

"Well, you'll just have to go back to town and fetch them. Can't have family staying in a hotel. We've plenty of room upstairs."

Sam glanced at Adam.

Adam smiled wanly.

"We don't wish to impose," Sam said.

"Hell, if I knew I had a brother in New York City, I'd have been there imposing on your hospitality years ago. Adam, too. Wouldn't we, Adam?"

Adam made a wry face at Josh. "I know you would."

"We really are quite comfortable where we are," Sam assured them.

"Adam, tell him he and his family have gotta stay with us."

"Josh is right. You oughta stay here," Adam agreed.

"As I said before, I don't wish to impose." Sam addressed his words to Adam. His voice was even and devoid of censure. "I understand my showing up on your doorstep unannounced is not something a person can take in stride. It took me months to come to terms with the fact I had a father and two older brothers. I am not here to disrupt your lives. We grew up strangers. You may prefer we stay that way. In fact, if it is your desire I do so, I can give the necessary legal papers to you now and leave immediately. Everything is in order, and you will have no difficulty transferring the money owed you to your accounts. When you feel you're ready, and I fully realize that may be never, you can contact me."

Adam knew he hadn't greeted his brother with open arms, but Sam's speech made him sit up and take notice of the effect of his reticence. He didn't even know why he was behaving the way he was, and he had no notion what to say to make Sam understand, but he tried. "You're right it will take some getting used to, but that doesn't mean I want you to leave. I don't," Adam stated sincerely. "I already like you, and I hardly know you. I'd like to get to know you better. Too many years have passed with us living under separate roofs. . . . As for the money, I don't want it."

"But it's rightfully yours," Sam protested.

Adam shook his head. "No. When our mother left, she stopped being my mother. She couldn't be bothered with me when she was alive. I don't want to accept anything from her now."

"The choice is yours, of course, but it's a considerable sum."

Adam shrugged. "If you want us to get along, don't try to force it on me."

"I won't," Sam pledged.

"Good. Then it's settled. You'll spend the night with us and tomorrow you'll return to town to fetch your wife and child."

"Adam, I know you wish to be hospitable, and I appreciate your offer, but I think you would be more comfortable if we remained in town."

Adam looked him squarely in the eye. "No. We've gotta lot of catching up to do, and I for one don't have time to be riding back and forth to town every few days."

Sam exchanged a questioning glance with Josh. Josh nodded yes.

"If you're certain."

"Yes, I'm certain—and the two of you can stop looking at me like I'm about to jump out of my skin. I'm fine. I just haven't gotten over the surprise, that's all. If you'll excuse me, I have a couple of things to tend in the barn."

By supper time Adam felt better prepared to face his brother. His feelings were still raw, but spending time alone in the barn had helped him collect his thoughts.

Sam was his brother. He deserved to be treated like a member of the family. Their father would have wanted him to be welcomed with open arms. Adam wanted to do the same. What he didn't welcome was having painful old memories stirred up.

The past was the past, and he had always found the best way to deal with it was *not* to deal with it. Now he was staring it in the eye, and he was scared and angry all over again. This afternoon, his mother's betrayal stung like a fresh wound. Hammering on the wagon rack he'd just repaired hadn't made the feelings go away, but the physical exertion had dissipated some of the tension knotting his muscles.

When he stepped into the dining room from the kitchen, Josh and Sam were entering from the parlor. The two men were engaged in animated conversation.

Adam took a deep breath and cheerfully commented, "I hope you two are hungry, because Rex has a pot of stew bubbling on the stove."

"I'm famished," Josh declared. "How about you, Sam?"

"The stew smells delicious," Sam complimented.

"Sam's been telling me all about his life in New York. Sounds luxurious, but I sure am glad we were raised out here. I know we got to have more fun."

"The West is definitely less restrictive than the East," Sam agreed. "It's one of the reasons my wife and I have decided we want to raise our family here."

Rex carried in a tureen of stew and a plate of biscuits. The brothers seated themselves at the table and began passing around the food.

Determined to make the effort to be sociable, Adam picked up the conversation where they had left off. "Is your wife also from New York?"

"No, she was born and raised in Wyoming on a ranch outside a little town called Heaven. I met her when I was looking for you and Josh."

"And, oh what a meeting," Josh chortled. "Her sisters bonked him over the head, hogtied him, then held him prisoner till the sheriff shot him to convince him to marry her."

Adam's eyes widened.

"Josh just gave you the short version of the long story," Sam laughed. "There's no denying our courtship was highly unconventional, but I assure you, I'm a very happily married man. Ella is the best thing that ever happened to me, with the possible exception of Josie, who ties for the honor."

"You sound like a proud father," Adam observed.

Sam beamed. "Ella says I'm going to spoil our daughter, but I don't care. A father has a right to spoil his little girl."

"I'm gonna go to town tomorrow with him to fetch them," Josh said. "You want to come along, Adam?"

Adam agreed, and the rest of the meal passed in pleasant conversation. Josh and Sam were already getting along as if they had known each other for years. Adam was jealous of Josh's ability to take everything life threw him in stride, but he didn't resent him for it. He just wished he'd teach him how to do the same.

Conspicuously absent from their table conversation was any mention of their mother. Adam knew he was the reason she wasn't mentioned, and though he disliked the notion they had been discussing him in his absence, he appreciated both men's restraint.

The three brothers talked long into the night, drinking coffee laced with brandy while sharing stories of their boyhoods, their father, the cattle business, Sam's rise of fortune on Wall Street. Just as he had during supper, Sam carefully sidestepped any mention of Margaret Carrigan.

Eventually the lateness of the hour forced them to retire.

Adam was feeling much better than he had when Sam first delivered the news he was their brother. He still hadn't gotten over the shock, but he found it impossible not to like him, and he was genuinely looking forward to meeting Sam's wife and daughter. Sam couldn't say enough nice things about them, and that was more than a little amazing considering what his wife's family had put him through. Ella Carrigan must be quite a woman to make a man willing to forgive having his liberty snatched away.

A knock at his bedroom door interrupted Adam's thoughts. He opened it to find Sam wearing a serious expression and holding a stack of small leather-bound books.

"I want to give these to you," he stated.

"What are they?"

"Our mother's diaries."

Adam took a quick step back. "I don't want them."

Sam's eyes met his. "I know—but I think you should read them anyway. All my life she told me my father had died before I was born. When I found out the truth, I was furious. I'll never approve of what she did, but her diaries helped me understand. Maybe they'll do the same for you . . ."

Though he appreciated Sam's good intentions, Adam continued to look at the diaries as if they were demons. "Why not give them to Josh first?"

"You need them more."

"But—"

Sam transferred the diaries from his hands to Adam's. "Don't read them unless you want to. I just thought you should have them, so when you are ready to know, you can approach the matter in your own way and time. I won't mention her to you again."

Adam silently watched Sam turn on his heels and walk back to his room. Whatever else he thought about his mother, she had raised his youngest brother to be a fine man.

Closing his bedroom door, Adam carried the diaries to his

bedside table. He sat on the edge of his bed, rubbing the palms of his hands together, staring at them.

He started to reach for the diary on top of the stack, then pulled his hand back. Tomorrow would be soon enough to start reading them. Tomorrow or perhaps the next day. After all these years, what was the hurry? It was already late, and they planned to leave for Helena at the crack of dawn. Dousing the light, Adam crawled under his sheets.

"Ella, Josie—I've brought guests," Sam called out as he ushered his brothers into his hotel suite. A moment later a lovely dark-haired woman cradling a baby in her arms stepped out of the bedroom.

"From the sound of your voice and the smile on your face, I assume your meeting with your brothers went well." Ella welcomed her husband with a kiss on the cheek and handed the baby into his waiting arms before turning her full attention to their guests.

"Ella, I'd like you to meet my brothers, Adam and Josh," Sam introduced them.

"I'm very pleased to meet you." Ella offered her hand.

"They've invited us to stay out at the ranch with them."

"That's wonderful." She smiled warmly at her husband, her hazel eyes shining, then turned back to his brothers. "Thank you both for your hospitality."

"Our pleasure." Josh flourished a bow. "Sam, are you sure all her sisters already got themselves hitched? If I could find myself a wife as pretty as this, I might seriously start thinking about settling down."

Ella blushed at the compliment.

"I'm afraid every one of them is taken," Sam said.

"I sure enjoyed hearing the tale of your courtship," Josh told Ella, his eyes twinkling merrily.

"Josh, the lady may prefer to avoid that subject," Adam chided.

"It's okay," Ella reassured him. "Sam and I have promised to always be absolutely forthright in our dealings with each other and the world. It makes life much less complicated. Besides, now that our courtship is all behind us, even I can see the humor in it—though I'd never want to go through anything like that again."

"If I knew the prize was you, I'd go through it again," Sam proclaimed. "A hundred times over."

Ella rolled her eyes, patting her husband's arm. "Since Josie was born, my husband has been suffering from a severe shortage of sleep, so you will have to excuse him. He used to be quite levelheaded."

Adam found Ella a charming woman and was inclined to agree with Sam that she was worth the misery he'd gone through. His brother was obviously extremely happy in his marriage. His entire face had lit up when his wife entered the room. Sam's pride in his daughter went without saying.

Adam and Josh spent the rest of the day showing their brother and his family the sights in and around Helena. They ate dinner at the Cosmopolitan Hotel, making plans to take a tour of the ranch when they returned home and to go on a picnic downriver the day after. When Adam learned Sam had previously made some profitable investments in a local mine and was contemplating making Helena his permanent home, he encouraged him to do so.

The next morning they rose early, so they could journey home during the coolest part of the day.

Adam was so busy getting to know his brother and his family during the next week, he barely had time to think, which suited him just fine. By concentrating on the pleasure of the moment, he could avoid thinking beyond it.

The diaries still sat unopened on his bedside table. Cammie still lived across the river. He knew he must deal with both, but he preferred to expend his energies on his brother's family.

The three men spent much of their time alone together, hunting, fishing, riding out to check on the cattle, but Adam found himself looking forward to the evenings as well.

It was unexpectedly pleasant having a woman living at the ranch, and even more pleasant to observe his brother's delight with his family. Ella didn't exaggerate when she said Sam spoiled their daughter. It never took more than a whimper to win a place in her father's arms. But who could blame him? Josie was an angel. Sam, Josh, and Adam took turns wrangling over who got to hold her. The only time her popularity waned was when her diaper needed changing or she awoke in the middle of the night. They generously shared Josie with her mother on these occasions.

Sam and his family had been with them a week and a half when Adam finally worked up the courage to open one of his mother's diaries. He had overheard Josh and Sam discussing their mother more than once, but they always changed the topic of conversation when he entered the room.

Almost as strong as his need to know the truth was his need to relieve his brothers of the burden his resistance imposed on them. He was a grown man, and it was time he faced the truth. Knowing why his mother had left him couldn't be worse than the years he'd spent smothering his sobs with his pillow so no one would know how badly he missed her.

* * *

Each night before turning out the light, Adam lay in bed reading the diaries. He told no one what he was doing, and appreciated Sam's willingness to respect his need for patience and privacy. Their father would have been proud to claim him as a son.

The diaries began a year before their parents had met and covered the years until their mother's death. His mother's words painted a portrait of a young woman deeply in love but filled with unrealistic expectations—especially concerning the life she would face in the West. She filled her diary with flowery phrases about the grand adventure upon which her handsome new husband had persuaded her to embark. Less than a month of living in Wyoming turned her effusive prose into tear-stained pages filled with despair.

She wrote of his father's love for their new life and how she had never seen him so happy, but mostly she wrote of her failings as a wife. She hated living in the wilderness, but because she didn't want to mar her husband's happiness, she kept her feelings hidden from him.

As a boy, Adam had believed his mother loved him with the same devotion he felt for her. It was why it had hurt so much when she left. Her diaries spoke of the same love he had once felt.

The closer Adam came to the date she had left, the harder he found it to force himself to keep reading. But he did.

Adam was surprised by how much his mother had anguished over the decision to leave her family. He remembered her as being cheerful right up to the day she was suddenly gone. One page she would resolve to be strong and happy for the sake of her husband and children. The next she would bemoan the loss of the comfortable life she had left behind, describing the texture of a silk glove or the refreshments served at a tea party in minute detail. Her diary went on like this not for months but for years. She was clearly a tormented woman.

What surprised him even more was reading the reason she had decided to leave her sons behind. She had left them behind because she couldn't bear to deprive their father of their companionship. She considered losing them just punishment for failing to love her husband enough to overcome her hatred of toil and isolation.

The more he read, the more Adam came to see how inaccurate both images were that he held of his mother. The laughing, contented mother of his early years was a facade. The coldhearted villainess who deserted her family without a thought for their welfare was equally false.

She had thought of them many times throughout the years. She felt deeply ashamed of what she had done, though she made it plain she believed she had made the only choice possible and would do it again.

As he continued to read the diaries, Adam kept hoping his mother would explain why she just hadn't told his father how unhappy she was and asked him to move the family back East, but she never did. She just kept insisting he belonged in the West and she did not. It occurred to Adam that his father had to have known when she left she would return to her home in New York. Adam had been so angry with his mother he had never thought to ask his father why he had never followed her.

In the weeks he took to read the diaries, Adam slowly came to realize he had never taken into account that his parents were also human beings. His loyalties had sided with his father because his father had stayed by his side—but that didn't mean his father was wholly right and his mother wholly wrong. Perhaps a seven-year-old boy could fail to recognize his mother's misery, but surely her husband must have noticed. Why hadn't he tried to do anything about it?

It was difficult for Adam to change his way of thinking after believing he knew things to be a certain way all his life, but he couldn't ignore how well Sam and Ella got along. Whenever they had a disagreement, they discussed the matter. He knew their recent decision to have a house built in Helena was a mutual one. They were a fine example of what a marriage could be. There was no reason he couldn't have one just like theirs, if he was of a mind to.

Adam had let his feelings about his mother get mixed up with his feelings for every woman to whom he'd ever been attracted, convicting them with the same evidence he'd used to judge her. He hadn't wanted to let himself love Cammie for the same reason. Only in Cammie's case he had fallen in love anyway.

And there wasn't a thing wrong with that. Cammie had come out West of her own free will—not out of a misguided desire to please anyone. She had come to please herself. Her head wasn't filled with fanciful notions. She was the most realistic woman he had ever met. Lord knew, she had no trouble telling him exactly what she thought, so he never need worry she would keep her feelings from him. The only problem he could see to marrying her was she didn't want to marry him.

Someone who didn't understand her as well as he did might judge that a significant drawback, but Adam didn't because he was fairly sure he knew why she didn't want to marry him. She was scared, just like he was. Only she wasn't afraid of abandonment—she was afraid he would turn into a man like her father.

It was time they both grew up. She wasn't his mother, and he wasn't her father. One of the things he liked best about

Cammie was her independence. He would never try to take that away from her. The trick was to find some way to convince her of that.

Too bad Sam didn't have another set of diaries to put her on the road to right thinking . . . but maybe he had something even better, Adam mused. He had Ella.

Adam knew Josh had already taken both Sam and Ella across the river to meet Cammie. He also knew the three of them had discussed his peculiar relationship with his nearest neighbor amongst themselves and behind his back on more than one occasion. By doing so, Josh had broken his promise to him that he would keep silent on the subject, but Adam had never confronted him because . . . partly because he was too embarrassed, and partly because claiming he didn't care about Cammie when he knew damn well he did would have made him feel like a fraud.

But that didn't matter anymore. What did matter was getting Cammie to stop and take a good look at what both of them had been doing and why . . . which brought him back to Ella and Sam.

If Cammie spent more time with them, saw how they got along together, she would realize that all marriages weren't predestined to end up with the man on the top and the woman on the bottom. A man and woman could be partners if they tried.

The more Adam thought about it, the more convinced he was that he could bring Cammie around to the idea of marriage . . . *if she loved him.* It might just be wishful thinking, but his instincts told him she did.

She was a smart, sensible woman. If he laid out the facts for her, she would see the truth just as he had.

First thing tomorrow morning, he was going to ride over and have a talk with her.

Twenty

Cammie yawned, rolling to her side. Her sleepy mind registered the sound of a horse neighing. Too close to be coming from the corrals, she mused. Must be one of her men returning from his Sunday revelry in town. She pulled the sheets up tighter under her chin, drifting back into the deep sleep from which she'd half awakened.

A minute later Cammie rolled over and glanced at her bedside clock. It was only quarter past three—far too early to even think of getting out of bed . . . but something felt wrong. What it was she couldn't say. Rubbing Lucretia's ears, Cammie drew in a long sighing breath, then coughed and abruptly sat up in bed. Did she smell smoke coming from the next room?

Vaulting out of bed, Cammie paused to place her hand on the door to test for heat. Finding it cool to the touch, she opened the door leading to the parlor. To her horror, she found the curtains and settee on fire.

Racing to the kitchen, Cammie grabbed a bucket of water and threw it on the curtains. She ran back to the bedroom. Yanking the bedding off the mattress, she flung it onto the seat of the settee, using it to smother the flames.

Cammie picked up two buckets and hurried to the well for more water. It was then she saw a man and horse rapidly heading east, clearly silhouetted in the light of the full moon.

Unmitigated fury supplanted the fear sparked by the fire. The instant she had seen the fire, Cammie had realized it could not have started unless it was deliberately set—but the need to put it out had left no room to consciously acknowledge the fact. Now that she and her house were all right, her thoughts converged on catching the man responsible for setting the fires and making him pay.

Pumping water into the buckets, Cammie dashed inside, pouring one bucket over the settee and dropping the smoldering curtains into the other to be certain the fires were completely out. It took her less than a minute to dress and grab her rifle off its rack.

She shouldn't have allowed herself to be lulled into a false sense of security so soon, Cammie scolded herself as she sprinted toward Bliss's corral. But it had been well over a month since anything had happened. During the time when the incidents were occurring, no more than a week passed between them. She had thought the ranch was safe. She was so sure of it, she no longer required a man to sleep in the barns and had allowed everyone to return to their usual routine. Sunday was the day she gave her men off, and most of them weren't even on the ranch. Whoever had been causing trouble before must have been watching and waiting for just this moment—and this time he'd meant to kill her!

Who hated her so much he would patiently bide his time, watching for the opportunity to murder her? Cammie could think of no one. It made no sense. But someone obviously did.

Cammie was so enraged that anyone would dare to sneak into her house while she slept and set fire to her home, hoping to burn her with it, she was beyond rational thought when she reached the corral. Saddling Bliss in record time, she set off in pursuit.

She was going to put a stop to this mayhem once and for all! To do that, she couldn't let the trail grow cold. She could no longer see the villain, but Cammie knew the direction of his cowardly retreat. Once away from the confusion of hoofprints blanketing the ground around the heart of the ranch, she should have little trouble picking up his trail.

Bliss covered the distance between the ranch and the place in the trees where the man had disappeared with powerful strides. When they entered the trees, the full moon shining through the branches revealed a path of broken twigs and shrubs.

Bliss seemed to instinctively know what she wanted from him. It was almost as if he could smell the horse they were chasing. They darted in between the trees, rarely slowing and never straying from the trail.

As she clung to Bliss's back, it crossed Cammie's mind that it would have been wise to alert someone at the ranch before setting off in pursuit, but it was too late now. She had her rifle and enough determination surging through her veins to give her the strength of ten women.

Nobody had the right to try to take her dream away from her. She had waited too long and worked too hard to get where she was.

A fresh surge of wrath heated her blood. When and if she caught up with the culprit, *he* was the one who would have cause to worry.

Adam was so eager to talk to Cammie about marriage, he only slept in snatches. Shortly before dawn he gave up altogether and got dressed. There were plenty of chores to do on the ranch to keep him busy until the hour was more respectable for paying a visit.

Everyone else was still asleep. Adam tiptoed down to the kitchen and started a pot of coffee. There were still four of yesterday's eggs in the pantry. Adam mixed up a bowl of flapjack batter, scrambling the remaining two eggs when his pancakes were ready. He hummed as he worked.

It was going to be a fine day. He could feel it in his bones. He wasn't so starry-eyed as to kid himself into believing Cammie would jump at the chance when he asked her to marry him. He was pretty sure she would balk at the idea—but he was prepared to be patient. He'd woo her with the facts. Point to Sam and Ella as a fine example of the kind of marriage he was proposing. Seduce her with brilliant displays of logic. That was the way to court a woman like Cammie Kendall.

When he finished eating his breakfast, Adam rinsed and stacked his dishes, then slipped out the back door. On the way to the barn, he glanced across the river in the direction of Cammie's house.

He froze.

A ball of flames glowed where her house was supposed to be.

"No!" Adam roared.

The sound of his own anguished cry jolted him from his paralysis and spurred him to action. Running to the bunkhouse, Adam pounded on the doors, shouting instructions to his men. He left them to rouse Josh and Sam.

"Josh! Sam! Cammie's house is on fire!" he bellowed as he raced up the stairs. "I'm taking the boat and as many men as I can fit into it over! Follow with the rest on horseback!"

Both Josh and Sam were at their bedroom doors and halfway into their trousers before Adam reached the top of the stairs. "We're right behind you," Josh called.

Adam hit the dock at a run. He picked up the oars while

his men and a flurry of buckets filled in every available space. The second the boat was untied, he put his shoulders to the oars.

While Adam was summoning help, a line of her men with buckets had formed between Cammie's house and the river. He felt better knowing something was already being done, but he hadn't caught sight of Cammie.

Adam told himself it didn't mean a thing. In the confusion a tiny woman could easily be lost in the crowd of men. He clung to the thought because to believe the alternative was unbearable.

Upon reaching the opposite shore, his men formed a second line, joining hers passing buckets of water from the river to the flames. Adam ran toward the house, shouting the same question to every man he passed, "Has anyone seen her?"

Every no felt like a cannonball striking his chest.

The house was completely engulfed in flames. If anyone was inside, there was no chance they were still alive. No one on the outside could get close enough to even try to go in.

Culver was at the head of the line of buckets. Tears streamed down his soot-blackened face while he heaved bucket after bucket of water onto the flames. "Nobody's seen her," he answered Adam's question before he asked it.

Adam knew if Cammie had made it out of the house, she would be right beside her men fighting the fire. Sick with grief, he took a place next to Culver and numbly battled the blaze.

When Josh and Sam arrived with the rest of the men, Adam stared at them with blank eyes and shook his head. They didn't need to ask what it meant. Forming a third line to the river, they mutely joined the fight.

Saving the cabin had been an impossible goal from the

beginning. Their purpose now was to keep the fire from spreading.

Adam worked in a state of disbelief. Reason told him she was gone, but he couldn't believe it. He didn't want to believe it. His hands continued to combat the fire, but his mind shut down. It was the only way he could keep going.

The sun had risen by the time the flames were completely out. In the end there was nothing left of the cabin.

Exhausted, Adam sank to the ground. He couldn't face the next task. Burying his face in his hands, he let other men sift through the smoldering rumble, searching for Cammie's remains.

Adam's eyes stung, but it was smoke, not tears, that made them burn. He couldn't cry. He didn't feel anything. There was nothing inside him except an awful void.

Something brushed up against his right side, and he glanced down. Lucretia's once white fur was now singed black on the tips, but he saw no sign of injury. She meowed loudly. Adam picked her up, cradling her in his lap.

"I guess you're gonna have to learn to be a man's cat now," he told her. "I figure she would have wanted me to take care of you." A lump clogged his throat, and Adam fell silent.

It seemed to be taking an inordinate amount of time to locate what was left of her body. Adam wanted it found. He wanted her wrapped in a blanket and . . . He couldn't finish the thought. He only knew he didn't want to see what the fire had done to her. He wanted to remember how she looked alive, with her eyes flashing and her lips curled into a defiant grin.

"Adam." Adam felt a hand on his shoulder and recognized Josh's voice.

"I was gonna ask her to marry me today," Adam murmured

without looking up at his brother. "Not like before when I didn't mean it, but really ask. Now it's too late."

"We can't find a body."

"What?" Adam's head shot up. Josh was grinning.

"I don't know where the hell she is, but she didn't burn in the fire. There would be something left of her, and there's not a trace," Josh declared.

Adam was on his feet immediately, but he was afraid to believe. "You're certain?"

"Yep. We've combed every inch of the place."

"Thank God!"

"My feelings exactly."

The news that Cammie was alive was so incredible, Adam's heart galloped in his chest. He grabbed Josh and hugged him so fiercely he lifted his feet off the ground. They danced around in a circle, whooping with elation until they were both so out of breath they were dizzy. Adam spread his legs, bracing his hands on his knees to keep his balance.

"I wonder where she is?" Adam spoke his thoughts aloud when he had recovered enough breath. "We oughta organize a search of the grounds."

"Sam is already doing it," Josh said.

"What a great brother!" Adam proclaimed.

Within five minutes it was determined that Bliss and his tack were missing. A few men remained near the site of the fire to make certain a concealed ember didn't flame the fire back to life. The rest kept searching for Cammie, though no one really expected to find her anywhere on the ranch.

Adam, Josh, Sam, Quigley Culver, and Carl Daley huddled to confer together in the yard.

"Did she mention she planned to spend the night with friends?" Adam questioned both Daley and Culver.

"No," both men offered. Culver added, "I talked to her up

at the house around ten o'clock last night, right before I headed for bed. That's why I was so sure she was in there."

"It doesn't make sense for her to get up in the middle of the night and go for a ride," Josh said.

"No, it don't," Culver agreed.

Adam proposed another theory. "Could she have decided to go to town? It's been hot. Maybe she rode in early to beat the afternoon heat."

"She always tells either me or Quigley when she's going to town," Daley insisted.

"Then where could she be?"

"Don't know, but I'm worried," Culver admitted.

"Since we don't know how the fire started, I don't think we should completely rule out the possibility of foul play," Sam reluctantly opined.

Adam grimaced, the joy of believing her alive blunted by new fears. "Let's check the stallion barns."

The five men went over every inch of the barns. There were no signs of a struggle. Adam was relieved but far from happy. He wasn't going to be happy until he could hold Cammie in his arms and assure himself she was fine.

"Maybe she woke up, saw the fire, and panicked," Sam ventured. "I had a friend in New York with a deathly fear of fires. Every time he'd hear the bells of a fire wagon, he'd fall to pieces—and he was a grown man."

"Cammie once told me the only thing she was afraid of was dying before she lived, and all my dealings with her bear that out as true," Adam contended. "If she knew about the fire, she'd see it was put out."

Everyone who knew Cammie nodded in agreement.

Adam stroked his mustache while he thought the matter through. "We know she's gotta be somewhere, but we aren't gonna figure out where standing here. I can't sit back and wait for her to come home on her own." Taking charge of the situation, he continued, "First, I'm gonna check with every man present on the property to confirm our suspicions she's nowhere on the ranch. Then I'm gonna start putting together search parties. My guess is we'll find Cammie wherever Bliss is. We know her horse's prints. Logic says if we break up into small groups and follow every set of tracks, we're bound to find her eventually."

Adam set off on foot, walking around the perimeter of the outbuildings. Josh walked the perimeter in the opposite direction. Whenever either man came upon Bliss's prints heading away from the ranch, they marked the spot with a small pile of stones. They then traced each other's steps to make certain neither had overlooked anything.

There were five sets of prints. Two were plainly several days old. Adam divided the men into three groups. He put Josh in charge of one, Carl Daley another. Borrowing a horse from Cammie's stable, Adam headed the third group. Sam accompanied him.

Adam's group followed the set of tracks going east. He was worried, but he pushed his feelings down. If Cammie was in danger he needed to be clearheaded.

The prints led directly to a stand of trees. There they began to mingle with those of another horse. Adam dismounted, examining the unidentified tracks more closely. Both these tracks and the one made by Cammie's horse seemed to be made at about the same time—but the horses weren't traveling together because one set was on top of the other. Cammie's horse was the last to travel this way. The pattern of the unknown horse was unusual. Adam called for his men to dismount. "Take a close look, boys. Any of you recognize these prints?"

Each man studied the ground in turn. After a minute

Bradley Stone, Adam's head wrangler, said, "Yeah—they belong to Jay Larson's buckskin. Horse got a bad hoof infection years ago when we both worked at the Four Bars ranch, and it scarred his back left foot."

Adam traced the outline of the print, his eyes darkening and his lips thinning.

Sam squatted beside him. "Do you know this Jay Larson?"

"Well enough to know I don't like the looks of this," Adam muttered.

"You reckon he's the one behind the trouble we've been having?" Elias Rutley asked.

Before Adam could answer, William Woodrow gruffly stated, "Never thought a thing about it before now, but I know he don't have a good word to say about Miss Kendall."

Adam's muscles tensed and his eyes narrowed. "Has she been keeping company with him?"

"Naw," Woodrow replied. "Leastways, not that I know of. He just likes to bad-mouth her 'cause she wouldn't hire him on as foreman."

"Have you ever heard him make any threats against her?"

"Would have told the sheriff if I had," Woodrow vowed. "Larson bad-mouths everybody in the territory who don't reckon him the greatest horseman ever born. Nobody's paid attention to him for years."

Adam knew of Larson's ego and his reputation as a chronic complainer. He raked his fingers through his hair, then settled his Stetson back on his head.

"Okay," Adam cataloged his thoughts aloud to solicit the other men's opinions. "This is what we know. Miss Kendall's house just burned to the ground from unknown causes. Larson doesn't like her. He was recently here and she's trailing him."

"Do you reckon he set the fire?" Bradley Stone questioned.

"I wouldn't swear to it, but that's my guess," Adam grimly stated.

"If you're right, and she caught him in the act, wouldn't she have called for help from her men?" Sam asked.

"That's the part I can't figure out," Adam admitted. "If she caught Larson setting the fire, she might work herself into such a fury she'd ride after him, but it doesn't make sense that she wouldn't alert her men about the fire. All it would take is one gust of wind and every building on the place could burn. She'd never leave her horses or her men at risk."

"That's true," both Rutley and Woodrow confirmed.

"Then how do you explain these tracks?" his own man, Peter McVay, inquired.

Frowning at them, Adam shook his head. "I can't—and I'm not gonna waste any more time trying."

Adam remounted and urged his horse forward. The rest of the men followed his lead.

Adam didn't know what kind of trouble he'd find at the end of the trail, but if Cammie needed him, he would be there for her.

Things weren't adding up right in his head, and that made him more than a little worried. So did knowing Larson was involved. The man had a mean streak. He wasn't ready to convict Larson without a fair trial, but his gut told him if Cammie caught up with Larson before they caught up with her, she was in imminent peril.

Adam spurred his horse to a faster pace.

When they crossed a stretch of grassland, Cammie rode Bliss as hard as she dared, but the man she was chasing managed to stay far enough ahead of her she still had no idea who he was.

The farther she rode from the ranch, the tenser she became—but if she turned back, she could lose the man altogether . . . and the next time he trespassed upon her ranch she might not be so lucky. If she hadn't awakened when she did, there was no doubt in Cammie's mind she would have lost her home and her life.

She wanted the arsonist caught, and the only way to do that was to find out who he was. Her temper had cooled down, and she no longer planned to confront him alone unless she could do so without putting herself in undue danger. What she wanted was a name or face to give the sheriff. He and his deputies could make the arrest.

The hoofprints she was trailing entered the trees again, forcing Cammie to slow. She followed them without difficulty for several hundred yards, then they stopped abruptly at the base of a steep granite wall. She studied the ground, but there was no indication which direction the horse and rider had taken.

Dismounting, Cammie lowered herself to her haunches to examine the ground more closely. At first she saw nothing, then she noticed an indentation beneath the carpet of pine needles. Brushing the needles away, she found a single hoofprint. Cammie swept away some more debris. She found nothing to the left of the first print, but the right proved more rewarding.

Just as it was dawning on her that the man she was trailing must realize he was being followed or he wouldn't have gone to the effort to disguise his tracks, Cammie heard a twig break behind her. She spun toward the sound and found herself face to face with Jay Larson and the bore of his Colt .45.

A gasp of surprise rushed from her throat.

"Stand up real slow like and back up against the wall," Larson commanded.

Cammie slowly stood. Her heart was pounding against her ribs, and her palms were sweating, but she refused to let herself be overcome by fear. Her situation was too grave to allow even a moment of panic. She glanced stealthily from Larson's face to her rifle, which was tied to Bliss's saddle. Even if she could reach Bliss, she would never be able to untie the rifle and take aim before she was gunned down.

"I said back up!" Larson spat, waving the Colt menacingly.

Cammie did as she was told.

He sighted her with his revolver, then lowered his aim to her heart and held it steady. "That's better."

"You set the fire." It was more statement than question.

"Yep."

"All the other things that happened—I assume you were responsible for those, too."

Grinning arrogantly, Larson nodded.

"Why?"

"You figure it out."

She searched her memory. "Since we've spoken on only two occasions, I haven't the slightest idea. I know you have little reason to like me. Neither were pleasant conversations, but—"

"Neither were pleasant conversations," Larson mocked. "You and your hoity-toity, nose-in-the-air ways don't know nothing."

"Then tell me what I should know," Cammie coaxed, pretending interest. If she could keep Larson talking long enough, maybe she could think her way out of this situation.

Larson puffed out his chest, marking each word with a flick of the barrel of his Colt. "I'm the best horse wrangler on both sides of the Rockies, but since you made me a laughingstock in front of all them men that day you was hiring, I can't get decent work nowhere round here. You done poisoned people's minds against me."

Think, Cammie told herself—think and stay calm. If she could persuade him he was mistaken, perhaps he'd let her go. Choosing her words carefully, she said, "I discussed you with only one person—and he warned me away from you, not the other way around. I'm sorry you haven't been able to find employment, but it has nothing to do with anything I've said."

"Liar!"

Cammie's heart dropped to her toes, but she kept her voice steady. "I'm telling you the truth. If someone has told you I'm talking behind your back, they are the ones who are lying."

"Sure would've liked to see you burn," Larson sneered. He raked his assessing gaze up and down her frame. "All that soft, creamy white flesh turning hard and black. Your blond hair blazing red. Them limbs writhing and you screaming out in agony." He licked his lips. "My, wouldn't that have been a glorious sight."

A chill ran down Cammie's spine.

"You reckon you know all there is to know about horses, don't you?" he continued to cackle. "Well, you're just a stupid woman. Coming here with your highfalutin notions and duping everyone into believing you know more than a seasoned wrangler like myself. I've watched the way they've flocked to your ranch, and heard them boasting about what a fine horsewoman you are and how you're gonna end up the richest female in the territory. It makes me sick."

Sick was exactly the word Cammie would use to describe Jay Larson. He had let his anger over the hiring incident fester into a canker. He couldn't see he had brought ill fortune upon himself.

Cammie wondered how to reason with him. Was it even possible to do so? The sinking sensation in her stomach told her no, but she had to try. Her chest constricted with each breath and she prayed her voice would not reveal her growing terror. "Disliking my method of training horses is hardly reason to murder me."

"Wasn't planning on killing you at first," Larson informed her. "Just wanted to get rid of you. I tried to be gentlemanly about it, doing little things to show my displeasure—but you don't know how to take a hint."

A man who regarded slashing tack and killing chickens as gentlemanly was clearly insane, but having already come to that conclusion, Cammie was able to maintain her unruffled facade. "I had no idea my presence here bothered you so much. Now that I do, I'm sure we can work out some arrangement agreeable to us both."

Larson's eyes shimmered. "You offering me the foreman job?"

Cammie struggled to infuse her tone with a convincing measure of sincerity. "I'm certainly willing to discuss the matter."

"You'd have to make me the boss of all your horses. Do everything my way."

"All right."

"And pay me double salary with Sundays *and* Saturdays off."

She pretended to consider his demand. "Yes, I could agree to those terms."

"And I want him." Larson pointed at Bliss.

Cammie stiffened. She would shoot Bliss before she let him fall into Larson's brutal hands. Even though she knew the moment she got away from Larson she'd ride straight to the sheriff's office and have the man arrested, it took every ounce of her control to say, "Of course he's yours. You're a fine horseman and you deserve him."

Larson's face contorted with rage. "Hah! It's too late to be making amends, Miss High and Mighty. Even if you was to promise to let me share your bed, I wouldn't work for you!"

Hoping her revulsion for his last suggestion didn't show on her face, Cammie forced out a dispassionate, "Why?"

" 'Cause I got my heart set on killing you." Checking the line of his sight to be certain it remained true, he stroked the trigger of his Colt.

"But you'll gain nothing if you kill me. If you're caught, you'll hang—and if you aren't, my death will change nothing."

"Sure it will. I won't have to watch you strut about like you reckon you're the Queen of Sheba or listen to another word of blather about you and your grand horses."

"What if I agreed to sell my land and move to some other part of the country? Wouldn't that accomplish the same thing?"

"I'd still know you were out there somewhere, and it'd rankle me."

"I bet you'd forget all about me in no time," Cammie cajoled.

He thought about it a minute before replying, "Naw. This way is better."

"Not if you get caught," she reminded. "I hardly think I'm worth the risk of hanging."

"I don't plan on getting caught."

"Neither did I, and I walked right into your trap."

"You sure did." Larson guffawed. "You ain't near as smart as you figure you are. 'Course, I knew it all along. Now me, I ain't that stupid. Nobody caught me before, and nobody is gonna catch me now."

"How can you be sure?"

"Because with you dead, there ain't gonna be no witnesses."

Cammie winced. No one was more aware than she of how foolish and shortsighted she had been to come after Larson alone. And, she was equally aware she was the only one who knew where she was and why. Fortunately Larson didn't know what she knew.

"There's something you're not taking into account," she said curtly. "I wrote a note before I left, naming you responsible for the fire and informing my men I was coming after you. If I don't come back, they will know exactly who to hold responsible for my disappearance."

For an instant, he appeared worried, but the moment was all too brief. "You didn't know it was me till you turned round and saw my face," he insisted.

"The smoke from the fire woke me up. When I went to the well to draw water to put it out, I saw you riding away from the ranch. How else do you think I was able to follow you?"

The worried expression returned to his face. He stared at her, speaking his thoughts aloud. "You might have seen something, but you didn't know it was me. And you didn't leave no note. The fire would've burnt it."

"I put out the fire before I left."

A grin spread across Larson's face. "Now I know you're a liar."

"What do you mean?"

"I saw your place burning."

"You can't have. I put the fires out. They never spread beyond the curtains and settee."

"Well, you didn't do a very good job, 'cause I seen the

whole cabin ablaze from a rise when I looked back. Same time I saw you was following me."

Something in his manner convinced Cammie he wasn't lying. Her eyes widened in alarm. "Oh, no!" The exclamation escaped her lips before she could stop it.

Larson laughed. "So even if you did write a note, there ain't no note now."

Cammie realized she had lost her gamble, and a deep sense of foreboding descended on her. Her house was gone. Soon she would be gone, too, and the knowledge numbed her. "You're going to shoot me where I stand, bury the body, and no one will be the wiser." With trembling lips, she outlined the events that were about to befall her.

"You got it just about right," Larson gloated. "Except I ain't gonna shoot you here. I know a better place."

"Where?"

"Some place they'll *never* find you."

Twenty-one

"Turn around and face the wall," Larson ordered.

The pounding of Cammie's heart accelerated, but she stood firm. If she turned her back to him, she wouldn't be able to see what he was doing—and not knowing would make whatever it was worse. "Why?"

"I need to truss you up before we take our little ride."

If she allowed him to tie her, she would be even more vulnerable than she already was. In the end it might not matter, but Cammie couldn't meekly accept this new impairment. "A big strong man like you doesn't need to tie me up," she flattered. "If I was foolish enough to try anything—which I'm not—I'm sure you could overpower someone my size without any trouble at all."

"Turn around!" Larson commanded.

Cammie refused to budge. "But you have a gun and I don't."

"You got that right—and I'll use it on you here and now if you don't stop stalling." Pressing the Colt to her forehead, Larson left no question he meant it.

She turned.

"Now put both your hands behind your back." He jabbed the back of her head with his gun. Cammie had little choice but to obey. As soon as she did, he lifted the gun and took a step back.

She could feel his eyes on her. Her ears pricked when he took another step. Then another. He was walking away. She assumed he was retrieving a rope.

While she grimly waited for him to come back with the rope, Cammie reached a decision. No matter what she did, he was going to kill her, either now or later. There probably wasn't anything she could do to save herself. But if she was destined to die, she was determined to do everything she could to make certain he was brought to justice for the crime. There must be a reason he preferred to kill her elsewhere, and Cammie saw no sense in making her murder convenient for him. If she was going to die, she was going to do it here.

Gritting her teeth, she mentally prepared herself for what she was about to do. Her chances of surviving the next few minutes were slim, but at least she would have the satisfaction of knowing she went to her death fighting. And there was the possibility that she could defy the odds, reach Bliss, and ride to safety.

He was walking toward her again. Cammie forced herself to take slow, deep breaths, readying her muscles. She had heard it said that fear was capable of increasing strength beyond its normal limits. If it was true, the magnitude of her fear should lend her the strength of an army. The closer he came, the more her resolve to resist increased.

The instant his hand touched her wrist, Cammie whirled around, catching him just below the ribs with her left elbow. Her right foot kicked hard against his shin while her fist slammed against the side of his face. The unexpected attack stole his breath, throwing him off balance. He dropped the rope. Cammie didn't see his gun.

She didn't have time to find out what happened to it. Spinning away from his outstretched arm, she ran for Bliss.

Cammie completed three steps and half of a fourth before

Larson tackled her. Screaming in protest, she clawed at the ground, trying to crawl away. Flipping her to her back, he flattened her with his weight. Cammie pummelled him with her fists, using her feet, knees, elbows . . . any part of her body she could wrench into service to dislodge him. Larson slapped her hard across the face.

Cammie was so intent on breaking loose, the blow barely registered. With a herculean shove she heaved his weight from her, tumbling so she lay atop him. With her arms and legs free, she was able to inflict greater damage, but not enough to gain her release. Larson returned blow for blow.

Groans and curses spewed from Larson's lips as they battled on the ground. Cammie shrieked with fury, praying someone would hear her war cry.

He pinned her to the ground again. If she was capable of deductive thought, the venom in Larson's eyes would have terrified her.

His knees were on her shoulders. Raising up, he brought the back of his hand down upon her right cheek, then her left. He struck her again and again.

Cammie arched her back, beat on his legs, twisted her head, trying to evade his hands, but it was impossible. Clenching her eyes closed, she braced herself for the next blow.

She was drowning in a sea of pain. She fought on, instinct rather than reason driving the movements of her limbs. Her ears rang. The red haze she saw behind her tightly shut eyelids began to dim at the corners.

Then she felt nothing.

When Cammie awoke, the first thing she was aware of was pain. Her head was throbbing and every inch of her ached. Something was hurting her stomach. She attempted to change position, but found her hands and ankles were bound. She tried to open her eyes, but only one eyelid would lift. Cammie peered through her one good eye, trying to orient herself to an upside-down world.

It took several minutes for her head to clear enough to absorb that she had been flung across Bliss's back like a sack of meal. That awareness brought back the reason she found herself riding her horse in such an odd posture.

Panic clutched at her chest, but she checked the urge to cry out. She licked her lips. Her tongue tasted blood.

Cammie told herself she should be grateful she wasn't dead. She was surprised to find herself still alive. But it was difficult to be optimistic when the only purpose she could think of for Larson not killing her when he had had the opportunity involved more pain and humiliation.

Still, she wouldn't allow herself to succumb to despair. It was what Larson would want. If there was a way to escape her death sentence, Cammie was determined to find it.

She was facing Bliss's hindquarters. Her gaze jerked to the spot where she had tied her rifle, but it was gone. She knew it was naive to hope Larson had overlook such an obvious object of self-defense—but for an instant, hope had nonetheless sprung to life in her breast. With her hands bound, she couldn't have made use of the rifle anyway, but she could have fantasized about picking her knots, grabbing the gun, and shooting Larson before he shot her.

Slowly turning her head forward, Cammie glared at him on his buckskin. He had tied a lead from Bliss to his saddle. That ruled out nudging Bliss in the ribs and gambling she could communicate her will to him through spoken commands during a headlong dash for freedom. She continued to stare at Larson's back.

He was whistling. The cheerful sound made her blood run

cold. Why hadn't he killed her? The question repeated itself in her pounding head. If he was worried someone would hear the report of his revolver, he could easily have strangled her. A corpse would be less troublesome than a live woman. Reminding herself she was not dealing with a sane man, Cammie blotted the question from her mind. Even if she could divine the answer, she knew she was probably better off not knowing.

Her thoughts wandered down another path. In a few minutes, perhaps hours, her life would be over. She wasn't ready to die. The prospect of facing the kind of death she envisioned Larson had in store for her petrified her. She kept praying she would wake up and find that discovering her house on fire and being captured by Larson were nothing but a monstrous nightmare.

Cammie felt like two separate people in the same body. One trembled with fear. The other watched what was happening like a member of an audience observing a play.

The analytical Cammie didn't feel fear or pain. She examined the facts and accepted her death as inevitable. She thought about the life she had lived.

In many ways it had been a far easier life than most people ever dreamed of having. She had grown up in a grand house with servants to do her bidding, elegant clothes, and all the money she could ever desire was hers for the asking. She had never wanted for anything . . . except the freedom to be herself.

She had found that freedom in Montana. She belonged here. Her little cabin had felt far more like home than the Virginia mansion where she had spent so many years. She loved her ranch. Cammie's swollen lips smiled.

It had been worth every sleepless night, every aching muscle, and every blister. Even knowing she was about to die did not diminish her pleasure when she thought of the joy owning her own ranch had given her.

Her life might be fated to be brief, but this past year she had lived it with gusto. She regretted nothing . . . nothing except her failure to explore what might have been had she opened herself up to the idea of falling in love with Adam Carrigan.

Her reasons for refusing to even consider the possibility they might be able to buck the dictates of society and form a union with rules of their own making suddenly felt petty.

All her life she had judged every man she had met using her father as the measure, never bothering to take the time to let them prove her right or wrong. How was that any different than her father condemning her to live life as an ornament because she was born female? It wasn't. Without realizing it, she had become what she despised. She had let her own preconceived notions of how the world was ordered to prejudice her against the male of the species without ever getting to know each person as an individual.

Adam Carrigan wasn't anything like her father. She knew that in her heart. Certainly he had a mind of his own—she wouldn't want a man who didn't have his own opinions—but that didn't mean he wouldn't respect her and allow her to live her life according to her own will.

And she did want Adam. She had wanted him from the first moment she laid eyes on him—and the more she got to know him, the stronger her want had become. She wanted him for a friend and a lover and a lifelong partner. If they couldn't resist the temptations of each other's flesh, marriage—not exile to opposite shores of the river—was the logical solution to their problem. If they were husband and wife, their attraction would no longer be a burden to be borne alone but a joy to be shared. They could make a marriage work if both of them were committed to the goal. She had let fear cheat her out of experiencing one of life's grandest adventures: *love.*

Cammie considered it extremely perverse of her brain to come to this conclusion now, when there was no hope she would ever see Adam again. She wanted a second chance to be with Adam. She wanted to know if the reluctant love that had blossomed between them could grow to be more if nurtured rather than denied. She wanted to be given back all the time she had wasted running away from her own feelings.

A tear slipped from her eye, but Cammie blinked back those that would have followed. Larson would never see her reduced to tears.

He would enjoy seeing her cry, seeing her beg for her life on her knees. It would intensify the pleasure of killing her. She would deny him that pleasure as her final act upon this earth.

Whatever he did to her, no matter how horrible, she wouldn't let him see her break down. *That would be her comfort and her revenge.*

Adam made no effort to disguise his distress as he and his men followed the trail left by Larson and Cammie. In his own mind he could envision what had happened on the Kendall ranch:

Cammie had been awakened by a noise and had gone outside to investigate. She spotted Larson, knew he shouldn't be hanging around her ranch, and with her usual dauntlessness had attempted to question him. He had taken off, and she set off in pursuit.

Adam's hands tightened on his reins. He could take a hickory stick to her backside for her lack of regard for her own safety. Surely she must have realized if Larson ran when she tried to question him, he was up to no good.

He had no proof Larson had started the fire, but it was too hot this time of year to keep a stove burning at night, so that ruled out a flue fire. Cammie wasn't the type to leave a candle or lamp burning unattended. If Larson set the fire while she was outside, it would also explain why she hadn't alerted her men to the fire. She couldn't alert them to something she didn't know about.

The more Adam thought about it, the more convinced he became that Larson was to blame for the fire. Had Larson lured Cammie outside to prevent her from being killed in the blaze or had luck saved her? Adam prayed Larson had lured her, otherwise . . . should Cammie catch up with Larson before they found her, she would be in mortal danger.

Cammie had no idea how long she lay bound to Bliss's back. The minutes ticked by in a blur of pain. She was torn between wanting the agonizing ride to end, and praying it would go on forever so she wouldn't have to face whatever torment Larson had in store for her.

Whenever panic threatened to overwhelm her, she used anger to crush it down. Anger fortified her. When they stopped, she would fight Larson until she drew her last breath—but he would never see her terror. She would go to her death with courage and dignity.

Without warning, Larson reined to a halt, causing Bliss to bump into the buckskin. Bliss pawed nervously at the ground and tried to rear. Cursing, Larson used the ends of the lead as a whip to regain control, striking Bliss's face repeatedly.

"Stop!" Cammie shouted weakly.

"So . . . you're awake," Larson observed, striking Bliss again. "Good."

Larson continued to lash Bliss. Unused to such treatment, it only made Bliss more unruly. If not for the ropes binding her, Cammie knew she would fall from his back and be trampled beneath his hooves.

With every blow Cammie's outrage increased. Bliss fought, but to no avail. Caught by the rope, he couldn't escape or strike back. Inevitably his efforts exhausted his spirit, and he stood quietly, his head drooping.

Larson grinned with satisfaction at the now-subdued Bliss. Sliding from his saddle, he tied the buckskin to the nearest tree. Using a knife, he cut the ropes binding Cammie to Bliss's saddle, yanked her to the ground, and dragged her by her arms a few yards from the horses. "Here we are," Larson announced.

Pushing herself to a sitting position, Cammie sat motionless while she waited for her dizziness to subside.

At first glance, her surroundings appeared no different than a hundred other spots they had passed. Scattered tufts of bunchgrass dotted a carpet of pine needles. A few boulders lay on the ground. Trees ringed three sides of the small clearing. Then she heard the distant sound of water, coming from far below. They must be on a cliff over the river canyon.

So this was how he intended to dispose of her body, she mused. She was no longer afraid. His maltreatment of Bliss had pushed her beyond fright. She was numb to all feeling, save one: contempt. "You're planning to push me over the edge, aren't you?"

"Yep."

"Before or after you kill me?"

"That depends."

"On what?"

"How good you treat me."

The gleam in his eye and the syrupy tone of his voice caused Cammie's skin to prickle. "What's that supposed to mean?"

Larson rubbed his chest and spat on the ground near her hip. "While we've been riding along, I decided I may as well take full advantage of the situation. I've had a hankering to give you a good poke ever since I met you. Might learn you some manners." He raised a hand as if to slap her, then frowned and dropped it to his side. " 'Course you ain't as pretty as you used to be—and manners ain't gonna do you much good where you're headed—but won't cost me nothing to give you and me a little fun before you go."

There was no question in Cammie's mind what he meant by his statements, and his intentions didn't surprise her. In the back of her mind, she had assumed it was the reason he hadn't killed her earlier. Raising her chin, she coldly muttered, "Go to hell."

"If you fight me, I'll make it worse for you." He loosened his belt. "May as well just lie back and enjoy it."

"That's like telling me to enjoy drowning in a trough of manure," she scoffed. "No woman ever born could enjoy having your vile hands upon her."

Larson's face turned an ugly shade of red. "There's more than one whore in town tells me I'm the best there is in the saddle."

"They're paid to stroke the egos of buffoons," Cammie said disdainfully.

"I ain't no buffoon!"

"You look like one to me."

"You wouldn't know a real man if you saw him!" Grabbing a hank of her hair, he wrapped it around his fist, pulling Cammie to her feet and up to his sneering face. When she refused to cower, he abruptly let go, kicking her feet out from under her. Unable to catch herself, Cammie hit the ground with a thud. Larson snickered. "Makes no never mind to me if you don't like how I poke you. Just remember, the more fun you give *me,* the longer you'll live."

Since Cammie's primary purpose in goading him was to enrage him to the point he killed her before he defiled her, his words had the opposite effect he desired. "Touch me and the only thing I'm going to give you is a swift knee in the groin. With any luck, I'll cripple you for life."

"You talk mighty big for a woman who ain't got a chance in hell."

Cammie shrugged. "Dead is dead."

"True, but if you're sweet to me, I can make the trip there hurt a whole lot less." Licking his lips, he began unbuttoning his fly. "Way I'm feeling now, I'm inclined to make your dying as hard as I can."

Cammie had no doubt he would, but she also knew he would do the same even if she groveled at his feet.

In a few minutes he would be upon her. Whatever she did to try to save herself, she had to do it now. Her gaze darted around the clearing, rapidly weighing her options.

She could stay where she was, but with her hands and ankles bound, there was no chance she could successfully defend her person against violation.

She could try to roll across the clearing and throw herself off the cliff before he touched her. This choice held far more appeal than the first, but the distance was considerable, and it guaranteed death.

She could roll herself under Bliss's hooves. Bliss was much closer than the cliff, so her chances of reaching him were greater. Cammie knew Bliss would never purposefully hurt her—but she also knew the danger she would put herself in if she sought refuge under his hooves. But at least with Bliss, she had a chance. And she could always hope he stomped Larson to death before he did her.

These thoughts raced through her mind in the space of a breath. Cammie waited until Larson dropped his trousers to his ankles—then stiffening her body into a log, she hurled herself toward Bliss.

"What the hell!" Larson bellowed as she spun away. He grunted when he tripped and fell over his own trousers. The sound heartened Cammie.

Ignoring the rocks and twigs scraping her flesh, she sped toward her goal. With each rotation, she could see Bliss's hooves getting nearer.

She had less than a yard to go when she felt a hand on her ankle.

Cammie kicked it off, but it grabbed her again.

"Oh, no, you don't," Larson snarled. "You ain't gonna cheat me out of my pleasure." Hand over hand he hauled her toward him.

Cammie kicked, bucking her legs. She smashed his fingers between her knees. But he held fast. Panic welled up in her, but she resisted giving in to it. Prying a rock out of the dirt, she pitched it over her head.

If it struck him, it didn't faze him.

His hands continued their spider crawl up the legs of her split skirt. He pinched her thighs. Cammie bit her lip to prevent herself from crying out.

With a sudden lunge, Larson threw himself atop her. Seizing her shoulders, he jerked her to her back, smashing her into the dirt with the weight of his body. His face hovered above hers. Balling her hands into fists, Cammie brought them down on his head.

He cursed her. Shackling her hands above her head, he

ground his mouth into her raw, swollen lips. Cammie's bile rose in her throat. It choked her, but she didn't give up the struggle.

Thrashing back and forth, she caught glimpses of Bliss straining at his ropes. She could hear him snorting and whinnying loudly. Cammie labored to inch them within striking range of the horse's hooves. Bliss was her only hope. She had to reach him. She had to deny Larson his way.

Again and again she brought her knees up, praying she would incapacitate him, but no matter how she twisted and turned, she couldn't hit her mark. Every time she made the attempt, Larson punished her by bringing a hand down hard across her face.

Cammie was still conscious, but her actions were those of a wild animal caught in a trap. She fought on because her mind refused to acknowledge she had lost.

Larson's wheezing laughter echoed in her ears. Using his teeth, he tugged at the top button of her blouse until the threads broke.

Spitting the button out, he bit off the next.

Twenty-two

"Whoa." Adam reined to a halt and jumped from his horse.

"It looks like trouble," Bradley Stone remarked.

"Sure does," Adam somberly agreed. The signs were unmistakable. The pattern of hoofprints showed both horses had stopped here, and the disturbance of the forest floor indicated a struggle had taken place. A path through the crush of pine needles—ending at the clutter of hoofprints—told of a body being dragged.

Adam clenched his jaw as a wave of dread washed over him. This was exactly what he hadn't wanted to find. Only the knowledge that now, more than ever, Cammie needed him to be strong kept him from giving in to his fears.

Squatting, Adam examined the ground more closely. His eyes fell upon a spattering of dark red droplets. Touching one with his finger, he swore, "I'll kill the bastard."

"What is it?" Sam asked.

"Blood."

Sam joined him on the ground. "Hers?"

"I can't say, but from the width of the drag marks, I'd say the body being pulled along was hers," Adam said dully. First, he had thought Cammie had burned in the fire. Then, he knew her to be alive. Now this. Had she escaped the fire only to be murdered? The grim evidence before him made it difficult to come to any other conclusion. Lifting a single strand of blond hair he found on the ground near his feet, Adam brought it to his lips. Despite the hot sun overhead, he shivered.

He glanced at his group of men. From the sober expressions on their faces, he knew they had reached the same conclusion he had. He bowed his head and stared at the ground.

Sam put a hand on his shoulder. "There isn't much blood. She might still be alive."

"I wonder where he's taking her and why?" Adam murmured.

"I don't have an answer, but I think the fact that she's not here is further cause to trust she's alive," Sam comforted. "If he killed her here, what sense would there be in taking her with him?"

As he looked up at his brother, a glimmer of hope shone in Adam's eyes, but it was quickly extinguished. "None," he replied. "Unless he knows we're trailing him."

"How could he?" Sam argued. "We've been making excellent time, but we still must be at least an hour behind him."

"True." Adam was grateful to hear a voice of reason. Abruptly rising, Adam faced the other men. "I don't know whether she's alive or dead, but till I know for certain, I'm gonna assume the best. I know we've been riding fast and hard, but we're gonna go faster. Keep your eyes sharp and your guns at the ready. We can't afford to make any mistakes."

Remounting, Adam set a punishing pace. Larson had left a clear path to follow, allowing them to push their horses to the limit. They had to reach Cammie before it was too late—if it wasn't already too late. Adam banished the thought from his head. Cammie was alive—he had to believe that. If he didn't, he would be of no use to her.

He ought to listen to Sam. He hadn't known his brother long, but he knew him to be an extraordinarily perceptive man. If Larson had killed Cammie, he would have left the body behind. The fact he'd made no attempt to cover his tracks said he had no idea he was being trailed. Even if he did know he was being followed, it still made more sense for him to leave her. Murder was a hanging offense. Why slow himself down with a corpse?

Adam wondered what had happened back at the granite wall. Had Cammie tried to confront Larson? Had he jumped her? Larson had to be guilty of something, or there wouldn't have been signs of a struggle.

And now Larson had Cammie. If he hadn't murdered her, it meant he'd kidnapped her. What Larson's plans were for Cammie he couldn't bear to contemplate—but whatever they were, Adam figured she didn't have long to live.

Thinking of Cammie terrified and in pain from the injuries Larson had already inflicted upon her made Adam's blood boil. He had no idea why Larson wanted to hurt her, but he knew his motives couldn't be justified. Larson always did have a hair-trigger temper. Most people didn't like him much and avoided him when they could. But it had never occurred to Adam that Larson was capable of stepping this far out of line. Burning down a house and kidnapping wasn't a case of flying off the handle—it was a calculated kind of evil.

Adam's gaze hardened. When he got his hands on Larson, he'd make him sorry he'd ever been born.

The trail began to circle north. They were now heading toward the river canyon. Adam's gut knotted. He knew the terrain too well, and his apprehension spiraled as several possible reasons for Larson choosing this direction flashed through his mind.

No one spoke as their horses galloped up the miles. There was nothing anyone could say.

Every ear was attuned to the slightest sound. Every pair

of eyes scanned the countryside, straining for a glimpse of a horse or rider.

Still alive. She had to be still alive. Adam refused to let doubt creep back into his mind. He refused to let her be dead. She had barely begun to live the life she had dreamed of for so long. It wasn't fair to take it away from her. It wasn't fair to take her away from him.

He loved her. He needed her. He wanted them to grow old and gray together.

A torrent of thoughts whirled in Adam's head—he had to find her. Nothing else mattered as long as he could make her safe.

Adam's ears picked up a faint rustling sound of dry pine needles. He thought it might be caused by his imagination or an animal but—

A horse neighed. A high-pitched *no!* rent the air. The scream of protest was immediately followed by the sound of a sharp slap and a gruff, "Hold still, dammit!"

"It's her," Adam shouted, spurring his horse toward the voices. Breaking into a small clearing, he saw Cammie wrestling on the ground beneath Larson. Larson had his trousers pulled down to his ankles.

Leaping from his horse, Adam drew his gun, cocking the hammer. "Get off of her, you bastard!"

The men with Adam dismounted, backing him with their weapons.

Larson let out a startled yelp. Flipping to his back he used Cammie's body as a shield, locking his arm across her throat as he slowly stood.

Rage burned bright in Adam's eyes as he stared at Cammie's blackened eye, bruised and swollen face, and torn blouse. She stared back at him, disbelief, relief, and a wordless plea for help glistening in her uninjured eye.

"Can't shoot me without killing her, too," Larson warned, glowering at them and their drawn weapons. Pressing his forearm against Cammie's windpipe to cut off her breath so she couldn't fight him, he shuffled the few steps to the spot where he'd discarded his gun belt and eased his arm downward until his hand touched his holster. In a single movement, he jerked his Colt out of the holster and himself and Cammie upright.

"Let her go," Adam commanded.

"Like hell, I will." Holding the gun to Cammie's head and keeping his arm across her throat, Larson dragged her behind a tree trunk.

A shot whizzed past Adam's ear. He dove for the ground and rolled for cover behind a boulder. The rest of the men took cover behind the nearest trees. Their weapons remained drawn, and they looked to him for guidance.

Adam quickly assessed the situation. He had to remain calm. He couldn't let his fear for her or his hatred for Larson cloud his judgment. Cammie was depending on him. Her fate was in his hands. He couldn't let her down.

Taking a deep breath, Adam said, "You're outnumbered six to one, Larson—and you have only five bullets left. Let her go and give yourself up."

"So I can hang?" Larson jeered. "Not hardly. If I die, she dies with me."

Adam had expected that would be his answer, but he wasn't ready to give up trying to reason with him. He had little confidence he could talk Larson into giving himself up—but it would keep Larson busy dealing with him and buy him time to think up a plan. Adam tried again, "Letting her go might not save you from a hangman's noose, but it might save you from burning in hell. Way I see it, you're gonna meet the Almighty either way. If I were you, I'd be worrying more about my soul along about now."

"Well, you ain't me, are you?" Larson hollered back.

"No, I'm not—but I'm still giving you good advice."

"If you're so smart, why the hell are you trying to stop me? The way I hear it, all that's standing between you and owning the whole valley is this high and mighty bitch I'm holding. My getting rid of her would be doing you a big favor."

Adam swallowed his anger. He wasn't about to allow Larson to provoke him into doing something stupid. Keeping low so Larson couldn't see him, Adam used his head to signal the other men to quietly begin moving from tree to tree and surround Larson. He still didn't have a firm plan, but one was starting to take shape in his mind. To distract Larson, Adam balanced his hat on the end of a stick and poked the top above the boulder he was crouched behind.

A shot rang out. It missed the hat and ricocheted off the rock.

Adam stuck up his hat again. Larson fired off another shot. This time the bullet hit its mark, knocking the hat off the stick.

A hoarse scream rasped from Cammie throat.

"Only got the hat, didn't hit me," Adam shouted. "You're down to three bullets, Larson. Ready to deal?"

"What kinda deal?"

"What do you want?"

"I want you and your men to get on your horses and ride on out of here," Larson declared.

"What about Miss Kendall?"

"She stays with me."

"No deal. I want Miss Kendall set free. Your life for hers. Let her go, and I'll let you ride out of here."

"Don't trust you—even if you let me ride out of here, there ain't nothing to keep you from hunting me down later," Larson growled.

"No, there isn't, but that doesn't mean I would. All I want is the woman. Give her to me, and I'll forget I ever laid eyes on you."

"You'll come after me," Larson insisted.

"Not if I give you my word I won't."

"Nope—if I let her go, I'm a dead man."

The truth was he'd make a deal with the devil if doing so would guarantee Cammie's safety, but Adam knew Larson was right. Once he had Cammie, he'd never rest until he brought Larson to justice.

Adam again used his hat as a decoy. Larson fired and missed. "Two bullets, Larson."

"That's one for you and one for her!"

"But you keep missing me," Adam reminded. "If I were you, I'd start seriously considering making that deal. Even if you shoot us both, you're a goner. Or are you forgetting the five men standing behind the trees directly in back of me? They're all good friends of mine, and they're not gonna take kindly to you shooting me. Might want to take some time to think about that."

"Don't need to think about nothing," Larson brayed.

The other men had moved into place. Adam considered taunting Larson into spending another of his bullets, but the man was desperate, and a desperate man did desperate things. With only one bullet left, he might not hesitate to turn the gun on Cammie.

The back-up plan he'd settled on carried its own risks, but Adam staked his hopes on the element of surprise. He wished he could tell Cammie what he was about to do, but if he warned her, he also warned Larson.

Peering around the bottom of the boulder, Adam caught Peter McVay's eye. Signaling with his fingers, he instructed him and the other men to count off ten and charge. McVay nodded his understanding, held up his palm to caution him to wait until he had relayed the message to the rest of the men, then nodded again when they were ready.

Adam counted off the seconds and charged.

Men rushed Larson from six directions, leaving him no place to hide. The report of gunfire peppered the air. Larson fired off his last two shots in rapid succession.

Cursing and throwing the gun away, he covered himself with Cammie, dragging her toward the cliff. Cammie brought the heels of her boots down as hard as she could against his shin. While they had been behind the tree, Larson hadn't had enough hands to hold her, the gun, and hike up his pants—and with his trousers still sagging around his ankles, the force of the kick toppled him to the ground. He took Cammie with him.

Before her mind registered that Larson had loosened his hold on her to catch himself before he hit the dirt, Adam was on top of him. Cammie rolled out of harm's way and struggled to her feet.

Elias Rutley and William Woodrow rushed to her side, helping steady her. Using his knife, Rutley sawed through the ropes binding Cammie's wrists and ankles. Woodrow removed his shirt, pulling her arms through the sleeves as he would a child's and buttoning it up to her chin.

Cammie barely noticed. Her gaze was glued to Adam and Larson. The two men wrestled in the dirt, fists furiously flying. They were evenly matched in height. Larson held the advantage in weight. Both wore murderous expressions.

Adam's fist connected with Larson's nose. Larson hit Adam's jaw. Over and over, they struck each other. One second one man was on top, the next it was the other. The sound of knuckles splitting flesh made a sickening pop. Clearly they were trying to kill each other.

The savagery of the fight stunned her. Larson was an animal, driven by insanity and the knowledge he had nothing to look forward to but a hangman's noose. But why did Adam put himself at further jeopardy? She had never seen such a ferocious look in his eyes. Didn't he realize she was safe? That they had won?

"Adam," Cammie called his name. "It's all right. It's over. Please stop." He didn't seem to hear her. She called his name again, this time louder. It had no effect.

With five men training their guns on Larson, there was no possibility he could get away. Cammie couldn't understand why no one besides her thought to intervene. Their guns were useless while the two men rolled end over end. No one could fire a shot without risk of shooting Adam instead of Larson. But they could pull them apart. Why didn't they?

"Stop them," she implored when Larson landed a nasty blow to Adam's belly.

The men around her shook their heads while Rutley spoke for them all, "No, ma'am."

"Why not?" Cammie cried.

"Sometimes a man is so full of feeling he has to let it out or he'll explode. You didn't see the look on Adam's face when he reckoned you were dead. We'll stop it if it gets out of hand—but right now the boss needs this," Bradley Stone explained.

"But he's getting hurt," Cammie protested.

"He's got the upper hand," Peter McVay assured her.

She turned to Sam. "You're his brother. Do something!"

"If it becomes necessary, when the time comes, I will," he promised.

Every time Larson landed a punch, Cammie flinched and had to stifle a scream. She didn't care what anybody said. Adam had saved her life. The least she could do was save him further injury. The time to stop them was now! "If you won't stop them, I will."

Taking a step forward, she prepared to launch herself into the fray, but two pair of hands restrained her.

"Let him be," Sam enjoined. "He'll stop when he's had enough."

Cammie tried to shake off the hands binding her, but both men secured their grip. If she hadn't been bound by the knowledge every man present had risked his life for her, she would have battled them tooth and nail. She didn't comprehend letting the fight proceed, but all five men were in agreement. They seemed to instinctively know something she didn't. In any case she couldn't do anything to stop the fight even if she wanted to.

Cammie's concern for Adam's well-being clouded the joy of her own rescue. When she had heard the approaching thunder of hooves and then Adam's voice, she was suffused with the most profound sense of relief she had ever experienced. It was squelched by her terror for Adam's safety the moment Larson grabbed up his gun. She cared nothing for her life if it cost Adam his, but she had had no way of telling him that. But, all that was over now.

Cammie had no idea how Adam had known she was in trouble or how he had found her, but she was too worried for him to waste time wondering about it. He was here. He had saved her. She could tell Adam the truth about how she felt about him.

Unless Larson did him some grave injury . . .

Adam heaved Larson to his back, straddling his belly. Larson grunted as the wind was knocked out of him. Blood lust filled Adam's eyes as he pummeled Larson's face. Larson writhed, lifting his arms to defend himself, but he could neither block the blows nor return them. His movements became progressively weaker. Mewling noises rose from his throat.

Cammie's fears for Adam turned to fear he was going to kill Larson with his bare hands. She had no sympathy for Larson. He deserved to die, but not this way. When Adam came to his senses, he would regret taking the law into his own hands.

Adam's fists continued to pummel Larson. Larson whimpered with each blow. His eyes were swelling shut, and his head lolled. He strained to raise a fist, but halfway to its target it went limp and slumped to the ground.

Adam *was* going to kill him, Cammie concluded with wide-eyed dismay. No matter what the others said, she couldn't stand mutely by and not even try to do something. Adam was plainly beyond reason. He needed her.

Just as Cammie renewed her struggle to escape the hands holding her back, Adam landed a final blow, stood up, and dusted his hands over Larson's still breathing body. "Get him out of my sight!" he ordered. "The sheriff can handle him from here."

The two men from the Carrigan ranch picked Larson up off the ground and carried him toward the horses. At the same time Rutley and Woodrow released their hold on her.

Cammie flew into Adam's arms. Disregarding the pain it caused her lips, she covered his face with kisses. Adam held her tightly against his chest.

Cupping his face, she kissed him without pause, though she was careful to avoid his rapidly blackening left eye, split lip, and bruises.

Elias Rutley and William Woodrow backed away from the effusive display of emotion from their usually dispassionate employer, joining Adam's men at the edge of the clearing. Sam smiled his approval of the couple's embrace, then discreetly followed to allow them a modicum of privacy.

"Don't ever give me a scare like that again," Cammie scolded between fervent kisses.

"Me scare *you?"* Adam protested, holding her even tighter. "What about the scare you gave me? It's a miracle you're not dead."

Cammie stroked the sides of his face, smiling up at him. "I'm not, thanks to you."

Adam scowled. "When I think what would have happened if we hadn't found you when we did—"

"He planned to throw me over the cliff after he—" Cammie couldn't quite make herself finish the sentence, and Adam's eyes told her she needn't. She kissed the corners of his lips. "Let's not talk about him now. I just want to stand here and soak in the fact that you're really here."

Adam persisted to scowl, but his voice was full of sympathy. "We don't ever have to talk about him if you don't want to—but I've gotta ask you one question."

"All right."

"What on earth possessed you to ride after him alone?"

The underlying note of rebuke in his voice was more than justified considering what her reckless actions had put them both through, and Cammie's contrition was genuine. She focused her gaze on the ground, shamefaced. "When I woke up and found my house on fire, I was so furious I couldn't think straight. Later my only thought was to catch a glimpse of the person who had set the fire so I could give a name or description to the sheriff. By the time I came to my senses, it was too late."

"You knew about the fire and didn't tell anyone?" Adam gaped at her.

"When I discovered it, there was more smoke than flames. I thought I had put it out," Cammie explained.

"Your house burned to the ground," Adam ruefully informed her.

She nodded. "Larson said he looked back and saw it burning." Cammie had a question of her own. Even though she was afraid of the answer, she had to know. "Did Lucretia get out?"

"I don't know how, but other than some singed fur, she's no worse for the experience."

Cammie eyes filled with tears. "Thank goodness. And the horses? How are they?"

"The fire didn't spread beyond the house. All of your animals are fine, which is more than I can say for you." He gingerly touched a bruise under her eye. "You look terrible."

Cammie gave him a crooked smile. "You don't look any too attractive yourself."

"Thanks a lot." Adam grinned back at her. "A man saves your life and all you can do is insult his looks."

"Adam Carrigan, even with a black eye and a split lip, you're the most handsome man I've ever laid eyes on."

"I'm glad you think so, because I aim to marry you." He caught hold of both her hands and held on as if he were afraid she might run away. "I was gonna give you a little time to get used to the notion, but if you're gonna go running off half-baked chasing down scum like Larson, I want you right by my side where I can keep an eye on you."

"Yes."

"What?" Adam gawked at her in amazement.

"Yes, I'll marry you," Cammie repeated, overjoyed she would get her second chance with Adam after all—and determined not to waste one minute worrying about why everything was unexpectedly turning out right.

"You will?"

"If your proposal is serious, I can think of nothing I'd like better than to marry you." She paused to kiss him again before she continued. "Of course, we'll have to get certain things settled first—but I'm confident we can work them out."

Though he appeared genuinely gratified she had agreed to marry him, a circumspect expression stole over his face. "Why the sudden change of mind? It's not because you feel beholden to me, is it?"

"I should think you know me better than that," Cammie gently chided.

"I hope I do, but it still doesn't make sense. I know why I changed my mind. I love you. I've known it for quite some time, but I didn't want to admit it, even to myself. When I read my mother's diaries I realized how wrong I was to let the pain of my past cheat me out of loving you." He brushed a leaf from her hair, and his gaze locked with hers. "But me coming to my senses doesn't explain why you've had a sudden change of heart."

"Back on the trail, when I was sure I was going to die, I realized the only thing I regretted was being afraid to acknowledge I'd fallen in love with you and pursue my feelings. Since I love you, and I want to be with you, the sensible thing to do is marry you."

"Why aren't you afraid anymore?"

"Oh, I am. I'm absolutely terrified. But I'm more afraid of missing out on spending my life with you."

Her answer satisfied him, and the tension left his body. "Then it's settled. I love you. You love me. We're getting married."

"All we need to do is discuss the terms," Cammie agreed.

"Terms?"

"The terms of our marriage," Cammie reminded. "I may be in love with you, but I haven't become a starry-eyed debutante willing to fall into the arms of the first handsome man who will have me without a thought for the future. And I want you to understand the kind of wife you'll be getting. After you hear, you may want to change your mind."

"Tell me your terms," Adam cheerfully commanded.

Cammie took a deep breath. "I want us to be partners, *equal* partners. When we have an important decision to make about our lives, we should both have a say in it. I have no problem with you retaining dominion over the cattle ranch as long as you respect my word as final on all matters concerning my horse ranch. I have no intention of taking up the role of a domestic, and expect to continue working with my horses much as I do now. I enjoy being challenged and despise being coddled. These feelings will not change. In short, I will love you with all my heart, but I will *not* be an obedient wife."

"I can see that," Adam replied, his tone and expression unreadable.

Cammie's heart skipped a beat. Had she gone too far, hoped for too much? She knew she could never settle for less, and that to be other than forthright would be a terrible disservice to them both—but despite her earlier statement, she had blithely assumed he would have no objections. Her lips trembling and her voice faltering, she asked, "Would you like to withdraw your proposal?"

Lifting her off the ground, Adam kissed her soundly on the mouth. "No. Pliant wives are as plentiful as bunchgrass. You are what I want."

Cammie's relief was so great that her knees nearly buckled beneath her when he set her back on the ground. Throwing her arms around his neck, she joyfully asked, "When do you want this marriage to take place?"

"Today," Adam declared. When Cammie raised both brows, he chuckled and reluctantly amended, "Okay, tomorrow."

"But we both look dreadful. Wouldn't you prefer to wait until your bride isn't sporting a black eye?"

Surveying her battered face, he gently tweaked her nose. "Looks to me like we're a matching set. I don't mind if you don't—and even if you do, don't forget you no longer have a house. You have to live somewhere. It may as well be with me."

"Your house *is* convenient to my horses."

"Our house," Adam corrected.

"Our house," Cammie echoed, liking the sound of it. "Shall we be married in the courthouse or a church?"

He considered the matter for a moment. "Why not both? We can have a judge marry us now; then when we're both looking and feeling more ourselves, we'll throw the biggest wedding the territory has ever seen."

Cammie beamed. "I like that."

Adam offered his arm. "Ready to announce our engagement to the world?"

"Yes."

As they strolled toward the men, Adam whispered in her ear, "I figure it's only fair to warn you that there's no changing your mind after we tell the others. Sam and Josh are as thick as thieves. When Josh hears we've decided to tie the knot, he'll never let us back out of it."

"Once I've made up my mind to do something, I never change it," Cammie said firmly.

"How could I have forgotten that?"

"Perhaps you're punch drunk," she teased.

"I've never been more clearheaded in my life," Adam proclaimed. "I love you Cammie Kendall."

"I love you, Adam Carrigan." Cammie leaned against him. "Let's go home."

Twenty-three

"No fair hogging the bride all to yourself." Josh poked Adam in the ribs and attempted to cut into the waltz.

"Nothing doing, baby brother. If you want a dance partner, find your own."

"Cammie, tell him to share," Josh cajoled.

Cammie grinned at him. "Now why would I do that? I'm exactly where I want to be."

Josh harrumphed. "First, I can't get the two of you together to save my life—now I can't tear you apart. You sure don't believe in doing anything in moderation, do you?"

"No," Adam replied, pulling Cammie's hand toward him and planting a kiss on the inside of her wrist.

"Between you two and Sam and Ella always hugging and kissing and making moon eyes at each other, I'm starting to feel like I'm drowning in a vat of honey. Gonna have to start seriously considering getting myself hitched up to a woman of my own as a matter of self-preservation," Josh muttered, stomping away in mock indignation.

"Poor Josh," Cammie chortled.

"He'll get over it." Adam pulled her tighter into his arms, spinning her through a series of dizzying turns.

Leaning her head back, Cammie laughed as she watched the colors of the flowers and ribbons festooning the ballroom whiz by in a kaleidoscope of color.

Two months had passed since the day of the fire. They had been married the next day by a judge at the ranch in a private ceremony.

These past weeks Adam and she had spent nearly every minute together. When Adam had said he wanted her where he could keep his eye on her, he had meant it literally—not that she had any complaints. There was nothing oppressive about the attention he paid her. It was delightful to share a roof and bed with her best friend.

Every morning they discussed their plans for the day over cups of coffee and tea. Adam was teaching her everything he knew about cattle ranching, from branding to roping to gauging the fluctuations in market prices. She had taught him a thing or two about horses. They took long rides in the afternoon together. More than once they had picnicked at the river canyon, then made love under the warm sun.

They had their disagreements. Both being strong-willed people, it was inevitable they would. But Adam never attempted to dictate her opinions or behavior. Each argued their position—offering facts to support their view—until they came to a compromise or agreed to disagree.

Today they had renewed their wedding vows with half the town as witnesses. Cammie was glad Adam had insisted they have a formal wedding and reception. The first time she had spoken her vows, she had been caught up in a stampede of high emotion. Her heart was full of love and hope, but also a goodly amount of trepidation. This afternoon she was able to make the same vows with utter confidence in the future.

Ella and Sam had insisted they be allowed to host the reception, and they had outdone themselves: hiring an orchestra, renting the ballroom, personally overseeing every detail of the decorations and refreshments. With Josie propped in one arm and a notebook in her hand, Ella had been issuing orders to the hotel staff like a general for days. Cammie liked her new in-laws.

The waltz ended, and Adam reluctantly gave Cammie over to the governor of the territory for the next dance. Several other gentlemen of high social standing claimed their right to dance with the bride after him.

Though Cammie and Adam were able to dance together on occasion, the long line of gentlemen eager to share a dance with the bride made these opportunities all too infrequent, and unlike Josh, they could not be put off without danger of giving offense. All Adam and she could do was smile at their respective partners and exchange longing glances across the room.

When Roy Higgins's turn came to claim Cammie's hand, he winked at her. "For a while there I was afraid I was gonna lose a good friend over that piece of land I sold you," he confessed. "But looks like I knew what I was doing, after all."

"Don't tell me you were playing matchmaker, too," she remarked as he led her through the steps of the schottische.

"Naw. All these years I believed Adam when he said he was a confirmed bachelor. Wish I could take the credit for bringing the two of you to the altar, but I was just trying to line my pockets."

"I admire your honesty," Cammie declared while step-hopping around him. "How are you liking living a life of leisure?"

"For the first few months I thought it was grand, but now I'm getting kinda itchy to put a few calluses on my hands," he admitted. "Thinking of buying myself another little spread east of town."

Cammie's eyes took on an eager gleam. "You'll be needing good horses to work your new ranch."

"And I bet you know just where I can buy some, right?" Higgins shook his head and chuckled. "Never misjudged a person so bad as you in all my life. I thought you were a pretty little know-nothing society gal with the sense of a mule, and here you're trying to drum up business on your own wedding day."

"After the ridiculous amount you overcharged me for my land, I have to keep my eye out for opportunities to turn a profit," Cammie twitted him.

"Oh, you'll turn a profit, all right. Them horses of yours are every cowboy's dream."

"Thank you, Mr. Higgins. Please feel free to express that opinion to everyone you meet."

The dance ended, and Cammie was approached by a new partner, then another. It was a long time before she found herself back in Adam's arms.

"So how do you like married life so far, Mrs. Carrigan?" he whispered in her ear, when they had settled comfortably into the rhythm of the dance steps.

"Other than not getting to dance with you as much as I'd like, I must say it agrees with me."

"No regrets?"

"Not a one," Cammie answered without hesitation. "What about you?"

"Taking you on as a partner is the smartest move I ever made."

"Are you speaking of business or pleasure, Mr. Carrigan?"

"Both. You've a hard head for business and soft body for loving. I especially like that little spot right below—"

Cammie's cheeks bloomed rosy red. "Shush. Someone might overhear you."

"I thought you liked flaunting your talents," Adam teased.

"Very funny. If you don't behave yourself, I'll be forced to share a few of your secrets—like the way you purr just like Lucretia when I rub your belly. What would the townsfolk think of you then?"

"They'd figure I was stupid for letting you dance with other men when I could have you up in our hotel room all to myself. How much longer do you figure it'll be before we can get out of here?"

"After all the effort they went to, I don't want to hurt Ella and Sam's feelings." Cammie craned her neck, trying to locate the couple. "I think we should wait until—"

Adam captured her chin in his hand and centered her gaze on his face. "They slipped out the back way over a half hour ago."

Cammie pretended to be outraged. "The wretches."

Adam's eyes twinkled. "Want to follow their fine example?"

The sparkle in her eyes reflected the glow of anticipation in his. "Let's."

Waltzing across the room and out the ballroom door, they paused at the threshold to wave at Josh. Then turning on their heels, hand in hand, they dashed up the stairs to their room.

Zebra Books and Kensington Books
proudly announce . . .

SUMMER DARKNESS,
WINTER LIGHT

by Sylvia Halliday

Coming from
Kensington Books Hardcovers in
early May, 1995

The following is a preview of
SUMMER DARKNESS,
WINTER LIGHT . . .

ADVANCE PRAISE FOR
SUMMER DARKNESS,
WINTER LIGHT

"*Summer Darkness, Winter Light* deals with the many faces of love—and obsession. I read it in one sitting and found it fascinating."

—Roberta Gellis
author of *Dazzling Brightness*

"*Summer Darkness, Winter Light* is an engrossing story of two people fighting the demons of the past to make way for the possibility of a future. Sylvia Halliday delivers a strong, emotional tale of the darkness of despair giving way to the bright light of hope."

—*A Little Romance*

"Funny, poignant, brimming over with bright dialogue . . . highly entertaining . . . an irresistible read that grips you from page one and never lets go. Clever, original . . . a thinking reader's romance. This one has it all!"

—Kathe Robin, *Romantic Times*

One

The wrought-iron gate was newly painted. Allegra ran her fingers over the smooth curliques, followed the cool, sinuous curves to the oval medallion that held the Baniard coat of arms. The carved leopard still raised a broken front paw. But after more than eight years of fresh paint—glistening black layers piled one upon another—the jagged metal edges had become rounded, gentle.

"Curse them all," Allegra muttered. "Every foul Wickham who ever lived." She clenched her teeth against the familiar pain. If only sharp memories could be as softened and gentled as the old iron gate. She reached into the pocket of her wide seaman's breeches and pulled forth a worn, lace-edged square of linen, yellow with age and mottled with stains the color of old wine, the color of dead leaves. Papa's blood—staining the proud Baniard crest embroidered in the corner.

Wickham. Allegra's lip curled in silent rage and bitterness. If there was a God of vengeance, a just God, her prayers would be answered today. Her stomach twisted with the pangs of hunger, and her feet—in their broken shoes—ached from the long morning's climb through the Shropshire hills, but it would be worth it. She reached under her shabby coat and waistcoat and fingered the hilt of the dagger tucked into the waistband of her breeches. All her pain would vanish when she confronted John Wickham, Baron

Ellsmere, false Lord of Baniard Hall. When she saw his look of surprise, then fear, then abject terror in the breathless, time-stopped seconds before she plunged her dagger into his black heart.

A sour-faced manservant came out of the lodge next to the high stone wall that enclosed Baniard Park. A thickly curled gray peruke covered his round head, and he wore a handsome livery of blue velvet trimmed with crimson—the Ellsmere colors, no doubt. He squinted up at the morning sun, peered through the bars of the gate and shook his fist at Allegra. "Get off with you, boy. You have no business here."

Allegra jammed her three-cornered hat more firmly over her forehead to shield her face from the gatekeeper's gaze. Her masculine guise had protected her clear across the ocean and through the English countryside all the way north from Plymouth. Still, to be discovered now, when vengeance lay so close at hand . . .

"I ain't doin' no harm, your worship," she mumbled, keeping her naturally husky voice pitched low, her accent common. "Just come up from Ludlow, I did. It were a long climb. And I'm fearful hungry. Thought I might beg a farthing or two of His Lordship."

"Pah!" said the gatekeeper with a sneer of contempt as he scanned her stained and ragged clothing. "Do you think milord can be bothered with the likes of you? A dirty-faced whelp?" He scowled at her dark eyes, her raven-black hair braided into a tousled queue, and her face still deeply tanned from the Carolina sun. "Leastwise not someone who looks like a black Welsh Gypsy," he added. "Be off, lest I give you a good rap on the ear."

Years of cruel servitude had taught Allegra how to feign humility, even while her heart seethed with rebellion. "Have a crumb o' pity, your worship," she whined. "I be but a poor orphan lad."

"Be off, I say." He pointed across the narrow, dusty road to a footpath that wound its way through a small grove of trees. "That way lies the village of Newton-in-the-Vale. There's a fine workhouse that will do well enough for you. A good day's work for a good day's bread, and none of your sloth and begging."

Allegra rubbed at her hands, feeling the hardness of the calluses on her palms and fingers. She wondered whether this self-satisfied, overfed man had ever known *real* work. Heigh-ho. There was no sense in quarreling with him. She shrugged and plodded across the road. The trees were thick in the coppice, crowded close together; their dark, summer-green leaves and shade soon hid her from the gatekeeper's view. She waited a few minutes, then stepped off the footpath and doubled back through the trees, treading softly so as not to alert the servant. Just within the shelter of the coppice, she found a spot that concealed her presence while commanding a clear view of the gate.

By King George upon his throne, if she had to wait all day for Wickham she would!

She heard the noise of a coach from somewhere beyond the gate—the rattle of harness, the squeaking of wheels—as it made its way down the long, tree-shaded drive that led from Baniard Hall. In another moment, the coach appeared in view and stopped at the gate; the team of horses snorted and stamped, eager to proceed. At once, the gatekeeper hurried to take hold of the iron gate and swing it wide. Allegra heard the word "Milord" uttered in deference, noted the blue and crimson she was certain now were Ellsmere colors on the coachman's ample body. Wickham's very own coach. Without a doubt, the villain himself was within.

Allegra's heart began to pound in her breast, like the thud of distant thunder before a storm. After all this time . . . She started to rush forward, then checked herself. No. No! She mustn't let her impatience cloud her judgment; she must think clearly. The coach was moving quite slowly through the open gate. Out of the view of the gatekeeper and coachman, she might be able to hoist herself onto the empty footman's perch in the rear and cling to the coach until it stopped and her enemy alit. But that might not be until they reached a village and the coach was surrounded by crowds. And then the job would be impossible.

She remembered a crumbling section of the wall that surrounded the park, where the stones had loosened. Perhaps she could make her way onto the grounds from there, wait for Ellsmere to return. No. The wall might be repaired after all this time. And, besides, she couldn't wait another minute. She laughed softly, ruefully. She had endured the long, slow years, the years of nurturing her hatred in patient silence. And now, to her surprise, she found that the thought of a few hours' delay had become unbearable.

What to do? The frown faded from her brow as a sudden thought struck her. She would accost him now, present herself as a harmless lad, win his sympathy, worm her way into his favor. He wouldn't recognize her after all this time. And then, when his guard was down, her dagger could do its work.

"Milord!" she cried, and dashed in front of the carriage. The coachman shouted and tried to avoid her; she held her ground and leapt away only at the last second. It had been such a narrow escape that her shoulder burned from the friction of rubbing against a horse's flank, and a passing harness buckle had torn the sleeve of her coat.

She began at once to howl. " 'Od's blood, but my arm be broken!"

She heard a string of foul curses from within the coach, then a deep voice boomed, "Stop!"

As the coach drew to a halt, Allegra clutched at her arm and bent over in seeming pain. Though she continued to wail, all her energies were concentrated on observing the man who sprang from the coach. She'd seen him once before—that long-ago, sweet summer at Baniard Hall. The summer she'd turned nine. The summer before the nightmare had begun. A man of stature, proud and haughty and cruel.

He was even taller than her misty memory of him, and the years had clearly treated him with kindness. His dark brown hair was still untouched by gray. He wore it simply, unpowdered and tied back with a black silk ribbon. His pugnacious jaw had a bluish cast, as though he'd neglected to take a shave, and his dark and somewhat shaggy brows were drawn together in a scowl, shading pale-brown eyes. His well-cut coat and waistcoat of fine woolen cloth covered a solid, muscular torso, and his legs were strong and straight. The fact that he looked so young made her hate him all the more: Papa had aged a dozen years from the time of the trial to the day they had been herded aboard the convict ship.

"Damned fool," growled the man. He sounded more annoyed than angry, as though it was a bother merely to deal with the lower classes. "Why the devil did you run into my coach, boy? I should break your neck, match it to your arm." He stepped closer and thrust out his hand. "Show it here."

The simmering hatred became a red mist before Allegra's eyes: the red, bloody dream that had kept her going through all the hellish years, through the shame and the suffering and the loss of all she'd held dear. She felt strength coursing through her body—the strength of righteous anger that poor Mama had never been able to find.

Now! she thought. For her pledge to Mama. For all the lost Baniards! There would never be a better opportunity. The gatekeeper was busy with his gate and the coachman was too fat to scramble down from his perch in time to save his master.

Allegra snaked her hand inside her coat. A quick thrust with her dagger and then—in the chaos of the unexpected, the confusion of the servants—she'd make her escape into the woods. "Die like the dog you are," she choked, and drove the knife upward toward his breast with all her might. With all the fury in her pent-up heart.

"Christ's blood!" he swore. He wrenched his body to one side and just managed to dodge the murderous blade. At the same moment he caught Allegra's wrist in a punishing grip and twisted it until she was forced to drop the knife. His lip curled in disgust. "Good God. You're not a fool. You're a bloody lunatic! Do you fancy the gibbet, boy?"

She bared her teeth in a snarl. "It would be worth it, to see you dead."

He laughed, an unpleasant sound, lacking in humor or warmth. "What a tartar. How does a boy learn such passion at such a young age?" He drawled the words, as though strong emotions were scarcely worth his own effort.

"I learned from villains like you," she said. She eyed her dagger lying in the dusty road. If she could just reach it . . .

"Oh, no, boy. You'll not have a second chance." Reading her intentions, he quickly stooped and retrieved the knife.

"Curse you!" Allegra felt her stomach give a sickening lurch. She had failed them all. All the ghosts waiting to be avenged. How could she have been so hasty and careless? Would there ever be another chance to redeem herself? Another chance to do what she must, and, after, learn to live again? In her frustration, she raised her hands to spring at the man's throat; she grunted in surprise as she felt her arms caught and pinioned behind her back. She struggled in vain, then twisted around to glare at the man who held her—a somber-looking young man who had stepped from the coach behind her. He was dressed in a plain dark suit, the garb of a steward or clerk.

"Hold your tongue, bratling," he said, "unless you mean to beg His Lordship's mercy."

"His Lordship can rot in hell, for aught I care!" She turned back and spat in the direction of the tall man. "In *hell,* Wickham! Do you hear?"

"Wickham?" The tall man laughed again and idly scraped Allegra's blade against the stubble on his chin. It made a metallic, rasping sound. "Wickham? Is that who you think I am?"

"You're the Lord of Baniard Hall, aren't you?" she challenged.

"That I am. But Wickham was ruined by debts nearly two years ago. The last I heard, he was in London."

"No!" She shook her head in disbelief, feeling her blood run cold. "Curse you, villain, you're lying to save your skin."

The steward gave a sharp jerk on her arms. "I told you to hold your tongue, boy," he growled in her ear. "This is Sir Greyston Morgan, Viscount Ridley. Baron Ellsmere sold the Hall to His Lordship a year ago."

"I don't believe you." But of course there was no reason to doubt him. She examined the tall man more closely. What a fool she'd been, allowing her passion to blind her to reality. He didn't just appear younger; he *was* younger, and considerably so. Perhaps in his early thirties. Wickham would be almost as old as Papa would have been today, or at least nearing fifty. She'd forgotten that, still seeing the man through the eyes of her childhood.

All the fight drained out of her. She sagged in the steward's grip, filled with an aching disappointment. To have come so far, and then to find another obstacle in her path, another barrier before she could sleep in peace . . . She stared at the viscount, her dark eyes burning with frustration and resentment. He should have been Wickham. "I curse you as well, Ridley," she said bitterly. "A pox on you."

"Now, milord," said the coachman, climbing down for his box, "if this isn't a rascally lad who needs a few hours in the stocks to teach him manners! Shall we deliver him to the beadle in the village?" He looked for agreement toward the gatekeeper, who had finally joined them.

Ridley looked down at Allegra's petite frame and shook his head. "He's just a slip of a boy. The stocks would kill him. A mere ten minutes with a mob hurling garbage and filth . . ."

"But you can't let him go, milord. He tried to kill you!" said the gatekeeper.

Ridley smiled, a sardonic twist of his mouth. "So he did, Humphrey. And I note you took your time coming to my rescue." His icy glance swept his other servants as well. "The lot of you. Slow as treacle on a cold day. Very shortsighted. If you'd let him kill me, you'd have had to seek honest employment for a change." He shrugged, ignoring his servants' sullen frowns. "Well, the lad wasn't the first to wish me dead. However"—he slapped the broad width of Allegra's dagger against his open palm—"the boy does have an insolent tongue, and for that he should be made to pay." He nodded at his steward. "Loose him, Briggs. I'll deal with him myself."

"But . . ." Briggs hesitated. "Do you think you're fit, milord?"

A sharp laugh. "Sober, you mean?"

"I didn't mean that at all," said Briggs in an aggrieved tone.

Ridley's eyes were cold amber. "What a damned bloody liar you are, Briggs. Now, do you want to keep your position? You'll not find another master willing to pay so much for so little. Loose the boy, I said."

"As you wish, milord." There was pained resentment in the steward's voice, but he obeyed.

The moment her arms were freed, Allegra looked wildly about, seeking a path to safety. There was none. The three servants hemmed her in, and Lord Ridley stood before her, a cold smile of determination on his face. He slapped the flat of Allegra's knife more sharply against his hand. Again, and then once more—a decidedly menacing gesture, for all his smiling. "Damn me to hell, will you, boy? Spit on my boots, will you? Someone has neglected your education, it would seem. I intend to remedy that." He slipped the knife into his boot top and advanced on Allegra. His long arm shot out and wrapped around her waist. With the merest effort, he lifted her and tucked her under his arm, like a farmer carrying a squirming pig to market.

Allegra writhed in his strong grip. "Bloody villain. Spawn of hell! Put me down!"

"If I were you, boy, I'd hold my tongue," he said dryly. "I have all day to educate you, and every fresh insolence will only earn you another painful lesson." He turned toward the woodland path.

"Where are you going, milord?" asked the gatekeeper, Humphrey.

"To find a suitable 'schoolroom.' Don't follow me. Grant

the lad privacy in his humiliation." Ridley laughed, a sharp, sardonic bark. "Besides, you shall hear his howls anon."

He carried Allegra into the grove of trees and stopped at last when he found a fallen log in a small clearing. He sat down and slung her across his knees with such force that her hat flew from her head and landed in a patch of bright green ferns.

Allegra grunted and wriggled in powerless rage, punching at his legs, his thighs—anything within reach of her flailing fists. It was like beating back a tempest with a lady's fan. His strong arm held her firmly against his lap. She felt his other hand at her rump, turning up the skirts of her coat; then his fingers were curled around the top of her breeches.

She struggled more violently to free herself. She didn't fear the thrashing—not even with the flat of her own knife, which the villain clearly intended. Punishment was nothing new to her. But if he saw the pale flesh of her backside, the womanly curves, he'd guess at once. And then what? What could she expect from this cold-hearted devil of a viscount? God save her, she hadn't guarded her virtue against the greatest adversities only to be raped by a man with nothing better to do on a July morning! With a superhuman effort, she wrenched herself from his lap and tumbled to the ground.

He reached down to pull her back. By chance, his hands closed over her breasts. "Christ's blood," he exclaimed, and dropped down beside her. "A *woman,* begad!" While she struggled in helpless frustration, he rolled her onto her back, straddled her and pinned her wrists over her head. With his free hand he explored her body, threw open her coat and tattered waistcoat and fondled her breasts through her full linen shirt. It was a leisurely, searching examination that clearly amused him. His mouth twisted in a smirk. "A very pleasing shape. May I assume your other parts are equally feminine? Or shall I find out for myself?"

She squirmed in disgust at his touch, her eyes flashing. "Let me up, you plaguey dog!"

He shook his head and laughed. "To think I very nearly beat you like a child. I should have realized . . . all that passion. Not childlike at all. But why waste your fire in anger? Why foul your lips with curses, when they could be put to better use?" He bent down, his face close to hers. His breath smelled of liquor, sour and pungent.

"Cursed rogue," she muttered. "Drunken sot. I would rather the beating than the kiss."

"Perhaps I can oblige you with both," he said, and silenced her mouth with his.

His lips were hard and demanding, rapacious in their greed, the desire for self-gratification. And when she groaned and bucked beneath him, Ridley chuckled deep in his throat, as though her struggles only increased the enjoyment of his mastery over her. Without releasing either her lips or her hands, he shifted his body so his considerable weight pressed upon her breast and his free hand rested on the juncture between her legs.

Allegra had a sudden, terrifying memory of Mama, gasping in pain and grief as Squire Pringle violated her frail body. She could hear again the animal sounds she'd heard, night after night in the dark. Hear her mother's heartbroken sobs as the master, satisfied once more, slunk away to his own bed. *No!* It mustn't happen to her. She was stronger than Mama. Hadn't she survived until now?

Despite her rising panic, she forced herself to think clearly. If Ridley wasn't completely drunk, he'd certainly had a great deal to drink this morning. His senses would be dulled, his reflexes numbed by alcohol. Surely she could outwit him if she put her mind to it.

With a sigh, she relaxed under him in seeming surrender. She even managed a moan of pleasure when he began to stroke her inner thigh, his large hand hot through her breeches. He grunted his contentment, softened his kiss, eased his hard grip upon her wrists. How easily gulled men could be, she thought. And if he was anything like the lecherous pigs in Carolina, no doubt he enjoyed kissing in the French manner. She prayed it was so. She parted her lips beneath his, hoping he'd understand and respond to her invitation. To her satisfaction, he immediately opened his own mouth and thrust his tongue between her lips and teeth. She waited a second—fighting her disgust—then bit down with all her might.

He let out a bellow and flew off her as though he'd been shot, sitting up to clutch at his bloody mouth. "Damned bitch!" he roared.

She gave him no chance to recover. She scrambled to her knees and drove her fist into his diaphragm with all her strength. He recoiled in agony and doubled over, gasping for breath. She was on her feet in a flash. She snatched up her three-cornered hat, pulled her knife from his boot top and turned toward the footpath. Her mouth was bitter with the taste of his blood; bitterer still with the knowledge that time was passing and she was no nearer her goal. Her stomach burned with hunger, and London and Wickham were long miles and days away. Somehow, that made her hate Ridley all the more. Ridley, with his careless, shallow lechery. What did he know of true suffering?

She retraced her steps to where he still sat, rocking in pain. "Filthy whoremonger," she said, and spat his own blood upon his bent head. When he looked up at her, she was pleased to see that the cold, indifferent eyes were—for the first time—dark with rage. "Laugh that away, Ridley," she said. "If you can." She turned on her heel and made for the safety of the trees . . . and the direction that would take her eventually to London and Wickham.

And bloody vengeance.

Sir Greyston Morgan, Lord Ridley, late of His Majesty's Guards and survivor of many an incursion against the Mogul Empire, gingerly rubbed the sore spot beneath his ribs and muttered a soft curse. He pulled out a handkerchief and wiped the spittle from his hair, grunting at the pain that small effort cost him. The absurdity of the whole episode served to temper his anger. "Ambushed, begad," he said, beginning to laugh in spite of his discomfort. He stuck out his tongue and dabbed at it, marveling at the amount of blood on the snowy linen. It was a wonder the virago hadn't bitten his tongue clean off!

"Are you hurt, milord?" Jonathan Briggs stood on the edge of the path, frowning in concern.

Grey struggled to his feet and glared at his steward. It was one thing to be outwitted by a wench. It was quite another matter to be caught at it by a servant. "Damn it, I thought I told you not to follow."

"We heard you cry out, milord." Briggs looked around the small clearing. "Where's the boy?"

Grey took a tentative step forward, relieved to discover that he could breathe almost normally again. "The 'boy,' Briggs, turned out to be a woman." His tongue was still bleeding; he stopped to spit a mouthful of blood against the base of a tree. "And a damned shifty bitch at that."

Grey watched in dismay. "Was it the wench responsible for this? I'll send Humphrey after her."

"No. Let her be. I'll wager she's halfway to London by now."

"What's to be done now, milord?"

Grey moved swiftly to the steward and leaned his arm on the man's shoulder. "Help me back to the coach and open that bottle of gin."

Briggs shook his head in disapproval. "But, milord, do you think it wise, so early in the day?"

He swore softly. "You tell me what's worth staying sober for, Briggs, and I'll stay sober. Until then, you'll keep me supplied with all the drink I need. And no insolence. Is that understood?"

Briggs pressed his lips together and nodded.

By the time they'd reached the coach, Grey was feeling a good deal better. At least his tongue and his ribs were feeling better. He wasn't sure of anything else. There was something disturbing about the woman. Something about her eyes, so large and dark and filled with pain . . . "Damn it, Briggs," he growled, "where's that gin?" He snatched the small flask from the steward's hand and took a long, mind-numbing swallow. Why should he let the thought of a savage creature with a dirty face get under his hide?

"Do you still want to go down to Ludlow, milord?"

"Of course. The blacksmith promised to have that Toledo blade repaired by today."

"Are you sure you don't want someone to go after the woman?"

"I told you, no!"

"But she tried to kill you. What if she should return and try again?"

"She wants Ellsmere, not me." He smiled crookedly. "I pity him if the witch should find him." He took another swig of gin and shrugged. "Besides, if she should return to kill me, I'm no great loss."

"Nonsense, milord. You're a great man, admired and respected by your tenants and servants. Everyone in the parish honors Lord Ridley."

Grey threw back his head and laughed aloud. "Such kind flattery, Briggs. You do it well, as befits a man of honor. But how difficult it must be for you. To serve a man you don't even like. You're the second son of a knight, aren't you? You were predestined to inherit nothing from your father except his good wishes. Well, a house steward is a fine calling for a man with few prospects and a good education. And money speaks with a loud voice, as I've learned." He leaned back in his seat and tapped his long fingers against the bottle of gin. "How much am I paying you?"

"Forty pounds, milord," murmured Briggs. He watched in silence, his solemn eyes registering dismay, as Grey downed the last of the gin.

The liquor stung Grey's injured tongue, but he was beginning to feel better and better. He chuckled softly. "What a disappointment I must be to you, Briggs. I think your upbringing was better than mine, though I, too, was the second son of a title. I regret that I don't suit your ideas of proper nobility here in Shropshire. But if you can learn to hide that look of disgust on your face, I give you leave to take another thirty pounds per annum. If not"—he shrugged—"it's simple enough to buy loyalty elsewhere, if one has the money." He laughed at the sullen look Briggs shot at him. "God's truth, I think if my brother hadn't died and left me his fortune and title, you'd be pleased to knock me to my knees at this very moment. But you're too much a gentleman for that. Too respectful of a man's rank, even if he's undeserving. Eh,

Briggs?" He laughed again as the steward reddened and turned away.

Grey closed his eyes. The rocking of the coach soothed him. And the gin had done its work. It was good to feel nothing but a comfortable hum in his brain. There was a surfeit of passion in the world, a stupid waste of emotion. He hated it. Hated caring, hated feeling. It was better to be numb than to suffer with rage and pain, one's soul exposed to the agony of the human condition. Raw flesh held to an open flame. Like that ragged, dark-eyed creature, who burned with an intensity he couldn't begin to understand. That he didn't *want* to understand.

"Briggs," he said suddenly. "Do you remember the red-haired serving wench at the Kings Oak tavern in Newton? Find out if she's still as agreeable as before. If so, pay her double what you did last time. Then see that she's waiting in my bed tonight."

"Yes, milord." Briggs's voice was sharp with disapproval.

Grey opened his eyes and smiled cynically. "She's a shallow, greedy whore, Briggs. I know. But—like the gin—she gives me what I want. Forgetfulness."

And plague take all sad-eyed creatures who overflowed with more passion than their hearts could safely hold.

* * *

SYLVIA HALLIDAY has written a dozen highly praised historical romances under the pseudonyms Ena Halliday and Louisa Rawlings. Her Louisa Rawlings books include *Forever Wild,* a finalist for the RWA Golden Medallion, *Promise of Summer,* which received the *Romantic Times* Reviewer's

Choice Award, and *Wicked Stranger,* which was a finalist for a 1993 RWA Rita Award. Born in Canada, raised in Massachusetts, Sylvia Halliday now makes her home in New York City.

* * *

Look for
SUMMER DARKNESS, WINTER LIGHT
in early May, 1995,
wherever hardcover books
are sold

HISTORICAL ROMANCES BY PHOEBE CONN

FOR THE STEAMIEST READS, NOTHING BEATS THE PROSE OF CONN . . .

ARIZONA ANGEL	(3872, $4.50/$5.50)
CAPTIVE HEART	(3871, $4.50/$5.50)
DESIRE	(4086, $5.99/$6.99)
EMERALD FIRE	(4243, $4.99/$5.99)
LOVE ME 'TIL DAWN	(3593, $5.99/$6.99)
LOVING FURY	(3870, $4.50/$5.50)
NO SWEETER ECSTASY	(3064, $4.95/$5.95)
STARLIT ECSTASY	(2134, $3.95/$4.95)
TEMPT ME WITH KISSES	(3296, $4.95/$5.95)
TENDER SAVAGE	(3559, $4.95/$5.95)

Available wherever paperbacks are sold, or order direct from the Publisher. Send cover price plus 50¢ per copy for mailing and handling to Penguin USA, P.O. Box 999, c/o Dept. 17109, Bergenfield, NJ 07621.Residents of New York and Tennessee must include sales tax. DO NOT SEND CASH.